MARK
DE BINDER

SERIAL
CONNECTIONS

White Falcon Group Publishing

Hancock, NH

First Edition—November 2007
Copyright © 2007 by Mark De Binder
ISBN-13: 978-0-9795897-0-6
ISBN-10: 0-9795897-0-3

White Falcon Group Publishing
Printed in the United States of America
10 9 8 7 6 5 4 3 2 1

Cover Design by Marcia Press

Dedicated To

Patricia Lacey De Binder

For the Spark of Life,

Hope for the Future,

And the Courage to Keep Pressing On!

Coming in 2008

Serial Entity

By MARK DE BINDER

White Falcon Group Publishing
Hancock, NH

www.whitefalcongroup.com

Prologue

New England 1988

"You idiot Henry! The kid could be dead already," Chase shouted, lunging at the FBI agent. "How in the hell did you let this happen?" Four other agents grabbed Chase Benton and held him back before he could make contact with Henry White, the agent in charge of the "Hacker" case. Henry jumped back at the assault, startled by the reaction of the private investigator, and moved behind his reinforcements.

"Benton, this could have happened to anybody," said Henry, his face turning beet red. "It's not our fault!"

Trying to break away from his captors while reaching for Henry, Chase yelled, "If that kid dies I'll make sure each and every one of you is locked up for incompetence!"

"Benton, I think you better leave now," said one of the restraining agents, inches from his face.

"I'll do better than that, bozo," Chase spat, pushing away from the men. "I'm going to catch the Hacker and bring Tom Longworth back before he gets killed like the rest of them."

Chase shook the men off, turned his back on the crowd of suits, and quickly walked away. *"We were so damn close!"* he howled at himself. The last four weeks were a blur, working night and day in the FBI office in Boston, and Chase could feel the wave of fatigue and oppression coming over him. A light drizzle had started to come down and the air in Portland, Maine was damp and cold. *"It won't be much longer until the snow comes,"* he pondered as the crisp moist air hit his nostrils. The facts, thoughts, and events of the last four weeks poured through his mind making him crazy as he crossed the large industrial parking lot to his car. Just an hour ago he thought the mission was going to be over. He couldn't understand how the FBI fumbled this one, nor did he really care at this point. His VIP client had been very clear to him: *"Chase, I don't care who is in charge of this case, I want you to use every method and means at your disposal to find my son."*

That was four weeks ago and based on his profile of the Hacker, Jonathan Longworth's son Tom could already be dead. And best case, had less than five to seven days to live. There was no time left. Chase felt a chill go down the back of his neck as he sped down I-95 South toward New Hampshire. Suddenly thoughts and pictures started flashing in his mind. He knew this feeling well. Noticing a rest area ahead, he pulled over to think—meditate was more like it. Chase closed his eyes and relaxed his mind and body until he lost himself to that world deep inside where he could see and feel things most people could not. This was not a new skill he had recently developed. Ever since he was a little child he had visions and thoughts of things he could not understand. His parents had always dismissed it as a very vivid imagination. It wasn't until he was 12 years old that his true abilities became apparent to others.

In 1970, on a hot summer morning he had walked into the house to find his mother sitting at the kitchen table crying. "Mom, what's wrong?" he asked, placing his hands on her shoulders.

"Your Aunt June just called," she explained. "Your cousin Josh has been missing since yesterday morning. They have looked everywhere but can't find him. Your father just left the office to drive out there to join the search party."

Without a moment's hesitation Chase responded, "Don't cry Mom, Josh is okay. He is stuck right now and calling out for help—they'll find him."

"Chase now is not the time for this," his mother chided, slowly lifting her head. "I know you mean well but there's no possible way you could know." Chase shrugged and walked back outside to re-engage the day.

That night after Chase had gone to bed his father called. "Honey, we have searched over two square miles and nothing, nothing at all!" he groaned. "I am afraid that if he is outdoors he may not make it through another night."

Sarah remembered her brief encounter with Chase that morning. "John, she began tentatively, "Chase had one of those moments this morning and told me that Josh is okay but is stuck somewhere. I dismissed him right away. I don't know... it's just sometimes I think his moments might be real..."

"Oh God, not again Sarah," John said. "We've been through this so many times! The boy just has a wild imagination. We are about to head back out. I will call as soon as we know anything. I love you."

Sarah stayed up most of the night worrying about Josh and praying to God that they would find him soon. She had just finished fixing Chase's breakfast when he came downstairs. Grateful that it was not Chase who was missing, Sarah went to him and gave him a big hug.

"Good morning Mom," said Chase as he stared at his plate and began swirling his scrambled eggs around.

"Not hungry today?" she asked.

"Josh is tired, cold, and hungry," Chase replied. "I just can't eat right now."

Sarah paused at the sink and looked hard at her son—he appeared tired, solemn, and withdrawn.

"Chase," she said, "Do you know where Josh is?"

"Not exactly, Mom. He is in a dark place and he's stuck and no one can hear him calling. There is water around him, lots of rocks, and he is very cold and scared. He feels real bad because he's not supposed to be there and is afraid of getting into lots of trouble."

Sarah put her hands to her temples and pressed hard. "What in the hell is going on?" she thought to herself.

Springing into action she commanded, "Go to the bathroom and get dressed, we're leaving right now." She gathered her purse and car keys and they began the two-hour drive to her sister-in-law's house.

The ride was very quiet. John had called that morning and said there was no news. The search party was becoming less optimistic by the minute. "What if?" Sarah kept asking herself. Things had become hopeless and she could not get the thoughts out of her head.

When Sarah and Chase arrived, police cars, ambulances, and 20 to 30 civilian vehicles clogged the small road. Sarah's sister-in-law June was on the front porch surrounded by friends and family. Her eyes had dark circles and were swollen with tears.

Sarah ran to the porch and took June into her arms. "Oh June, I am so sorry," she said as she squeezed her hard.

"Sarah I am so glad you're here," June gasped. "Tim, John, and the rest of the men are at their wits end. They have looked everywhere. The dogs ran out of trail over near the small quarry and they thought he might have fallen in somehow." She began sobbing uncontrollably as Sarah kept her tight hold, afraid that June might collapse.

"They have three boats and divers in there now and have just finished dragging the entire pond," June uttered, her body quivering. "Nothing, nothing at all..."

Chase took a seat on the front steps. "Tell them to keep looking," he said barely audible. "He is there, and he is cold, wet, and scared."

Pulling away from Sarah, June looked down at Chase's back as he sat there.

"What did you just say?"

"He is there Aunt June, you just can't see him," Chase replied. "He is very afraid now and very cold." She hurried down the stairs to look Chase in the eyes.

"What do you mean Chase? Talk to me!" she demanded. Chase turned, silently questioning his mother. She gave him a loving nod of permission. Chase turned back and addressed his aunt.

"Aunt June, Josh is okay, but not for long. I don't know exactly where he is, but he is in the dark with water all around him and he is frightened because no one can hear him."

"My God!" June whispered. She was well of aware of Chase's "moments" as they called them, because she had lent a mother's ear and advice to Sarah many times. Suddenly, a look of astonishment mixed with sheer terror came across her face.

"We have to get to that quarry now!" June exclaimed, grabbing Chase by the hand. She stopped suddenly looking for the police dispatcher serving as the communications hub.

"Betsy, quick! Come here!" Jane called excitedly. "Call Captain Turner and tell him not to take the boats out of the quarry yet. Tell him I'll be there in ten minutes to explain." Betsy pulled out her walkie-talkie as Sarah, June, and Chase disappeared down the trail.

When they got to the quarry, Tim, John, Captain Turner, and a few others were looking down over the 50-foot cliff into the water below. A small zodiac was just leaving the beach with a pilot and diver. They had already been packing up when the Captain hailed them on the radio and told them to head back out. The men turned around when the two mothers and small boy came running through the clearing.

"Sarah!" John exclaimed to his wife. "What are you doing here? What's this all about?"

June interrupted and explained what Chase had said. The Captain dropped his head with a look of disappointment. "June, I know you are desperate," the Captain began, "but every minute we waste…" He cut himself short as Chase walked over to the edge of the cliff and pointed to a place on the north wall of the quarry.

"Josh is in there," Chase said quietly. All the adults stared in utter disbelief.

"Charlie! Send the boat over there," June demanded of the Captain, "and have that diver take a look right now!"

The Captain picked up his walkie-talkie and ordered the boat over to the north face. Chase kept pointing while the boat moved slowly along the bottom of the steep granite wall. Suddenly dropping his arm, Chase whispered, "There!" The Captain ordered the boat to stop and the diver to look around. A sudden chill went down his spine as he noticed that the major water line was a good 15 feet above the current water level.

"Well, I'll be damned!" he said more to himself than to the others. "The water is lower than it usually is because of the dry spring we had." The others came to the same realization.

At that moment the diver took a rope out of the boat, tied it off to one of the cloth rails and disappeared again below the surface. The radio crackled as the boat's pilot reported to the Captain. "Charlie, there's a small opening or cave about three feet below the surface," he began. "He is going in to check it out." The Captain ordered the other boats to head to the area and to bring the medic. As they arrived, the diver was just coming back up. He took off his mask waving furiously up to the crowd, issuing the thumbs up! The crowd responded with cheers and gasps of joy. Chase's mother and father saw Chase smiling quietly to himself.

A few days later, Chase was watching his neighbors' horses frolic around in the field. Mr. Marks, the horses' owner, appeared from nowhere and sat down on his side of the fence.

"Good morning, Chase," he said smiling.

"Hi, Mr. Marks," Chase responded, looking up at the older man. Although Mr. Marks was only 27 years old, to Chase he was an adult and looked huge.

After a brief silence Mr. Marks commented, "Chase, you did a wonderful thing the other day helping the police find Josh."

"How did you know about Josh?" Chase asked, making a funny face. As far as Chase knew his parents never really talked to Mr. Marks or his wife because they were a bit odd and kept to themselves.

"The real question," said Mr. Marks looking intently at the boy "is how you knew about Josh."

"I don't know," shrugged Chase. "Things just kept popping into my head. Did they pop into your head, too?"

"Well, let's just say we were working together on this one, Chase," he replied smiling, and walked toward his house. Chase did not realize it then, but in years to come, Wesley Marks was to become one of the most loved and important people in his life.

The sound of heavy rain brought Chase back to reality for a moment. He quickly went back down into a semi-trance and thought about the Hacker. As his mind began to focus, pictures began blinking into his subconscious mind. At first he could see a rather large log cabin situated deep in a heavily forested area. The logs were medium brown and seemed worn as if they had little or no maintenance. The cabin had a large two story main section, one-story wings off of each side, and a long porch across the front. On either side of the door Chase could see large picture windows. Off to the left he noticed a large propane tank and scattered junk—old rusting car parts, corrugated roofing, and other stuff he could not recognize. An old water well was on the right with a rusty hand pump, a worn path indicating that the pump might still be active. The cleared sections of the yard were tall and overgrown with weeds and small fir trees. There was no grass or shrubs to speak of.

As he focused, he could see the back of the house, its gently sloping land leading to a well-beaten trail heading into the woods. All of a sudden a new image flashed in his mind. A man in his late 20's was curled up into a ball in a bare room. He was tied up from behind with the lashings connecting his hands and feet. *He must be alive Chase thought, or why the restraint?* A face flashed in front him at the same moment—a face he knew well now that the Hacker's employer had given them a copy of his corporate ID. At this moment, the Hacker was wearing a light blue t-shirt and jeans, stood about 5'11," with short brown hair, and looked pretty well built. He was pacing the cabin, deep in thought. In the same breath, Chase saw another image. This time the Hacker was wearing hunting fatigues and a hat, and was pushing a man out the back of the cabin into the yard.

After Chase had figured out the profile and identified the man, the FBI immediately sent four teams to talk to relatives and acquaintances. His real name was Edward Feeney, born and raised in Quincy, Massachusetts as a foster child. He dropped out of college at the age of 20 and had no known relationships with females or others for that matter. A loner, he had not been in contact with anyone in his foster family for over six years. According to his foster mother, while Edward was in his second year of college something happened causing him to turn away, withdraw, and become almost hostile. About nine months later he simply disappeared. They did not try very hard to find him because he had been difficult at best. They tolerated him because they had made a commitment to themselves and God to raise and take care of the boy no matter what.

The last picture that came into Chase's mind was that of a smaller building, not built of logs, but rather more contemporary materials. It was a single story with very small windows and one door. Chase could not see any roads or trails around the building, which was odd as he could not place the location. He felt a chill go up his spine and an oppressive wave of fear wash over his body. He hoped to God that the image of his VIP's son being pushed out the door of the cabin was in the future... and not the past.

Chase knew the log cabin's location from tax receipts they had found in Edward's primary house on the South Shore. Just hours before, a team from the local police had pronounced the cabin empty— with no sign of activity. Chase knew they were there, though. He backed out of the parking space and continued down Route 95 south. Once he crossed into New Hampshire, he turned on Route 101 west for the hour long ride.

Once he got to the small town of Wilton, New Hampshire, he began looking for the small dirt access road that would lead him to the cabin. The road he was on looked more like a coastal back road rather than one sixty miles inland. The shoulders were sand, with sparse overgrowth just beginning to wither from the late autumn frosts. After two miles of searching, he noticed a rural marker on the left. *"This is it!"* he thought, and peeled off the pavement heading down a long and darkened dirt trail. According to the map, the cabin would be almost 1½ miles into the woods. Chase pulled his car over into the brush after a mile, and got out to look around. The forest was thick, with freshly fallen leaves providing a carpet along the forest floor.

"The leaves are nice and damp," he noticed. *"They'll provide a certain amount of stealth when approaching the cabin."* Chase knew that if the leaves were dry and crisp, it would be impossible to get close to the cabin unnoticed. He planned his strategy carefully—if he went barging in he was sure to be spotted, as Edward knew they were on to him and would be watching closely. Chase sensed that Edward had actually been nearby when the local police had gone by earlier in the day.

Springing to action, Chase popped the trunk and pulled out a large plastic container filled with his bow hunting gear hoping the Hacker would mistake him for a deer hunter and let him pass. Chase took off his leather jacket, shoulder holster and shoes and quickly got dressed. He clipped a holster behind his back with his Glock nine-millimeter

handgun, pulled on his camo top, and laced his boots. Lifting his Fred
Bear compound bow from its case, Chase put six broad head tipped
arrows into the side-mounted quiver and began his hunt.

It took about twenty minutes for Chase to get within 200 yards of
the cabin. He stopped and waited quietly, listening for the sounds of the
forest and for those of humans. The woods sounded pretty normal.
Squirrels and chipmunks were scurrying around and the birds were
singing—not making sounds of alarm. Chase began to concentrate. He
could not see or feel the Hacker in or near the cabin, so he casually
walked out of the woods into the clearing.

Walking deliberately to the water pump as if he needed to quench
his thirst, Chase looked around. He noticed an old wooden ladder lying
against the side of the cabin. Laying his bow carefully on the ground,
he picked up the ladder and began to climb to the roof.

Peering into a second story window, Chase convinced himself that
all was clear. He carefully slid the window open and stepped into a
bedroom. He stood quietly for a few moments listening to his new
surroundings—nothing. To the right was a neatly made bunk bed, and a
dresser made of solid oak. The door was slightly ajar. Chase stepped
through the door and looked out over a railing into the living area
below.

He took note of the staircase and railed walkway, and again
stopped to listen. His mind flashed with deja vu as he entered the other
bedroom. Closing his eyes, he could see the image of his VIP lying on
the floor. Chase sensed the hostage had been here earlier in the day, but
had been gone for some time now. All at once he was hit by a wave of
terror and pain, while fear shot through him as if it was his own feeling.
Images of people began to flash through his mind—men, women,
teenagers, old, young, married and single. He fell to his knees as
dozens of faces flashed before his eyes, along with visions of their
torture, pain, and death.

Disoriented, Chase stood up. "*I hope to God I'm not too late!*" he
thought, poking around the room. Finding nothing, he headed slowly
down the stairs to the large living area, containing several red couches
and a 12-point buck head mounted over the fireplace. Off to his left he
could see the kitchen wing and the wood stove that served as the
cabin's source of heat.

As Chase turned to explore the other wing he felt something crash
into his head, blinding him and sending him to the floor. His Glock was
knocked out of his hand and the last thing he saw was Edward Feeny
swinging a large cut log toward his head.

Chase's head was throbbing as he regained consciousness; he realized he was in the room upstairs, lying on the floor trussed up just like the others. He wiggled and rolled around to test the tightness of his bonds—they weren't going to come off easily.

Quieting his mind, Chase remembered tucking a small hunting blade into his boot as an afterthought. If he could slip it out he might have a chance. He rolled onto his belly tilting his boots and wrists toward the ceiling. He could feel the knife sliding down the neck of his boot. As it finally fell out onto the floor, Chase rolled onto his side and felt around until he touched the straight edge. He sawed at the rope around his wrists until the last thread snapped free.

His head felt like a cantaloupe. A good-sized knot protruded from his forehead and he could feel the dried blood caked on his cheek and neck. Finding the bathroom, he splashed cold water on his face, head, and neck, washing away the pain and the blood. As he headed downstairs, Chase couldn't figure out why he hadn't felt Edward's presence earlier. But he was sure that the guy who almost beheaded him was Edward.

"No time to dwell on it now," he thought as he headed outside to retrieve his bow. Scanning the back yard, he spotted the trail that he had seen earlier in his mind. Three sets of footprints worked themselves down the damp, leaf-covered path. Two sets stopped ten feet down the trail and turned back abruptly. *"The police,"* he thought, *"must have taken a quick look and headed back."* The third set was very fresh and disappeared around the corner.

Following slowly, Chase kept quiet as he advanced about 300 yards down a gently sloping hill into the valley below. Suddenly, the tracks veered off to the right directly into the woods. As he followed into the trees, he noticed some movement about 40 yards ahead. Just then, a shot rang out exploding against a tree one foot above his head. Wishing he had his Glock, Chase dropped low to the ground, realizing that the shot had come from his own pistol! Crawling to the left to avoid another shot he heard someone begin running and stood up to continue pursuit.

He eventually came to a small brook and noticed footprints going into the water. Searching the woods ahead, Chase saw nothing. He was about to cross the stream when he noticed a wet rock along the side about 25 feet downstream. *"Smart,"* Chase thought, *"he walked through the water to throw me off!"* Instinctively he crouched just as another shot exploded from further down the incline. This time it was a clear miss.

Chase's mind flashed to the other, smaller building he had seen in his vision. He sensed that the other building was heading up from the cabin not down. The Hacker was leading him AWAY from the other building! He had not been out cold for that long, and must have surprised the Hacker, causing him to duck down the trail.

"The important thing is to find the VIP and get him to safety," Chase thought as he ducked behind a large hemlock tree. Taking off his hat, he stuck a long stick into the ground behind some ferns and placed his hat on the stick. An old trick yes, but it worked every time. Pulling an arrow from the quiver, he loaded it into the bow, put on the mechanical trigger, and waited.

In less than a minute, Chase saw an arm come from behind a tree almost 50 yards away. It would be a long shot, but he did not want to kill the Hacker—not yet anyway. He wanted far too much information from the guy, especially if his hunch about the VIP's whereabouts was wrong. He preferred to wound Edward, and more importantly, get him running even deeper down the valley. Looking through his peep sight, he placed his aim between the 40- and 60-yard range pins. He was not a marksman, but he did believe in luck. He gently squeezed the trigger and launched the arrow silently through the forest.

He could see the arrow like a tracer as he followed the bright orange and green tail feathers blazing down the slope. His shot would be close. The angle he was shooting from would put the arrow right into the Hacker's forearm, disabling his shooting arm and sending him fleeing down the hill. BINGO! Chase saw the arrow brush the arm and plant itself into the soft wood of the tree. His instincts were right— Edward flinched and let out a soft cry of pain as he turned and fled through the trees.

Chase didn't waste a second grabbing his hat and headed back toward the cabin. He figured he had a half hour before Edward would figure out what was going on. Stopping back at the log cabin, Chase looked around for another trail. Nothing! *"Shit I am so close I can smell it!"* he muttered.

Remembering the uphill direction leading to the other building, Chase started moving slowly along the edges of the clearing, stepping back to look at the ferns bordering the forest. He could barely see ten different entry/exit points along the perimeter. *"This guy is smart,"* Chase noted, recognizing that Edward used the scatter method of covering his trail. Only a discerning eye would pick up those subtle hints, preventing most anyone from finding the second building. His adrenaline pumping, Chase started running through the woods, always heading up slope.

Twenty minutes later, Chase found what he was looking for. Getting as close as he dared, he looked through the window. There in the darkness he could see two rooms housing a table, small sofa, wood stove, and large two-door locker. Checking his watch, Chase decided he did not have any time to fool around. Carefully opening the unlocked front door he pushed his bow through first. He didn't believe there was more than one person involved but one never knew. Stepping through the door, Chase looked around quickly and carefully for any danger. Seeing and sensing nothing (not that it mattered much having gotten his head knocked off at the cabin) he picked the door on the right and opened it.

Jackpot! The VIP's son was in the room lying down on a cot, tied by his wrists and feet. He was gagged with an old cloth and was obviously not drugged up—at least not anymore. Chase was struck by the fear in his eyes; whatever he had been through in the last four weeks, he was scared to death. Quietly calling out his name, Chase told him he was there to help. Getting out his small blade, Chase cut the bonds one by one and removed the gag.

"Tom, we need to get out of here quickly," Chase hissed. "Can you walk?" Tom spit and could barely utter any words after being gagged for so long.

"Y-y-yes," Tom choked, as he raised himself up from the cot trying to stand. He was a little wobbly, but it didn't take long for the adrenaline to kick in when Tom realized he was being saved. Chase asked him when he had been moved from the other building.

"Late yesterday afternoon, I think," Tom rasped. "He's had me in the cabin for days or weeks," he continued, having no idea it had already been four weeks. "The asshole's been giving me some kind of injection and I've been out of it most of the time. Yesterday afternoon the guy came running into the cabin in a panic, untied my bonds, and led me here. He was obviously afraid of something."

"Is he the only one here?" Chase asked.

"Yes," said Tom. "He would be gone for days at a time then come back and give me some food and water." Chase studied Tom carefully, noting that his dark brown hair was matted and greasy, his shirt torn and stained, and his pants were soiled with excrement causing a very bad odor.

"Okay Tom, I managed to get this guy out of our hair for a little while but he'll be back any minute. We have to get out into the woods and try to get back to my car. Are you sure you're up to this?

"Yeah," Tom answered with a look of desperation. Chase took him by the hand and led him to the front door. Pausing for a moment, Chase settled his spirit and focused on Edward's whereabouts. A picture came into his mind. Edward was driving down a back road not too far from where they were.

Chase was not sure if the vision was present, past, or future, but decided they needed to move quickly. Darting out into the trees, Chase led them back down the valley, skirting around the log cabin to the far road where Chase's car would be waiting.

They had just moved behind the large propane tank when a shot rang out and grazed Chase's shoulder. Pushing Tom down into a bed of ferns, he took cover behind a pile of junk. Another shot hit the piece of galvanized roofing he was behind and bounced right by his head. Ducking down, Chase gathered his thoughts. The shots were coming from a second story window in the cabin. Edward had a good line of sight but did not have any spare ammo for the gun, and four out of nine shots had already been expended. Loading his bow, Chase moved away from the pile of junk taking cover behind a small fir tree. Stealth was his advantage now! Pulling down his face mask, Chase took advantage of the approaching twilight. He whispered to Tom to stay down and keep quiet as he moved about 30 feet further down through the forest.

Chase could barely make out Edward's figure peering out the window. He knew he would only have one shot and had to make it count. Drawing the bow, he held his breath and waited for the Hacker's impatience. Finally, Edward inched closer to the window and took a hard look out. Chase could tell he was having trouble seeing in the coming darkness.

Edward held out the pistol and took three random shots into the woods around the tank. "*Shit,*" Chase thought hearing a grunt coming from the ferns. "*Tom has been hit!*" Tom did not get up or move as the Hacker leveled the gun in the direction of the grunt. Chase let loose his arrow. The projectile soared through the air with lightning speed piercing Edward's chest before he could even hear it coming. Chase watched him fall back and heard him cry in pain. He ran over to see about Tom. He was lying still, with dirt and mud covering his face.

"Tom, are you okay?" Chase asked.

"Yes, I was lying here when a shot landed right in front of my face," he answered. "Dirt flew into my eyes and blinded me."

"Let's get out of here," said Chase, breathing a sigh of relief. "I just got a clean shot and hit the guy. Hopefully he's not getting up."

Chase led him into the yard and headed toward the road. Fifteen feet from freedom they heard the front door squeak. Turning around, they froze at the sight of a bloody figure in the doorway, a Glock in his hand, and an arrow sticking out from his shoulder. Edward fired a wild shot. Guessing that there was only one shot left, Chase pushed Tom to the ground. Wobbling, Edward fell back against the door and raised the gun one more time. Chase had already loaded the bow, drawn, and was sighting as they both fired their weapons. The bullet whizzed by Chase long before the arrow hit its target. Edward and Chase both watched the arrow sail across the lawn. It seemed to move in slow motion before it pounded the Hacker in the chest pinning him to the front door. Edward's face did not show pain but rather serenity, and then suddenly, his lips curled into the most evil smile Chase had ever seen, his eyes rolling into the back of his head. Chase knew that the look on Edwards face would haunt him for the rest of his life.

Chapter 1

Seattle, Washington---17 Years Later

When the solid door opened, he could feel the draw of air rushing up from the depths of the musty stone corridor. Thinking back, he realized this place had been quite the find. With a twisted smile, he recounted finding the house he now owned. About a year after he bought it, he was searching the building plans at the town hall to see if he could build additions for his extracurricular activities, but found something odd. There were spaces in his house that were not accounted for in the original drawings. After carefully studying the layouts, he broke through a wall in the cellar and discovered a stone passageway that wound down almost 200 feet below and behind his house. The passageway ended at the foundation of a second house, diagonal to his. The walls were made of thick, ancient cobblestones, the color of dark gray ash. Every five feet three sided archways of heavy oak beams provided support. After the archways, stairs led down to the next level, the pattern repeating itself all the way to the house at the bottom of the hill. Lengths of granite provided a firm and sound flooring. Further exploration revealed four good sized rooms off the passageway. All of the rooms were made of stone and each was buried under at least fifteen feet of dirt, fill, and heavy bushes running down the "no-mans" land on the sharp incline between the houses. One of the rooms even boasted a jail. His curiosity piqued, he researched the deeds for both properties and learned that the original builder had been a famous bootlegger back in the 1920's. The property had been used to store illegal products and to house all kinds of activities that were not meant for prying eyes.

There had been a rudimentary electrical system which he had subsequently ripped out and replaced with a modern one. He upgraded the master circuit breaker in the main house and connected a main lead to a secondary breaker in the passageway. This way, casual inspection would not give away the fact that wires were running into the wall.

Inside the house, he made sure he had major electrical appliances in every room so that his electrical bills, being higher than normal, would again stand up to inspection—he just never turned those devices on. He bought a very elaborate security system which included video, audio, and infrared detection that could be controlled from his laptop, PDA, basement, or inside the passageway. His PDA was especially handy because he was away frequently and could control lights, temperature, and some specialized equipment from anywhere in the world.

After six months of renovation, he felt satisfied that the place was ready. The four rooms had been cleaned out, gutted, and completely renovated to his needs. The walls and ceilings had been covered with soot and ash from many years of oil lamps being used as the primary source of light. He had found all sorts of great memorabilia left behind when the place had been sealed including oil lamps, crates, and half-empty barrels of whiskey. In the room he now used as a workplace, he had found a hidden wall safe standing five feet tall and three feet wide. Using a web site to decipher the combination, he still remembered the day he found all kinds of accounting journals, client ledgers, a very old Smith and Wesson six shot revolver and $1,200 in hard currency—all of which were in pristine condition. The owner must have abandoned this place in a hurry and never come back.

The first room on the right was the old jail cell he had converted into the holding room, where his victims were kept while alone. Even though the walls and ceiling looked more like a dungeon than anything else, the room was decorated nicely and looked warm and cozy. The room was designed for either passive or aggressive restraint and he had included an active water system allowing for shower and toilet functions. The drainage for the system was simply a leaching field underneath the hill. He had removed the iron bars and door from the original structure and replaced them with a contemporary steel reinforced door that was electronically locked or unlocked with the push of a button recessed into the passageway wall. There was also a concealed latch on both sides that would take a very well-trained eye or extraordinary luck to find. The floors were covered with wall to wall carpeting that helped reduce noise and cold. The bed, love seat, and reclining chair were each rigged with restraint systems.

Down the first flight of stairs after the holding room was the "clean" room as he called it. This was a very sterile room with the same steel door structure as the first. Inside however, there was no carpeting or furniture. Instead, two metal morgue-class gurneys with straps were neatly lined up against the back wall. A large steel wash basin with two sections on either side stood in the corner, along with three double door lockers containing medical and chemical supplies. An elaborate system was mounted on the far wall, with four different colored canisters, wires, blowers, and small plastic tubes running in all different directions. He had added a washer/dryer, small electric stove, refrigerator, and wooden pantry. An oval surgical light on a swivel arm hung from the ceiling.

Down yet another set of stairs, was the best room of all. He called it the "fun" room. Unlike the first two rooms, this was decorated in traditional Japanese, with three by six foot Tatami mats covering most of the granite floors. A platform with a huge futon mattress covered with large satin pillows sat in the center of the room, with white floor pillows scattered around the platform. To the left of the bed a small wooden cabinet containing a jade Buddha, candles, and a scroll written in Kanji adorned the wall. In an alcove on the right was a small bathroom and shower.

In his workroom—the last room in the passageway—a traditional Japanese desk sat 18 inches off the floor, with a thick pillow in place of a normal chair. A flat screen computer monitor, keyboard and mouse sat on the desk. On the wall behind the desk an ornate hand carved mount sported two Katanas cradled gently in felt-covered pegs. A small cabinet housed a server, printer, and high end stereo system. A second Buddha altar, this one larger and more elegant, sat to the left of the desk, flanked by long tapestries inscribed with a single Kanji character.

For two years he had waited patiently for the owners of the connecting house to put the place on the market. He quickly purchased it through a dummy entity he had set up years ago to keep his abnormal activities secret. Although he had used the passageway's hidden rooms while the second house was still occupied, he was only able to stage one of his "concubines" every few months. It was very dangerous because of possible noise and the fact that he had to use his own house as the entry and exit point.

Five years, two houses, and 27 concubines later, he was feeling very bold knowing that the FBI was on to him. They had even searched his house on two different occasions but came up empty-handed— thanks to his own modifications of the foundation walls. Fortunately they had not used dogs yet, although he was sure even the dogs would come up blank because of the sanitization process he underwent every time he went into and out of the passageway.

Tonight was the third-to-last step with his current concubine, Tanya Richie. She was not the prettiest of the girls, but she had a very sensual body that really got him hot. She had not shown any adverse reactions to the chemical dusting system he used to ready the girls, either. The expertly-mixed chemical cloud could be activated from six different places and took only two minutes to dissipate, giving him access to a harmless, willing woman for about 45 minutes. He found that most of the girls had a hard time recalling the details of the sessions, although they could feel the effects on the areas of the body. Tanya had the right personality for this. After the dust cloud took effect, she was not only willing, but actually became the aggressor wanting to unbury all her hidden lust and desire for her new master. He would be sorry in the morning if things did not work out with Tanya, for the fourth step was that of cleansing. He had already chosen the method of termination if needed, and was searching for a new dumping site for her about twenty miles northwest of the city. As he punched the activation button, he was anticipating the fun and games for the evening...

Chapter 2

Providence, Rhode Island

Yellow police tape stretched around the front of the old warehouse in downtown Providence, Rhode Island. State and local police vehicles were strewn among the fire, ambulance, and city coroner trucks along the closed-off street. Special agent Bob Fellows pulled into an empty spot and began to survey the layout. The warehouse was an old three-story building that had been condemned some years earlier and had so far escaped the mad renovation craze revitalizing downtown. An old sign just over the second story windows suggested that the building had been a meat distribution center decades ago. This made sense, because directly behind the building were the remnants of the old rail line that connected Providence to Boston and Portsmouth to the north, and Waterbury and New York City to the south.

Flashing his FBI badge, Agent Fellows followed the local officers into the front of the building. *"God, this place smells,"* he thought, scanning the antique architecture. To the left was what must have been the administration offices. The walls came up halfway where glass took over up to the ceiling. Old furniture was scattered about, but for the most part the building had long since been cleaned out one way or another. Bob could see blue police tape blocking the rooms and hallways, sealing off areas where footprints might damage the evidence. *"One of the first cops on the scene must have been on the ball,"* he thought. In Bob's experience, the blue tape usually came out after 20 people had virtually walked all over the evidence. The forensic teams had also created paths through the areas where general traffic could walk without worrying about covering up evidence. Through one of the blue areas he saw the person he was looking for—Lieutenant Seville Waters. She was directing a few cops and making some notes into a hand held electronic device. Seeing Bob, a half frown and half smile came across her face. Bob extended his hand to Seville and at the same time kissed her on the cheek. She blushed at the greeting, feeling the other officers looking at them. Everyone in the room could tell Bob was a fed and the feds always made the local cops uneasy. Without hesitation Bob said, "It's good to see you again Seville. I'm sorry it is under these circumstances, though."

Bob and Seville had met a year earlier in Las Vegas during a week long seminar on profiling serial killers. Both were single at the time and before half the seminar was over, they had formed a bond. Their last three days were spent not attending many of the remaining sessions, but rather in one or the other's hotel room. At the end of the conference, they had both made bold intentions to continue the newly-formed relationship when they returned to New England. However, after a few rushed dates between Boston and Providence, Bob's schedule precluded any lasting commitment.

"Let's try to catch up later," replied Seville. "Right now I want to fill you in on what we have here. Based on the two bodies we found it looks a lot like the Lumber Jack's calling card. We're not sure how long they've been here or even where they come from yet," she continued. "We're running missing person reports in Rhode Island, Massachusetts, Connecticut, Vermont, and New Hampshire for the last two weeks. One of the bodies is over in the back in an old meat locker, and the second is on the third floor in an old storage area. I really mean torso. Both of them are missing heads, arms, and legs and we haven't found the extremities yet. According to the local precinct cops, a homeless guy came running out of here just after midnight screaming that Aliens had landed and were conducting obscene science experiments on people. The cops came in to investigate and after finding these two they called in the troops and cordoned off the area. Bob, I need to know right now what the FBI's intent is. If you are planning to take this crime scene over let me now or we are going to keep sifting through the pieces!"

Bob frowned. "Henry White, the head of the FBI serial unit, sent me down to take a look at the place," he explained. "I need to call in a recommendation within the hour to the Boston Bureau and to Henry down in Virginia. So far it looks like your team has been on the ball— which frankly is unusual for the locals. Let's take a look around Seville. Our forensics team already has 3 Lumber Jack sites under its belt and I would like to call them in to help you all out".

"Alright Bob," said Seville raising an eyebrow. "I just don't want to spoil the good work the team is doing. You know I have worked damn hard over the last two years building a serial capability. These guys are good and I want to give them a shot to prove their stuff. As a matter of fact, I would like them to work with your forensics team anyway because it's good cross training. Just please tell your crew to work with us instead of right through us like we don't exist." *What an arrogant SOB,* she thought to herself. *How did I get tangled up with him in the first place? Then she remembered it was all about being lonely. Thank God she had decided to make some major changes in her life.*

"Good enough, Seville," said Bob pulling a white facemask over his mouth. He headed to the meat locker for his first examination of the remains...

Chapter 3

Jaffrey, New Hampshire

The early morning twilight was so beautiful. Chase had gotten up at 5:00 am sharp, put on his hunting gear and headed out the back door onto the state forest reserve. Today was opening day for bow hunting. Chase had spent the last four weeks scouting a 90 acre area for deer trail, scrapes, rubs and other signs that might lead him to the big trophy buck he had run into a couple of seasons ago. Last season, he had spent the entire six weeks looking for that big buck, had found his sign and even received confirmation from a jogger one day who had seen the gigantic 12 pointer while running down the bike trail. He never even got to encounter the very sly, nocturnal, easily-spooked creature. This year he hoped his scouting would pay off early in the season so he could enjoy the outdoors without this all-consuming obsession.

Years of traveling through this forest allowed Chase to get almost anywhere in the pitch black without a flash light. Today his destination was the far north corner where he had found the big buck's trail near a large stream. He suspected that the buck was feeding in the forest during the night, and then swimming across the water at dawn to bed down for the day without risking predators or hunters. Chase quickly put his climber together and scurried up a tall hardwood tree that would give him ample shooting options. Once he got up about 20 feet, he positioned the climber, attached his safety harness and settled into the seat. Ten minuets later he barely heard the soft but firm footsteps slowly advancing through the woods. The sound was coming from his left, which would make for the best shot with the bow. Looking through the vent in his scent proof hood, he watched carefully for any movement. About 30 yards away the brush moved and he saw a very large deer step through the thicket into a small clearing. His heart thumping, Chase readied the bow and began to draw the string back. As the deer emerged, he saw that it was a very big doe, not his prized 12 pointer! Too early in the season to bag an antlerless deer, he let loose the strings and put the bow to resting position.

Carefully listening once again, he heard another set of footsteps off to the right. Sure enough, through the thick trees he could see what looked like slowly-moving branches about 45 yards off. It had to be the buck! His heart racing, Chase thought the situation through. He needed the buck to continue advancing toward the tree stand for at least another 20 yards to make sure he could get a nice clean shot in the kill zone. However, the buck was moving off in a diagonal direction—he would never get a shot if he continued that way! Thinking quickly, he quietly removed a doe call from his jacket pocket and let out three quick bleats. Fortunately, the doe had come another ten yards closer. The buck stopped cold in its tracks as he saw the doe advancing. As luck would have it, the early rut was starting and the buck took interest in the doe. With a single bound, the buck changed direction and advanced fifteen yards toward the doe. Shooting right handed Chase had to make some body gyrations in order to position for the shot. It would also not be a good idea to try to get the buck to come across the front of the stand because he knew how easily they spooked. "*Another 10 yards,*" he thought, pulling the string back so slowly he could barely tell it was moving. Just then, another doe came into a clearing straight ahead of the tree stand and also caught the buck's attention.

Chase could not believe it! Ninety-nine percent of the time he was out hunting he saw nothing at all. Now when the trophy buck he had been stalking for three seasons was right here, every deer in the woods seemed to be around to screw it up. "*Time for drastic measures,*" he thought as the buck moved away from the stand. Projecting out along the buck's path he could not find a shooting lane for a clear shot. This time he decided to get the buck riled up. He pulled out another cylinder—a buck call—and gave it two deep draws creating a loud and low male deer grunting noise. Again the buck stopped. The deer could not see the other buck that just grunted, but was sure he did not want that buck sharing the does in this little neck of the woods. He charged around, his 12-point antlers high, and rushed toward the tree stand. "*Not too close,*" Chase coached as the big buck charged. Looking frantically for the other contender, the buck stopped about 20 yards from the tree, pausing near the first doe. A tree blocked Chase from taking a nice broadside shot. Holding his breath, bow fully drawn, Chase waited for what seemed to be an hour as the buck carefully advanced one more step beyond the tree. *Thwack!* Chase released the trigger on the firing mechanism, watching the camouflaged arrow leave the bow at an exciting speed, its florescent green and yellow feathers acting as tracers as it sped toward the target. He could barely make out the arrow as it entered into the side of the buck right behind its front leg. The majestic animal grunted upon the impact of the arrow and careened away from the scene into the dense forest.

"Three long years and I finally got the sucker!" Chase exclaimed, as he caught the white tails of the two does fleeing toward the water. A splash, then another splash told him that the does were swimming across to one of the many marsh islands on the other side of the stream. He made a mental note to add that crossing to his hunting journal as a possible spot for the future.

Chase could feel the blood coursing through his veins with the rush of the moment. He would wait a little while before tracking the animal to make sure it was dead. He did not want to keep bumping it further into the woods. Eventually, he lowered his bow to the ground and climbed down to the forest floor. It took a moment but soon he found the back end of the arrow sticking out of the soft ground. Pulling the arrow out, he saw that it was covered with a bright red viscous fluid from tip to tip. It was a clean hit, penetrating the liver or lungs at entry and with a little luck it struck the heart on the way down.

Replaying the sequence through his head, he jumped as his cell phone rang. "Damn!" he mumbled, "I forgot to turn this off before the hunt." Chase thanked his lucky stars the call had not come just 30 minutes earlier.

"Chase, this is Sam, I'm down in Providence. Late last night, two bodies were found, both missing all their extremities including the heads. Looks like the Lumber Jack has struck again! Other than the torsos, there is no evidence at all at the scene."

"The Lumber Jack, huh?" quizzed Chase. "He is one nasty I would love to get out of commission soon. Didn't you just schedule the executive team meeting on him? Chase thought, *"These two would be victims number 28 and 29, and the first time more than one torso was found at the same scene."*

"Yes Chase, the team and I think we have pinned the guy down. He lives on the Cape but also has a place up in the woods in Maine. His name is Emit Ferguson, no priors *but,* I just ran into Bob Fellows of the FBI. He came down from the Boston office, and he is very interested in all the information we have on the Lumber Jack. He wants us to go downtown this afternoon to meet with him and a detective from Providence. I played stupid for the most part, but told him we could probably meet him at his office downtown after lunch today."

"So they want to grill us, huh?" asked Chase. "I don't think I mind on this one because this guy needs to be caught quickly. Go ahead and tell Bob that we will meet him later on. Listen Sam, not to be callous, but do you know that big trophy buck I have been trailing the last few seasons?"

Sam interrupted and said, "Chase, you know that we would all love for you to get that buck so we can stop hearing about…."

"Listen!" Chase practically shouted through the phone. "I just got him! No shit—30 minutes ago. It is going to take me a couple of hours to track him, dress him, and haul him out of here. I'll meet you at our office by 11:00. We can head downtown from there. Have Louise make sure the case is all wrapped so we can review it later on. Also, tell her we may have to do a remote connection so we can brief the FBI."

There was a brief silence on the other end. "You got the buck? *THE buck?*" Sam cried. "I don't believe you! You had better bring that bad boy back because if I don't see it with my own eyes, well, you know…"

"You will not only see it, you can help me check it in at the deer check station on the way into town. See you in a few," Chase replied, closing his cell phone and slipping it into his pocket. Thinking twice, he pulled it back out, turned it off, and replaced it again. Nothing, not even the Lumber Jack was going to ruin the rest of this moment for Chase.

Chapter 4

Seattle

Tanya could not tell what time it was or even how many days she had been there. Her head pounded like a New Year's Day hangover and her eye sight was blurry at best. She had a vague memory about a man she had become very intimate with. An oriental man she was sure, but could not guess whether he was Chinese, Japanese, or what. He had not treated her badly and this simple fact gave her a shred of hope. It could have been days, even weeks since she had been abducted. The last thing she remembered before arriving here, was riding down the elevator in her apartment complex as she was heading out for the night to meet her friends. Somehow this guy had taken her from there and moved her here, without any physical violence. Now that her senses were coming back, she was starting to remember things. She remembered sitting in a vaulted room hearing a rush of air suddenly blasting down the corridor outside. She could feel the chill of air moving that had otherwise been stagnant. At the same time, she could see a smoky mist coming out through a number of nozzles protruding from the high ceilings. The last memory she had involved a different room—with a large bed in the middle, music playing, and a bathroom with a two-person shower. She had been having sex with this man, and enjoying it immensely. She could still feel the tingles as she thought of just how unabashed she had become with this man she did not know, taking him in ways that she had only joked about with her girlfriends. Remembering this, she started to feel her body. Bruises and sore spots suddenly revealed themselves to her as she saw in her mind's eye the things they had been doing. An odd thought raced through her mind as a vision of a very small penis came into view followed by another penis that was quite the opposite. How did he do that? Were there two men? She could not remember the details. As she curled up in a fetal position on her bed she heard that rushing sound from the hallway again. Oh no, he's coming back! What's next? Maybe he is going to set me free now! Tanya looked up at the ceiling at the nozzles waiting for the mist to appear but it did not come. Was she going to be spared the drugs this time?

Suddenly terror grabbed hold of her and her eyes darted around the room quickly, looking for something she could use as a weapon. She found nothing. Her heart was pounding and she had all but forgotten about her aches and pains, as instinct and the need to survive took over her every breath. The sound of footsteps came down the stairs and stopped in front of her door. She could see his eyes peering at her through the horizontal slot, a vaguely familiar voice saying hello. Then he opened the door and walked through. She prayed that she was dreaming—this was the man who had taken her from her life—and violated her. The anger was forming deep down in her belly, taking control of her mind and body as she realized that he was done with her and had come to finish this somehow. She was not meant to leave this place alive. Without thought or care, she lunged off the bed at the man in a desperate attempt to catch him off guard and put an end to this nightmare. The man stood at the other end of the room, no expression on his face as she rushed towards him. His blank stare seemed to turn into one of disappointment as Tanya moved within five feet of him. To her horror, he raised his left hand and released two string-like projectiles that pierced her chest. The voltage from the stun gun knocked her down, turning her mind into white noise as her senses left her one by one and she collapsed to the floor.

Masanori looked at the woman on the floor, his insides filled with rage. Each time he arrived at this critical point with one of his concubines he experienced the same thing—rejection. Just once, he wanted the woman to accept him, come to him in love, and tell him that they could be together forever. What was wrong with these women? Did they not realize what they could have? They could be anything, do anything, and have anything if they just loved him! A tear came to his eyes as he thought about Tanya. She was very pretty—not stunning, but pretty. She could have been the girl next door, with her blue eyes and light skin with a few freckles here and there. Her light blond hair was soft and long enough to flow across her breasts. "*She could have been the one,*" he lamented, as he sat down wiping the tears from his face. His eyes lit up thinking about having her one more time, but thought better of it and moved on to the fourth step. Even though all of the girls had rejected him, he insisted on treating them kindly—even to their deaths. He carried Tanya out of her prison down the hall to yet another room. Laying her out on the surgical table in the middle of the room, he strapped her onto the cold metal slab. He only had a few more moments before she might wake up. Pulling out a bottle containing clear liquid, he picked up a respirator mask and pulled it over his head. Carefully unscrewing the cap, he poured a small amount of the liquid onto a clean white cloth. Quietly placing the cloth over her mouth and nose he said goodbye to Tanya.

Chapter 5

FBI HQ--Quantico

Henry hit the intercom button on his phone set and his admin Grace announced the call from Bob Fellows of the Boston branch. He hit another button and said "Bob, what have you got?"

"I just left the Providence crime scene and it sure looks like the Lumber Jack. Two bodies in different areas of the meat warehouse, both are missing all the extremities including the heads. I went through the entire scene and having been to three other Lumber Jack sites I would say it fits the MO. I did run into Sam Johnson from Serial Connections as you suspected. He was not very cooperative either. I invited him, Chase Benton and Seville Waters from the RIPD to the Boston office this afternoon to have a come to Jesus meeting regarding the Lumber Jack."

"Bob, I have reason to believe that the Serial Connections group has been making a lot of progress on the Lumber Jack case and several others we are working on. I want you to get very close to them and especially to Chase. As a matter of fact, I want you to cancel the meeting at your office, get Seville Waters, and meet Chase at Serial Connections Headquarters. I want you to have a very good look around up there and want a report on the top three cases they are working on with as much background info as you can get. Take down my cell phone number and call me day or night." Henry commanded.

Bob said, "I can do that. Are these guys up to anything I need to know about? Why the special attention?"

Henry replied, "I am under a great deal of pressure to get the Lumber Jack, Maryland Devil, and the Samurai cases solved quickly and by us. I want to make sure that we are taking the lead on each case and that when they break it is *this* agency that breaks them and not Serial Connections. Get any and all information you can from Serial Connections and merge the data with ours. You might want to selectively give Chase some information so that it looks like we are feeding them. I will help you on that front."

Bob hesitated and asked, "Just who are these guys? I have heard of them before and even met one or two Serial Connections operatives. They seem to be on the up and up. Do you have any background on them?" Henry sat back in his chair, put his feet up on the desk and gave him a personal history on the organization. "About 17 years ago there was a VIP in the Boston area whose son was kidnapped by who we know now was one of the most successful and sadistic Serials ever. The case had been kept very close to the vest all along because we believed the body count from this guy was into three figures. The team I was leading decided early on not to let this one into the media because widespread panic could have prevailed. Fortunately, the Hacker (the nickname we had given him) did not have a signature on his work. Many of the victims hit the press but to the casual observer, they seemed to be random slayings not connected at all. We had discovered a year or so into the case some evidence that linked at least nine of the random killings to the same person. That's when we opened the file for the Hacker and put together a special team."

He continued "I led that team and we spent the next two years connecting as many unidentified slayings as we could to the Hacker. In two years, we were fairly certain that more than 35 victims might be his handy work. He was good, real good. We had begun to connect the victims but we were no closer in two years to figuring out who the guy was and where he was working from. Most of the 35 victims were from the New England area so we concentrated our efforts in Vermont, New Hampshire, Massachusetts, and Rhode Island. Through our forensic studies and missing persons reports were able to determine that he held his victims for as much as five weeks before killing them then discarding the bodies. As far as we knew he would always dump the bodies in a public place where they would be found within a few days. Even to this day we do not know exactly how many killings he was responsible for and if he dumped bodies in remote places."

"Anyway, we got a call one day from the Governor of Massachusetts. He told us that one of Boston's wealthiest and most powerful men had reported his son missing. The Governor was pulling in everyone he could to help this guy. After our initial interviews we reported to the VIP that we thought his son might have been abducted by the Hacker. The son fit the general profile of the 35 victims we had connected to him so far. After we briefed him on our Hacker file he went ballistic. He couldn't believe that there was nothing we could do. He was told we would put 20 new agents on the case but felt hopeless anyway. That's when he hired Chase Benton. Chase was a private investigator. Not the usual type you think of. He specialized in missing persons and had a very successful track record. Four of his cases involved serials that ended up being caught as a result of his work."

The VIP brought him into the case and insisted we share our case files with him. For the first few days the relationship was very tense as you can imagine. But then things started to happen. Chase has this uncanny sixth sense about things. It is like he can feel and see things that don't exist. In just a week he had put together a profile of the guy that was unbelievable. According to Chase, the Hacker was from southern Vermont, was college educated, had a professional job that required travel around the New England states and had a severe personality complex that drove him to "eliminate" people that he thought were better than him. So inside of a couple weeks we had a profile. Chase conducted a briefing session with all our agents and we got to work. Time was running out though. It had been almost four weeks since the VIP's son had been missing and we knew that we had five weeks tops to find the kid. Chase took 10 of the agents and started connecting the dots from the 35 cases we suspected were the Hackers with the VIP's son. We got lucky. In a few days we found the connection. Office equipment! Chase was the one who figured it out. He had seen three or four things in his mind that could be common denominators between the cases, but office equipment was ringing in his head. He had us check every company that all the victims worked for with the corresponding office equipment and found they all had the same supplier for copy machines, faxes and so forth. A detailed look showed all of them had been serviced by the same technician over the last five years. We had the guy. He lived in a small town in Vermont just over the border from Massachusetts but was traveling at the moment. We got a warrant and raided his house. It was empty with absolutely no trace of any evidence. We contacted his company to find out where he was and they told us he was currently up in Portland Maine doing routine maintenance on several large accounts. We all raced up there, staked out his hotel and the three companies he was supposed to be working at and came up with nothing. When we called his company back we learned that he had called in and someone told him we were looking for him.

We got skunked badly but Chase was right back into the thick of it before we even knew what was going on. While we were at his house in Vermont Chase had uncovered an address on a tax statement for a cabin in Southern New Hampshire. He didn't tell us because we had just totally fucked things up. The rest happened very quickly; within six hours the Hacker was dead, the VIP's Son was found barely alive, and psychic/forensic evidence was gathered that confirmed most of the 35 cases we were working on and 20 we had not linked. According to the report filed by Chase he had played cat and mouse in the woods with the Hacker before taking him out with a hunting bow. Anyway, after the dust settled the VIP approached Chase and offered to set up a permanent trust fund of more than $100 million dollars for Chase to start an organization dedicated to the profiling and capture of serial killers. That was seventeen years ago. Since then the Serial Connections foundation has grown considerably through government and private endowments. They have what is considered one of the most comprehensive databases on serials in the world, and have identified and captured or led authorities to capture over 100 of them." Bob whistled through the phone as he listened to Henry's story about Chase and Serial Connections.

Bob said, "Henry, what do you think they have on the Lumber Jack?"

"I don't know" answered Henry, "That's what I want you to find out for me. I know they have a file on case, but I am pretty sure they do not have a comprehensive profile on the individual yet. That means we still have a shot at bringing this asshole in ourselves." Henry then reminded Bob to keep him posted on anything interesting materializing through Serial Connections as he hung up the phone.

Henry White looked around his office at the decorations, commendations, special citations, and other memorabilia from having served the FBI very successfully for the last 22 years. He had seen just about everything an FBI person could see and done an equal amount. 15 years ago he was asked to join the national team that profiled and hunted down the worst of the country's serials. To this date he had been involved in or responsible for the arrest, capture, or death of over 17 of the most wanted serials in the country. Highly regarded inside and outside the FBI as one of the leading experts on serial crime, Henry taught many law enforcement seminars for state and local police departments on profiling, setting up, and catching these modern day vampires. *Chase and Serial Connections have got to go,* thought Henry. *He has been stealing my thunder way too long. I am so tired of that son of a bitch getting all the glory and making my department look like the keystone cops. I need to have all their bandwidth on the Lumber Jack case just until I can get things rolling here....*

Henry finished putting a video tape and letter into a white Federal Express envelope when he pushed the button on his phone. "Grace!"

Henry shouted into the intercom system. "I have a FedEx package here that has to go to Seattle immediately. Would you please drop it downstairs for me?"

Chapter 6

Ocean City/Gaithersburg, Maryland

The killer sat at his dark colored desk, his feet up on the windowsill as he looked out over the boardwalk and into the frothing waves of the Atlantic Ocean. His mind began to wander as he thought about his next ritual. The family he had picked out was at this very moment cleaning the rental unit where they had stayed on vacation for the last week. Check out time was 10:00PM and after having spoken with them that Wednesday, he knew they were planning on spending the morning here doing some last minute stuff with the kids before heading back to their home on the outskirts of Gaithersburg.

He had stopped by earlier in the week to check out a supposed electrical problem in their unit so he could meet them and get to know them better before he executed his plans. The father was an average guy, medium build, strong but not trade strong. He was good looking he supposed, but certainly not model material. His gut protruded with the telltale signs of a beer drinker, and sure enough even at 11:00 in the morning on the day of his visit, Dad was already nursing a Budweiser. The wife on the other hand, was definitely model material on the outside. She was about 5'9," medium length brunette hair, sharp and attractive facial features and a figure that was carved by many hours at the gym. When she answered the front door, she was wearing her bathing suit top and a wrap around her waist that was sheer and not very concealing. It was hard for him not to check her out up and down definitely liking what he saw. When she opened her mouth though, the external beauty seemed to drift away. It was clear she had not gone to Harvard and when she spoke, that awful Maryland backwoods accent came out loud and clear. He was not concerned though because it was not her mind he was after.

The two teenagers were fairly predictable. The boy was about 15 years old and in that awkward stage where you could tell his body was trying to sprout but had not quite gotten there. He was already in his knee high swim trunks and looked like he was dying to get out to the beach for a day filled with bogey boarding. The girl was a little older, looked more like her father than mother, sported a very pimply face, and was generally disinterested with everything around her. She had begun to blossom into womanhood and had the makings of her mother's great figure.

After checking out the circuit breaker in the unit, the killer struck up a casual conversation with the parents. They would be checking out on Saturday at 10:00PM and spending most of the morning here in Ocean City before making the four hour trip back home to Gaithersburg. Both of them had taken a couple of extra days off from work so that when they got home, they could lazily unpack and unwind. He had coaxed them into talking about their house as he gently pried some very important information from them. They had no security system, no pets, and the closest neighbor lived about 400 yards down the road—perfect.

Looking down at his watch he saw that it was time to leave. If he planned the trip right he would get to the house about three hours before they did. This was good. It was important for him to have a lay of the land in order to conduct his very exact ritual. He got up from his desk, tidied a few things on the top and walked out of his office. He walked down the street a couple of blocks away and unlocked a door that led into a storage garage. He hopped into a 7 year old green Ford sedan with Virginia license plates, pushed the button on the garage door opener, and headed down the main street to the causeway over to the mainland.

In just over four hours he found himself driving slowly by the driveway marked #147 Cotton Wood Street. He continued driving for about a mile to survey the area then turned around and headed back. He spotted an old grass road into the woods not too far from their house that he decided to back the sedan into so the car would not be visible from the road. Getting out, he took his knapsack and walked through the woods along the road until he was across the street from #147. Listening carefully for cars or people and satisfied there were none, he casually walked out of the woods, across the road and up the driveway to the house. After he did a quick walk around he checked the obvious places for the spare key. Sure enough, in the backyard he picked up an ornamental frog sitting on the stone pathway to the kitchen door and found a key. *People are so predictable!*, he mused, as he replaced the frog and entered the kitchen door. Inside the house was quiet and the air was stale from being vacant all week. He spent the next 30 minutes going from room to room, making mental notes of furniture placements, beds, bathrooms, doors, and windows. He opened and closed every door to test for squeaks as well as creaks in the floors. Next he went down to the cellar to search for his hiding place. The door to the basement had no locks on it so he was certain he would have no trouble getting back up after nightfall. Downstairs was dark and musty. A workbench was in the far right corner as he came down the stairs. As he walked around, he found an old section of the cellar wall that went halfway up and opened into a crawl space underneath the attached garage. This is it he thought.

He opened his backpack and took out four little electronic devices and went back upstairs. He placed the first one in the kitchen on top of one of the cabinets. Next he went upstairs and put one in each of the three bedrooms, concealing them from eye sight. He took one more look around upstairs and carefully planned the sequence of his ritual massacre. Then he headed back down to the basement, got into the crawl space and began the long wait.

Chapter 7

Jaffrey

"Good Morning, Serial Connections" the woman said politely into the phone. "Karen, this is Chase, how are you today?"

"Hey Chase!" Karen said excitedly. "I heard you finally got that big buck you've been obsessing about. Congratulations!"

"Thanks," he said, "I'll fill you in on all the details later."

"You'd better" she exclaimed with a sarcastic tone, "We've been listening to you whine about that deer for years!"

"Listen Karen, I just got a call from Bob Fellows from the Boston branch of the FBI. Sam and I were going to meet him downtown after lunch but he wants to come out here instead. He's bringing along a Lieutenant from the Providence PD as well. Could you please call out and get sandwiches and stuff for the meeting?"

"Sure Chase, where are you now?"

"Sam and I are on the way to Bonds Corner to check Mr. Buck in. After that we are headed over to West Jaffrey to the butcher to have him fix us all up some nice steaks, burgers, and jerky. You had better get the company grill cleaned up; we're going to be eating like kings until Christmas!" Chase said excitedly.

"What luck" Karen replied, "See you around noon?"

"Yup, oh, and if they get there before us, please give them the grand tour. They are coming over specifically regarding the Lumber Jack. You can show them the portrait room but don't take out the Lumber Jack portfolio until we get back—OK?"

"You got it boss!" she said as she hung up the phone.

Karen looked at her watch, it was 11:00. She picked the phone back up and called downtown to the deli and ordered lunch for eight. The phone rang again. "Good Morning, Serial Connections," she said in her soft but firm voice. "Well, good morning to you sweetheart," the voice said over the line. "Tom! She exclaimed! "Are you in town yet?"

"Not yet but on my way. I get into Logan airport around 3:00. Up for some company?" he said.

"Oh I don't know," sighed Karen into the phone with a big grin on her face. "It promises to be a long a day, I'm stuck on a new program Chase installed on the network, and quite frankly I haven't missed you at all."

"You naughty girl," Tom said back in a sly voice. "Just for that I might forget to pick up that lavender oil for the massage I promised you," and snorted into the phone.

"Darling," she said, "If you were to forget the oil, I would have to insist that you sleep out on the porch with the bugs!"

"I'll tell you what," Tom said, "I will pick up some dinner on the way over to your place and we can have a bite or two."

"Or two? You bite me and you're a dead man! Sounds great sweetie, I'll see you when you get in, drive carefully—Love you," and she blew a kiss into the phone.

Karen glowed. The flush in her checks highlighted her long auburn hair and Celtic facial features. She was just about to turn 37 years old and could not remember ever being so deeply in love with a man. She had been working very hard on her figure and weight over the last two years. Dropping 85 pounds and getting to the gym almost every day had transformed her into a blossoming woman that most men found irresistible to look at when she walked into a room. Looking out the large window in front of her desk she daydreamed about her evening with Tom.

Shaking loose of her new found mood, Karen picked up the phone yet again, pressed the intercom button and began speaking. "Attention all geeks, perverts, and loners, a quick announcement from the front desk." all the employees loved the intercom system. They did not entertain guests very often at headquarters, and they used the intercom once in a while for playful meanderings. "First and foremost, if you have not heard yet, our one and only, fearless, charming, debonair, fatally attractive founder and leader finally got that buck he has tortured us with for the last three years." Pausing, Karen listened into the building as cheers, boo's, and other out of character hoots and hollers came rafting out from the offices.

"I have been informed by the Chief himself that unless you are an incorrigible Vegan, you will be eating venison burgers, steaks, and jerky until Santa arrives in December. Secondly, and most seriously, we have two visitors coming in around 11:30 or 12:00 today. Agent Bob Fellows from the Boston branch of the FBI and a serial Detective from the Providence Police will be gracing us with their presence. They are here regarding the Lumber Jack, so everyone please bone up and have all current materials pulled together just in case we are called into an all hands meeting. I also ordered lunch enough for all of us, V(enison)LT sandwiches, Bambi Chips, and Cream of Doe Soup," Karen finished.

The last two messages elicited further moans and groans from the rank and file. It was a sad day when they had to entertain the FBI on current cases. Inevitably, the FBI was here to second the results of their hard work and very sophisticated intelligence gathering. Everyone at Serial Connections new the drill by heart: Never divulge more information than asked for, always look to Chase or the Senior Intelligence Officer of the firm for a nod before answering, and never, ever, let them see you sweat. Chase usually met with the visitors first, compiled mental notes of what they were after, and then called the group or individuals into the conference area and Chase answered only the questions that he felt comfortable revealing the answers to.

*****

The ride from Providence to Jaffrey started out quiet. Bob finally broke the ice and said "So Seville how is the job? You've been the head of special homicide for almost two years now."

"Bob," Seville said with a quiet under tone, "I resigned my position three months ago. I am currently on the job temporarily until we find the Lumber Jack."

"What? What do you mean resigned?" Bob said with sincere concern.

"Bob, I've been on the force for twenty years. I stopped having a life about 18 years ago. My family doesn't know who I am any more. My brother and sisters all have nice spouses, kids, and jobs that let them be at home, have hobbies, interests and raise their families. Every time I go to a family event, if I even show up, they all barely know who I am. My nieces and nephews ask why I don't have kids or a husband and I just don't fit in. When I was younger I used to do so many things. Today I work. That's it. So I decided that I would take my pension after 20 years, retire, take a bunch of time off to see what's out there in the world and then decide what to do with the rest of my life."

"Whew," Bob sighed. "But I always thought you loved what you do? You have risen through the ranks higher and faster than most women in the country. You could go all the way! Why throw that out now?"

"Because things change Bob… Like I said, I feel like life is passing me by. I do love what I do. If I could continue doing it and find a life I would for sure. But it doesn't look like that's going to happen."

Bob started thinking to himself that he was in the same boat, 43 years old and nothing to show for it but two divorces, no kids and no life.

"I know how you feel Seville. My marriages were great at first, but after the honeymoon and all the hours I work I just couldn't keep up with the relationships. The problem is I love what I do too much and would rather be lonely than without my career."

Seville was thinking back to when they had dated; Bob had put them on the backburner too, even though he had promised not to. She understood first hand exactly what he was saying.

She continued, "So, as soon as the Lumber Jack is caught I'm outta here as they say. I just hope I can make it to the end. When I resigned I knew it was going to take awhile for the actual departure date but things keep dragging on. Every day I keep saying to myself that this is the last day. I don't know else to tell you."

"Well," said Bob, looking over at Seville through the corner of his eyes, admiring her beauty and kicking himself in the ass for what he just said to her, "Have you thought about what you would do? I mean, after 20 years in law enforcement your options might be somewhat limited."

Seville paused, and then answered, "To be honest, I have thought about so many things that my head is spinning. Like I said if there is any way to stay in the business I will find it. If not, I might just become a security consultant or PI. Who knows?"

Seville looked up and saw the town sign for Jaffrey. "What a nice little New England town," she exclaimed!

"Yes," said Bob, "I haven't been through here in years and the place looks exactly the same. I used to come here on my annual pilgrimage to the Jaffrey fireworks festival in August. I keep reminding myself that I would love to come back for that some time."

Seville heard a faint hint in what Bob just said, but she didn't take the bait. Instead, she looked down at the directions and said to Bob "Bear right at the next right after the large white house."

"White house? There is nothing but white houses in this town!"

"True," she agreed, but there is only one right fork in the road— here." Seville had been pretty nervous traveling with Bob. She had come to realize that their little fling last year was just that. It could have been more but like Bob had just said, they were both consummate professionals first. She had been grateful for the intimacy though. If she had fallen head over heels for Bob, she was sure things would have been much different. Bob had not brought up the past as of yet, but she could feel that he was stirring inside, not sure what to do. She decided to let the sleeping dog lie.

"Take this next left, then we are looking for a..., she paused, "Totem Gate?" "What is a Totem Gate?" she asked.

"I guess we'll see when we get there," Bob answered, driving on down the winding back road. Just after the odometer clicked one mile, they saw it on the left. A well maintained and groomed estate lawn came into view with high cast iron fences running along the road and back into the property. They could see a road snaking down to the street and soon came upon the entrance. *Amazing,* they both thought at the same time. The fence ended up on either side of the driveway and where the traditional brick gate posts would stand were the most unusual monoliths. Each post stood a good 15 feet high, were made out of very large logs with a diameter of around five feet. The posts were beautifully carved with animals and ancient American Indian hieroglyphs. On top of the first pole stood a very regal and wise looking wolf; atop the second pole was a Falcon, wings spread, both talons gripping the sides of the pole with great strength and determination. Seville looked up at the Totems and a chill went up and down her spine. She had seen Indian Totems before in pictures, but these........something began to stir deep inside her.

Bob stopped the car for a moment so that they could take in the very unusual sight. Looking ahead, the driveway was at least a quarter of mile long with no building in sight, but he could see the breathtaking bald top of Mount Monadnock just a mile away. He put the car in drive and headed down the hard packed dirt surface towards who knew where. Finally, in about two tenths of a mile they came around a slight curve and encountered a fork in the road. A small sign in the middle of the fork said Serial Connections and pointed to the left. The road on the right wound around and disappeared up a hill in the distance. Coming around yet another curve they saw the Serial Connections headquarters. They were both expecting to a see a traditional antique white colonial structure keeping in step with the motif of the town. Instead what they saw drew breaths from both of them.

"Wow," Seville muttered. In front of them and off to the right was a large hill, forested on either side. Centered into the hill was what looked like a three or four story concave glass walled building with gorgeous terraces running along the floor line of each level: Even though it was autumn, long flowing plants hung gracefully down from the terraces creating a very serene and quiet look. From the bottom of the structure to the top, each floor was set back about 15 feet further than the one below creating a cascading effect that was brilliant. Each floor was also shorter in width by about 20 feet, the total effect causing the observer to follow the structure up to the pinnacle which was a glass domed roof towering above.

They parked the car and headed towards the front door. Karen met them in the ornately decorated foyer, hand outstretched, and a beaming smile on her face.

"Hello, you must be Special Agent Fellows," taking his hand and planting a firm handshake. "Welcome to Serial Connections, my name is Karen Kelly, I am the office manager and slave driver around here," she said with a sly look. "And you are?" Karen said looking into the eyes of Bob's guest.

"Oh, excuse me," said Bob. "This is Seville Waters, Head of Special Homicide with the Providence PD." Karen extended her hand to Seville and issued the same warm welcome. "Seville is here at our request because of the trouble yesterday in Providence. It clearly looks like the Lumber Jack. Henry White, the Executive Director of the FBI Serial division expressly asked us to come up to talk about the Lumber Jack case with Chase."

"Yes, that's what Chase told me on the phone awhile ago," Karen said, not able to take her eyes off of Seville. Karen could have sworn she had seen Seville somewhere before but could not quite place it. Seville had the most stunning dark brown hair, cut long, almost to the middle of the back and tied in a plain, neat French braid. Her face was sharp featured, yet soft, with a slight olive complexion and the deepest blue eyes she had ever seen. If Karen had not gotten "slim and toned" she would have been extremely jealous about the figure she was looking at. Seville was wearing a black turtle neck pull over that left nothing to the imagination. Her breasts were medium in size but were high on the chest and very firm. Her waist was slim, with a perfectly contoured slope to her well rounded and firm hips and butt. *On second thought, I am jealous!* Karen mused to herself. Karen looked up and saw that Seville was a little flushed and embarrassed by her longer than normal sweep up and down. Without further pause Karen said to Seville "Have we met before? I mean really, you look so familiar!"

Seville recovered well, and as she gave Karen the once over too, she replied, "Sorry but I don't think so; I don't get up to this neck of the woods very often."

"Oh well," Karen said. "Listen guys, Chase is running a little behind and he asked me to go ahead and give you the nickel tour while we wait (she did not bother to tell them why he was late, she would leave that to Chase's discretion. Her job was simply to Serve and protect). We ordered lunch and we can eat later while we're talking."

"Sounds good," said Bob as Seville nodded her head to echo the thought. Karen began with a short spiel on the rather large endowment of $100 million dollars left to Chase by Jonathan Longworth almost 17 years earlier. Since then Serial Connections had received at least as much through Federal grants and private benefactors. The land that we are on was a separate gift by a wealthy local land owner and personal friend of Mr. Longworth. The property is roughly 40 acres and boarders on 300 acres of local conservation land and 90 acres of state forest property. The hill that our building is joined to was once a local quarry that has not been used for over 30 years. The building itself was designed by Chase and she pointed to a large framed picture on the wall. Next to that picture was a splendid multi-floor log cabin with a dome on top of it similar to the one on this building. Having given the tour dozens of times, Karen read their minds as they looked at the picture of the cabin.

"Yes, that cabin is the top of this building. The dome and the fourth floor of this building is Chase's residence. You probably noticed his driveway forking off to the right as you came down the road."

Bob Fellows let out a low whistle admitting that he was truly impressed. Seville looked interested but did not say a word. Karen took note. The foyer they were in was round and decorated with tasteful tan leather couches and chairs and numerous pictures and artworks covered the walls. Leading over to the west side Karen stepped into a very large 1000 square foot function room. Along the back wall was a plasma display screen. The room sported a conference table at one end, and couches and chairs similar to those in the foyer. Karen commented that this was where they hosted company parties, training sessions, or other events that required the space. Pushing a button on a control panel inside the podium sent a motor whirling somewhere and a 15 foot section of the back wall quietly slide into its frame. Lights immediately came on showing a series of long tables, each with 5 flat panel displays, keyboards, and mice. In the back of the room stood another podium and a blank wall that could drop a white board, screen, or plasma TV. The room could hold up to 30 people comfortably for a training class or seminar.

Karen pushed the button to close the wall and led them back out into the foyer. She pointed to the other side at various hallways and doors.

"Over there are private conference rooms, rest rooms, and phones," and she walked over to the elevator. Next to the elevator was a futuristic looking console with an oversized hand print on it. In back of the console were two camera lenses pointing right over the pedestal. Karen asked Seville to step up to the console, place her right hand in the hand print and look at the camera. As quick as a flash, a display blinked on with an electronic profile. At the top left was Seville's department photo from the Providence Police Department, to the right of that was the photo just taken by the camera. Below the first picture was a set of 10 fingerprints, also from her police file, the five finger prints of the right hand were lit bright green. Next to that was a digital picture of her right hand taken just then by the reader and the five finger prints on that hand were lit bright green as well, indicating a pure match between the two sets. And finally, below everything else were three pictures of Seville's eyes. The first one was the regular picture, the second was of the pupil only, and the third was the retina scan. After Karen was satisfied she punched a code into the console, hit a particular sequence into the number pad and a marquee flashed across the screen blinking the words "two hour guest pass, hosted access only," a digital clock starting the backwards count to 0. "Bob, you're next," Karen said as Seville stepped to the side and let Bob move in. In about two seconds, Bob's profile shot up onto the screen. His had an additional military photo and set of finger prints. All three sets of prints glowing green. Again the marquee flashed the status message and the three of them walked over to the elevator. Karen did not push any buttons but once they had been standing in front of the elevator for just a few seconds, a bright red light over the elevator door turned green and the doors opened.

Karen said "Two please" and the elevator quickly lifted and came to a stop. As the doors opened, the view of the woods and the mountain jumped out at them as though they were right there. Karen spoke: "This is the main work area, about 5000 square feet in total. Except for the computer folks up on the third floor the rest of us work here." Seville walked over to the unusually shaped floor to ceiling windows and looked out onto the property. Karen stepped up behind her, pushed another button somewhere on the wall and the large pane of glass in front them slid up on tracks and stopped about eight feet overhead. As soon as the door stopped, Seville could feel a forceful, slightly heated air flow coming from both sides of the opening creating a force field across the opening to the outside terrace. They all stepped out into the warm fall day, the sun beating down from a low angle just to their right. The terrace was about 15 feet wide and curved around all the way from one side of the hill to the other. Tables and chairs were expertly scattered in places that offered either sun or shade depending on the time of day. Looking up, Bob noticed that the concave windows from the third floor overhung and covered about half of the width of the terrace offering shelter for the tables and chairs.

While peering over the side, both Karen and Seville noticed a maroon pick up truck coming down the main driveway and veering off to the right up the other road. Seville looked at Karen with a quizzical look.

Karen said "Yes, that's the boss and he should be joining us in about 20 minutes, just enough time to finish up the tour." Karen then walked back inside and over to a set of double glass doors. After all three of them had been scanned by an unseen device over the top of the door it slid open. "This is the portrait or profile room as we call it," she pointed out as they entered another very large room "and where we will be meeting with Chase when he gets here." The room had two tiers divided by a single step that curved all the way around the outside of the room. Bob and Seville noticed tracks in the floor on the second tier coming from both sides and disappearing under walls on either side. In the center of the room was an oblong conference table surrounded by 10 very nice black leather swivel chairs. Up on the second tier right dead center was a half wall with a very large plasma TV and two smaller ones underneath. On either side of the conference table and about 15 feet apart were what looked like viewing stations. Set back about five feet from the step on the bottom tier, each of the four stations had a black three person couch, brown wooden table, and matching chairs on either side of the couch. Each was facing the second tier and looked out through the windows.

Karen said, "This is where we will go over the Lumber Jack case." In the meantime I have one more room to show you before we begin." She turned around and walked to the far right hand side of the room, where there was a single door with the letters PD etched into it. To the left of the door, a single set of tracks led under the wall into the room. Bob looked at the sign on the door and said "PD? You have your own Police Department here?"

Karen smiled and said, "Hold onto your hats ladies and gentlemen, you are about to enter the twilight zone." A device over the door scanned the group again and the door marked PD slid into the wall to the right. Bob and Seville followed Karen into a different world. The room was more like an estate house than an office building. It was bright and cheery and a third of the ceiling was a skylight that let the outside ambience flow in. 1000 square feet, the room had three sections. A console similar to the one in the last room was centered to the left with tracks leading to it and around it. Pastel colored fabric chairs and couch formed an oval around the console with an ornately hand carved coffee table in the middle. On the far wall in the room were ceiling to floor, hand built, light oak bookshelves and cabinets. Visible on the shelves were many differently shaped and colored candles. Beautiful abalone shells were placed around what looked like decks of cards. In the center of the room was a round circle of straight back oak chairs with a small wooden table covered in red felt. On top of the table was a large white candle, unlit but very used, wax drippings running down the sides. The walls in this room were a very light colored ash, obviously hand finished and very expensive. All around the room were miniature versions of the large Totems guarding the driveway. 25 in all, each was hand carved, painted, and had a different creature posed on the top. The White Eagle, falcon, bear, wolf, coyote, mountain lion, snake, beaver, shark, dolphin, deer, otter, moose, and more. Seville got that same feeling she had at the entrance to the driveway as she glanced around at the seemingly familiar objects.

After letting Bob and Seville absorb the essence of the room as she had been trained to do, Karen spoke softly, "This is the psychic developments room. Bob, I am sure that you have heard that Chase has a sixth sense, a gift if you will, that enables him to see and feel things that others cannot. This room is used for psychic meditation on the cases we are working on. Chase manages all aspects of the psychic business and has a Director reporting to him that runs the day to day operation. They work with a number of outside consultants either off site or right here when a case warrants clairvoyance. Most people are very skeptical about the psychic aspect of what we do but our major benefactor, Mr. Longworth, not only believes it, he and his son are beneficiaries of the work. As of today, every single case we have closed was solved directly or indirectly because of this very unique capability."

"For the most part, this team works on our top ten cases. When we first introduce a major case, Chase and the team come here to view all the information, look at site photos, feel and touch any materials from the site that we can get our hands on, and do whatever it is they do.

Often, Chase will take the team to a case site before they come here so they can connect with the energy of the victims and most importantly the killers. I have never been in here during any sessions and really can't tell you more than that. Whenever the team makes a connection to the case, whether it is imagery, feelings, thoughts, or what ever, that information is cataloged and appended to the electronic case file. Let's go out into the other room and wait for Chase. Would either of you like some coffee, tea, or soda?"

Chapter 8

Ocean City

The Sawyer family's Toyota SUV was fully loaded and headed over the causeway back to the mainland, a four hour drive, with the reality of another vacation week coming to an end. Kevin Sawyer was driving and had already begun his daily ritual of no less than 15 Budweiser's. His wife Susan had just passed him a cold one that rested between his legs and once he had guzzled the first half, his dour mood began to slowly ebb away. Susan, knowing the pattern well, figured that they could at least get home before the funny and well adjusted Kevin went one beer over that magical line and turned into a raving monster.

Katie and Russell sat quietly in the back seat watching a DVD movie on the 10 inch screen hanging down from the ceiling. Each one was sporting a pair of wireless headphones which spared Susan and Kevin the agony of listening to Scary Movie 3 just one more time. They had a nice rock and roll radio station playing up front with a cadre of CD's ready for that two hour stretch of the ride where good music stations were few and far between. Susan had been thinking of the trip. Kevin had not blown up much at all this time which was good but she new damn well that it was probably due to exhaustion and heat. The beer had gone right through him. One of the reasons they vacationed in October was that the weather and the water were still warm AND not that many people were around. Years ago Susan had had enough embarrassment with Kevin's behavior to begin lobbying for out of season trips.

She was actually looking forward to the next few days. Kevin had informed her yesterday that he was going to take Russell and the boat down to the Chesapeake for some last minute fishing. They would leave tomorrow and come back Tuesday morning. *Perfect*, she thought, I can get unpacked, get the laundry done, spend some time with Katie, and not have to worry about the monster. She was concerned about Russell though, as she suspected that Kevin was already making him an alternate drinking buddy on their ever more frequent fishing trips. God, she couldn't wait until the kids left home. She would be packed up and gone before anyone knew what happened. She put in a Phil Collins CD, handed Kevin another Bud, settled back into the seat, and started daydreaming about her future.

Chapter 9

Jaffrey

When Chase walked into the room, Karen, Bob, and Seville were sitting down at the conference table with hot coffee steaming up from their mugs. "Good morning everyone," said Chase with a very large and pronounced smile on his face. He walked over to Bob Fellows, shook his hand and said "Hello Bob, its good to finally meet you. I've heard of you at the Boston Branch. I followed the work you did a couple of years ago on that psycho from South Boston, what was her name again?"

"We called her the Widower," Bob explained. "She had started by knocking off her first two husbands, got the taste for killing, then expanded out to casual dates she was meeting at the local bar scene."

"*That's* right," Chase exaggerated, having pulled up the file of that case in his mind. At that moment he looked over at their other guest, and took a quick glance as Bob introduced her.

Bob looked over at Seville and said, "Chase, this is Seville Waters from the Providence Rhode Island Police Department." Chase held out his hand as Seville turned to meet him.

"Hello Chase, this is quite a place you have here!"

"Thanks," Chase said. "I hope you all enjoyed the tour," looking over at Karen and giving her a nod of thanks.

"Karen showed us around and we are both still absorbing everything we have seen so far," Seville said.

"Especially the PD room Chase," Bob uttered with a sound of certain skepticism in his voice. Chase momentarily ignored Bob as he refocused on Seville. He did a double take and all of a sudden he drew in his breath, heart racing, trying to keep the shock off his face. *Why is she so damn familiar!,* he thought to himself as he quickly regained his composure.

"Bob and Seville, it is no secret that here at Serial Connections we believe in using every means at our disposal in order to successfully profile and capture some of the most dangerous killers in the world,"

Chase began. "And yes, to that end we employ what most people call the supernatural in order to get the best possible results. You are not alone in your thinking that ESP, clairvoyance, and other spiritual methods are suspect. Many of our staunchest supporters today were just as skeptical or more so until they saw the work we do here first hand. Our combined approach allows us to profile, identify, and capture killers 30-50% faster than traditional methods. Believe me, if it *didn't work,* this building would not be here, over 134 killers would still be out on the street killing, and we would not be having this meeting."

Seville spoke up, "Chase you have to admit that this supernatural stuff has been used to try to solve crimes for decades. The results have been less than useful in all but a few nationally acclaimed stories. Why do you think your results are different than all the cases we have heard about?"

"Good question Seville; there are actually quite a few very distinct reasons. First, many of the stories you have heard about are people that may or may not have true psychic ability. Secondly, if they do, they are working under conditions that are not conducive to success. Often they come forward because of a vision or a thought they had and the law enforcement agency they approach is basically laughing at them and putting out such a negative energy that the psychic cannot possibly be receptive. I feel bad for those people who truly have the gift because their intentions are good; they just haven't put themselves in a position to succeed. At Serial Connections, we have a highly focused, expertly trained, and very gifted group of psychic individuals. We provide the ideal conditions, culture, and support for psychic receptivity. Eight out of ten times, the cases we work on were initiated by us and we control the process from start to finish. That means the psychic portion of our capability thrives to the point where we get some pretty amazing stuff. In the cases where we are brought in, I make sure that our program, methods, and needs are fully understood and agreed to by the requesting agency before we say yes."

Seville jumped in, "Chase you said that 80% of your cases are initiated by you, but from what I have heard most of your cases are also being worked on by local or federal law enforcement."

"You're absolutely right Seville, think about it. Of the top ten cases going on today, at least three different groups are working the case, the locals, FBI, and us. The reason you're here today is a great example. Serial Connections did not discover the Lumber Jack. He was discovered by a local agency after a trend surfaced. When Serial Connections decided to add the case to our hot list, we started from scratch using our own methods but also incorporated public domain information regarding the case. In this way we keep our case pure in terms of outside distractions, bad or misleading information, agendas, and any pre-conceived notions by other groups. For instance, after our meeting today, I will wash the information we exchange, throw out stuff that my instincts and training flag as noise, then append our case file with information that is then shared by our team."

"Bob, let's say you come in here today under a great deal of pressure from Henry White to break this case. Henry may have tainted your instincts or direction because of an agency agenda for certain results or timing. In this case, you might close your mind or start subconsciously ignoring facts, information, or methods that might be contrary to the agenda of your boss."

"Our mission at Serial Connections is very simple. We profile, identify, and capture mass murderers. We do not succumb to pressures of time, agenda, profit, or duress. It is this philosophy that enables us to work better, faster, and with much greater results, our only constraint being that we work within the confines of the law."

"Now let's move on. Serial Connections is far from being a Saturday side show at the carnival. We have three major pieces of the business that work in concert on any case. The other two areas are equally if not more important. Upstairs on the 3rd floor is one of the most sophisticated computer centers you will find anywhere. It is not NSA or CIA class breadth or depth wise but our computer system, database, applications, and network *IS* the most sophisticated in terms of how we manage and use the data as it pertains to certain types of criminal elements."

"Our network, as you saw when you went through our security system is very comprehensive. Bob, did you expect to see your FBI and military profiles come up on the screen? Did you notice how fast the system pulled your records, pictures, fingerprints, AND conduct a fingerprint and picture match?"

Bob answered "Yes I did see it Chase, and, no I did not expect it at all, let alone the speed. How you were able to do that?"

Chase continued on. "In addition to a very powerful and fast network, we have developed a suite of in-house applications that are not available on the commercial market. It still amazes me to this day that with two in house people and some nominal contract work our team was able to produce a main application that not only ties data together from dozens of disparate data bases, but can also analyze and compare information with lighting speed."

"We call the application Clairvoyance or Clair for short. Clair has four major components to it. First is the data collection, merging, and cleansing aspect. Once we pull data in from a search or feed, it is cleaned, reformatted, and added to our central repository. We have 100's of terabytes of storage from all sorts of data sources like the FBI, CIA, NSA, DEA, State and Local Police Agencies, all the military branches, IRS, Immigration, etc. We also have taps into information from all the major news sources, cable stations, and web sites. This module was named Vortex because it will suck in almost any kind of data in any format."

"Module two of Clair is the Information Mapping Program which we call IMP. This is the code that takes information such as photos, scanned images, fingerprints, forensic reports, DNA codes, blood types, hair analysis, even text descriptions, and can analyze and match them against any other piece of information we have. For example, if a written description of a person comes into the system, Clair will translate that information into a coded picture that is then used as the reference for a full search against the image repository. We can even render a picture of the text description that can be printed or attached to case files."

"The Profile Manager or PM is the hub where most of us work the entire system. New Cases are opened in one of two ways. First, Clair, as she is fed inputs from the data sources, has been trained to identify new or evolving events going on that might indicate the beginning of a new case. When she does, an inactive case file is generated, matched against the data and case repositories, similarities noted, if any, and then routed to our investigative staff via a workflow system. Cases with similarities are routed to the investigator(s) working the similar files. An investigator can merge the new case into an existing one, open the file as active, or keep it marked inactive. All others are grabbed by investigators based on geographic or profile interest. Secondly, we input case files by hand. The Lumber Jack case was opened and input into the system after a call from the Rhode Island State Police about 18 months ago for example. Actually, Clair had opened a file on the Lumber Jack about two weeks prior to the call. When we input the new case from Rhode Island Clair immediately matched the two and the investigative group merged the files."

"All of us have access to the PM but there are different security levels of case access based on job, seniority, and area of expertise. On some occasions we even provide temporary access to outside entities when there is a severe life or death situation going on real time."

"Vortex, IMP, and PM were the three original programs designed for the entire organization. We had a major usability issue pop up with our psychic personnel that caused the development of the fourth application, Shaman. When we first tried to interface our psychic personnel to Clair we hit a major wall. You see, during a session, whether it is a single person or a group exercise, the psychics might see vivid images like a house, a person, a place or an action which often flash before their mind's eye. It is critical that we capture as much detail as possible and we found that after a session, which can be very exhausting, our personnel could not remember all of the details and sometimes confused the sequence of events. The same holds true for sounds, tastes, smells, and textures. Feelings like happiness, sadness, anger, joy, and fear come and go like wild fire and might be attached to a specific person or event. It was almost impossible to translate these visions into Clair after the fact."

"So we developed Shaman. The primary interface is a headset and microphone, the same kind major call or customer service centers use. The voice and AI program behind it is where the magic occurs. First of all, we have amassed a dictionary of keywords that are common to psychic identifiers. When an input session happens, Shaman records the input from the headset and pre-loads the information into IMP. The program looks for keywords like see, saw, feel, touched, etc. and then transforms what it perceives the information to be into either an image or descriptive text or both. So the user might say into the speaker "I see a house on a hill, it is blue with white shutters and looks like a colonial. People are around the house, four people in all. One adult female with an average build, blond hair, and wearing blue jeans and a halter. Two male adults are chasing her, one is heavy set with black hair and the other is tall, skinny and bald. Both are wearing jeans and leather jackets. There is one small child hiding in the bushes. She is about six year's old, light blond curly hair, and wearing a blue sundress. The two females are afraid and scared. The men are angry, enraged and very anxious."

"From that input, Shaman would create an image of the house based on stored information regarding colonial architectures, add the two colors of blue and white and place it sitting on top of a hill. Things like trees, cars, bushes, fences, swing sets or pets are added into the picture too. The descriptions of the people are matched with a huge database we have with gender specific body, hair, eye, height, weight, and face profiles, then renditions are created. Once a session is over, the user or users can then go into the case file in PM and actually edit the information. This is a powerful tool because once a user sees Clair's interpretation of what they saw or felt it jogs the memory allowing the user to edit the images, add more detail, change things around and get pretty damn accurate portrayals. We have matched many of the Clair's interpretations to actual crime scene photos and forensic evidence after the fact."

"The last tier of the pyramid is our investigative staff which has two groups. Group one is the analytical staff who primarily works with Clair. Our analysts interface with external agencies and are responsible for analyzing, updating, adding, deleting, and monitoring case files. They do travel but only to crime scenes that are already under scrutiny. Our analytical staff does not carry weapons of any sort and are not licensed to do so. They are the brains of the investigative staff and have extensive training in profiling, forensics, database systems, and a good working knowledge of how to manage and when to bring in the psychic team."

"Our external investigative team is another story altogether. You could liken them to glorified bounty hunters. They all pack and are trained equally on the analytical side but have past histories with law enforcement, military special ops, spook agencies or all of the above. I personally recruit, train, and manage this staff of only the brightest, highly skilled, capable, and stable individuals. Our inside staff pairs up with the outside staff to form case teams. Together the team decides what the overall case strategy is going to be and any outside work that needs to be done like surveillance or canvassing is done by the external agent. Once the team gets to the point where we think we have a match and want to make a move, we have a team and executive meeting where the plan is laid out, assignments made, and we go out and get the bad guys."

"Come on over to the work area and let's pull up the Lumber Jack Case and you can see for yourself how all this comes together. *Chase could still not take his eyes off of Seville, wondering why she stirred him so…*

Chapter 10

Gaithersburg

Through the haze of half sleep, the killer could hear noises starting to filter into his headset from the eves-dropping microphones he had placed around the house. The sound of footsteps began reverberating through the floor board's overhead as he shook the sleep from his head, stretched his cramped muscles, and began to focus on his victims that had just arrived home. He was feeling great; this family was an ideal set up for him. The wife, kids and drunken husband he was counting on to pass out later on in the evening, were just too good to be true. He had played the ritual over and over in his mind dozens of times before drifting off to sleep in the basement. For the next couple of hours he would listen to the family going about its business, getting a feel for each one of them. Where they spent most of their time, who they interacted with, how they interacted with each other, and later on, where each one was settled in for the night, so he could emerge from the cellar and swiftly and quietly take each one hostage for the final redemption.

His mind started to drift back to when he was 12 years old and living with his mother and deranged stepfather in West Virginia. They had married two years before, three years after his real father had been killed in a bad car accident. His mother was beautiful, simple, and very religious. She had met his stepfather at an evangelical tent meeting and they had courted for about six months before announcing their marriage. At first he liked the man who had taken him under his wing and attempted to fill the void his real father had left. It did not take long though for the man to show his true colors to the family.

One night, while he was sleeping in his room, he heard loud voices coming from their room. Getting up and going to his door he could hear his mother's frightened voice telling the man to stop what ever he was doing. It did not last very long and he had not heard a word coming from his stepfather so he let it pass. It was a couple of months later when it happened again, and his mother sounded much more frightened and he could hear other strange noises coming from the room including some harsh commands being barked at her by the man. This time he snuck out of his room and went down the hall to listen. His Mother was crying and the man was doing something to her but he did not know what. Soon, it was over and once again he thought nothing of it.

The next day he did not have the courage to ask his mother what had happened because he did not want her to know he had been listening to them. But he did notice that she had become very withdrawn and sad. He was not sure what to do. His stepfather was acting weird too and he decided to just stay out of the way.

For the next several months he had paid very close attention to what was going on. His stepfather had stopped doing things with him and was leaving for work everyday and coming home late at night drunk. His mother was beside herself most of the time and was spending a lot of time praying when the man was not at home.

Then one night it got really bad. He had gone to their door and found it open slightly. When he peeked inside he gasped in horror seeing his mother splayed out with her arms and legs tied to the bed. He could not see his stepfather and was trying to look around when the door whipped opened and he was grabbed by the neck and pulled into the room. His mother was whipping her head from side to side saying no, no, no, don't let him see me like this," tears streaming down her swollen face. "Shut up whore," the man yelled at her and threw him into a chair beside the bed. "Boy, your Mother is a whore. She has been giving herself to men during the day while I am off working to provide for you. It is about time you see what happens to whores like this."

Chapter 11

Jaffrey

Chase, Karen, and their guests walked over to the work center area and Chase directed each one to sit down. Sitting himself, Chase then said "Hello Clair."

"Good Afternoon Chase," a soft feminine voice said over the speaker system in the room.

"Clair, we would like to see the full working case of the Lumber Jack please," Chase said in a very pleasant and clear voice.

Karen gave Chase a funny look knowing that he rarely opened up the full case file for *anyone* outside of Serial Connections.

Feeling Karen's concern and anticipating Clair's response, Chase quickly chimed in "Clair, please give Bob Fellows and Seville Waters temporary security clearance for the Lumber Jack file only. Clearance is to be terminated at the end of this working session."

Almost immediately the room walls to each side of the master console began sliding open and disappeared into the recesses. At the same time, on the right side, a six foot tall, four foot wide screen began silently sliding across the room on the tracks built into the floor. On the left side two panels of the same size began moving towards the console as well. The two closest panels pressed into and locked themselves to the center console on either side. The third panel kept moving until it locked into its sister panel on the left. Once they were connected, all four units came to life and Clair announced that everything was ready.

Chase said "Thank you Clair: Bob and Seville sit back, relax and leave the driving to Clair."

Seville looked over at Chase and saw that he had settled into his chair, arms on the leather rests, his eyes closed gently. She found herself drawn to him, staring at his distinctive facial features, a mix between European and Amerindian with a well defined and very handsome Roman nose. She loved blue eyes and his were a unique pale blue that penetrated deeply but delicately when he looked at you. His hair was a light blond color, cropped short and parted slightly from right to left which matched perfectly with his six+ foot obviously well shaped-frame. Earlier when he had smiled at her she had thought it was the most beautiful smile she had ever seen. He looked totally at peace with himself and the world around him as he sat there listening to Clair begin her summary of case file #389. Seville paused, smirked softly, and then looked up at the screen as the Lumber Jack started to unfold before her eyes.

Clair began to recite the formal case information, and the screens on the four panels began to populate with graphical icons, maps, artist renditions of a man, and thumbnail pictures both real and computer generated of people, places, and things. Clair had already gone over the logistics of the case file; case number, date opened, by whom, agencies involved and current status when it began moving logically through the entire portfolio.

On the master screen the words 'Case analyst' popped up, followed by a picture of a middle aged-woman with short, blondish red hair. Under the picture the name Katherine Goddard appeared with a small profile under it that Clair began to read to the group. Another picture came up along side of her of a stately, hard looking man. His name Clair said was Samuel Johnson. He was labeled 'Field Investigator', and had a profile which was pretty impressive.

"Samuel A. Johnson, born March 27, 1963 in Baltimore Maryland, attended West Point and served in the armed forces for 6 years specializing in intelligence, surveillance, and other clandestine activities. Samuel went on to college to study criminal law enforcement at the University of Maryland, graduated with honors, and became a private investigator in the greater Washington D.C. area for the next 10 years until he was recruited by Serial Connections five years ago."

Both profiles then disappeared off the screen and a third popped up showing the picture of an older woman, maybe in her late fifties. Her hair was long and silver and pulled back into a pony tail that hung down to the middle of her back. Glasses framed her gentle and kind face and a slight smile emanated a glow that was hard to keep your eyes off of. Her name, the caption said was Veronica Newton, and Clair spoke on; a native of Massachusetts, Reverend, and long time spiritualist. Mediumship and pyschometry are her main practices, and she currently teaches psychic development at a number of different forums. Veronica has been affiliated with Serial Connections ever since it was formed 17 years earlier, and is a Director of, teacher, mentor, and coach for the psychic team portion of the operation.

When Clair was done with Veronica's profile it was collapsed over to the side of the screen to join Katherine and Samuels's thumbnails while both Seville and Bob sat perfectly still, both in awe of the presentation format of the case.

Chase chimed in real quick, "From here on in we will see the meat of the case including all the possible scenarios, leading to the conclusions of the case team. As a matter of fact Sam and Katherine have called for a sting meeting which means they are 90% sure they have identified the Lumber Jack and are ready to go in to get him."

Seville said very seriously and with a touch of anger, "You mean you already know who the guy is? How long have you known about him?"

Chase thought about her tone then said "Seville, the case analysts just came to their conclusions late last night BEFORE we found out about the latest murders in Rhode Island. We were scheduled to meet tomorrow night and have moved up the meeting to later this afternoon. I want both you and Bob to stay for that meeting if it's ok with you."

Bob answered quickly, "Chase, I would love to but I have to get back to the office in about two hours for some other matters. Seville, Can you stay for the meeting?"

"Absolutely, I will just need a ride back to Providence," as she looked over at Chase.

"I'll make sure you get back," smiled Chase. "As a matter of fact, knowing what I know now, we will probably be moving in on the Lumber Jack early tomorrow. Bob, I'll call you later this afternoon after the meeting with the logistics."

"Great," concluded Bob, "I will make sure my team in on standby for tomorrow. Where will we be heading?"

"Let's have Clair continue and I am sure we will figure that out," said Chase.

Bob and Seville suddenly became aware that the presentation had automatically stopped when they had all started talking.

"Go ahead Clair" said Chase as he sank back into his chair, closed his eyes, and continued on, contemplating the Lumber Jack.

Clair began summarizing the Lumber Jack case from the date it first opened with statistics on how many cases had been attributed to the Lumber Jack; how many they suspected, genders, backgrounds, and more. Then on the main screen a picture came up of a blond woman. Her name was Kimberly Clark; she was 28 years old, had lived in Newbury Port, MA, was employed as a hairdresser, was not married and had no children. She had been reported missing three days prior to a torso being found in an abandoned building in Revere MA. The screen began displaying pictures of Kimberly's body. Her naked corpse was chest up with little or no marks on the chest, abdomen or sides. The head, arms, and legs were all missing and there was no blood around the corpse, suggesting that the murder had occurred elsewhere AND that the murder had been committed at least 24 hours earlier. More pictures came up on the screen. Kimberly had been rolled over on her stomach and again there were no marks on the back suggesting beatings or torture.

Close up shots of the areas where the extremities were missing, showed jagged edges that suggested a rough and violent tool was used to remove them. As Clair continued to bring up victim after victim the group began to see the not so random patterns emerging from the profile. At last, the latest case from Providence came up on the screen. Samuel had been very quick and diligent in getting the pictures and information into the system. The screen populated with thumbnail prints of the crime scene that Bob and Seville had been through just that morning. Seville got the shivers up her spine seeing the pictures again but especially after having viewed all the other victims' profiles of the case. *This case viewing format is excellent*, she thought to herself. *What better way to see and feel what is going on than to see the big picture and the minute details all in one presentation! They did a very primitive version of this back at her precinct hanging pictures on the walls and such. The comparison did not come close though. This was truly awesome.*

After the victim profiles, Clair switched modes yet again and populated the main screen with a large number of thumbnails containing both pictures and text. She announced that they were about to walk through the perpetrator profiling files. Bob and Seville looked at each other sensing that they were just about to get to the meat of the case analysis.

"Clair," said Chase all of a sudden, "Let's skip over the normal analysis leading to our conclusions and go right to the conclusions. Please include the supporting documents and approach used by the team to weed out potential perps and to identify the most likely suspect."

Without responding, the main screen suddenly re-populated into three sections of thumbnail information. Clair began to walk them through the final case conclusions.

First, a text file jumped up on the screen. It was a profile of the individual that had been culled from a long list over the months and was labeled the "Lumber Jack."

Gender:	Male
Age:	34 years old
Race:	White/Caucasian
Height:	5'11"-6'3"
Weight:	200 lbs
Hair:	Dark Brown, medium length, slightly wavy
Eyes:	Dark Green/Hazel
Face:	Taut/Irish/European
Build:	Toned-medium to strong
Marks:	Single tattoo, upper left shoulder, pagan
Occupation:	Tradesman, woodcraft, carpentry,
Location:	Multiple—Maine, Cape Cod, Massachusetts
Status:	Single, divorced/separated, 3 children
Religion:	Catholic

Chase interrupted again and explained to Bob and Seville that the culled list was the combination of efforts of all the internal groups. The physical characteristics were largely the result of multiple sessions with the PD group, with hours of analysis of their psychic expressions, and interpretations by the psychics themselves combined with Clair's inputs, and validated by the investigative team.

"For example, the Lumber Jack's height, weight, tone, and physical appearance were the result of an intensive session with me, Veronica, and one of our remote psychics. We received three independent readings, merged them together, and came up with the most commonly matched attributes. Then the analytical team matched actual forensic evidence with our findings to make sure that there was some level of validation. If the body weight for example was 100 lbs, Samuel would have tossed that right back at us because there is no way a 100 lb person could be manipulating the bodies from abduction to murder to discard."

At once an elaborate series of illustrations popped up on the screen and began displaying themselves in 3-D format. At the top was a head shot of the Lumber Jack that moved about like a real video of a person. The head moved from side to side, up and down, and rotated to show all possible angles and features of the portrait in animated mode. Even the facial features moved to mimic what the face would look like smiling, laughing, yelling, distracted, alarmed, scared and so forth.

A smaller picture of the head to the left rotated in exactly the same motion as the larger version except certain things kept changing. The hair length went from long and pulled back, to buzzed all the way down to the scalp. Mustache, beard, goatee, glasses, sun glasses were shown to portray a wide variety of possible appearances. Then the head minimized and the body jumped up on the screen. Again, to the left was a smaller version of the body that turned, walked, ran, and mimicked the larger picture but with slightly different variations to weight, posture, and muscle tone. The larger picture began the animated process of walking, bending over, reaching up high, and other gyrations to help the viewer complete the mental picture of what this person might actually look like in the real world. When the body rotated to the left, they could all see a brightly colored tattoo on the left shoulder. The tattoo was some kind of pagan image depicting domination. Then to complete the scenario, the head and body pictures merged together forming a surrealistic view of the man that everyone in the room was desperately trying to find. Bob and Seville sat riveted to their seats as they met the man called the Lumber Jack for the very first time.

Bob looked over at Chase and exclaimed, "This is unbelievable Chase, to get such a workup from so many sources! My question is; how do you know where to find the person you are looking for?"

"Excellent," said Chase as he continued on. "First, remember that we are tapped into all the major databases in the US and most from around the world. Once we received this picture and the team was satisfied with the result, we sent Clair out looking. Our system has pre-indexed most of the data bases with physical descriptors so that the search is very quick, producing a list of about 150 possible candidates that actually live in the region we are looking through. Once we have the master list, Katherine starts a visual comparison and further culls down the list to about 30. At this point both teams get on the ball again. Samuel actually starts in the field locating and taking pictures of the 30 people and up-loading them into the system. As they are added, the psychic team, each on their own, does their thing with an on-line version of pyschometry and before you know it we have usually narrowed down the list to one or two perps. In the rare case that a picture is not coming up with matches, the psychics need to work that much harder, trying to figure possible locations, houses, buildings, landmarks and so forth that Samuel can then go check out."

"It turns out that in this case, our prime perp's photo was found on multiple systems including the Registry of Motor Vehicles in Massachusetts, the US Air Force, and a mug shot from Maine. Once Samuel went out in the field and collected photos of the guy's two houses, himself, his truck, van, and some other stuff, Clair then matched these photos with the case file renderings from the psychics. The two houses matched pictures rendered and even the truck he drives came up positive. All of this just happened over the weekend too, in case you were wondering."

Then on the screen the 3-D rendering of Lumber Jack morphed real time into a picture of a flesh and blood man. "Allow me to introduce Emit Ferguson."

At the same time the screen filled up with text data like before.

Name:	Emit Charles Ferguson
DOB:	January 17, 1972
POB:	Albany, New York
Current Residence:	192 Breakwater Street
	Truro, Massachusetts
Second Residence:	P.0. Box 564 (23 RT 82)
	Bethel, Maine
Occupation:	General Contractor
Height:	6'0"
Weight:	198 lbs
Eyes:	Hazel
Hair:	Brown
Marital Status:	Single, Separated, 4 Children
Spouse Name:	Elizabeth Green Ferguson
Spouse Residence:	27 Sand Bar Street
	Falmouth, Massachusetts
Children:	Mary 8, Emit 6, Gregory 5, Susan 3

Bob spoke up first, "Chase is it safe to assume that you have a short list of others that might be the Lumber Jack?"

Chase replied, "Of course we do Bob, but in our experience once we get to this point we are in the 95% accuracy mode. If for some reason we have two really close suspects, we will split the case in terms of surveillance and other activities until we can disqualify one of them. In the case of the Lumber Jack, suspect number two is a distant second, which means he would be a real stretch suspect that we would work only if we had not bumped into Emit."

"Interesting," Bob muttered to himself as he continued to study the profile information displayed on Clair's screen.

Seville asked, "What is Emit doing right now and where is he?"

"Samuel told me this morning that Emit was in Truro as of late last week. He has not been under constant surveillance yet and his proximity to Providence is probably not a coincidence. Samuel is checking missing person records from Maine, New Hampshire, and Northeast Massachusetts; because we feel that the two victims must have been brought down with him from up north. It's funny though, as soon as we got a bead on him, the psychic team has been drawing a blank. I had Ronni—sorry, Veronica, take a quick look at the profile pictures of Emit and the Providence victims about an hour ago and she was coming up blank—which is very unusual. I am going to try to do some work on this later this afternoon as is our remote man down in the Islands," said Chase.

"Remote man down in the Islands?" quizzed Seville.

"Yes, his name is Wesley. Wesley and I go way back but it's a long story we can get into some other time. Wesley is a key part of the team. He retired to Saint Bart's some time ago but is still very active with us and his own work."

Bob said, "What happens when the psychics draw a blank?"

Chase looked a bit funny then said, "Bob, I really don't know. Sometimes one or more of the team does blank out. But that is why we have a team, so that when one is down, the others can pick up the ball. There is no rhyme or reason for it, it just happens once in a while. We will wait and see what Wesley and I pick up later."

Bob looked over at Seville then checked his watch. "I have to get going now; can you guys call me later to let me know of any progress?"

"Sure," both Chase and Seville chimed in.

"By the way," said Bob, "We are working on two other cases that we could sure use some help on. We have a serial in Maryland and another in Seattle that have risen up to our hot list. Henry asked me to see if you are working on these cases too."

"It sounds like the "Samurai" in Seattle and who we call the "Devil" in Maryland. Yes, we are on both of those cases. A summary meeting is planed tonight on the Samurai case and we are getting close on the Maryland Devil," explained Chase.

"Well, would you mind just giving me a quick overview? I have to call Henry on the way back to Boston and he is sure to ask," said Bob.

"Clair, please pull up the public summaries of the Samurai and the Maryland Devil," Chase said into thin air. The Lumber Jack disappeared off the screen and two sets of pictures and information jumped on in its place. "Clair, I will do the summary," Chase said cutting the computer off as it began speaking. "The Samurai lives on the outskirts of Seattle in what was once a very prominent neighborhood. You can see on the left the composite we produced using similar methods to that of the Lumber Jack. We were able to match the composite with the Immigration Department files. Masanori Fukui immigrated to the United States 10 years ago from Tokyo, Japan. Through research and an affiliate in Tokyo we learned that Masanori is the son of one of the Yakuza's major crime bosses. It seems that Masanori and his blood lust were too much even for his father. He was disowned from the family, given a modest trust fund of nearly 10 million dollars, and shipped over here."

"We think he's responsible for more than 30 disappearances and murders over the last eight years or so. It also looks like his frequency is heating up to two-three women per month. He has a puppet company but basically lives on the interest of the trust fund and has plenty of time on his hands. His MO is pretty basic. He abducts a woman, keeps her three to five days, murders her, and then discards her along the side of a road. The bodies are always partially buried so that they will be found quickly. The method of killing is usually through chemicals and the victims have for the most part been through the wringer sexually."

"My field operative has been working the case for months and she has not been able to find out anything that is going to help us. Also, and you should know this Bob, you guys have been on to him for quite some time. My field gal said that your local Seattle office has been on premises twice with warrants but have found nothing."

"That's not surprising Chase, I told you Henry has a few key cases that he has got to close fast because he is taking way too much heat. Ok, how about the "Devil' as you call him. I have not heard of this one yet," said Bob.

"The Maryland Devil," Chase continued. "He is one hellacious predator. He stalks entire families from Maryland, Delaware, and Virginia, breaks into their homes, and stages the most gruesome ritual murders you will ever come across." Chase was watching Bob and Seville pour over the information on the Devil as he sat back and thought for moment.

Seville glanced at Chase and asked "Why isn't there a real picture of the Devil yet?"

"We currently have three prime suspects and are getting pretty close to narrowing it down. The Devil investigators are shaking down some last minute input from the psychic team for validation and verification. We hope to close in on this one soon. As a matter of fact, both the Devil and the Samurai are right in the middle of a cycle as we speak," Chase said with a cracked voice."

"Cycle?" said Seville, noticing his change of tone.

"Cycle is the word we use for the period of time that we think the killer is active. Meaning right in the middle of an event or events," Chase said with a look of sadness on his face. "That is the hardest part of this business, when you know you are getting so close yet you also know that the perp is out there torturing and murdering innocent victims."

Bob checked his watch again, cleared his throat and began to stand. "Chase and Karen, I can't thank you enough for all the help. I am sure Henry is going to be very pleased that we are getting closer to the Lumber Jack and that we are going to take action tomorrow. I will also tell him about the Devil and the Samurai."

Before they could speak, Bob looked over at Seville who was staring at Chase and he felt a chill of jealousy run down his spine. *I can't believe I let her go. Maybe I should offer to drive her back to Providence myself. I don't care if she listens to the conversation with Henry as long as she cannot hear him. He could feel himself getting angry. He could see the look on her face as she watched Chase.*

Chase and Karen got out of their seats and Chase got a funny look on his face for a second glancing at Bob. Bob held out his hand to shake Chase's and when Chase took it a wave of feeling went right up into his arm. Chase was expert at this though and did not show any signs of what had just happened. He just continued to shake Bob's hand then let Karen into the circle.

Karen spoke to Bob, "I'll walk you out Bob. I have to go upstairs anyway to check some things and get the group together for the Lumber Jack briefing."

Bob looked over at Seville ignoring Karen and said "Seville, I was thinking that I could drop you off in Providence then head back into Boston. It was kind of rude of me to abandon you here."

Seville smiled at Bob saying "You know what Bob; I really would like to stay here to meet with the Lumber Jack team. I'm sure Karen can find a hotel room nearby" and glanced over in Karen's direction.

Now Karen smiled and said "Seville, the arrangements have already been made. We did not have the chance to see the guest cottages we have on the side of the hill around the building. We use them for visiting VIP's, our field investigators when they are in town, and the psychic group often uses them because they frequently work very late into the night and it's not practical or safe for them to drive home."

Bob's face had turned a beat red listening to this conversation, and Chase, having read the situation pretty clearly was now amused at the little soap opera going on.

"Fine," Bob said, trying to regain his composure and started to head over to the door. "I will see both of you tomorrow. Thanks again for your hospitality Karen."

Karen walked Bob out through the doors into the foyer and they disappeared down the elevator. Chase and Seville suddenly found themselves in a very awkward silence and Chase decided to break the ice.

"Seville, we have about 30 minutes until the meeting starts. Would you like me to show you to your cabin so you can get settled in a bit?"

"Sure," Seville said, thankful that he had broken the ice. She followed Chase out into the foyer and out through the sliding patio doors they had gone through earlier. The day was still so beautiful and the sun was just starting to head down behind the forest in the distance. They walked along the deck until they got to a very large hand carved wooden door set in the solid rock of the hill. Chase put his hand on the receptacle and the door slowly and silently opened. At the same time, old fashioned gas lights lit up a tunnel that wound down and to the left away from the building. Seville was still amazed with everything she had seen today and found herself not surprised at all at this very unusual passageway wondering to herself where this would all lead.

Chapter 12

Boston/FBI HQ

"Bob, Henry is on the other line but I know he wants to talk to you so please hold" Grace said as she pushed the park button on the phone set. Bob had waited a good 30 minutes after leaving Serial Connections before calling Henry. So many things were swirling through his mind when he left, that he had had to sift through them and come up with a plan before he made the call. Seville was really in his thoughts. How in the hell could he have let her go, and now, how in the hell would he get her back? And then there was Chase Benton. He had become rather fond of Chase, despite his undercover mission for Henry, until Seville had clearly chosen between the two. Now it would appear that he was going to have to side with Henry and perhaps even use Henry to get Chase out of the picture some how. *But how,* he was thinking as he could hear the phone being picked up through his ear speaker.

"Bob, it's Henry. How did the meeting go? What's going on with the Lumber Jack?"

"Hello Henry," replied Bob, as he had just finished thinking through his problem. "The visit to Serial Connections was unusual to say the least. The place they have there is in one sense the most sophisticated crime lab I have ever seen and on the other hand one of the spookiest. I mean the whole place is set up to center around Chase and his group of misfit psychics."

"Don't let yourself be fooled by the psychic piece Bob; it is real and from all accounts very effective."

"Perhaps Henry, but I still can't believe that 90% of the operation revolves around the paranormal. Anyway, the core information we are looking for is right there. Seville and I got a full briefing on everything they have on the Lumber Jack and they are making plans as we speak to move in on him tomorrow."

"Tomorrow!" Henry bellowed, "That means they know who the guy is and where he is? How in the hell did they figure that out so fast?"

"Pretty much the psychics" said Bob, "They walked me through the entire case process starting with dozens of potential perps, boiling them all down through deduction, and coming up with a guy named Emit Ferguson."

"You said they are making a move tomorrow? What is the chance of us getting this guy tonight before they show up?"

"I already thought of that," said Bob. "We could and maybe it is the right move but, we ran out of time before we were able to get as much detail on the Maryland and Seattle cases. If we do charge in, we can kiss the others goodbye in terms of getting any more info out of Chase."

"What about Seville?" Henry said in a softer voice realizing that she was in the car with Bob.

"You don't have to whisper Henry; Seville is still at Serial Connections for the sting briefing." Bob said realizing the bitterness in his voice.

"Perfect, we can keep her on the inside to continue to get information for us on the other two."

"I don't think it will be a good idea for me to be on the wrong side of the fence Henry" said Bob. He was thinking to himself that if Seville thought he was a rat, he wouldn't stand a chance with her. After all, she clearly liked Chase and the Serial Connections team and would probably place her loyalties there. And in light of her retirement she would have nothing to lose in terms of being politically correct or not.

"Seville is a short timer, I found out today she retired three months ago and is hanging on until the close of this case before she leaves. She can leave any time she wants to as a matter of fact and I don't think she would play with us."

Henry blurted out, "What does she think she is going to do when she leaves? Does she realize that having me black list her means she might never work in law enforcement again?"

"Whoa Henry, slow down a bit, She doesn't even realize what's going on here. Of course she would care, but after talking with her today it is unlikely she wants to get back into law enforcement at all. I don't get the feeling that we can trust her with our intentions and that if we are going to use her for information she has to have at least me to trust."

"What are you saying Bob?"

"It just struck me. If we go ahead and pull in the Lumber Jack ahead of Serial Connections, it has to appear that I was not part of the decision or even there. I have to come out clean. After this, Chase is not going to trust me anymore anyway, but he might trust Seville so *she* will need to trust me in order to push information through. Either way I need to appear to be close to Chase and on his side. The fact is that they are supposedly very close to solving the Maryland and Seattle cases too. It should not take more than a couple of three weeks before all three cases are wrapped up. If that's right then we might just be able to pull this off."

Henry paused on the other end of the line to think for a moment. "How much did you get on the other two cases Bob and where are you now?"

Bob was just cresting the hill on RT2 east looking at Boston in the distance. With the setting sun to the west the sky behind the city was a perfect deep blue, the lights of the city just starting to twinkle; "I am almost back in Boston. They think the guy in Seattle is the same Japanese guy we are onto. They are almost ready to plan a sting on him within a few days. The Maryland Devil, as they call him, has not been narrowed down yet but Chase feels they are close. He would not drill down on a lot of information on either of those cases yet—trust issues."

"Alright," Henry said, "Let me get this straight. They are holding what they call a sting meeting for the Lumber Jack tonight and are planning on taking this Ferguson guy tomorrow. They are close on the Samurai but not as close on the Maryland devil."

"That's right," said Bob

"Ok Bob, listen up, here's what we are going to do."

Chapter 13

Jaffrey/Peterborough/NH

"Hello, Serial Connections, this is Karen speaking."

"Karen, this is Bob Fellows, I need to speak to Chase please."

Karen was thinking that Chase and Seville were off at the cabins and she really didn't want to disturb them so she said "I am sorry Bob, Chase is off with Seville somewhere on the campus. Is there a message I can give him."

You bitch! Bob thought to himself. She knew exactly what she was doing. It did not take a psychic to see her reaction to Seville and Chase all afternoon. She was helping to play cupid. "Karen, I just got off the phone with Quantico and they want me to come back out to your place to be part of the sting meeting so we can better coordinate resources tomorrow. I need to stop in at the office for about an hour and will be back up there by 9:00PM. Please tell Chase and the team to wait until I get there."

Karen saw the chance for a shot at Bob "Ok Bob, I will let Chase know but he may want to go ahead with the meeting anyway because everyone is almost here."

"Karen, please find Chase and have him call me immediately."

"Bob, I will give Chase the message and if you don't hear back from him assume he has decided to wait for you."

Bob was furious at Karen but kept composed while he said "Karen, that's an excellent plan. Will I see you later on too?"

"Not sure yet, my significant other is back in town from traveling and we have plans so I will have to see what the boss says. See you later on Bob!"

"Good Bye," she heard Bob say with a slight twang in his voice. She was smiling now but the smile soon faded as she realized that she *did* have a date tonight with Tom. He should already be at her house. Shit, what crappy timing. She looked down at the phone system and hit the intercom button. "Chase, please dial 102. Chase—102 please."

Within a few seconds she heard his voice saying "yes" on the speaker. She quickly explained Bob's call and his request. "What do you think?" she asked. Chase was paused on the other end and she could tell that he was doing more than just thinking about Bob and Henry.

"Let's go ahead and move the meeting back to 9:00. I will fill you in later on what I just picked up."

"Sounds good" she said. "Oh Chase, I almost forgot, Tom is back tonight and we had plans for the evening. I don't want to miss the meeting so do you mind if I leave and come back later? Dinner and refreshments have already been ordered and will be here shortly."

"No problem, just make sure you come up for air long enough to notice the time because if you're not here I will send Samuel out to drag you back!"

Karen chuckled through the phone and said, "Look who's talking Vision Quest Man, don't stay down in the courtyard too long with Mother of Air!"

"Jesus, that's it" thought Chase to himself. Leave it to Karen to figure it out. No wonder she has been playing Miss Matchmaker all afternoon. Seeing his favorite deck of Tarot cards in his mind he looked at the "Mother of Air" card. She was a beautiful American Indian with long flowing dark hair, soft but intelligent eyes, and a radiance that was warm and caring. Chase had told everyone that he was waiting for her in the flesh every time they kidded him about being single for so long. There was something about the picture of that woman that had seemed familiar to him and he had never been able to put his finger on it. Now seeing Seville and the amazing resemblance he had to wonder!

"Touché dear, have fun, and I will see you later. Hey, by the way, did you get that new application up and running yet? I am going to need to do some special data mining tonight and will need that new interface."

"I was right on it when all hell broke loose here today. I'm sorry; I will call Tom and tell him I will be very late."

"Don't you dare," said Chase. "You get going; he's a computer whiz isn't he? Maybe he can help you from home."

"Thanks Chase, I won't let you down and will see you in a while." Karen hung up the phone with a huge smile on her face.

*****

Karen pulled into her driveway after the short 10 minute ride from the office to find Tom's light green sports car parked around to the side. She was so excited to see him. They had been going out for almost a year after having met through an on-line dating web site. Things had started out slowly at first. Tom was a computer network consultant and he was always on the road. For the first two months they must have only seen each other five or six times. Then he was working on a local project for a couple of months and hardly traveled at all. During that project they spent a lot of time together and fell head over heels for each other. He had a nice place down on the South Shore and when she could manage the time off they had spent days walking the beach, sailing, and getting to know each other.

Things were changing now though. She was starting to get a case of the "lets get serious" thinking and she was not sure how he felt about that. Neither of them had kids and Karen knew for sure that she wanted to settle down and have a family some day--soon. Tom on the other hand loved the rapid pace of his job, the travel, and the excitement of not having to work a 9-5 job everyday. She was not sure how a tighter commitment would sit with him and also if he would be a capable husband and father. So for now, she just basked in the relationship and believed that if it was meant to be then it would be. She had been tempted many times to solicit the aid of one of the psychics to see the future but thought better of it because she did not want anything spoiling the moment.

As she got out of her car, she noticed that the lights in the house were not on but that there was a flickering glow coming from the living room window. Karen could feel the heat building inside her. It had been almost three weeks since they had been together and she was ready. She was not sure just who was going to get ravished tonight. As she approached the doorway, it slowly swung open and a bouquet of flowers magically slid through the door. Taking them in her hand and pushing the door open further she saw Tom standing there dressed only in blue paisley silk boxers. She gave him an exaggerated twice over. He stood almost 6' tall, had short cropped brown hair, and a frame that had seen the gym more than once. His bright white smile peeked out through the dim light and she could actually smell his scent as she melted right into his arms.

Pressing her legs hard into his, Karen dropped the flowers on the floor and they began exploring each other's lips as though they had never kissed before. Tom's hands ran through Karen's hair and gently but firmly pulled her into him. Karen found his chest and began sliding her hands across his muscular breasts. Her sighs became moans as she melted completely away. Tom lifted her off the floor and carried her into the living room where candlelight danced across the throw pillows he had placed along the carpet. Setting her on her feet, his hands found the buttons on her blouse and expertly undid each one until he slid his warm hands inside and caressed her strong and toned back. Karen undid the clasp on her bra and could feel her swollen and throbbing breasts break loose from their bondage as she pressed them into his.

"Oh Tom," she moaned as his knee began rubbing her special place gently back and forth as they danced to the quiet music in the background. In a trance, Karen felt her jeans being pulled down to the floor. Her panties were soaked and her sweetness floated in the air around them. Tom gently laid her into the pillows and they embraced fully on the soft cushions. Their hands were moving along forbidden places, causing shivering anticipation to the point where Karen could take no more. She threw Tom on his back, straddled him, and began kissing him and rocking back and forth across his hard penis. She slid her hand between her legs, taking him in her fingers and guiding him to her waiting lips. He was throbbing as she lowered herself completely and deeply.

"Karen," Tom called out softly. He could feel her warmth and wetness engulf him as she took him all the way and began grinding her hips. As her passion heated up so did her tempo. Karen couldn't control herself and as Tom took her breast into his mouth she came and came again until she felt his body tense, his penis swell, and his hips push up into her core. When he let loose she could feel the heat and his penetration, causing her to scream one last time as she pushed down, melding their bodies into one.

*****

Seville marveled at the courtyard where she and Chase sat to talk. The medieval motif surrounded them. The six "cabins" as they were referred to, were more like thatched huts straight out of a King Arthur movie. The courtyard itself was paved in cobblestone with small island gardens sprouting all kinds of plants and herbs. The antique gas lights had come on when the sun finally set behind the trees off the river and illuminated the gardens and the cedar trees growing on the periphery. A small stream meandered along the entire length of the courtyard, polished stones adorning the shallow bed.

"Chase, is it just me or do you have one of the most vivid imaginations of anyone I know? This place is unreal!" Seville said with a tone of approval.

"I can't take all the credit," Chase said. "I did design the entire place in terms of the buildings and grounds but I had help on the decorative aspects. I asked Veronica to help me out here and in the psychic development room you saw inside. My request to her was simple. I gave her cart-blanc to create the most effective and conducive environment possible for herself and the team. Wesley also got involved and did the actual design layout of the courtyard and the quarters based on Veronica's desires."

"The only stumbling block I ran into was with Jonathan Longworth. At first, he wasn't buying the design concept. I had to work him for months until I got him to realize that in order for the Foundation to attain its goals we needed to create ideal working environments for all the employees. I basically explained that the computer center was designed around the IS people's expectations and needs, the office around the office personnel, and hence the psychic team should also have the ambiance they needed to be happy and successful. Thank God he saw the logic in that because he sure couldn't feel the rightness of it in our terms."

"The huts are remarkable Chase, I mean they look and feel like ancient dwellings until you look a little harder and find the modern conveniences tucked away. I love the refrigerators hidden behind the wall shelves and who would have known that a modern bathroom was on the other side of the wall tapestry!"

Chase grinned and said "What did you think of the dirt floors?"

"Honestly, I could live without them. They must be cold in the winter."

"Not at all, the floors are actually concrete with radiant heat. The dirt is a special mix of clay and loam that compacts and stays down without kicking up a lot of dust."

"I can't wait to meet Veronica," said Seville as she focused on a waterfall like noise coming from behind them and around a corner.

"What's that sound Chase?"

"Ahh! That would be my favorite feature of the courtyard and my doing. Give me your hand and close your eyes."

Seville reached out for Chase's hand and he gently pulled her to her feet. She felt like a little kid closing her eyes as he led her down the cobblestone walk. As they moved closer, she was sure she heard a waterfall and babbling water. He guided her up a set of winding stairs that seemed to go on forever until all of a sudden she could feel mist on her face and hands and the sounds became a roar. She could sense that the outside light had dimmed quite a bit through her closed eyes and a slight chill ran up her arms as the air liquefied around her.

Chase let go of her hand and moved behind her holding onto her waist and whispered into her ear. "Ok Seville, open your eyes!"

Seville slowly opened her eyes and as she did, a wave of disorientation swept over her causing her to loose her balance. Chase held on tight as she got her bearings and realized they were up on the very edge of a large ledge, in the middle of a beautifully lit waterfall, looking down and out over a deep blue pool roiling with bubbles and currents, a light mist rising gently from the surface and swirling around with the moving water.

Chase took his hands from around her waist and she realized that he had really been holding onto to her, not flirting as she had originally thought. It didn't matter though; her groins were stirring in a way she hadn't felt for some time. It felt *real* good. She couldn't resist herself when she said "Chase, were you just flirting with me?"

Chase blushed as he moved next to her on the platform and replied "Seville, if I hadn't been holding on to you like that you would have gone for a swim for sure."

She smiled and gave him that "Oh right" look.

"Ok I'm nabbed!" Chase exclaimed. "I wasn't going to show you the pool just now but since you asked what that sound was…."

"Nice try bucko," she retorted. "Yea, that's right, it's entirely my fault!" She grinned and looked into his deep blue eyes.

"Of course I was flirting Seville but I am serious about you taking that swim if I hadn't been holding on," he said.

"I love swimming anyway," she said smugly. She was toying with him and thoroughly enjoying herself.

"Really now" he smiled, returning her joust. He got a funny look on his face that turned into a wicked grin. He reached out, took her hand, and before she knew it she was screaming and they were plunging 15 feet into the clear blue water below.

*****

Karen was standing in the kitchen, minus her clothes, putting Chinese food in bowls for her and Tom. She had cleaned up a bit in the bathroom after they had made love again. This time more slowly and for much longer. She kept shivering as aftershocks swept up from her loins and she wished she did not have to go back to work tonight. Tom was at her computer, also naked; checking out the new network data mining interface Chase had asked her to have Tom help get set up for him. When she came over to Tom at the console he was busy typing setup commands into the screen marked with Chase's user name "Shaman". Tom was always a big help with this stuff and Karen was very grateful that he loved the work so much because she did not enjoy the computer work and did not like to impose her burdens on Tom.

After she set down Tom's bowl, she playfully pecked his nipples with her chopsticks making him lose concentration for a moment.

"You better not get me started again babe, or you ARE going to miss that meeting at 9:00. Speaking of time did you notice that it's 8:30 already?"

"Yeah sweetie" Karen sighed as she gingerly raked her fingers through his scalp wanting to continue her sexual assaults. "I am going to head in and get dressed, ok?"

"Sure babe, it's going to take me a while to get his app up and running but I should be done well before your meeting is over and then I'll be waiting here just like this for your return."

Karen bent down and kissed him on the head then disappeared down the hall into the bedroom. She stood there looking into the mirror for a moment. She liked the way she had gotten her body back into prime shape. Her breasts were still nice and firm and her waist and hips were very proportional helping her feel super sexy. Enough of that, she thought and grabbed her panties off the pile on her bed and slide them up her long legs and snugged them into place. As she picked up her bra she got an evil thought. Throwing it back on the bed she grabbed her jeans, snugged them up too then went over to her dresser and picked out a very thin, low cut, pullover light green blouse and dropped it over her head. Looking in the mirror again she smiled and said "perfect".

She grabbed her purse and keys and walked over to Tom to say goodbye and when he saw her he almost fell off the chair. "I thought this was an office meeting sexy?"

"You see, it worked," she smiled back at Tom.

"What worked," he answered back with a questioning voice.

"I am trying to protect Chase from a bad guy tonight and thought I would try a little diversionary tactic."

He smiled up at her and said "What ever floats your boat babe. Just remember me sitting back here waiting for you—ok?'

"Thanks Honey, I will see you in a while—Love you."

"Love you too!"

*****

Seville was laughing so hard her sides were bursting. She had not felt so good and so free in a long, long time. Had this been any other time or circumstance she was sure she would have drawn her service revolver on Chase and had him cuffed in seconds. But swimming along with him made her feel happy and she felt very safe around him even though he had almost drowned her. As they swam up to the stairs at the far end of the pool, Seville realized that she had not packed any clothes for the trip because she had been expecting to ride back with Bob earlier that afternoon.

"Chase, what am I going to do about my clothes and hair? I don't have a blow dryer or clothes to change into!"

As Chase helped her out of the pool he replied "I think we can take care of you. I know that the cabins all have spare sets of clothes and all the comforts of home somewhere." As Seville stepped out of the water Chase realized just how beautiful she really was. He was seeing not only her physical beauty but an inner spirit coming alive in her, her aura full of bright colors. Her smile was bright and genuine, and he could feel nothing but wonderful energy coming from her. He glanced at her body, her wet and tight clothing left little or nothing to his imagination. She was pulling her long black hair around in front of her and squeezing the water out from the top to the bottom.

He took her hand once again when she was done and they began walking beside the courtyard stream towards the cabins in a wonderful silence. As they came around a corner they happened upon an older woman with long gray hair and glasses sitting under one of the lamps reading a book. Peering up over her spectacles, the woman looked up at the two apparitions walking toward her with her eyes wide open in surprise. She was shocked to see Chase soaking wet in his street clothes and was even more shocked when she saw a black haired beauty by his side in the same condition.

Without missing a beat she offered "Good evening Chase, wonderful night for a swim, isn't it?"

"Hey Ronni" said Chase still dripping and obviously spinning an explanation in his mind. "I would like to introduce you to a friend of mine," he said.

"Hello Seville, my name is Veronica Newton"

Both Chase and Seville glanced at each other wondering how she had known Seville's name before the introduction.

Veronica smiled at them knowing exactly what they were thinking and said "Don't worry Seville, Karen left me a note before she left that I might find the two of you down here, I already knew your name."

"Phew," spouted Seville half under her breath as she reached her hand out. "It is a pleasure to finally meet you Veronica. Chase has told me so much about you."

"You might as well just call me Ronni, Seville. It will be far too confusing having to answer to different names around here!"

"Thanks Ronni, I do appreciate that. I love the name Veronica though; it was my Mother's middle name."

Both Chase and Ronni picked up on the "was" and decided now was not the right time to pursue the obvious. Ronni looked up and down Seville again and said "Seville, come with me, I have some things you will be wanting before the meeting. Chase, you had better go get cleaned up yourself. We will meet you upstairs by 9:00."

"Chase bent over and kissed Ronni on the cheek and said "Thanks kiddo, I'll see you at the meeting." He shot an admiring look at Seville who was still beaming from their very spontaneous adventure. "Don't get cleaned up too much Seville, I like the life guard looks quite a bit."

She gave him a quick shot in the arm before he walked off to a different corner of the courtyard and disappeared into a wooden door that she had not noticed before.

Ronni noticed the question before it came and said "That leads up to his place on top of the building.," as she pointed her head upwards suggesting to Seville she take a look. Seville turned her head and looked up the massive hill and saw lights coming out from a few very large windows four stories above them.

"That's the log cabin I saw in the picture in the atrium this afternoon?"

"It sure is. I guess you haven't been up there yet but you'll find it's quite impressive and is much more than a home to Chase. It's really the center of his universe."

"That almost sounds lonely Ronni, does he have a life?"

"Oh quite the opposite Seville, he has a wonderful life, he is a very rich person in many ways, and I am not talking about money. What I mean by the center of his universe is that he designed his home in such a way that he can easily tap into all the energy sources he needs that make him who he is."

"You mean he used Feng Shui?

"Not at all, and as a matter of fact, as you have probably noticed, Chase practices spiritual rituals from his North American Indian and Aborigines ancestors."

"Aboriginal?" Seville said with a quizzical look.

"Yes," said Ronni, "I will let Chase get into that piece with you some other time. Come along dear, it's almost 9:00 and we have to hurry."

Chapter 14

FBI HQ/Boston/Gaithersburg

"Where are you now?" asked Henry from his cell phone.

"I'm in Boston" the man said back. "Samuel came back up here early this morning and has been hanging around in Jaffrey all day."

"We have a new development. I need you to get back out to Seattle ASAP. Chase and his crew are onto the Samurai and should be planning a move within the week. I need you to get out there and set up as soon as possible." Henry said.

"What about the Lumber Jack?" the cold voice said with a tone of disappointment.

"I have that situation under control. I have a small team from NYC going to pick up Emit Ferguson tonight down on the Cape, and by the time Chase figures out what we did it will be too late and we will have gotten the collar."

"Emit was my pick too," said the man. "I have a man out in Seattle, are you sure you don't want me to stick around another day or two to see how things pan out here?"

Henry snapped back, "No, I want you out there and on top of Chase's people AND Masanori Fukui. You know the drill, if you think Chase's people are close to moving in on the guy, grab him and keep him safe until you hear from me."

"How did you find out about Emit?"

"I have a man on the inside at Serial Connections; the problem is that after they find out about our little trick, that resource all but goes away. But, like I said, once we get the Lumber Jack I get some critical mass and what you do in Seattle becomes even more important. I am sure Chase will be watching his butt very closely out there."

"Henry, did you get that forensics stuff out to Seattle today?"

"Yes, Grace dropped it in the FedEx box this afternoon using a blind account. I am going to send the other package out to your guy in Maryland on Monday. If all goes well I might be able to send a little bit more information to each one after the weekend. We'll see what happens up in Jaffrey tonight."

"Thanks Henry, the more my guys know the better. By the way, we all agree that Chase's field people are top notch. We have to really keep our distance with them and have planted tracking devices on their vehicles to keep tabs on them. After this is over I have been thinking about approaching at least two of them to join my outfit. And don't worry, if I do they will never know about the Serial Connections job. All my guys are top notch and they know to keep their job to themselves no matter what."

"We'll talk about that one later," said Henry. "I will call you on Monday in Seattle to check in." Henry folded up his personal cell phone and dropped it into his jacket pocket.

It is finally coming together he thought. Getting the Lumber Jack tonight will put us back in the limelight and get everyone off my back. And Serial Connections; if I can beat them to the collar just a few times I will never have to listen to anyone again calling us incompetent or incapable in comparison. I hope Tim and his people can set things up well in Seattle and Maryland. I knew we were right about Masanori Fukui. It is just a matter of timing now. If I can get Tim to stay one step ahead of Chase's people we will be able to pull in that collar too. The Seattle team is still on standby and I will be able to call them as soon as I get the word from Tim that they have Fukui contained. I need to keep focused on Boston and Seattle and then pull out all the stops on this guy in Maryland. Being so close to home and the Capital, I want that one to be a sensational story!

*****

Tim hung up his phone and turned back to the computer. He was looking at a screen filled with information regarding the Lumber Jack. He was cycling through the thumbnails of all the people associated with the case; Chase, Samuel, Katherine, Susan, Dug, Veronica, and Karen. Other than Chase, he actually liked the Serial Connections people for the most part; too bad they were on the wrong side of the fence. He looked at the picture of Bob Fellows and thought what an idiot the guy was. A typically dry, boring, by the book FBI suit. When he came to Seville's picture he double clicked on it to enlarge the photo. Ever since he had seen Seville at one of the crime scenes nine months ago he had fallen head over heels for her. He had spent many hours since then daydreaming about being with her someday. *Someday soon he hoped!*

On the top right of the screen a small window with a map and a red blip on it popped up. He toggled through it until he came to the one marked the "Devil" and made it full screen. As the map enlarged, it showed the greater Maryland region all the way to the coast. He hit the zoom button over the red blip and found himself looking at Gaithersburg Maryland and a long country road out in the middle of nowhere. Then he checked out where Emit and Masanori were. It looked like Emit was right where he was supposed to be but Masanori was traveling. His blip was moving North East of Seattle about 20 miles outside the city. Tim quickly toggled through to another screen and saw that Chase's investigator, Susan Kincaid's car was still sitting down the street from Masanori's house. *What are you boys up to tonight?* He thought to himself smiling before shutting down the computer to go pack for his trip.

*****

Over the last half hour the house had grown very quiet. He could tell that Kevin was upstairs in the family room, TV on, but could not tell whether or not he was passed out yet. He considered that for a moment and decided it would be easier to bring the others downstairs than it would to be to bring Kevin upstairs so he modified the plan in his mind just a little. *Got to be flexible in this business* he mused to himself. The girl was in her room on the phone talking to one of her girlfriends about all the hunks she saw at Ocean City and making up tall stories about one or two of the guys she supposedly was with down there. She had been on the phone for an hour now and should be done soon. Mom had been in bed reading, he guessed, because all he could hear from her room was the periodic turning of pages. She had taken a shower and dried her hair a while ago and was hopefully in bed for the night. The boy was either typing homework on the computer or on-line with his friends as the only noise from his room was the incessant sound of the keyboard clacking away. *It's time,* he was thinking. *Everyone is where I need them to be.* Keeping the ear piece in, he crawled out of his basement hideaway and stood for a few moments to regain his coordination after lying flat for almost seven hours. He dropped his back pack on the floor and began doing stretching exercises to limber up a bit while he kept listening for any room changes upstairs. Once he felt awake and limber, he reached down to open his pack. First, he brought out an eight ounce bottle filled with a clear liquid that had no markings on it. Next, he reached in and brought out a small 4x6 inch plastic box with a flip top on one end, opened the top to reveal a piece of sponge like material inside and while holding the container away from his body, opened the bottle of liquid and poured about half of it into the container then closed the lid. Once the container was all set, he pulled out 10 leather straps and laid them out on the floor at his feet.

Equipment all set he dug deeper into the backpack and pulled out a bundle of clothes wrapped in a very large table size silk cloth. Taking off his shoes and socks he pulled silk slippers over his feet then removed the rest of his clothing uncovering a flawlessly hairless body from head to toe. Then he wrapped a thin belt around his waist and inserted an ivory handled knife with a very sharp, double sided six inch blade into a sheath. The last piece of clothing was a long black and purple hooded robe completely covered with white embroidered crosses all of sizes that hung down to the floor.

Ready to go, the killer went through the plan one more time in his head, moving from room to room, person to person, seeing in his mind the actual sequence of events right through to the moment of redemption for each of the four victims. A trance like calm came over him as he moved silently through the cellar, up the carpeted stair case, and into the kitchen. He could still hear through his ear piece and all was quiet upstairs on the second floor. Moving slowly around to the doorway into the family room he could see the light from the wide screen TV dancing on the walls in the darkened kitchen. Kevin's head was sticking up part way over the top of the couch when he approached the man sleeping off his all day drunk. He stood over him from behind the couch for a few moments while he imagined the brutality this man had caused his family and wishing that someone had come along to save him and his mother when he was a child. He took the small plastic box from a pocket in his robe and held it around to Kevin's face and placed it over his nose for just a few seconds. Kevin didn't even flinch as the chemicals did their work with amazing speed. Looking at his watch, the killer saw that he had about 45 minutes until the dose wore off.

Carefully and thoughtfully he went about setting up the room just the way he liked it. He placed three chairs in a semi-circle around the large area of the floor in front of the couch and placed the comforter and fleece blankets from the couch on the floor in front of the chairs. He removed all of the man's clothing and picked him up off the couch and placed him on one of the hard back chairs, securing him to the chair with two of the of leather straps. Kevin's head was slumped forward, hanging down onto his chest, bobbing up and down to the rhythm of his breathing.

Suddenly, he heard the girl stirring in her room, getting out of bed, opening her bedroom door and starting for the stairs. The killer quickly went into the kitchen and hid behind the partially opened pantry door waiting for the girl to descend. *Excellent—now I won't have to haul her downstairs.*

Katie had been on the phone for well over an hour and had gotten hungry and thirsty. She hated coming downstairs when her father was down here at night, so she moved as quietly as she could down the stairs, listening for any activity. She paused for a moment at the bottom of the stairs. The TV was on but other than that she heard nothing else and decided it was safe to sneak into the kitchen by going around through the dinning room. She didn't turn on the lights knowing that with the glow from the TV in the family room there was plenty of illumination. When she opened the refrigerator door, she felt a sudden chill go up and down her spine and shivered, even though it was well over 80 degrees in the house. Grabbing a can of Diet Coke, she began rummaging through the trip leftovers her Mother had put back in the fridge. Nothing looked appealing, so she quietly shut the door and turned to go into the pantry. The door was slightly ajar and she thanked God that she wouldn't have to make any noise to get into the small room. As she pulled back the door handle she glanced over to the family room to see if her father was passed out and froze in horror at the sight she saw through the door. In a split second, she was wondering what the hell he was doing strapped naked to a chair and all her senses began to electrify with fear and danger. She quickly turned to flee the room when something hit her in the face and an arm grabbed around her and held her close. The scream that was on the tip of her throat was cut short by a stinging sensation moving through her nose and mouth. The hooded face in front of her was dark and void of emotion as she collapsed into his arms and went to sleep.

Two down and two to go; Richard thought as he finished setting Katie up in the chair next to her Father. She had smelled so sweet and young as he carried her into the family room to undress her and put on her restraints. He could still feel the stirring within him and shook it off so that he could focus and concentrate on his next move—the boy. He made no assumptions and considered each one of his victims dangerous until he could subdue them with his special chemical mix. He touched his face lightly and felt a scar running down the side of his cheek left as a gift from one of his first victims. He had thought himself superior in strength back then and did not realize the effects of adrenaline rushes brought about by terror. He was much more cautious now and considered everyone to be a threat until they were under his control.

The boy—he would have to move in quickly before the kid could make a sound and alert his mother who was sleeping down the hallway. Once he had the boy knocked out, he would go for the mother before taking them both downstairs. His paced quickened as the anticipation started to take over his thoughts and actions—*I must hurry*—stepping into the hallway upstairs he walked over to the boy's room and listened through the door and with his ear piece. The keyboard was still clacking away and the killer visualized the layout of the room. The desk and computer were over to the left and the door swung open to the left meaning he would be blind as he opened the door to the bedroom. His only hope was that the boy was too engrossed in his chatting to notice the door opening. The knob turned easily and noiselessly as he pushed it open very slowly into the room.

Russell was just hitting the enter button to send along his latest response to one of his buddies asking him if his dad was going to let him drink on the fishing trip, when he saw the door slowly opening behind him in the reflection of his computer screen. He smiled and fidgeted ever so slightly as he thought of Katie trying to get close enough to steal a glimpse of what he was saying to his friends on-line. They had played this game for years and to this date she had never been able to sneak up on him. He pretended to keep typing a message as the door opened about halfway and a figure came slinking around the door. *Nice touch sis,* he thought when he noticed the robe she was wearing to conceal her identity from her brother. *That must be her Halloween costume—nice. I wonder what she's wearing underneath he thought. She is so hot! Too bad she's my sister; every guy in school would pay me a hundred bucks to be in my place right now.* He decided after the last thought to let her get closer then spin around and pull the robe open. *She was sneaking in on him after all*—It had been years since he had seen her naked but she drove him crazy walking around half dressed in her bra and panties or towel—*just one peek he thought and then he could let his buddies know exactly what they were missing and he would become a legend for getting a glimpse.* He tensed his body and thought through the move as she approached him slowly from behind. He continued typing mindlessly into the keyboard, watching her approach out of the corner of his eye.

When the killer got close enough, he looked at the computer screen and saw what the boy was typing. His instincts kicked into over drive as he read the garbage being produced on the screen—in an instant he knew what was going on as he could see the boys eyes watching him in the reflection. At the same time, the boy spun around with a huge grin on his face and pulled open the man's robe with a look of total anticipation. The look turned to horror as the thought of his sister's beautiful naked body turned into the stark reality of a naked man—his father briefly flashed in his mind before his face was covered with a hard plastic object that stole his breath away.

"Holly Shit," the killer thought after he grabbed the boy from falling and placed him on his bed. *"What in the hell was he doing?"* He quickly composed himself and decided it was not important—he got the kid with little or no noise. He waited a few minutes for his breathing to slow then walked over to the computer. Looking at the instant messenger application on the screen, he decided he would have to log the boy off so that his friends would think he was gone for the night.

Alright he thought, now for Mom. He found himself smiling as the anticipation of the next couple of hours hit him like a brick. He was never happy with this reaction but could not help himself. He was the avenger, and an avenger should not delight in the things he was about to do. *But, an avenger must like what he does in order to do it well* he chanted to himself to allay the feelings of guilt starting to wash through him.

Mom's room was down at the other end of the hallway. He had a special treat for Susan and maybe for the daughter too. Now the noise didn't matter, all the others would be out cold until he woke them with smelling salts. He boldly walked right into her room and found her asleep in bed, bedside light still on, and a book lying across her chest. She was not covered as it must have been at 85 degree's in the room. Her legs were well tanned and the tee shirt she was wearing was hiked up over her waist showing off the lovely hips and skimpy panties. He gently pulled the book from her hands and watched her breasts rise and fall with her breathing. *She is so beautiful, just like you Mom* he found himself thinking. He began to stroke her hair softly and her eyes began to flutter open at the sensation.

When she came fully awake the thought of a dream entered her mind, but a hand was still moving through her hair and she pulled away violently at the sudden intrusion. It took a second but she recognized the face buried in the hood and found her self saying "What are you doing here?," as she instinctively started to slide away from him on the bed. "Susan, you have nothing to fear. I came to rescue you and your family from your life of hell."

"Get the fuck away from me Richard, what in the hell are you doing in my house! Keeeeviiin!" she screamed, "Russell! Help me!" she gasped realizing with a sunken feeling that there was no one to help her. "Katie!" barely came out of her mouth as the tears began streaming down her cheeks sensing with all her heart that she had already lost her precious children and that a nightmare beyond her wildest imagination had yet to begin.

"Susan, please be still," he begged. "I thought you would be happy to see me and to finally be free."

Her sobs turned into uncontrollable shaking as she felt the will to fight surrender to the thought of joining her children in death. She began to pray to God that it would be quick and painless.

Chapter 15

Jaffrey--Cape Cod, MA

Chase looked down at his watch and saw it was 10 minutes to 9:00. He was just putting on a new shirt and said "Clair, please show me the case meeting room". A large flat screen monitor on his wall that had been a lovely mountain brook spilling down over rocks blinked into a wide angle view of the meeting room. After putting on his sandals, he sat back in the chair and closed his eyes for a moment.

Henry is really making a mess of things. Bob does not know how to shield himself and left his psychic wide open when he and Karen were talking on the phone earlier. He plans on coming back here to get more information on the Samurai and the Maryland Devil, and, Henry is in the process of having Emit picked up right now! Henry doesn't realize that our foundation is only concerned with getting these criminals off the street and if they pick up Emit first, so be it. I don't care. What I do care about is the way they use our information. At the surface level our stuff looks very good, but without repeated verification and validation, our information could lead to major disasters. I have explained this to people for years and they still just don't get it.

So now Henry is taking matters into his own hands and I hope to God things work out. I can't believe Bob though. When he left here this afternoon, other than his very obvious feelings for Seville, he felt like he was on our team. I wonder what Henry said to him that changed his mind.

Looking at Bob and Karen in the meeting room on the screen, Chase got a chill down his spine. Just then a picture of a man came into his mind who was taking the legs off a man. The man had his back to Chase in the picture so he could not see what the man looked like except that it was not Emit Ferguson! Another picture flashed in his mind of the meat warehouse in Providence and the same man throwing down one of the bodies they had found this morning.

Jesus, thought Chase. *Where in the hell did that come from? He had been trying all day to get a hit from Providence and got nothing at*

all. This is not good. Henry's team is on the way to the Cape to pick up
Emit and he may not be the guy at all!

Chase sat back in the chair and tried to relax but nothing more was
happening. It was as if someone had turned on a faucet for a few
seconds then turned it off. Glancing back at the screen he noticed that
Samuel, Katherine, Ronni, and Seville had just walked into the room
and were making introductions. At that moment it felt right to let the
meeting continue the way they had planned and he was going to clam
up and let Bob play through his little deception. Ronnie would know
better though, maybe I should talk to her before we start.

He picked up the phone and hit the button marked "Karen" which
caused Karen's cell phone to vibrate. He could see her react to the
sensation on her belt and excuse herself from the crowd to pick up the
phone. "Yes Boss," she said softly through the mouth piece.

"How was your big date tonight? If I'm not mistaken you have
quite the glow and smile on your face."

"Chase, it was wonderful, not enough time though," Karen let out a
big sigh.

Chase was looking at Karen on the screen and noticed the top she
was wearing and he started to gasp through the phone "Good God girl,
what is that you are wearing? Did you forget to put something else on?"

Karen giggled through the phone as she had forgotten all about the
top she was wearing to distract Bob Fellows. She quickly explained her
plan to Chase who simply said "You are a piece of work kiddo. What
would I do without you?"

"Probably stay single all your life," she shot back through the
phone.

"Alright, listen up. Could you please tell Ronnie in private to come
up to my place and tell everyone else that we will be starting a few
minutes late?"

"Why, what's up Chase?"

"I'm not sure Karen; I need to talk to Ronni about something"

"About Seville?" Karen said with a sly tone in her voice.

"No, it's about the Lumber Jack, something is going on I can't
figure out and I need to get a better handle on it before we meet. Please
keep the group entertained until we return. Why don't you ask Clair to
play a quick re-run of the case to get everyone back in the zone, and
Karen?"

"Yes"

"Make sure you sit right in front of Bob during the meeting. You
look awesome!"

He could see her blush on screen and knowing that he was watching sent him a glance over at the camera with a thumb up in the air to confirm.

Chase didn't really approve of what Karen was wearing but her heart was in the right place and he made a mental note to speak with her about it some other time. As he was watching Karen pull Ronni aside, he glanced to Seville who was talking to Samuel, Katherine, and Bob. Seeing her hair still wet from their little dip in the pool made him smile. Ronnie had obviously helped her pull it back and braided her hair in Celtic fashion and the long black mane ran down to the small of her back. She was wearing one of Ronni's favorite medium outfits. The long black dress fit around her waist perfectly, hanging down to her ankles, and a purple lace shawl draped around her shoulders accented the outfit and undoubtedly kept her warm in the cool autumn air. Ronni sure knew what she was doing, as she had dressed Seville up to get his attention and to keep Seville's obvious womanly charms hidden from the general public i.e., Bob. *Ronni doesn't miss a trick* he chuckled as he walked out of his bedroom, down the stairs, and into his library where he knew Ronni would appear any second now.

Just then a panel in his library opened and an elevator door slid from left to right. As quietly as a mouse, Ronni stepped out, walked into the room, said hello to Chase, and then took her favorite chair over by the fireplace.

"Its wonderful weather we're having" Ronni said casually as if nothing in particular was going on. "I told Charles I might spend the night out here and that I would call him later to let him know. Are you coming to the beginner's class tomorrow?" she said in reference to the weekly Sunday afternoon psychic development class she held downstairs.

"I'm not sure yet. There is so much going on right now I might have to bow out, but since you are going to be here I would like to get the rest of the team together to have a working session on current cases. I don't think we can or should wait until the regular Wednesday night gathering. Wait a minute; you knew I was going to the Cape tomorrow with Samuel to pull in Emit, why did you just ask if I would be here for the class?"

"Bob Fellows is such an open book that he might as well have just told everyone the truth" said Ronni in a matter of fact tone. "I don't like what's going on one little bit but I will say that I would much rather know about it than get blindsided by those guys."

"I should have known," said Chase smirking. It had been a very long day and he was feeling pretty drained and not quite on the beam. "Somehow Bob succumbed to Henry and his deviousness from the time he left here this afternoon to the time he came back tonight. I wonder if Henry is holding something over him or what?"

"I don't think so. Bob seems to have one thing on his mind and I get a strong feeling that it's that subject matter and its underlying agenda that is driving him. As a matter of fact I got the feeling that he is the one using Henry more than Henry is using him."

"Interesting," Chase said into space not really looking at anything in particular.

They both knew that the subject matter was Seville and that Bob was sending out a ton of negative energy in all directions, actually doing quite a bit of harm to himself and those around him.

"Seville told me downstairs she and Bob had been together briefly a couple of years ago but that it never really worked out so they parted ways and that was that. Today was the first time they've seen each other or spoken since," Ronni offered.

"Seville told you that?" Chase said with an astonished tone in his voice.

"Well, I did ask her." Ronni said with a smile on her face. "It was not hard to read that he was involved with her energy today."

"You must have had a chat with Karen—didn't you?" He said, challenging her to tell the truth.

Looking over at the fire Ronni said to the flames "We did have a brief chat on the phone when she called to tell me about the meeting tonight."

Chase suddenly realized that the original meeting was for late this afternoon and that Ronni had been hanging around since then. "I owe you an apology Ronni, you were sitting around waiting all evening after I moved the meeting back and I was out frolicking around."

"Not to worry Chase. Karen and I talked on the phone before I left the house. I decided to stay anyway because I wanted to catch up on some reading, and besides, when was the last time any of us have seen you frolic!"

For the first time Chase was beginning to see just how much his team really looked out for him. True, they had been trying to set him up with women for years but he had never seen them go to the extremes he had seen today.

"Ronni, I can't describe the feeling I get about her. It's as if I have known her for a long time and have been waiting for her to come back. It just seems so natural."

"Remind me to take you on a guided meditation on past lives tomorrow. I would be willing to bet that you two have been together before and I think I know when and where."

"Oh you do, do ya, then why don't you just tell me."

"That would spoil it. I'm sure you will think of it long before I get you on the couch, because if I can remember it after all these years with my memory, I am sure you can if you would just relax a little."

"Every party has a pooper, that's why we invited you...." Chase chanted knowing that she was absolutely right. He would make sure he spent some time on that tonight before he went to bed. It just wasn't coming to him at the moment.

"Ok, back to business." He said, seriously changing his tone. "Something is not quite right in spookyville. While I was upstairs earlier a valve opened in my mind for just a couple of minutes and I had visions that the guy who did the Providence murders was not Emit Ferguson. It was really weird Ronni; the pictures literally appeared from nowhere then disappeared again. I couldn't see the guy because he had his back to me but I knew that he was not Emit. What do you think that's all about?"

"It could just be an over worked mind Chase. You know that all of us got positive hits on Emit as the Lumber Jack and that when more than two of us hit on the same thing it usually means positive validation. Was there anything else about the visions that made them unusual?"

"Something else was there too Ronni. I got the feeling that I was being taunted AND I got the deja vu feeling but couldn't place the event. I wonder if Emit has an accomplice that we don't know about and this guy in the pictures is just starting to show up on our radar."

"It could be" Said Ronni, "Not likely though. At least one of us would have picked up this guy before, especially Samuel because he has been keeping tabs on Emit. On the other hand, Samuel was not with Emit the last four days because he was busy doing the disqualification work on the number two and three perps. But either way, a second person does not feel right."

"It doesn't feel right to me either" said Chase. "But something is going on Ronni; I just can't put my finger on it yet."

"What are we going to do about downstairs? Ronni said, bringing Chase back into the present.

"We go along with Bob for now. If my instincts are right, Clair is going to pick up on the police communications regarding the group sent to pick up Emit. If that happens I can't wait to see the look on Bob's face in the meeting."

Ronni nodded her head as if feeling the same truth and said "What are you going to do when that happens?"

"What I always do" said Chase with his serene smile "Play it by ear! Come on, let's go join the circus."

*****

Special Agent Tom Sands was conducting a radio check to make sure his three team mates were all in place. They were wearing their FBI S.W.A.T. gear and had made the long ride up to the Cape earlier in the evening. Next to Tom stood the Chief of Police of Truro, Tony Grazzo, a small man with a large gut protruding from under his flack jacket. Agent Sands could never understand these backwoods cops and why some of them just didn't take care of themselves. He would not want to go into a dangerous situation with this man or the other two Truro Cops he had met. So far he had convinced them to be observers of the bust and had them waiting with him at the van. In just a minute he would leave the two and join his team for what he hoped would be a routine bust.

The call he got this afternoon from Henry White had been most unusual. After his conversation with Henry, Tom made a call to his local superior to make sure everything was on the up and up. They were simply to drive to Cape Cod and take into custody a man named Emit Ferguson who lived in Truro. Henry told him that Emit was the prime suspect for the Lumber Jack killings and that they suspected he was behind the Providence killings uncovered that morning. Once they had Emit in custody they were to take him back to New York to their lock-up and let the Boston forensics team Henry was sending down go over his place for evidence.

Tom made sure the truck they were given the description of was in the driveway of the house and had all his men stationed around the yard in strategic locations. There was only one light on in the house, up front, where a living room or family room might be. No other lights or movement had been seen over the last 20 minutes of the preliminary stake out. Tom was just about to give the order to move in when a blue sedan turned onto the street about a block away coming in their direction.

"Hold on guys," Tom said into his ear piece. "Let's wait until this car goes by." But the car did not go by; instead it turned right into Emit's driveway and parked next to the truck. Tom watched two men get out of the car and walk around to the trunk the driver had popped from within the car. "Hold your positions" Tom said into his headset as he thought about what the next move was going to be. He had not been told about any other people but because this guy was supposed to be dangerous, he didn't think it would hurt to pick them both up.

"That's Reverend Peters of the Unitarian Church" Tom heard Tony whisper to him.

"What" Tom said incredulously?

"That's right, it's John Peters, and he's the local pastor of the Unitarian Church. I heard some one say that he has been away for a few days on a men's retreat. Look's like he and Emit are just getting back."

"Shit" Tom said to no one in particular. *It figures, this was supposed to be a quick in and out mission. According to Henry this guy was supposed to be home not away at a retreat. This smells bad.*

Decision made, Tom said into his speaker. "Ok guys, we have a potential friendly with our perp. Listen up. We are going to go in on the count of three. Susan, you take the driver of the vehicle, he is supposedly a pastor so don't rough him up, just get him in cuffs quickly. Randy and Brian, you get the suspect. Get him down fast and get the cuffs on. We will be on top of you in 10 seconds and once the two are in restraints all three of you get into the house immediately and check it for any one else. Copy?"

Tom listened for all three of them to return a check before he began his count.

"Well Emit that was not exactly the best retreat I have ever been on but it sure was nice to get away for a few days," John said as Emit retrieved his suitcase out of the trunk of his pastor's car.

"I don't know" said Emit, "I got a lot out of it, especially the sessions yesterday. They were pretty intense and gave me a lot to think about for the next couple of weeks. It was good to get away too. I really liked the hike we made on Wednesday. The leaves couldn't have been any better."

"That's for sure. I had been praying for some time that the weather and the leaves would cooperate with us."

Just then the pastor was knocked to the ground in the driveway. As Emit looked on in amazement, he heard more footsteps coming right at him from his blind side. For an instant he thought about trying to run, but his instincts said better as two bodies crashed into him and had his face planted firmly in the gravel.

"What in the hell is going on" cried the pastor as he briefly struggled against the unforeseen assault. "Who are you people?"

"FBI Sir" said Agent Ward, as she clicked the cuffs on the pastor's wrists.

"Emit, what's going on?" John said to his long time friend.

"Hell if I know" Emit barely squeaked out under the pressure of his two assailants. Just then three more people came running up to the driveway and the first three got up quickly and ran towards the house.

What are they doing here? Emit was thinking. *They won't find anything here that's for sure. I better just play dumb for now until I figure things out.*

"Emit Ferguson?" the man in charge said to the figure lying on the ground beneath his feet.

"That's right Officer; can you please tell me what's going on?"

"I am placing you under arrest for murder," said Agent Sands as he left Emit lying on the driveway while he picked up the pastor and brought him to his feet.

"Murder? What in God's name are you talking about?" Emit shouted at Agent Sands.

"Mr. Peters, my name is Agent Sands from the Long Island Bureau of the FBI. We are here to place Emit Ferguson under arrest for multiple murders. I am sure you have nothing to do with this but I must keep you under restraint until we get a few things resolved."

"Agent Sands, are you sure you have the right man? Emit and I just got back from a four day retreat in western Mass. What murders are you talking about?"

"Mr. Peters, there was a double homicide in Providence this morning and the FBI at the highest levels thinks Emit here was involved in those and others."

"That's absurd agent, Emit has been with me literally 24 hours a day since early Wednesday morning. How could he have possibly committed murder?"

"I didn't commit any damn murders!" Emit hollered at the men.

"Mr. Peters, I am just doing my job. We will be taking Emit into custody while we conduct a formal investigation. Now, I need to check on a few things before I can release you Reverend, so please just sit down right there and I will be with you as soon as possible."

Just then two blue vans drove up to the front of the house and six men and woman poured out of the vehicles, as one of them approached Agent Sands."

"I'm forensics Chief Turner from Boston. Are you Sands?"

"That's right" Sands said extending his hand to the man. "Please have your people wait right here until my team is done clearing the premises."

"No problem" Turner said looking around at one of the vans. "Hey Charlie, get out the tape and start doing the front of the house from the sidewalk will ya?"

"Sure" the man acknowledged and went to work rolling yellow crime scene tape from a tree on the end of the property.

"Excuse me Turner; I need to check in with the home team for a minute. Let me know when my people come out of the house."

Agent Sands walked away from the group and hit a button on his speed dialer and was soon talking feverishly into his cell phone to the man on the other end.

Agent Ward came over to Sands while he was still talking to Henry White. "Tom, the house is clear and clean. Other than some empty Bud cans in the kitchen, this house doesn't have anything out of place or anything suspicious."

"Thanks Susan" he said as he relayed the information to Henry. "Tell Turner from Boston that his team can go on in."

"So Henry, it looks like we have real problem here. Unless the pastor is involved with Emit, we have just made a huge mistake. I can either keep both of them, let the pastor go for now and question him later, or let them both go. It's your call."

Henry was still shaking on the other end of the line. He had been tricked and had two dozen eggs all over his face. Chase Benton would never see the end of his wraith now! "Tom, you guys stay put and let the forensics guys do a good sweep of the place. Don't forget the truck and any outbuildings. Put the two guys in the house under watch and have your team pitch in. We are already there so we might as well be thorough even if we fucked up. I am going to make some calls and will get back to you as soon as I can. Make sure Emit stays in restraints, and make damn sure the pastor is at least comfortable. If they need to eat make it so."

"Ok Henry," Sands said disconnecting the call and turning back to the abortion Henry had gotten him into.

*****

When Chase and Ronni joined the meeting, the group was just wrapping up watching the section of the Lumber Jack report which had already been slightly amended with more forensics input from the crime scene in Providence.

Chase opened the meeting; "The Lumber Jack team thinks we are ready to go in and take Emit. Samuel, would you mind giving us a brief summary of the criteria that has led to this conclusion?"

"Sure Chase, as you all know, we had narrowed down our prime suspects to three people as of two months ago. Katherine and I have done as much due diligence in the field as we possibly could. I have spent the last week disqualifying the other two. For example, Emit is the only one of the three who could have physically been at all of the body disposal sites we have cataloged up until two weeks ago. The other two guys, even though there was a great deal of proximity, were disqualified because of verifiable whereabouts. What I mean is, one of the guys travels a lot and on at least three different occasions he was in a different city far enough away that he could not possibly have been involved with the abduction, killing, or disposal of that particular murder. At face value that does not disqualify him completely but if you can follow the logic it is a sound method of narrowing down the field."

Seville jumped in "Samuel, are you saying that as far as you know Emit was the only one who was in physical proximity to the victims 100% of the time?"

"Yes Seville, all of the victims we investigated including Providence. The other two guys would have been a severe stretch to peg on these. Emit, however, has been on the Cape or in Massachusetts for the last two weeks. After hearing about the murders early this morning I took a detour and went to Truro to see if he was still in the area. I did not ID him specifically, but his truck was still there in the driveway. I know that sounds a little loose, but don't forget we back up each other here with other sources of information. Ronni and her team got positive hits on Emit being our man during other sessions."

Ronni stole a glance at Chase thinking about the conversation they'd had just a little while ago regarding Chase's vision of someone else being in Providence.

At that moment Bob Fellow's cell phone went off and without so much as an apologetic look, he picked it off his belt, looked at the number, got up and started walking for the door out into the atrium. *I was hoping this call wouldn't come until later. Henry better have good news because I am going to have to do some dancing when I go back in there.*

"Henry, it's Bob, how did it go on the Cape?"

Chase was looking over at Bob as he was walking out the door. He observed Bob pull the phone away from his ear, the way some one does when being yelled at, and thought that to be very interesting.

Chase addressed the group while Bob was outside "Alright guys, we have a new situation which has popped up. Seville, this may be an unreasonable request for you, let me know now if it is, but we need your help." *Then he filled in the team on what he thought was going on with the FBI and with Emit regarding Providence.*

"So, I have two guys in cuffs, one, the pastor of the local church, and a solid 40 alibis for both that they were in western Massachusetts since Wednesday on a God damn men's retreat!" Henry shouted into the phone at Bob.

"Jesus Christ" Bob muttered into the phone. "Henry, I don't know what to tell you. Serial Connections is convinced Emit is the guy. We just started the meeting a few minutes ago to go over the case material one more time before the planned pick up tomorrow."

"Planned pick up--Yeah right" Henry huffed. "I should have let them get egg on their faces and then come in to mop up the mess myself!" "What's the plan now Bob?"

"Henry, how quiet was the pick up down there?"

"As quiet as it could possibly be. We asked the locals to keep if it off the radios."

"Good, keep it that way. I am going to head back into the meeting like nothing happened to check what else I can get. I don't need to know now Henry, but I would like to let them go ahead with their plans tomorrow. Can you cut Emit loose?"

"I can. I am still waiting for the forensic reports from the Cape and his place up in Maine. If they both come back clean, he can stay in his house for the night."

"Great Henry; let's go with that and I will call you on my way back to Providence with Seville later on tonight."

"Alright Bob, no more screw ups!"

"Yeah," Bob muttered to himself, closing the phone, thinking for a second, and then heading back into the meeting.

"Everything ok Bob?" Karen asked from her chair sending a little jab Bob's way.

He gave Karen a funny look like *why would YOU be asking me that* and replied "Sure, it was one of my case officers calling in. They needed a warrant."

Chase and Ronni both knew that he was lying to them and Chase decided to launch the new information regarding his hit tonight alluding that Emit was not in Providence. He suspected that they had already picked him up and that he had an air tight alibi. It felt right, so he went ahead. He was very curious to see how Bob would respond to this.

"Samuel," Chase said, "Up until today, the findings of the team point very strongly to Emit Ferguson as the Lumber Jack. Is that correct?"

"Yes," said Samuel, Katherine nodding her head in agreement.

"I need to throw something out on the table." Chase said very seriously. "Just a little while ago I got a very strong hit that Emit was NOT the guy who did the Providence murders."

Everyone in the room came to full attention when Chase announced this piece of information.

"What in the hell do you mean?" Bob asked incredulously.

"I mean just what I said Bob, no more than one hour ago I got a VERY strong and intense visual on the Providence site and Emit was not the guy."

"But you told me this afternoon that you guys were sure of Emit and tonight's meeting was to plan on bringing him in!" he said in a very angry tone.

"Easy Bob, what you just said is true, but a big part of the agenda of this type of meeting is to re-qualify everything. We don't just barge through the barn door without making sure that we have the right guy. Even if I had not gotten that hit, which we will discuss shortly, we may have decided not to make a move yet. Karen; how many times have we had a sting meeting that ended up postponing or altering our plans?"

Karen adjusted her upper posture and turned to Bob and said "At least 40% of the time. This meeting is the most serious of our meetings. Our goal is to do it right and not make foolish mistakes. We are talking about people's lives here Bob. We don't mess around and we don't let others mess around with our work." Adding that little piece at the end to let Bob know she was on to him.

"Especially on the psychic front," Ronni chirped in. "Our piece of this puzzle is very complex and the approach we have devised over the years is predicated on a strict system of checks and balances. Psychic work is NOT a perfect science, and sometimes there are negative forces out there working against us. We have to be very cautious and very discerning about every little piece of information we end up using as part of a case validation. The fact that Chase just got a very contradictory piece of information is upsetting to me."

Seville said to no one in particular "Psychic bad guys?"

Bob looked over at Seville and was still really pissed about her new wardrobe. He had commented on it earlier. She had simply told him that she had fallen into the large pool by the guest houses and that Ronni had been kind enough to lend her some clothes while hers dried. He had not been able to question her further because Karen had moved right in and diverted the conversation. I will talk to her about that on the way back tonight, he thought.

"Unfortunately yes" Ronnie replied. "Imagine the work we do here. We are the good guys *but* we are not the only people in the world who use psychic abilities. Also, there are negative energies out there that are not human that love to mess around with good work. So that is why we have to be so careful."

Bob cut back in being very impatient "So, net this out for me, are you going to pick up Emit tomorrow or not?" he said starting to think this was a bunch of mumbo jumbo.

Chase solicited his team with a look to offer up an answer and Samuel spoke up "I don't think we can. Like I said earlier, I have not had positive contact with Emit for over four days, and in light of what Chase just said, I think he and Ronni need to do some more work on it. My vote is no."

"I agree with Samuel," Katherine offered making a quorum.

"Well, there's your answer Bob. It looks like we get back to the drawing board. You should probably call the troops you set up for tomorrow and let them know they are on standby for now," said Chase.

"Obviously," Bob muttered, clearly thinking hard about something important. "Ok, for my edification, can you explain to me how you were planning to pin this on Emit if you were going to pick him up tomorrow?"

Samuel started to speak but Chase gently interrupted him "Bob, it is hard to say for sure. Again, that is one of the topics we were going to talk about tonight. Picking up a man on a whim just doesn't work. We were going to decide tonight if and where we could find the evidence we needed to make the collar stick. That will have to wait now."

"Seville, can I see you outside for a moment? Bob asked clearly agitated.

She glanced quickly at Chase while saying "Sure Bob" and walked out with him to the foyer.

"What do you make of all this Seville, I mean you have been here all day, are these guys for real or what? I put my neck on the line today"

"Of course they are Bob. Why would you ask a thing like that?"

"Because" pausing for a minute debating on whether to tell her about the sting. "Henry had Emit picked up tonight--against my wishes."

"What!" Seville said with a tone of complete disgust. "How in the hell could you let that happen Bob!" Seville said with surprise even though she had already been informed of that potential.

"It wasn't my fault Seville. Henry went right around me after I briefed him this afternoon. I knew nothing about it until that phone call I just got."

"Yeah, and my name is Lady Godiva!" she said with venom in her voice, scowling at Bob.

"I swear Seville"—"Bob, don't even go there." she yelled at him. "You can take your friggin lies and shove them right up your ass!"

"Seville, what do I have to do to prove I'm not lying? Get your stuff; we can talk about this on way back to Providence. I will excuse us in the meeting and meet you downstairs!" he ordered.

"Are you insane? You lied to me when we were dating Bob. You never had any intentions of following through with *US*. I was just a one week stand for you and you think I'm going to believe you now? You can drive back to Boston by yourself, but if I were you I would find the balls to go back into that room and tell them what you did."

Bob looked at her with a sad face and said "I'm not going back in. I'll wait downstairs for five minutes and then I'm leaving. Last chance Seville."

She looked at him as though he had three heads. *This man doesn't have a damn clue.* "Don't bother Bob, it'll be a cold day in hell" as she quickly turned and walked back into the conference room with her new friends.

Chapter 16

Seattle

Masonori sat at his desk in his chamber room looking at the computer screen. He was on Map Quest searching out a route to take Tanya to her final resting place. He finally found a good location where he could drop her body without much danger of being caught, but where she would be found pretty easily. He exited the program and sighed. Just an hour ago he had laid Tanya out on one of the steel gurneys in the clean room and had performed his ritual prepping of her body.

He realized that in today's forensics world there was no way to completely get rid of evidence but he had devised a process that would at least give the forensic teams a run for their money. It took him about an hour to do it, making sure the process left no traces in her or on her body, and then had zipped her up in a sterile body bag and brought her down to the end of the passageway by his second house. This was really the hardest part for him. He had really liked Tanya and seeing her lying there on the table, beyond help, and having to clean her entire body made tears come to his eyes. *One of these days a woman is going to embrace me for who I am and come out of this place with me upstairs instead of through the garage downstairs. It will only be a matter of time before I meet a like minded woman who will just love me. Someday...*

Hitting another icon on his desktop brought up a surveillance program on his screen. At once eight windows opened showing outside views of both his houses, each one sweeping back and forth in a pre-determined pattern. Scanning the pictures to make sure his getaway with Tanya was clean; he noticed a light grey sedan about 200 yards down the street from his main house. Using the mouse to zoom in on the car he found it to be occupied by a woman who looked to be in her mid thirties. He had been expecting to see her. An anonymous e-mailer had sent him a short profile and warning just a few minutes before. He was very concerned about the e-mail, but it appeared that whoever sent it was on his side.

Fukui-san,

You do not know me, and never will, so don't reply to this e-mail or ask. At this moment there is an undercover agent watching your house. She is in a silver Honda, has brown hair, green eyes, athletic build, and carries a handgun. She does not work for a government agency but rather a private foundation that wants people like us annihilated!

Her name is Susan Kincaid, and she is a highly trained field operative for this organization I spoke of. You should use every precaution if you choose to deal with her one way or another. It would appear that they, along with the FBI, have been keeping a close watch on you. I admire you for keeping so cool and determined in your quest knowing that your days might end soon.

I may send you more information or not, as they are on to me as well.

Good Luck My Friend—Happy Hunting!

He snapped a picture of Susan using his remote outside camera, and stored it on his computer. He would look into this more carefully tonight when he got home. Continuing his scan, he noticed that his usual getaway from the second house was clear. He decided to put on a little show for Susan before he left and went back up to his house. It was just turning dark outside as he turned on the porch lights and stepped out through the front door. Without looking at anything in particular he walked down to the front lawn, picked up a newspaper that had been deposited earlier in the day, went to the mailbox, grabbed a few letters, and walked back into the house. Then he turned on the living room lights, pulled down the shades, and turned on the stereo system to a local jazz station.

Making a quick show walking around through the lights, he headed back down to the passageway and into his office to check the security cameras one more time before leaving. All clear, he turned off the monitor and headed down the stairs to the brown zippered bag that contained Tanya. He picked up the bag and headed through the security doors and into the second house. Going right into the garage he decided to take his station wagon. On top was a luggage carrier which was only window dressing. The carrier was empty but the back of the wagon was semi-filled with camping gear that would serve two purposes; if he was ever pulled over, the body bag would be concealed under the camping gear and the gear would corroborate his story about being out for a couple of days camping. On the back of the wagon, a mountain bike hung from the brackets as an added widow dressing. He loaded the bag into the wagon and covered it completely with his gear, got in the car, put on his hat and glasses and backed out into the street. The drive would take him about 30 minutes with no more than 10 minutes to dispose of the body, then 30 minutes back. He was looking forward to sizing up Susan later as she definitely fit his profile and was rather good looking. The question was would he abduct her and see if she loved him or just kill her? In a flash his decision was made, and a wide grin spread across his face as he cautiously drove out of the city.

While he was driving, he started thinking more about Susan. He quickly forgot Tanya and was now annoyed that she was going to take up any more of his precious time. He was tempted to just drop her behind a store somewhere but it was Saturday night and the streets were already busy with people. *Stick to your plan Masanori!* A small voice said in the back of his mind *Susan will still be there when you return and we can have a lot more fun!* He shuddered at the thought and recognized the wisdom in the voice. After all he had not come this far by being stupid. He took a right at the next light and continued on his journey all the while devising a plan for Susan. He had never had an opportunity like this and would have to be extremely careful in order to abduct her and keep whoever she was working for and the FBI off his tail. Then it came to him. He picked up his voice activated PDA and started surfing the net to figure out where Susan lived and as much more information about her as possible.

Chapter 17

FBI HQ/Cape Cod/Jaffrey

I am sticking my neck out pretty far with these guys from Serial Connections, Henry thought to himself. Bob had just informed him that the jig was up and that neither he nor Seville would be able to get any more inside information. He had asked Bob about Seville and only got a sharp reply that she was really pissed off about their Lumber Jack sting and he didn't consider her to be an asset any more. Henry finished typing a message into one of his personal e-mail accounts and hit the send button. *That should help a little bit. I have to keep everyone on their toes to make sure Chase doesn't get to make these three collars.*

He switched over to his FBI e-mail and opened a new mail from the forensics team up in Boston. It said that after looking over the house on the Cape and hearing from the team in Maine they had found absolutely nothing to implicate Emit in any crimes. *God damn it. I thought for sure we were going to get him and start the ball rolling for a change. Now I have to let Emit go, take the heat on Monday about a false bust, and still explain why there's no more progress on the other two cases either. Shit!*

Bob was supposed to send Henry a detailed report in the morning about what he had learned about all three cases while in Jaffrey. He would pass it along to Tim as soon as he cleaned it up a little bit. He sat back in his chair and thought for a moment. Bob had said that Chase had come up with doubts about Emit at the last minute. *Could he be playing cat and mouse with me or was that a real change in direction? Emit wasn't in Providence after all and that is a pretty good indication that Chase had the wrong guy anyway, and as far as Henry knew, Chase was not aware that Emit had been on a four day retreat with his Pastor. I think I better let things play out a little more with Emit or whoever it is. I feel much better about Seattle today after getting a few things set up there. Maryland is still a wild card but Tim's guy down there should be getting closer any time now.* Henry picked up the phone and called Agent Sands on the Cape.

*****

Agent Sands was in the Kitchen of Emit's house talking to Henry while Emit and the Pastor were being watched closely in the family room by the rest of his team. The forensics crew had just packed up and left a few minutes earlier and the Pastor's hysterical wife had just shown up as a result of Emit's neighbors seeing him being cuffed out on the driveway. Agent Ward was trying to explain to her what was going on and that her husband was not being held as a suspect when Sands stepped back into the room.

"Alright folks, I just got off the phone with the top guy at FBI headquarters. It seems the anonymous tip we got today was some kind of hoax. Agent Ward, please take the cuffs off our guests and have them sit back down on the couch." Sands waited until Agent Ward uncuffed the Pastor and Emit. "I have been asked by the FBI to extend our sincere apologies and you can rest assured that we will do everything in our power to trace the call we got today."

"Does this mean we can go home now?" Asked the Pastor who was holding his wife's hand looking over at Emit.

"Yes Pastor, would you like to have an escort home?"

"No thanks" he said to the very embarrassed FBI Agent.

Emit chimed in "Just what was it you thought we did officer?"

"Well Mr. Ferguson, it wasn't the both of you. It was just you. We got a call today from an anonymous person claiming you were the Lumber Jack. If you don't know, the Lumber Jack is a serial in the New England area that has done some very nasty killings. You can imagine that when we get a tip like the one we got today it is a matter of life or death and we have to respond accordingly."

"I can see your point officer but I still don't like the fact that you scared the hell out of us tonight. My attorney isn't going to like this one little bit!" Emit spurted out, putting on a little show for the crowd.

"I'm sure he isn't sir. I will leave you my card and feel free to have him or her call me with any questions. This kind of thing is unfortunate but like I said very necessary."

"Come on Charli" the pastor said pulling his wife to the door. "Emit, thanks again for a great trip. Let's catch up tomorrow, I would still like to talk some more about that seminar you went to."

"Sure enough John, you and Charli drive safe and I am really sorry about the sour ending to the trip."

"Good night everyone" he said as they walked out the door.

"Mr. Ferguson, once again we are sorry for the intrusion. Please give me a call if you have any questions about tonight."

"Ok officer, I will walk you all out."

Emit walked his unwanted guests out the front door and waited on the front steps until the last car disappeared down the street and the last of his nosy neighbors retreated back into their houses before he turned and walked into his house, beads of sweat running down his forehead. *Jesus--what the hell! If I didn't do the Providence murders than who in the hell is out there pretending to be me?*

*****

Chase and the group were just getting back together after Bob abruptly left the meeting when Clair announced an on-line message from field investigator Dug Masters in Maryland. Chase accepted the message and Dug's face appeared on the wide screen in front of them.

"Hello everyone" Dug said to the group he could see through the video conferencing camera on top of Clair's console.

Everyone nodded their head or made some kind of remark to Dug from their seats. Chase took a second to introduce Seville, explained why she was there, and mentioned to Dug that she had full clearance for any discussions.

Dug looked into the room as he spoke "We might have a big problem on our hands. I got down to Ocean City this afternoon to check on Richard Fox after I got through with the other top three contenders and have spent all day trying to track him down. Nothing; No one has seen him. I took a peek into the rental office, it was closed, and he was not there and it didn't look like he had been there for a while. He's not at his condo on 142nd street, and hasn't been seen at any of his favorite Saturday night hangouts yet. Funny though, his Beamer is still in the street outside the office. I think we might have an active cycle on our hands."

"Clair" Chase said into the air. "Can you please pull out the evidence walls on the Maryland Devil?"

Immediately the group heard a soft whirring sound from the room beyond and the sliding doors opened to the right of them. Two panels began the journey out to the master console and joined themselves to the Lumber Jack panels already in place. Unlike the others though, one of the panels had shelves which contained hard evidence, pieces of clothing, a keychain, and some odd looking leather straps. Chase looked over to Ronnie and gave her the nod. She got up and walked over to the case and took out one of the straps and the key chain. Both items were suspected to belong to the Maryland Devil.

She walked back to her seat and put the items on the table. "Seville, could you please pick up the straps and tell me what you feel or see?"

Chase looked at Ronnie again not having to wonder what she was doing. She was already testing Seville to see just how receptive she was. He went along with it for the time being.

"Karen, how about you pick up the keychain and tell me what you feel" Ronnie said. Karen, unlike Seville knew what Ronnie was doing. She had been practicing with Ronnie for over a year now in her development classes and was becoming more practiced at pyschometry.

Seville picked up the leather strap and held it in her hands looking over at Ronni. "Just close your eyes and relax Seville, and tell me what you see or feel no matter how ridiculous you may think it is" Ronni offered casually.

"Clair, please record session" Chase said again into the air. Karen began talking out loud. "I see gates, fence gates, a woman lying on her back crying, and icebergs! After another moment Karen opened her eyes and said "That's it Ronni, gates, a woman on her back, and icebergs."

"Good job Karen, how about you Seville?"

"I don't see anything really, just lights dancing around behind my eye lids. I do feel repressed though. It's as if I got very sad all of a sudden." She opened her eyes and put the straps back on the table.

"Chase, your turn" Ronnie said passing over the keychain and strap.

Chase picked up the strap first but didn't close his eyes as the others did. He let his thoughts go into a trance and focused on picking up the energy from the keychain. "Car, green sedan, 4 door, older, Virginia license plates, can't read the numbers, male driver, long winding back road, I feel anticipation, anger, and excitement." He stopped and put the key chain down and picked up the leather strap and entered back into his trance. "A boy and a girl, chairs, father?--chair, big room with fireplace and couch, straps, woman on floor bleeding--cuts, boy crying—bleeding--cuts, girl dead—bleeding--cuts—trying to pass but afraid." Then he snapped out of it and shook his head slightly. "That's it Ronni"

Ronni picked up the strap and held it gently in her hand. Like Chase she just stared into space. "Ocean…., waves….., window…., desk…., small two story garage on a busy street…Robe—

black.....crosses—white....blood—crosses—red. Ronni dropped the strap on the table without paying a bit of attention to the others in the room, picked up the keychain and held it in her palm. "Blue car—fast—near garage..." Ronni stopped talking and everyone thought she was done when her eyes opened wide and she almost screamed. She dropped the key chain immediately, closed her eyes, and began whispering something.

Chase picked up on what happened. He could feel that she had just been communicated to, but by what or who he no idea. He let her finish putting up her shields against whatever had just invaded her. She opened her eyes and looked at Chase and he nodded to her to continue. At this point there was no reason to keep whatever happened from the others.

Ronnie composed herself and said "Man, mid thirties, black hair, pinned to a wall—bleeding—talking---"Veronica, I'm coming for you!"—then blank." She relaxed in her chair for a few moments, the whole room keeping still and quiet.

Chase broke the ice and said "Clair, please process".

In about three minutes the full screen of Dug minimized into a small window in the top right hand corner of the screen. "Seville, this is where we try to help Clair with imagery and content based on the session we just had. Since you didn't actually see anything you won't be prompted for input."

First on the screen came Karen's stuff. Pictures of gates appeared and Karen said to Clair "Number 3," telling Clair that the picture she saw closely resembled that particular gate. Next, illustrations of woman lying on floors came up. Karen looked at the pictures carefully and chose one with a woman, wearing no clothes, black shoulder length hair behind her. Lastly up came pictures of icebergs. Karen directed Clair to one in particular and stopped.

Within a few minutes, a word with a question mark replaced the pictures.

Gaithersburg?

Dug was the first to respond. "Gaithersburg? Does that mean he is in Gaithersburg? Where did Clair come up with that?"

"Might be" said Chase, it looks like Clair took a symbolic view of Karen's information. Gates+woman+iceberg = Gait-her-ice-berg = Gaithersburg" he said looking at the screen and waiting for the next section to come up. Then pictures filled the screen with various Ocean views from land. Dug noticed some of the pictures he had submitted as part of the Devil case. Ronni looked at the pictures and said #12 and #14.

Next pictures of cars filled the screen. Chase called out #19 which was an old green Ford sedan. Ronni called out #47 which was a blue BMW. The cars went away and up on the screen came a whole series of male illustrations. Ronni called out #25 and Chase called out #10 and noted it was for the driver of the sedan and then called out #15 for the male/father figure he thought was a victim. Then the screen populated with crosses of different shapes and sizes. Ronni picked one in particular that was white and looked at the red ones and said "no matches for red crosses". The process was repeated for robes, garages, busy streets, the man pinned to the wall and then Clair put something gruesome on the screen. A body sitting strapped to a chair with dried crosses cut into the flesh all over the arms, legs, face, and torso. Both Ronnie and Chase voiced agreement. Then Clair went to work for a few minutes processing all the data.

Dug chimed in while Clair was working. "Ronnie, the pictures you picked out in particular all point to Richard Fox. The beach pictures you picked out are the view from his office, and the Blue BMW is the same kind of car he drives. I don't know about any green sedan with Virginia plates but I can run it against a few names."

Seville looked at Ronnie and said "Clair has a database of pictures for each case you are working on. Haven't you seen these pictures before? Doesn't that prejudice your clairvoyance at times?"

"Seville that depends; part of the training I put myself and the other team members through is the ability to block out known things during sessions. It's not easy, but doable. Also the psychic team does not arbitrarily look at pictures like the ones Dug loaded for the case. We only access them AFTER we have a session. I had not seen pictures of a blue BMW regarding this case before nor was I aware that one of the perp's offices overlooked the beach with a particular kind of view. And, as I said to Bob earlier, this is not a perfect science, but let the results speak for themselves. This organization is responsible for capturing dozens of very nasty killers that totally alluded government agencies!"

"Ronni, I was not criticizing, I was just exploring for my own edification. I am trying to understand how all this works and I think the results have been incredible!"

Just then Clair came back to life to present the findings. Seville sat back and marveled at the process that Chase had built over the years.

She was thinking that he should wrap all this up and start selling it to government agencies. Then she thought about them working with the psychic components of the process and canceled that thought right away as Clair began presenting information.

Possible Hostage Locations
Gaithersburg, Maryland
Ocean City, Maryland

Possible Perpetrator
Richard Fox
Owns Blue BMW
Office on Boardwalk—Ocean City
Owns vacation rental company—Ocean City Views
Secondary Residence—Rehoboth Beach Delaware
RMV Records—No matches—green sedan
RMV Records—Positive—2003 BMW 745i Blue--MD

Possible Victims
Credit Checks by Ocean City Views—last 6 months--Gaithersburg
Peter Baldwin
Jonathan Feldman
Debra Grady
Tom Mason
Tom Newburg
Kevin Sawyer
Olivia Trainor
Mark Wagner

Credit Card Usage—Ocean City—within 7 days
Kevin Sawyer—Only Match
Hotspots—Restaurant
Nigel's--Liquor
Water World—Amusement
Ocean City Gifts—Retail
Nigel's—Liquor
Nigel's--Liquor
Sports Wear—Retail
Red Lobster—Restaurant
Nigel's--Liquor
China Moon—Restaurant

Boardwalk Rentals—Rental
SuperSave—Food Outlet
SuperSave—Food Outlet
Nigel's—Liquor
Outback--Restaurant
Nigel's—Liquor

Last charge—3:15 today—Mobil-Easton Maryland--Gas

Possible Victim Profile
2 Adults—2 Children

Kevin Sawyer—Age 43
Susan Sawyer—Wife—Age 42
Katie Sawyer—Daughter—Age 17
Russell Sawyer—Son---Age 15
Address:
147 Cotton Wood Street, Gaithersburg, MD
Home Phone—301-999-9999

The last thing Clair put up on the screen caused them all to stop short for a moment. An illustration of a large family room with cathedral ceilings, brick fireplace against the back wall, large sectional couch, and good size bay window became the backdrop as one by one the scene was drawn. Three People were sitting in chairs and appeared to have straps holding them in place. The young females head was drooping down to her bare chest as if resting. The other two were male, one younger and the other obviously the father or at least twice his age. On the floor was a female who looked like the picture Karen had seen just a few minutes ago. All of them were bleeding and a closer look revealed red crosses dripping with blood cut into their flesh. Kneeling on the floor next to the woman was a figure draped in a long black robe with white crosses embroidered into the fabric, his hand sweeping across her flesh with a long object.

The team remained quiet for some time then Chase spoke up and asked Clair to stop for a moment. "Any questions at this point group?"

Seville was sitting on the edge of her seat as she watched the team and the computer work their magic. She was stunned. What they had just accomplished would have taken fifty man hours or more with mixed results at best. She knew that nothing was for sure yet but at least they had logically boiled things down.

"Chase, we need to call the locals in Gaithersburg. I am almost four hours away and if this is an active cycle maybe we can get the guy." Dug said.

"Who has jurisdiction in Gaithersburg"

"Montgomery County Police"

Clair, dial the Montgomery County Police emergency number.

They all waited while they heard the tell tale tones being dialed in the computer system.

A dispatcher was heard on the other end. "Montgomery Country Police emergency line, Officer Randall speaking, this call is being recorded."

"Officer Randall, my name is Chase Benton and I am a private detective. One of my men is in Ocean City Maryland and we think that a series of murders might be in progress at a residence in Gaithersburg."

They heard a very low and brief sigh on the other end. "Mr. Benton, the number you are calling from is where?" Officer Randall asked looking down at the caller ID not recognizing the New Hampshire area code.

"Officer, our headquarters are located in New Hampshire. That is where I am calling from, one of my agents, Dug Masters, is on the other line calling from Ocean City Maryland. The guy we think is committing the murders is the Maryland Devil which I am sure you are aware of."

There was a slight pause "Of course Mr. Benton, why do you think there is a murder being committed in Gaithersburg right now by the Devil?"

"Officer, we don't have time to go through all that, we've been investigating this case for months and are not able to get to the site in Gaithersburg and believe it is a life or death situation. You will find us on the up and up and simply need you to send a cruiser out to 147 Cotton Wood Street to check the place out. Kevin and Susan Sawyer and their two children live at that address."

"Mr. Benton, please hold while I transfer you to the supervisor on duty. I am going to alert a nearby unit to approach but standby."

"Thank you officer!" Chase said with a breath of relief.

"Lieutenant Willis speaking, this call is being recorded."

Chase repeated his message to the Lieutenant and waited for his reply.

"Mr. Benton, are you aware of the penalties for making false calls?"

Chase interrupted the man and said, "Officer, I have a federal PI license number and that number is NH439-405-2. This call is for real, and I thank God it is being recorded *he added for effect*. Officer, we are not sure, and like I said my man is four hours away from the house. This is not a random crank call." he said, voice becoming irritated and pitched.

"Ok, Ok" the Lieutenant said. "Do you believe the perpetrator to be armed and dangerous?"

Chase rolled his eyes at the group and answered the cop "Armed we are not sure-- dangerous—if he is the one who has murdered seven families in the last six months, then I would say so."

"Got it, I am going to dispatch three vehicles to the residence. Stay on the line please."

"Yes, we'll wait" Chase said asking Clair to mute the phone system. "Dug, are you able to get out to Gaithersburg if needed?"

"Yeah, I was just doing a Map Quest to the address. I can be there in about four hours, but what if he has already come and gone, I might be better off to wait around here and try to spot him when he returns. If the Sawyers put gas in their car at 3:15, they made it home by 6:00 or so and he could be half way back here for all we know."

"Let's see what the cop says."

Seville looked up at the screen. While they were on the phone talking to the police, Clair had replaced the last scene with another that sent a chill up and down her spine. A man, dressed casually in jeans and a regular button down shirt was against a wall with his arms spread out in a cross like fashion. The arms were bleeding in various places and she realized that there were nails or spikes in his arms and hands holding him to a blank white wall. His head was dipped slightly and his eyes were rolled up as if looking out over glasses on his nose. A grin on his face looked like the devil incarnate and she wondered why Clair didn't put horns on this rendition. His mouth was actually moving as if he was speaking.

Ronni noticed the picture next, sat up and embraced her assailant without the momentary fear she had shown before. She spoke to Clair "Clair, make the hair about an inch longer, height about two inches shorter, build is ok."

Clair did the modifications and Ronnie nodded in agreement and said "Save". Everyone in the room was looking at the picture now, particularly Chase and Karen.

"He looks very familiar" Karen offered her face looking indifferent.

"Yes" said Chase as he turned to look at Ronni. "Does this guy ring any bells for you?"

"Not really, he just looks familiar in general. He looks almost generic to me."

Both Chase and Karen nodded to this statement as a truth explaining their recollections.

"Mr. Benton? Are you still there?" a voice boomed breaking the relative silence of the last 10 minutes.

"Yes officer, where are we?"

"You guys are going to have a lot of explaining to do. Our units just called in. They just found the family at the house. They are all dead Mr. Benton, and there is no sign of a perpetrator anywhere."

Chase's face had suddenly turned from hopeful to very sad looking. He glanced around the room at everyone, then up to Dug. "Officer, I am sending Dug Masters to Gaithersburg right now. Like I said, he is in Ocean City at the moment and it will take him a while to get there."

"Where is he staying" the officer replied.

"I'm on 35th Street and Main, at the Sea Breakers Motel." Said Dug from his remote connection.

"Please go to the lobby, a State Police car will meet you in five minutes and take you to a waiting helicopter. We can't wait four hours."

"Go ahead Dug, give me a call on my cell later on after you're done at the scene and everyone is briefed. Officer, you have the phone number here, call me if there is anything I can do."

"You can tell me one thing" said the officer. "How in the hell did you know this was going on?"

Chase decided it would be better to put Dug on the spot later as all his people were well trained at presenting Serial Connections to law enforcement agencies. "Will you be at the crime scene officer?"

"I am on my way right now."

"It's a long story, when Dug gets there he will provide full details for everyone."

"Very well." The officer said and disconnected the line.

"Dug, when you get there, our friends from the FBI will be there also. I have to assume that Henry White will be aware of this within the half hour and will be looking for one of us at the scene. Provide basic information to them only; give the state police officer who picks you up information on the green sedan. Richard Fox is still only a suspect of ours and we don't have any proof yet so don't mention him. If the FBI presses you, which they will, send them my way immediately."

"Got it boss!" Dug replied. "I hope I didn't spoil everyone's evening" he said in a very sincere tone.

"Dug, this is the reason we're here. Great job! Hey, by the way, when you get to the site and after you let the feds grope you for a few minutes, spend about 20 minutes with the data gator, and upload the file to Clair."

"No problem, thanks Chase, I will check in later."

The group remained quiet and reflective for a moment when the silence was broken by someone coming in through the atrium door and walking over.

"Hey Lindsay!" Karen said breaking the silence and putting a half smile on her face.

"Hi guys, sorry I'm late, I was at home when I got paged and got here as fast as I could. I patched into Clair on the way over and listened to most of the session but lost my signal about 10 minutes ago. What happened at the end?"

Chase introduced Lindsay to Seville as Dug's counterpart on the Maryland Devil case then spent a few minutes briefing her on what the police found and letting her know that Dug would be sending up a data file as soon as he could.

"God Chase, we were so close to getting in his way. I hate to think about that poor family and the rotten timing of it all. I need to go over the analysis file Clair just put together from your session. Is Dug going to brief the cops on who we're looking for and how about a vehicle? Did we get a positive on the green sedan you saw?"

"Not on the car Lindsay, but we do know that he has anywhere from a one-to-two hour head start on us from what we know. He could be anywhere at this point. We'll have to wait to hear back from Dug. Would you mind viewing the file from your office? We were just wrapping up on some Lumber Jack stuff when the shit hit the fan and I don't want to lose focus on that."

"Sure, no problem, can we use this room after Dug sends up the datagator info?"

"Absolutely, it looks like it's going to be a long night in Jaffrey!"

Chapter 18

Gaithersburg/Seattle/Ocean City

Dug Masters was belted into the front seat of the State Police patrol helicopter. They had flown over the Chesapeake Bay about 20 minutes earlier and were now approaching Gaithersburg. Out in the distance he could see emergency lights flashing from at least 20 vehicles lined up in a straight line along an isolated road on the outskirts of town.

The pilot announced that he was going to land on the sports field of the local elementary school and that Dug was being met by FBI Special Agent Connie Thompson. When Dug heard this he dropped his head down and thought; *Jesus, they don't waste any time. I was hoping to get a look a round the place a little before talking to the FBI guys.*

Captain Frazer looked at him and smiled "Sucks to be you. Have you ever met Agent Thompson?"

"No" said Dug "Is there any way I can jump out of the bird over the house or something?"

He laughed "Connie—um I mean Agent Thompson is fondly referred to as the Ice Queen's Mother!"

"Ice-bergs and Ice Queen's—I knew I should have gone on vacation this week."

"Ice-bergs?" asked the pilot.

"Oh, nothing, I'm just not looking forward to riding with a suit. I have a lot to do and they tend to get in the way."

"Maybe you're right in general, but not Connie, rumor has it she's one of a kind in the Bureau, and has a bust rate higher than anyone in the region. Not to mention she's a total loner. No one at the agency will partner with her and I guess that's just the way she likes it. Tell me before we land, we heard you're the ones who called in the murders tonight. Who are you guys?"

"We're just a group of private eyes focused on serials. That's all we do and we do it very well. Serial Connections is the name of the group and we are based out of New Hampshire, I live in Bethesda and work a few cases on the eastern corridor from Maryland down to Florida. Here's a card for you. Any word on how I'm going to get back to Ocean City in a couple of hours?"

"Won't be me I'm afraid! I have to get the bird back for patrol, but I'm sure if you're nice to Agent Thompson she'll be more than happy to schlep you back to the coast."

"Where's the local Greyhound bus terminal?" Dug said smiling.

"Here we go said the pilot" and Dug could feel the bird start to descend into a well lit area about a mile from the murder site. As he looked down he could see two vehicles out on the field, one obviously a local cruiser and the other a green car that looked like a round turtle from 600 ft. up.

"Is that what I think it is?" Dug muttered.

"Yup, looks like a Beetle. I hear she likes to drive real hard!" he said chuckling to himself as he got focused to land. The big bird was just touching down and Dug never got the chance to ask him what he meant about "driving hard" and just prayed he wouldn't have to find out.

Dug opened the copter door, turned to thank the Captain for the ride, stepped out, ducked under the rotating blades and ran over to the police cruiser next to the green Beetle.

"Are you my ride?" he yelled at the police officer leaning against his vehicle.

He shook his head back and forth and pointed over at the Beetle, the driver barely visible behind the glass, and obviously anxious to get going.

"Officer I need to get to the site fast and need your lights, the Beetle can follow us" Dug said with a voice of authority. He ran up to the other side of the cruiser and hopped in the front seat. "Come on let's go!"

The officer was clearly confused but the ploy worked and they zoomed off down the field onto the school access road. *Whoever this is, he must be pretty important to get dropped off by a state bird* the cop thought, and headed off towards Cotton Wood Street.

Dug saw him look in the rearview to see if the Beetle was following, felt him slow down and said "Officer, forget the Bug and get to the site as quickly as you can please." The cop wasted no time flooring the car and leaving the Bug in the dust.

Captain Frazer was watching the whole thing as he slowly lifted the copter and saw Dug do an end run around Connie. A very wide grin spread across his face, his head nodding with approval; *the guys got balls, but I wouldn't want to be in his shoes in a few minutes!*

Dug was delivered right to the front door of the Sawyer home and when he got out of the cruiser he noticed what a zoo the place was. Getting dropped off by a Montgomery County Police cruiser and flashing his Federal PI badge got him through the door with no questions. If he timed things right he had about five minutes before Agent Thompson came bellowing through the front door, so he set out to find Lieutenant Willis first. He asked a badge walking by him who said Willis was upstairs so he walked up into the hallway and found him talking with a couple of forensics guys with plastic bags in their hands.

"Lieutenant Willis? I'm Dug Masters from Serial Connections and I was just dropped off a few minutes ago."

Before he even looked up he said "Agent Thompson find you yet?"

"Kind of, I just wanted to check in with you to let you know I'm here. I'll be downstairs working the scene when you're ready to talk."

"Got it," the Lieutenant said.

Dug was starting down the stairs when he saw her. She was standing near the bottom of the stairs looking straight at him with a look that could have stopped the armies of Troy. He continued down the stairs and decided that he had to make this quick. Chase was anxious for the data report and didn't want to keep him waiting because they might be able to get back on the trail of this guy real quick and she was just going to waste his time.

"Clarice? Clarice Starling? Is that really you? I haven't seen you since Arkansas! You look absolutely yummy!" Dug bellowed as he got to the bottom of the stairs, trying to work his way around her.

A very firm hand reached out and grabbed him from behind spinning him around so that they were looking into each others eyes from no more than 12 inches away. "Unless you'd like me to put the muzzle back on and throw you in the cage for a few days, I'd stop and listen to me for a moment Dr. Lector." She spat at him speaking very clearly and with just a touch of southern accent.

"Agent Thompson, my name is Dug Masters—Serial Connections. I'm not trying to give you a hard time, but my boss and his team in New Hampshire are waiting for some case data from me so that we can get back on the trail of this guy as soon as possible. We don't want to have to come to another scene like this ever again. I need 20 minutes to collect some information then you'll have my undivided attention. As a matter of fact, will you drive me back to Ocean City when we're done?" he said with a tinge of sarcasm.

Thompson looked at Dug, giving him the once over, sensed that he was at least being sincere and commanded a compromise. "I'll walk along with you while you get your information and then we WILL talk. How's that."

"Deal" Dug said pulling a camera bag off his shoulder and taking out what looked liked a video camera that had all kinds of other stuff attached to it. He put a neck strap over his head first and let the device dangle on his chest about midway. Next he put on a head piece that looked like an NASA controller head set. He reached down to the device, pushed a button on the top right and a small control panel of lights came alive. Once he was satisfied that the unit was functioning, he looked at Agent Thompson who had an amused look on her face, and began walking into the kitchen area following the traffic pattern.

When they entered the family room there were only two people left and it appeared like they were taking blood samples from the victims. Dug panned the device all around the room, the expression on his face stolid and professional. He began to speak into the microphone, describing any detail that a photo might not pick up and mapping his thoughts with the imagery he took. In front of them was a scene right out of a cheap Hollywood movie. At first it looked like a gathering, three people sitting in chairs lined up in a semi-circle facing a large sectional couch. The couch was unoccupied though and as Dug moved around to the right the camera picked up a woman's body lying on the floor, arms and legs spread out and tied to furniture with rope. Stopping the camera Dug took a long look around the room. He had to let the magnitude of what happened here sink in before he could continue. Even though he was seeing this for the first time, he had seen much of this scene on his laptop just over an hour ago in bits and pieces, and every time Ronni and the team created a picture like this that ended up becoming a reality it caused a major shock to his own psyche.

The camera came back to life and he moved it slowly up Susan Sawyers body starting from the toes, then up the legs to her thighs, which had deep cuts and were swollen and bruised from a brutal sexual assault. The vertical shaft of a cross had been cut deep into her flesh from the sternum to the top of the pelvis. The horizontal shaft cut through her belly button from side to side. Her breasts had been cut in the same way, and the last cross came down her face from the top of her hairline and cross sectioned from cheek to cheek across the nose.

122 MARK DE BINDER

Dug moved the camera to the right exposing the first chair and what was left of Kevin Sawyer. He too had been carved from head to toe with crosses, but the cuts looked much deeper and more jagged, almost like the cutter had taken out a fit of rage on the fathers body. From the looks of the blood on the mother and father, it was clear they had been alive for a great deal of the torture for all but a few of the cuts had freely flowed blood. Dug paned the camera at the foreheads of each body. Etched into the front right side of each was a capital "R" that had barely bled at all. That must have been the final act of the killer before he had fled the scene. He scanned the daughter's body with the camera and it appeared she had been spared sexual abuse but it was clear she had watched some of the torturing. Her face was swollen from fear and crying, the eyes still slightly bulging from the sockets, and cuts exactly like her mother's still had a bright crimson glow.

Moving to the last body, the teenage boy, the camera picked up something completely different. The boy's throat had been severed and unlike the others the "R" carved into his forehead was on the left side, and the blood that was dried and caked on him looked newer than the blood spills of all the others. Dug mentioned into the microphone that maybe the boy had been forced to watch the entire ritual prior to the murderer working on him. Then he touched the still damp leather straps covered in blood and amended his note to confirm that the boy was killed last.

Finished with the body documentation, Dug carefully walked through the entire house cataloging every possible item he could because anything could trigger a reaction from the psychic team. After finishing the upstairs and the basement he headed outdoors. Agent Thompson was patiently following him and watching very carefully for Dugs reactions to everything. She marveled at the precise fashion in which he talked into the machine, using one word descriptors or simple phrases to describe everything he saw. He wrapped up in the garage getting pictures of the Sawyer's two vehicles parked side by side inside.

Finishing the session, Dug flipped up a small antenna on the side of the unit and hit yet another button with his finger. Thompson assumed that he was now uploading the data back to his people at Serial Connections

"Alright Agent Thompson, may I call you Connie?" Dug said keeping one eye on the upload process and the other looking up at her.

She gave him a glance, and for some reason felt that she could let her guard down a little with this man. "Connie would be fine. Let's go inside and find a quiet place to talk for a while." She turned and walked towards the house without waiting for his reply suggesting that this was another command and not a friendly gesture. Dug watched her slightly stocky and muscular body walk towards the house, her typically short blond hair, salon perfect, shinning in the outside lights. He had noticed her vivid green eyes earlier when they confronted each other in the hallway and putting it all together could fully understand why she had been dubbed the "Ice Queen's Mother". They went into the living room on the other end of the house and sat down in two chairs by the fireplace. Connie broke the silence by asking about the machine Dug was breaking down and starting to put back in the case.

"We call it the datagator," he said energetically, looking up to see what her response would be. "Our resident computer genius, Louise Penta created this as a field input device to the very sophisticated computer system we use to collect and analyze data about serials. Clair is the name of the computer system and as a matter of fact, Clair is probably crunching this file as we speak."

"I understand the camera, the harness, the headset, and all, but what I didn't get was your input style. You were using very short descriptors and sometimes thoughts and feelings as you described things and events. What is that all about?"

"Well, first of all, we have trained Clair as a computer based forensics expert if you will. She is trained to process and analyze all kinds of inputs; spoken words, pictures, video, illustrations, graphics, forensic reports and tons more. When we input data we use a language and input style that make it quick and easy for her to process information correctly. *He decided to keep the psychic aspect out of the conversation with her as long as possible because he didn't feel that she would be receptive.*

"So when do we get a report back from this computer system?" Connie asked with a sincere but naïve tone.

"We? You mean I as in me, not you. Look Connie, I don't mean to be rude so please don't take this personally, but I have been asked to stay away from you, not you, but the FBI. It seems one of your bosses who shall remain nameless tried screwing us royally and might have risked losing one the most dangerous serials we happen to be hunting right now. To top it off, we had invited your people to our place in New Hampshire today to share information on that case in hopes of bringing the guy in together and you took the information and tried to get the suspect behind our backs, and failed miserably. You ended up putting a local pastor in cuffs for two hours who has 40+ people as an alibi. And to make it worse, if this guy Emit is the Lumber Jack, now he knows we're on to him and he might become impossible to catch!"

"Sounds like you're talking about Henry White, Dug, and if you are, I don't blame you one little bit. Henry has a reputation as a cutthroat; some one that will go to any lengths to satisfy his own agenda. I just want you to know that even though I report to Henry on a dotted line basis I do not answer to him nor do I wish to further his political career at the FBI by tramping over the good guys like yourselves."

"Gosh Connie that sounds just like story we got from Bob Fellows today from the Boston branch; You two related at all?" sarcasm teaming from his mouth.

"Look Dug, I've been on this case for five months and all I have to show for it is my reports from murder scene to murder scene—I am no closer to getting this bastard today than I was then, and every lead has turned up worse than dry. I am not your typical FBI agent Dug, that's why I'm considered to be a loner and why no one wants to work with me. I actually have a conscience; I don't drive any agenda other than wanting to bring in the bad guys, and I won't run over innocent people or backstab to do it. All I'm asking for is a chance. Yeah, it's a long shot but you may need help down here; things are going to start moving pretty fast."

"I don't know Connie; it's not my call anyway. I work for a great guy and we all run a tight ship. After what happened today it would be very hard for me to risk a situation that might cause the Devil to get loose." Then Dug remembered that Chase had asked him to have the suit down here call him if they wanted to discuss any more information sharing or partnering. He kinda liked this gal; she had spunk and he could feel that she was telling the truth, and it wouldn't be a bad thing to have a little help on this one when he got down to brass tacks with the killer. He looked at Connie and saw her staring at him like a little puppy wanting more treats.

"Ok Connie, I'll tell you what. I'm going to call the boss, Chase Benton, and tell him what you want to do. He'll want to talk to you on the phone and after that conversation if he says yes, we can work together, but only with as much information as he gives me the ok for, and only for as long as he says. If he says no, you hand me back the phone and we part company—deal?" he said as he extended his hand hoping that Chase would be able to do his magic on her and read the situation correctly.

Connie looked up at Dug and carefully thought about his proposal. She knew about Chase Benton and the fact that he was a psychic even though she had not told Dug she knew. She decided to make a peace offering and before she took his hand said "Dug, I am very familiar with Serial Connections and Chase Benton. I have never met Chase but I have heard all the stories about his psychic abilities, and if my intuition is right that's how you got hooked into this event tonight. I just want to let you know that I know, and that I'm willing to talk to Chase anytime," and she held out her hand to meet Dug's.

"You're ok Connie, I hope you get past the boss—I really do" and he pulled out his phone, hit the speed dial for Clair's connection system, looked back at Connie, and walked off into the corner for some privacy.

While Dug was talking on the phone Connie watched him pacing back and forth on the floor. *He was kinda cute she thought*, checking out his tall slender build, short cropped brown hair, mustache and beard. He dressed like a throw back from the sixties, with tattered jeans, pull over wool sweater that had seen better days, and old leather sandals that would be too cold to wear this time of year. She shook off the feeling. It had been a long, long time since she had been with a man and wasn't sure she liked the feelings stirring inside her so she redirected her focus and began to mentally prepare for the talk with Chase—not that it would do any good.

She was still watching Dug when she saw him take the phone away from his ear, fold it, and put it back in the side holster. Her heart sank to her knees as she started thinking about plan B. She just couldn't let this opportunity get away from her.

Dug walked up to her with a blank expression on his face and said "You never did answer my question."

She looked at him quizzically, thought about it for a moment, and then lit up with a big smile. "Let's get going, with my turbo Beetle we can be back in Ocean City in just under three hours!"

*****

It had been a long day and Susan was finally heading home from the eight hour stakeout of Masanori Fukui's house. She had seen him twice during the day, each time he had come out through the front door and done something outside. She couldn't get rid of the feeling that each of his appearances had been just that—a show. But her electronic gear didn't lie and the noises that were coming from inside the house verified that he was indeed inside. They were expecting him to make a move anytime now and except for a few trips out to the market, hardware store, and bank he had been pretty inactive over the last few days, even when she was not there, according to the surveillance bug she had planted on his car a few weeks ago.

Fortunately, her house was not that far away and once she got on the highway it was only a 15 minute ride. If he were to take off, she would be alerted and could get back on his tail pretty quickly using her in-dash navigation system that had been modified with a direct link to Clair back in Jaffrey. She had been poring over the missing person reports Clair had fed her while she sat in the car. At this moment there were four young women within a 150 mile radius that had been reported missing in the last week, any of which fit the profile the team had put together on Samurai victims. The problem was the proximity of the woman in terms of the time and place of the abductions and the known whereabouts of Masanori. Only one of the four girls, Tanya Richie, could have possibly been abducted by Masanori, but even she was a stretch because technically, according to the equipment, he had not been near her last reported location.

Her PI instincts told her otherwise. This guy continued to give her the creeps and each time they found one of his victims conveniently on the side of a road or behind a dumpster somewhere, her determination to bring him in kept her energy level at peak. She was thinking about going over his background file once more after a bath when she pulled into the mouth of her driveway which wound into the woods about 200 yards and up a slight slope. She had bought the place almost eight years ago as a refuge from the world, the isolating effects of no neighbors, woods, streams, and mountains a prime ingredient of her daily serenity. Talking to the voice activated computer system on her dash board she said "house lights" and the porch light, area light, living room, and kitchen lights came on bathing the secluded home with a nice warm feeling of security.

Going into the front door, Susan put down all her stuff on the hallway table and went into the kitchen to check her voice mails and to tend to the cat's litter box, water, and food. When she saw no light on the answering machine she kept walking over to the corner muttering to herself "nobody loves me today" and bent down to pick up the bowl of water and to empty the cat food dish.

"I love you Susan!" a man's voice said behind her in a soft, delicate manner.

With lightning speed the items in Susan's hands dropped and her arm reached behind her back for the belt holster. Just as her hand touched the leather case she felt a foot drive into her side with amazing force, taking all the wind out of her and slamming her into the wall. Before she could get to her knees and recover from the sudden attack, a fist bludgeoned her square in the chest sending her down again, forehead striking the window sill, blood starting to drip into her eye from a deep gash. Susan feigned a collapse and surrender in hopes of getting the attacker to come in close enough for a shot. At this point she had no idea what this person wanted or what he was going to do, only that he needed to be stopped.

Putting her gun hand to her forehead to hold the cut and beginning to cry seemed to slow down the ferocity of the attack so she went a little further and curled into the fetal position while thinking of what to do next. She saw the legs of the man slowly move into view and without thinking swung her leg out and swept it into the side of the his knee causing it to buckle inward. The man let out a howl of pain and stumbled back a few feet. Susan managed to roll out into the open room and flex herself up into a crouching position when another foot came out of no-where picking her off her feet and crashing her into the face of the oven, glass shattering all over the floor. Stunned and dazed she slowly opened her eyes and saw the man who had been beating her senseless. He was smiling at her and as she felt the vice of his hand squeezing a pressure point on her neck she heard him say "It's nice to be loved Susan."

*****

The water was gently lapping the side of the boat Dug and Connie had commandeered for the stake out of Richard Fox. It was almost two in the morning now, and they had just settled into their positions potentially for an all-nighter. The drive over had been very interesting for both of them. They seemed to hit if off and within an hour of starting out they knew more about each other than most people did. Both of them as it turned out were loners and had kept focused on just a few parts of their lives. Dug on one hand was an artist by calling and had gotten into the PI business purely by accident 10 years ago when he had answered an ad for a part time job for a large law firm that needed investigators for all sorts of criminal and civil matters. The job paid well, and Dug had found it to be an exciting secondary career eventually expanding his hours to a more full time role. His reputation in the D.C. area developed quickly. During that time he had been put through extensive training by his employers and had learned all about firearms, martial arts, surveillance techniques, and other trade crafts.

The hours also afforded him the time he needed to continue embracing his passion—art.

He had been approached about three and a half years earlier by a man wanting to talk to him about a very private foundation that focused purely on serials and that had intrigued him. Dug was the type of guy who needed to be passionate about what he did and although the work he was doing for the legal community was satisfying, he felt that he needed to take it to the next level. He met with Chase on the phone first and after a lengthy conversation and a good feeling in his gut, decided to make the trek up to Jaffrey New Hampshire to meet and see first hand what Serial Connections was all about. He ended up accepting a position during that trip and never turned back. Although popular with the female crowd, Dug was very particular in his tastes and very shy about approaching woman so his opportunities had been few and far between over the years. At 37, he kept driving his passions hard, and was pretty content with his life.

Connie on the other hand was quite the opposite. Every since she was a teenager she had dreamed of being in the FBI. Her grandfather had been a career FBI man and he had spent a good deal of time with her growing up telling her all kinds of stories and making the Bureau look very alluring to a young and impressionable girl. When she got into high school she sat down with guidance councilors' and mapped out everything she was going to need to do to make sure she ended up an agent. When Connie was 17 years old her grandfather was killed on the job by a drug lord during a bust. Connie had been devastated but soon turned her grief into a headlong desire to take his place someday in the agency.

Colleges around the country tried in vain to recruit Connie but she had set her sites on Georgetown University, her grandfather's Alma-Ata, and had graduated with the highest honors before being recruited by the FBI. She had followed his footsteps explicitly except for one thing. Although extremely talented and focused, he had been a very social and extroverted man, a great husband, father, member of church and community. Connie though, had become the proverbial introvert in the quest for her goals. She had ignored the callings of youth, and bypassed the rugged high school years of peer pressure, temptation, drugs, alcohol, and boys. She was not unattractive at all, but her lack of presence in the social scene had buried any desire to work on herself on the outside. Her hair had always been cut in the sports fashion, as sports had become her physical training ground, and more often than not she was labeled a dike by those that did not know her or understand her.

At 29 years old she was still practically a virgin and had never held a relationship that lasted more than a few months. Her reputation as a lesbian furthered itself by the obvious omission of a male partner in her life. Every time she dated a man, her fear of sex was so great that she could not let her hair down and as such, never really got to the point of sexual intimacy. At the Bureau, she was indeed a loner. At first she did ok with partners but as they started comparing notes with peers they realized her partnering abilities were deficient and every one of them ended up requesting a new partner. Eventually Connie's superiors stopped trying to pair her up, partly because she did not play well with others but mostly because she seemed to excel on her own and had developed into an exceptional individual contributor.

Shortly after they had finished baring their souls to one another, Chase had called and asked him to plug into Clair for a summary of what the team came up with after reviewing the file Dug had sent earlier. Even though Connie was driving she could barely take her eyes off the small monitor Dug held up on the dash. Clair had munched the file first and had presented the summary findings to Chase, Seville, Ronnie, Lindsay, and Karen. Katherine and Samuel had gone back upstairs to figure out a plan for the Lumber Jack. The group had done their thing and come up with two very important pieces of information. Chase had noticed it first, actually beating Clair to the punch, which always got Chase sparked up. After the screen had been loaded with still shots of the crime scene, Chase had looked at the garage picture and had noticed the same green sedan they had picked up in the earlier session. As he was just about to ask Clair to run the registry information for those plates and car, Clair shot up a window showing that the plates were registered to the Sawyers but that the green sedan was supposed to be a maroon Chrysler convertible. The killer had switched cars and plates!

Next, and most importantly, they had done their psychic thing and Seville had come up with a hit that no one else got. At first they wrote it off, but when it was mentioned to Dug as an afterthought, the group heard him say "Oh Shit" into the microphone. It turns out that Richard Fox did own a very expensive powerboat that he kept docked pretty close to his Ocean City office. Dug had gotten so worked up that morning trying to find Richard at his usual haunts he had forgotten to check the dock to see if the boat was there.

The group had decided it would be a good idea to do two things. Chase asked that Connie call in an APB on the missing Chrysler. They still didn't know what the plate numbers were for the car but it was all they had. They also suspected Virginia plates. Secondly, Dug suggested that they head straight for the marina when they hit Ocean City and if the boat was not there they would stake the place out over night. If it was still there they would do a little more checking around town for Richard. They all agreed and Chase and the group signed off and Dug was instructed to keep in touch with Clair, who would in turn keep the rest of them posted.

They had cruised by Richard's office and found the BMW still sitting where it had been all day and then driven right to the marina and sure enough his boat was not in the slip. Dug had considered waking up the marina owner to get permission to camp out in the stern of a boat diagonally across from the empty slip but thought better of it. Richard was very well connected around here and he was certain that a ship to shore phone call would be placed if he did, so they had parked the Beetle, watched the marina for a while to see who if anyone was around, then picked out a boat and started their vigil.

Chapter 19

Bethany/Jaffrey/Salem/Seattle

Richard had driven the distance from Gaithersburg to Bethany in the blink on eye. He had still been in a trance like state when he arrived on the outskirts of town about a quarter mile away from where his boat had been moored earlier in the evening. A close friend had used the boat for a little indiscretion with a cute blond he had been shagging from the office during the day. Richard and his friend Luke had made these arrangements many times before, and if Luke knew what his real motives were he would probably commit suicide. He had called Luke last weekend after he decided on the Sawyers as his next family and faxed Luke the game plans for this trip. Luke was always grateful to have a good friend like Richard who was thinking about him and looking after his interests.

The plan for this weekend was to have Luke pick up the boat in Bethany at a secluded area right outside of town in the morning. Richard had input a trip into the boats computer to take Luke and his guest on a tour of the Chesapeake that would last most of the day and on auto pilot they could enjoy each others company below deck for most of the time. He had left one of his credit cards, pullover sweaters, sunglasses, and baseball cap and had strongly suggested to Luke that he stop down in Fig's Landing to gas up the boat and get a few supplies for him using his credit card and to wear Richard's garb while doing it. He said he would be back to pick up the boat by 9:00 PM and that Luke should moor it in the same place he had picked it up.

Actually, Richard had lifted his car for the weekend a few days before down in Richmond and left it in Bethany. Luke had picked him up that day and driven him back to Ocean City. This morning, Richard had been on the boat by 4:00 AM, powered her to Bethany, moored her up, hopped in the old green Ford Taurus and drove it back to his hideaway garage down the street from the office.

After he climbed aboard the boat he did a quick check around to see if everything was in order. On the captain's chair was his baseball cap, sunglasses and sweater. He pulled them on, then went and looked in the fish keeper in the stern. In the water were eight fresh flounder, a half dozen good sized soft shelled crabs, bait fish, and chicken bones. In the beer cooler next to it were two cases of Budweiser, a bottle of Jack Daniels, and a few cokes. *Luke had done well,* he thought to himself. Everything but the fish and crabs should have been purchased at the Marina in Figs Landing with his credit card. The seafood should have been picked up with cash at a special place he had told Luke about.

Satisfied all was in order, he pulled up the mooring and anchor and went back to the Captain's station and set the auto pilot for home. *This boat was the best dam investment I ever made, some day it's going to save my ass.* Once he was sure everything was all set he began his victory celebration and cover up. *First things first,* he thought as he cracked the bottle of Jack and a beer and took long pulls from each to get things going. While he was getting the buzz on, he started a big pot of water on the propane grill, began opening cans of Bud and randomly pouring them all over the boat. He crumpled the empties and tossed them around the deck and down into the cabin. He looked at his watch and figured he had about 50 minutes until he was home. Next he went to the fish tank, pulled out the cutting board and started cleaning the flounders, one by one, putting the filets in very large plastic baggies, making sure that enough blood and guts got all over the place, then heaved each corpse out into the water. *By the time he got to his slip things would look just perfect.*

*****

After his fourth yawn in a row Chase realized it was getting late and that he had been up well before the sun this morning. He had all but forgotten about his prize Buck... They were just finishing up the meeting and he couldn't get Seville off his mind—and everything else for that matter. *What a day,* he reflected; *I need to go upstairs for some quiet time.*

"Well guys, looks like we're going to have another big day tomorrow and I think we should all try to get a little shut eye. Seville, how are you holding up? You must think we're all certifiable by now!" Chase said, unsuccessfully trying to hold back a yawn.

"Stop trying to make yourself feel better Chase, you guys are so far past certifiable, it scares the living crap outta me." She said with a huge grin on her face. "Seriously though, this may sound kinda sick after everything that went on today, but I can't remember feeling this alive in a long time. The work you're doing here is amazing and I'm extremely grateful just to have participated for one day."

"Two days" Karen spurted. "You're our prisoner remember, and I'm sure you won't be getting home until very late tomorrow night. As a matter of fact I think after your performance tonight you should quit your day job, move upstairs, umm I mean here to Jaffrey, and join the team!" She was still giddy from all the romance going on in the midst of chaos and was still reveling in her own little adventure this evening and despite the hour, couldn't wait for round two with Tom when she got home.

"Easy girl" Chase said to Karen with a big smile on his face. "You're in deep enough shit as it is, and if I ever catch you coming to work looking like that again I'll…" and he trailed off.

"You'll what? Change the dress code in the employee handbook? I'm shaking in my boots Chase," as she gave Ronni and Seville a quick wink. "I'm going to hit the road guys, call me if anything comes up and I can scoot back over. Ronni, you're in charge while I'm gone, and please make sure everyone gets tucked in." and after a round of hugs sauntered off through the doors for the night.

"Well Ronni, it's about dinner time for you! Do you have stuff to eat downstairs?" Chase said in reference to her status as the resident night owl.

"Oh I think I'll come up with something. Are you hungry dear?" she said looking at Seville, knowing that it would be best for Seville and Chase to separate for the rest of the evening.

Seville took the cue and said "I'm starving; I didn't realize how much energy this work takes. Do you have any cheese and crackers?"

"I brought all kinds of goodies knowing I would be here for a few days. I think we should have a small feast before we retire."

"A few days? That's the first I've heard about you camping out here for a few days. What's up with that?" Chase asked before he could catch himself already knowing the answer.

"Woman's intuition" she said as she walked up and gave Chase a big hug. "See you in the morning *after* 10:00AM."

Chase walked up to Seville, took her hand, and gave her a kiss on each cheek. "Good night Seville—I'm very happy you were here today. I'll see you in the morning. Ronnie? Would you show her how to use the page system when you get to the hut? I'm sure she'd like a nice hot cup of coffee long before we see you up!"

"Sure enough—night"

Seville looked into Chase's eyes then walked off after Ronnie.

*****

Chase went up the back stairs to his place to get some things done before he turned in for the night. The shackles on the back of his neck wouldn't quit, and this was causing him a great deal of discomfort, blocking him from moving through whatever it was. Something really bad was going on and he felt as though he had little or no control over it. In fact he knew he had no control over it. In times like these his thoughts went to his teacher and friend, Wesley Marks, who had practically raised him on his spiritual and psychic path. Wesley had shared with him that being in control is both a blessing and a curse. He remembered being told one day that the true path to learning, knowledge, and success was to be able to swim through any situation with no control at all, just by sheer instinct and divine guidance. Wesley's own experience was that when he tried too hard to gain control of a situation he ended up blocking the powers that enabled him to see the multitude of opportunities in that situation, thereby limiting or relinquishing the true path to success. *Easier said than done!*

He knew it was too late to call Wesley on the system. It was Saturday night, actually Sunday morning, and the Marks protected their Saturday nights with a passion unless it was a matter of life and death. Well this was, but this business always is, so he decided to defer a call until the next day. Wesley and Ashley had moved down to the Saint Bart's years ago for their retirement and Chase missed having them around on a daily basis but they managed to video conference at least twice a week just for social visits. Ashley was a psychic too and periodically got into the fray with them on certain cases, but for the most part she was a teacher. Ashley had actually introduced Ronni to Chase many years ago and Ashley and Ronni continued to team up to keep the psychic capability at Serial Connections up to date and on their toes. Ashley's primary mission in life it seemed was to constantly bust Chase's gonads regarding his celibacy and lack of interest in finding a female partner, and she did a very good job at it. But Ashley, more than anyone knew that Chase was holding out for a very special woman, he had just not met her yet, and Ashley respected that a great deal, because she knew he could have any woman he wanted.

Chase went right to the shower to clean up and get some soothing heat on his body to help release the built up tension of the day before he meditated on the events of the past 14 hours and sought direction.

Taking his silk robe and throwing it on, he made his way to one of his favorite quiet places. It was the room he had built facing Magic Mountain, his name for Mount Monadnock, also over looking the medieval courtyard Ronnie had designed down below. The view of the courtyard, waterfall, and pool provided him with a great deal of serenity, and Magic Mountain was a huge source of energy and power for him to draw on. He walked over to the floor-to-ceiling glass windows and opened the door to the outside terrace.

The moon had turned full and the air was a brisk 45 degree's as he pulled up a cushion and sat down cross legged to begin his cleansing process. Reaching into his robe sleeve, he pulled out a long tied up stick of white sage, lit the end, and let the soothing smoke cover his entire body. The energy of the night was fantastic, as the bright moon was just about to go over the mountain and he could see quite clearly the bald top at the far left of the mile long ridge running across the mass of rock. He had turned on the stereo and drum music filled the air around him with a supernatural presence and peace of mind. He could hear the waterfall below beating the rocks in a consistent and powerful rhythm as he closed his eyes and let his mind and spirit wander through space until he found his power place.

He was walking along a seldom used trail in a grassy meadow, surrounded by the sweet fragrance of wild flowers and the cool night air. The moon was so bright that the entire valley below was lit with an iridescent glow that could be seen for miles. Off in the distance was a small hilltop where four unmoving monoliths rose into the night. The pillars were carved from an ancient stone, each one facing the four directions, north, south, east, and west. Chase walked up the small hill and entered the sacred ground, taking his place in the center of the circle next to a small fire ring that illuminated the four, 10 foot tall pieces of granite.

Facing the east pillar, he acknowledged the Coyote carved into the stone and the picture of a river winding through a sparse forest. The Coyote and the water represented his youth, family, and emotions in the cycle of life. He had made the transition from youth to warrior in his late teens but still drew upon this boundless energy to maintain balance in his spirit. Thanking Coyote, he turned to the southern pillar and smiled at the picture of a deer mouse eating a berry. The mouse was feasting on the spoils of war, sitting on top of a fallen tree in a field. Etched under the mouse was a large pillar of flames shooting up into the night sky with furry and passion. Warrior energy! The mouse was small yet tenacious and was the most hunted creature in Mother

Earth's menagerie yet survived time and time again against all odds. The flames represented power and strength in the warrior's life. Tipping his head towards mouse he turned to the west and saw the great white bear walking away and into his cave of ice and snow. Under the carving of the bear was the earth rotating around the heavens, suggesting the supernatural wisdom of the ages. Bear spirit was that of the magician and shaman, being able to navigate life situations with knowledge, cunning, stealth, and the ability to draw upon the universe for answers to all things. He took a moment longer here, then smiled at the bear and completed his circle facing the northern pillar. A large snow owl perched high in the branches overlooking the wind blowing across the face of time, forever cleansing and all knowing.

Kneeling on the ground in front of the fire and placing his hands in the cool earth, he asked for the blessing of Mother Earth and silently praised her existence in the spirit world. Rising to his feet and raising his arms and outstretched hands to the heavens, he thanked Great Spirit for all things and asked to be a channel of his healing power and love to all. Relaxed and contemplative, Chase placed his hands over his heart and thanked his own spirit for remaining open to possibility, serenity, and gratitude for all things.

Taking a seat on a stone facing the third pillar, Chase sat quietly, contemplating his cycle of life. Wesley had been coaching him over the last six months on his transition from south to west, from warrior to magician, from fire to earth. He had spent all of his adult years in the warrior cycle and the transition into the realm of magician was both time consuming and difficult for him to master. In essence he was changing his pure energy self, the one who ran headlong into life full of ego, self determination, and physical strength into the energies of persuasion, attraction, wisdom, and stealth.

He asked his totem animals to join him and soon heard the soft but firm footsteps of wolf spirit coming up the hill. White Fang gently leaped onto one of the stones surrounding the fire ring and sat on his haunches, nose in the air smelling the midnight air for friend or foe. White Fang had been with Chase since his childhood and was never far from his human friend, offering advice and wisdom to overcome all kinds of situations and challenges. Behind him Chase heard the air being moved by an unseen body gliding down to earth, huge wings suddenly coming to life, stopping the forward motion and bringing the raptor talons to rest on the other side of the ring. White Beak preened her feathers, glanced at her friend the wolf, nodded to Chase, and perched intently by the small fire waiting for the spirit guides to arrive. The spirit of the falcon always amazed Chase who had called on White Beak many times to assist him in finding lost things, helping lost spirits find the light, and during his warrior years, helping him blind his enemies with the fury of her talons. On many occasions Chase had become White Beak and had learned to fly, hunt, and soar high in the clouds.

Not long after the three had begun to warm themselves by the fire, a barefooted man appeared from around the fourth pillar, small in stature, the wild haired, bearded man was no more than 4'10" tall and walked with short purposeful strides. As he sat upon a stone to the right of Chase, he didn't look at or speak to any of the entities gathered around the fire. Instead, he pulled a small lizard from a pouch tied to his loin cloth and skewered it on a stick and began roasting his meal in the white hot flames. Chase looked at the man whom he called ghost, knowing that as an ancient Shaman he had lived many lives in the flesh over eons of time, and had finally merged his physical self with the energies of the universe, no longer limiting himself to time, space and human constraints. Ghost had come to Chase as a spirit guide long ago as he began to show prowess as a shaman apprentice. Chase had been working on soul retrievals and asked for a sprit guide to accompany him to the underworld. Ghost had shown up at the entrance to the sacred cave and took Chase safely into the other realm, helped him find the lost soul, protected Chase against some evil lurkers, then helped him find his way back to the surface. Since then, Ghost had taken him under his wing and showed him things that most modern shamans could only dream about.

As the group watched Ghost tear the meat from the lizard with his yellow teeth, the air about them stirred as a warm western wind blew through the third pillar and a lone figure appeared sitting on the last stone directly across from Chase. A wise and simple man, dressed in a long hooded robe, magical by nature, mystical by necessity, friend and ally of Kings, slayer of the wicked, seer of the future, advisor to all and slave to none, Merlin gently tipped his hood at the esteemed gathering and smiled that never ending smile into the flames.

After they had settled, Chase spoke softly to the group gathered around his fire and explained that he felt that the coming days would be a test of his transition to the western direction. He shared that he was nervous because the test would be in the physical world and people's lives might depend on his skills and abilities to discern forces he had clearly not come up against in the past.

"Chase, our past is the pillar we stand upon today. If we have navigated our lives in thoughtful and progressive ways, which you have, then the pillar on which you now stand is certainly high enough to see tomorrow." Merlin offered.

"Thank you Merlin," Chase offered his teacher, "The tomorrow I see is one of chaos, death, loss, and destruction. I can feel forces working against my efforts and I am seeking wisdom and discernment to change what I see."

"Ah" Merlin muttered under his breath "Your destiny is not about changing the future. No one can do that, not even the Divine Creator. Your destiny is about how you embrace the present. Our actions have been etched in stone since the beginning of time and cannot be changed. What happens in the coming days or weeks has already passed since it was already known."

"What you say Merlin sparks an interesting thought. If the future is already known and has already passed, then those energies must exist somewhere."

"Of course they do Chase, and you already know that. Those of your clan who can see the future have found the channel into those energies before. But the paradox still remains; seeing the future is different from changing the future."

"Then I must be prepared for the present armed with an open and receptive spirit, so that I do not block out the possibilities with pre-conceived notions."

"Well said, and yes you are correct. The fact that you are here separates you from most men in that you prepare for battle with spiritual rigors when most only prepare at the egol and physical levels, if at all—mere animals they are.

The Wolf and the Falcon raised their heads at this last comment. Merlin smiled at them and offered an apology.

"There are things that can be known about the future that will shape your destiny. The question is how you use that knowledge. If I were to tell you one thing about tomorrow, would you focus your mind solely on that thing? I would hope not because that would be your undoing. Instead, you would integrate that thing into the very fabric of your being so that it becomes not so much knowledge as it becomes instinct, thereby allowing you to embrace any present situation with an open spirit."

As they were talking Ghost pulled a small tube from his belt and with little movement or effort put it to his lips, turned to his left and blew into the tube. In an instant, a bird, black like that of the raven fell from atop the first pillar. It had been sitting in the shadows away from the light of the fire. As the bird hit the ground it began to dissolve into the earth and disappeared from sight. Ghost tucked the tube back into his belt and began drawing pictures in the soil with his stick.

"It looks like our friend found an intruder" Merlin said to Chase and the others.

Using the dirt as his paper, Ghost began to draw pictures and symbols to speak to the group. At the top was a fish with a large body, big teeth, and an antenna coming out from the head and hanging out in front of the fish. A bulb tipped the end of the antenna and lines coming from bulb suggested a source of light. A second figure close to the first but below and to the left was that of a raven, similar to the one that had just visited them. To the other side was the picture of a lion, also close to the fish but below the fish and the raven. Around the three figures he drew three smaller figurines that looked like hyenas in their hunting pose, teeth bared, blood dripping from their mouths. He finished the drawing by placing a symbol next to each of the three main figures. The fish and the lion were men, and the dark raven was a woman.

As if someone had rung a bell, the guests around the fire began to leave one by one. Chase sat staring at the drawing and looked over at Merlin "What's your interpretation of this" he asked in a quizzical voice.

"Ah, my interpretation of that won't do you any good" he said.

"Sure it will, I trust your instincts and perceptions."

"That you might Chase, but in this case that message was meant for you and you alone. It's your interpretation that's needed for your destiny." And he disappeared just as fast as he had come.

Chase moved over and studied the drawing closely, wondering what all the pieces meant. If he had looked over his shoulder just for an instant, he would have seen the face of Merlin floating over the third pillar looking down at him smiling.

When Chase opened his eyes the moon had already traveled behind Magic Mountain, but the night was still very bright and full of energy. He sat and pondered the message Ghost had given him, and thought about the intruder. Some force had been powerful enough to find and enter his power place and this bothered him just as much as the psychic assaults Ronnie and he had experienced earlier in the evening. Instead of dwelling on what he didn't know he thought about what he did understand. The fish was clearly the Angler Fish, it swam and lived in deep dark places and used the power of attraction and deception to catch its prey. This thought sent shivers down his spine as it conjured up evil and manipulation. The lion could be almost anything or anyone but at the root the lion was a leader, wielded authority, was strong, was a hunter, but used brute strength and speed more than stealth. The raven was troublesome, because it conjured up thoughts of black magic and deception, someone or thing that traveled in the shadows with little or no need for light.

The hyenas around the other characters were just bloodthirsty scavengers. They preyed on the innocent and had no conscience in doing so. And there were three of them centered about the other characters. This could be the three serials they were after at the moment. But that couldn't be because they had been drawn as secondary figures in the picture. The lion, fish, and raven must be the Lumber Jack, Maryland Devil, and the Samurai. The question was going to be which one was which, the message clearly trying to help him figure out how best to approach each one and the twist he was not expecting was that the raven was a woman. A powerful and deceptive woman! But that didn't make sense either. All three of the serials they were after were thought to be men. So how and where does a woman fit in?

Just as that thought floated through his mind he noticed ripples in the pool below and changed his gaze to follow them to the source. Under the waterfall he saw a person, a woman to be exact, standing under the falling water, head tilted back, and hands running through her long dark hair. Her body glistened in the water and reflection of the lights. As he watched she sank down into the water and slowly swam across the pool obviously savoring the warmth of the water and the refreshing feeling against her skin. At the other side she walked up the stairs and out onto the patio and took a towel off a nearby rock. As she turned to face the pool, Chase could see her fullness as clear as day. Her shoulders were strong and muscular, her breasts full and firm, her waist curved gently in and out to meet her very proportionate hips and legs. He stood up as he was getting ready to go back in for the night when Seville sensed him and looked up to the balcony. She did not see him when she first came to the pool because he was sitting back from the edge. She looked up at him with a strong gaze, and let the towel that had been partially hiding her slip to the side, making him an offering and letting him know that they would soon share a bond. She smiled at Chase; he smiled back, turned and walked inside.

*****

"Things are in motion nicely, I have been able to reach and connect with both Ronnie and Chase. They are both very strong, especially the woman. She has already sensed me and the man was able to shut me off while he was in a trance." The woman said into her phone.

"What are the chances that they will find you out completely and be able to shut you off altogether?" the man's voice on the other end of the phone said with a sting.

"They may be able to detect me when I invade them but they should never be able to find out who I am. Also, the curtain I put around you is very strong and it would take a miracle for them to bring it down so as to see or feel you. This is a very interesting project sir; I have never run into such a group as this before. So many of them and so strong! They are well protected and will be formidable opponents."

"Well, I have to assume that your pay is equal to the project, is it not?

"Oh, yes sir, I was not posturing for more money, but just letting you know that you have certainly picked an interesting bunch."

"And you will be able to complete this project for me without the help of anyone else, as we agreed"

"Yes sir, at least no one else that you would ever run into, or want to, unless of course I wanted you too."

"I don't have the time or patience for your veiled threats. I have no fear of spiritual things. I only retained you because of my opponents and their beliefs. What about this new woman in the picture. Is she a threat or should we just concentrate on the others?

"For now, she will be more of a threat on the physical plain, which is your business. She is very strong psychically though and I sense something very ancient and almost brutal about her powers, but they are dormant—for now. I will keep my eye on her and let you know if that changes. The fact that she is around the others could very well accelerate her conscious awareness of her past and the energies she can tap into. As a matter of fact, she will become a good source of information because she does not feel or sense my intrusions yet."

"What of the man down south? You have not mentioned him at all?"

"He is apparently not very engaged and seems to be very weak in his abilities. Perhaps he is ill, but whatever the case, I do not feel him as a threat. It is the other two that are keeping me on my toes."

"Very well, you have the latest instructions; I would suggest you follow them without hesitation as I will be depending on your actions blindly. Let me know immediately if anything changes and I will be in touch regarding that other matter soon."

"You're the boss," she said as she heard the phone disconnect on the other end. *Fool,* she thought, the man had no idea what they were up against. She had honestly never come up against such strong presence in her life. It was going to take all the abilities she could muster to stay on top of them and successfully steer them down the path he wanted them to travel. *We'll see!*

*****

Masonori had taken his time getting back to his other house. The trip to drop off poor little Tanya had gone well and with no disruptions. His mind had been on that e-mail and Susan Kincaid all night and he felt like he let Tanya down because he had not been thinking about her. Although the thought of having Susan was very appealing, she was not a candidate for his long term plans, she would just be a fling and he was not sure if he was being set up or not, and couldn't for the life of him figure out who this anonymous person was or what their agenda was.

He shook off the thoughts for now. He had lots of work to do. For one thing he had not yet cleaned the Dungeon from Tanya's visit and he was a stickler for cleanliness and order. Before he went to work though, he sat down at his computer to check his mail and the perimeter of his fortress for more intruders. As he switched on his surveillance program, he saw the pesky FBI team still outside the main house down the street. He really didn't need equipment to know they were around as they were like clock work and showed up in the same vehicle at the same time every day.

Satisfied that all was well, he went to his e-mail program and other than some junk mail, there were no more communications from his mysterious ally. He opened the last e-mail from the person and read it again. Something was not right but as long as he played his cards well, he would continue to use this person for potentially helpful information.

He opened up another file set to his desktop, clicked on a file name and up popped the picture of his next date. After Tanya and the last few women he had decided to change his plans a little bit. He had originally figured that older single women would be more receptive to him because they would be lonely and tired of man hunting. But the reverse had been true. They were already set in their ways and did not have the open mindedness to see the potential of being with him. He opened the pictures of Greta he had taken a couple of days ago, she was in her mid twenties, long brown hair, medium height, and looked damn good.

He studied the profile he had put together on her over the last two weeks. Today would be a perfect day to pick her up based on her schedule and he was very much in the mood after Tanya and the thought of having Susan Kincaid. *She'll do nicely*, he mused as he closed up the files and started to prepare mentally for his new adventure.

Chapter 20

Ocean City/Saint Bart's/Seattle

Richard was pretty buzzed now as he made the final approach to the Marina off the southern tip of Ocean City. He glanced back over his shoulder and smiled in approval at the way he had set up the boat to look like he had been out partying all day. He checked the radar screen and depth finders going through the channel and as he was looking down a flash message began blinking on the screen. *What the hell*, he thought through the glaze in his eyes.

Warning!
*Richard, the FBI is waiting for you at the dock. There are two of them, and they have been to your playground in Gaithersburg. They only **suspect** you though, and have no real evidence that it's really you. I know better!*

Stay cool and go through with the little deception you and Luke put on today and they will not be able to keep you. You left the Gaithersburg site clean? I will be in touch again later--A friend.

A friend my ass! Who in the hell is that! Richard began chanting to himself as the rage and fear built up inside him. He throttled way back on the engines and let the boat just slip through the water for a moment as he thought through what he just read. *That message could have come from the FBI, and they could be taunting me into running or something. I had better just keep going into the dock and see what happens. I have my tracks covered anyway—who was that?* He cursed under his breath, throttling back and guiding the boat into the back of the Marina to his empty and awaiting slip.

Dug and Connie had been waiting about 45 minutes and for the most part had been quiet so as not to let anyone know they were stowaways on the big power liner just 30 yards away from where they hoped Richard would soon dock. At last they saw the running lights of a boat enter the channel a few hundred yards out.

"Here he comes" said Dug as he sat to attention and started to shake off the cool night air.

"Are you sure that's his boat?"

"Pretty sure, it's heading in the right direction; he would've cut to the right more if he were coming down this alley, and besides, it's very late, it has to be his boat. Let's just hope he's on it."

"Let's go get him!" Connie said softly as she stood up.

Dug grabbed her hand and pulled her back down. "Sit still. If he sees us before he has the boat docked he could take off real quick."

"Sorry" Connie said a little embarrassed. She was anxious to take this guy and needed to settle down.

"That's ok; just remember that we don't have a positive on the guy yet. We are going to approach him and question him for now. If he runs we take him. If not we wait to see how the interview goes. Just the fact that we are talking to him is going to change the dynamic here quite a bit. At the very least we'll be able to put a curb on him until we can investigate further and come up with concrete evidence."

"I still don't understand how you guys work" Connie said frustrated.

"Remember our main goal Connie. To stop the killings; usually, if we haven't come up with evidence yet, we approach the person like we are now, and that puts a temporary hold on their activities because they know we're onto them. And, once we get this close to a perp, the psychic team has always been able to pick up something that leads us to proof. I know that sounds back ass-wards but it works."

"All right Connie. He's backing into the slip. Let's wait for him to shut down the motors and tie off the boat."

As soon as Richard finished pulling in and tying off the last line he heard footsteps walking quickly down the dock. *Here we go!*

"Richard Fox?" said the male voice as the two people approached the side dock along his boat.

"Hey what's up!" he slurred while stepping back clumsily into the back of the boat. "Want a beer?" he said while fishing out one more and popping the top. "Hey, do me a favor will you? Chuck me over the hose there and turn on the water. I've got to wash her down a bit. It was a rough day out there."

Dug looked over at Connie and nodded to her to get the hose. "Rough day out where?" he said to Richard.

"Everywhere! Went down to Fig's Landing to do some flounder fishing and cut loose a little after a real long rental season up here!"

"How did you make out?"

"Not too bad," Richard said pulling out the bag of fillets from the same cooler the beer was in. "Got some good soft shells too. Hey do I know you? It's kinda late out here.

"The name is Dug Waters, and this here is Connie Thompson. I'm a private investigator and Connie is with the FBI."

Connie brought the hose over and laid it down on the side of the boat being careful not to get too close to Richard and keeping her gun hand free just in case.

"FBI huh? I know it's late, did somebody complain that I wasn't back yet? Or are you guys busting me?"

"Nobody's complained about anything Richard. A family that was vacationing down here this week and renting one of your units has been found murdered; we're just checking around a bit and talking to everyone who might have been in contact with them."

"Murdered? Here in Ocean City? Was it at one of my places?" Richard rattled off real fast.

"Nope, not here, they had already made it home today to Gaithersburg. Looks like whoever did it had been waiting for them."

"Good God detective, I only had one family in from Gaithersburg, the Sawyers, was it them?"

"I'm afraid so Richard. Why don't you have a seat and let's talk about the Sawyers," Dug said as he noticed the heavy smell of booze on the man's breath. The boat was totally trashed and Dug was trying to tell the difference between an all day outing and a victory celebration. Connie had joined them on the boat and he could see her taking close mental notes of the condition of the boat.

"When was the last time you saw the Sawyers Richard?"

Richard looked up thinking and said "It was Wednesday morning. They called complaining about the electrical system and I had to stop by to check it. They were due to check out this morning."

"So you didn't see them today at all?"

"Nope, usually the tenants just leave the keys in the unit and the cleaning service picks them up and returns them to the office when they're done."

"Hey this is a really nice rig you got here Richard, I bet it has one of those really cool radar tracking systems. Do you mind if I take a look at it?" Dug asked.

"I still can't believe the Sawyers were murdered. On Wednesday they seemed to be having a great time." He looked up as if just hearing the question asked and said "Sure you can look at the system. Dam thing has saved my ass more than once out there on the water. Worth every penny I put into buying it." He walked over to the Captain's wheel and turned on the Loran systems. "This thing can do just about everything but skin fish!" as he started to toggle through all the screens.

"Would you mind showing me the replay of today's trip Richard?" Dug said knowing that this system kept a log of each journey.

Richard toggled a couple of screens and a chart came up showing a very long line starting from about 1/4 mile outside the Marina going way down south, turning around, heading over to Figs Landing, then making it's way back up to the same marker where the trip had begun.

Dug noticed the discrepancy of where the beginning of the line started but wrote it off to Richard just being careless as to when he turned the system on and off. He noted that the entire trip would have taken at least eight hours of travel time and if Richard had stopped anywhere or been fishing, that could have racked up anywhere from 10 to 14 hours, pretty much putting him out of the running for today's murders—on paper. "Did you drink all this booze by yourself? Connie offered up from behind them. Looks like you had one hell of a party out on the boat today.

"I told you I was celebrating the end of rental season. I always take her out for a little blast on the last day. Been a tradition for years."

"Did you stop anywhere today, I mean on land, or were you just out on the water?" she said.

"Just stopped for some gas and supplies down south."

"Where was that Richard?"

"I drop into the Figs Landing Marina when I'm down in that area. God they gouge you on the gas prices though." he said with anger in his voice.

"Got a receipt for that?"

"Sure" he said reaching into his pants pockets and pulling out a handful of loose credit cards, license, and papers. Richard fumbled through everything until he produced a credit card slip and handed it the lady.

"Gas, beer, whiskey, and munchy food," both men heard her recite. "$137.00? That's a lot of money for a pit stop!"

"Tell me about it! The gas alone was $98 bucks. I should've gotten more supplies up here at Ted's before I left; he always gives me a local's discount."

"You were out alone all day?" Dug asked.

"Yeah, but that's not always a tradition. Last year I had a few friends along for the day and we had a blast."

"Where were your friends today Richard?"

"Kid stuff, birthday parties, soccer games, you name it."

Dug looked over at Connie; they had made up signals beforehand to suggest outcomes. Dug nodded his head to her suggesting that they wrap up and leave for now. Connie had been thinking the same thing and nodded in agreement.

"Alright Richard, glad you had a good time. Where are you going to be later today in case we need to talk to you?"

Richard pulled out business cards and exchanged them with Connie and Dug. "Hopefully I'm going to be sleeping for a while. I'm still shocked about the Sawyers; they seemed like a nice family. They've been renting from us for the last few years and always at the end of the season. I have all the records at the office if you need to see them."

"We probably will Richard; one of us will be calling you this afternoon." Offered Dug with just enough authority to let Richard know that he was more than a source of information to them.

Richard went back to work cleaning things up as Connie and Dug climbed off the boat and began headed down the long dock back to the parking lot.

"As soon as he leaves, I want to come back real quick and get some pictures of the boat and dock to send up north, it shouldn't take too long." Dug said.

"What's your read on the guy?"

"He either has a great alibi or he knows how to build one. I want to check out Figs Landing tomorrow to verify it was him down there getting gas and food. The time on the slip said 4:00 PM which would make it impossible for him to be in Gaithersburg. Whoever was at the Sawyers had been waiting for them inside the house. I'm sure of it."

"How do you know that?"

"Just a gut feeling Connie. Let's drive off and come back in a little while."

"Ok Dug. Hey, let's go over to your hotel and get me a room for the night. That should give him enough time to finish up and leave."

Dug just nodded as they got into her car and drove off.

Back on the boat, Richard had a worried look on his face as he walked over to the onboard computer system, turned it off, and then headed back to his condo.

*****

The moon was high in the sky and the light was flooding through the skylight window into the master bedroom of the rather odd looking house in the Saint Bart's. Just as the light was about to hit his face, Wesley Marks opened his eyes wide and sat straight up. He looked over at his wife, Ashley, who was still sleeping soundly, and quietly slipped out of bed, went into the bathroom to relieve himself, then headed to the other side of the perfectly round house to his office and computer system.

He had gone to bed only two hours ago as he had been remotely connected into the computer system keeping an eye on what was going on up in Jaffrey. He had been a little concerned with the FBI showing up out of the blue, but reminded himself that everything happens for a reason. He had not talked to Chase at all today for more reasons than one. He had been coaching Chase on a very important life transition over the past months and part of that coaching called for the old Indian "sink or swim" philosophy.

So far Chase had been doing just fine even though he was not going to tell him that in so many words. He had been uneasy all day for another reason. Even though their top three cases seemed to be coming to a head all at once, there was something else far darker going on in the background. Earlier today, and yesterday, for that matter, someone or something had tried to read him psychically. Whoever it was had been shielded and Wesley could not bounce the waves back to find out who was invading his space.

He had used one of the very lessons he was teaching Chase to counter the assault. As soon as he felt the presence trying to read him he had shut down a great deal of his psychic power and turned his mind to very mundane things like shark fishing and chores around the house. He had basically put up a false shield so that whoever was looking at him would not get an accurate reading of his strength or what he was really thinking about. So far it seemed to work. When the perpetrator tried to read him again today his chameleon shield went right up and he just let the person probe him like he was totally unaware of the invasion.

On top of this feeling, he was getting a very strong sense that there was a lot of deception going on all around them. He had just awoken from a dream where he saw web upon web upon web being spun around a tower. He had to imagine that the tower was Serial Connections as there had been a big mountain in the background and the tower itself was bright and full of light colors. The webs being spun around the tower were all different somehow. Three of them altogether, each was being spun with a different pattern and each had a different strength to it implying a unique source for each one. It made sense to Wesley that for now it meant that there were three different entities trying to screw with the efforts of the Serial team, each of those entities were after different things, and using different methods to obtain them. The webs themselves implied deception, being used by all three of them in order to trap their prey. He got the shivers after thinking about this, which for him was a clear validation of the message.

He pulled out his pendulum, a piece of paper and pencil, and started to dowse the situation for more clarity. First he started by asking permission to seek answers in the spirit world by saying "Can I? Should I? May I? A firm YES came back. Then he asked that he be protected from any energy or entity that might cause him harm and further asked that he remain undetectable during the session. Then he began his questions and let the pendulum do its work:

Are there negative entities trying to do us harm?	Y
How many entities are there?	4
Are these the Serial Killers we are hunting?	N
Are they dangerous to us and others?	Y
How many?	3
How dangerous are they?	1=10, 1=8, 1=7
Is entity one a female?	N
Is entity two a female?	N
Is entity three a female?	Y
Is entity four a female?	N
Do these entities have psychic ability?	1=Y=4, 2=N, 3=Y=10, 4=N

Should these entities be destroyed?   1=Y, 2=Y, 3=N, 4=N

Wesley stopped for a moment to consider this startling news. There were four entities present that were all trying to get at Serial Connections some how. Entity number one, a male, was extremely dangerous but only marginally psychic. Entity number two, also a male, was very dangerous, but also not psychic. Entity number three, a female, was not as dangerous, but VERY psychic. The fourth entity seemed to be harmless on all counts and that was a curious thing. He thought a bit more then asked a series of questions before consolidating the answers:

Do these entities know each other?

1=2
1=3
2=1
2=4
3=1
4=2

Entity one, the very dangerous entity, knew both of the other dangerous entities. Entity two knew entity one and four. Entity three knew entity one, Entity four knew entity two. Wesley studied this for a moment then scratched on his paper:

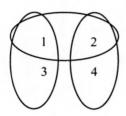

It appeared that the really dangerous entity (one) knew both the other dangerous ones (two and three) but *they* did not know each other implying that entity One knew a lot more about what was going on than the other two. Entity one was also not as psychic, so entity three, the female, seemed the logical candidate for the psychic assaults and somehow she was paired up with entity one—not good.

His gut was telling him that one was somehow the ringleader, but that two was also in a position of power. Three was being driven by one and four was being driven by two. *Minions perhaps?* Entity one and two were bad enough that they needed to be destroyed!

Satisfied that he had gotten all he was going to get for now he turned to his computer, pulled up e-mail, and started writing a note to Chase.

Good Morning Chase!

I trust all is well in your journey. I get the feeling that you have begun to become grounded in your new life direction and might be ready to put your new skills to the test—I hope this is the case! Do you remember many years ago when there was a ripple in the psychic community regarding deception? There were energies and entities that

*were disguising themselves psychically in order to penetrate our ranks
and wreak havoc with the good work we were doing at the time? It is
happening again!*

*My senses are telling me that we have become pawns in a game of
life or death the likes of which we have not encountered before. Three
of our most dangerous serials have all of a sudden become very active
and are within our grasp. This has never happened before and I do not
believe it's a coincidence. There are forces trying to drive us in certain
directions based on their understanding of our mission, moral
obligation, and past behaviors. Their agendas just became clear to me.
Destroy Serial Connections!*

*They are using the serials as a foundation to set us up Chase. The
problem is that there is more than one and each is coming at us from a
different place. One of the forces may be trying to destroy us
figuratively, but the other is trying to do so literally! We are in a time
where we must all be completely receptive, totally shielded, and
guarded in our every move. We will have to act in order to protect the
innocents. That is what they are counting on so we must assume that
each action on our part could be leading us into a trap.*

*Remember that your transition from warrior to magician does not
mean that you will not need your warrior skills. Listen to your inner
voice and let the magician guide you and the warrior protect you!*

> *Wesley*

He hit the send key and thought; *the next few days will be very
interesting and very dangerous. Chase has done an excellent job
building and protecting his team over the years, together we should be
able to navigate this maze and come out whole at the other end—I
pray.*

*****

The alley had the distinct smell of beer coming from empty boxes
piled up outside the back door of the bar Greta managed. Masonori had
pulled in about 20 minutes ago and parked right behind her new Mazda
sports car in his station wagon. The last three Saturday nights he had
cased the place from across the street; each time Greta had come out at
exactly the same time, and was always alone. He knew Greta was
coming by the sound of the big heavy metal door being slammed and
locked behind him. Knowing that she had to walk right by him on the

way to her car, he pushed down the button to lower his window all the way and picked up his weapon off the front seat. As he watched her approach through the side view mirror he tensed up, looked around one more time for signs of people, then got his weapon in the ready position.

Greta couldn't wait to get home. Another Saturday night had just gone by in her life and she was getting pretty sick of the routine, especially when she couldn't join her friends on the weekends to go out and party with them. As soon as she was through paying off the very expensive car she drove she would quit this job and return to having a life. She noticed a blue station wagon parked behind her car and thought that it must belong to a drunk who took a taxi home. *Funny, I don't remember calling any cabs tonight.* The back of the wagon was full of camping gear, blocking her view into the passenger compartment so she couldn't tell if anyone was inside.

She decided to be cautious and give the vehicle a wide berth but as she circled around the side of the wagon she noticed the open driver's window, and fear instantly sent goose bumps up and down her body. Panicking, she stopped in her tracks and froze trying to figure out her next move. Just before she turned to run out into the street a vaguely familiar voice called out the window. "Greta! I just want to talk to you for a moment—please don't be frightened!"

"Listen mister, I got mace. Don't come near me!" Greta squealed lifting her key chain and taking hold of a small plastic aerosol container attached to the ring.

"Greta, Greta, you aren't going to need the mace. Please put it down and just listen to what I have to say" Masonori said calmly as he opened the car door and slowly got out of the vehicle. When the Japanese man got out of the car, Greta relaxed just a little recognizing the man as a regular customer. He had been coming to the bar for months and was always a gentleman and tipped her very well.

"John!" Greta said relieved that at least she knew who this intruder was. "What are you doing out here so late? I didn't see you inside tonight. What's going on?"

"Greta, we've been eyeing each other in the bar for quite sometime. I figured it was time for us to start getting serious. I wanted to invite you over to my place for some soft music, a little wine, you know, just to get to know each other better."

"What are you talking about John? Her caution and fear returned after hearing his desires. "Listen, I think you're a great guy and all, but I have a steady boyfriend, you know that. As a matter of fact he's meeting me here any second to take me to breakfast." Greta lied, trying to throw the man off.

"But you've been coming on to me Greta. I don't understand."

"John, I don't think I've been coming on to you at all. I treat all my customers the same, you included. Maybe you'd better get back in your car and leave before Jason gets here. He might not understand this and you wouldn't want to be around if he gets pissed off. He's gets really jealous."

Anger began to swell inside Masonori's head as he listened to the girl reject him and deny what he knew had been a growing relationship between them. His face turned red and the gun in his right hand, still hidden from Greta began to twitch in his fingers. "Greta, I'm only going to ask you one more time. Please come to my place! I can give you so much more than that jar head boyfriend of yours."

"Forget it John. I'm going out in the street to wait for Jason. I'll use this mace, I swear it!" Greta cried out to the man, knowing that she was alone and that her boyfriend wasn't coming at all. Looking behind her towards the street she made a slight turning movement preparing to run when Masonori brought his right arm out into view and she saw the gun for the first time.

"Greta, we can do this the easy way or the hard way. Please make it easy," he appealed to her one more time.

Desperate, Greta pressed the push top on the mace and sent a stream of the illegal substance towards her attacker. Missing him completely her face turned to horror as the gun fired and two darts sailed through the air imbedding in her chest. She felt a blinding charge surge through her body and before she could run her knees collapsed sending her to the pavement.

Chapter 21

Jaffrey/Cape Cod/Ocean City

It was just before 7:00AM when Karen turned into the long driveway of the Serial Connections complex. She had expected to be up very late the night before but when she got home expecting to find Tom, all she found were some flowers and a note that he had been called down to Atlanta on an emergency call, he was very sorry, and would definitely make it up to her. This was not the first time he had taken off during one of his short visits but she had learned to get accustomed to it no matter how hard it hurt. It was just as well she thought because things were really heating up here and Chase was going to need all hands on deck.

As she headed down the driveway, her mind wandered to Chase and Seville. She was so happy to see that Chase was finally interested in someone and could only imagine what the next few days would bring in terms of this blossoming romance. She had a good feeling about Seville, and honestly was a little jealous. Even though she was madly in love with Tom, Chase had always held a special place in her heart and her fantasies, having kept her awake on more than one long cold winter night. Just as she pulled into her parking spot she was wondering if they had gotten together last night or not, then remembered that Ronnie had spent the night and the likelihood of that happening with her on guard was slim to say the least. She couldn't help but smile as she palmed the kiosk beside the front door of the building and trotted inside to start what she didn't know was going to be a very long and grueling day.

*****

Chase was entering his study when Clair came to life and announced that Karen had just signed in to the office. He wondered why, not expecting to see her until much later in the morning. He decided to invite whoever was here already up for homemade breakfast and coffee. It had been a while since he had brought the troops up from the office to enjoy the breathtaking view of the mountain from his cabin on top of the hill. He walked over to the phone and paged Karen then heard back;

"Yes Boss?"

"Hey, I'm glad you're here....I think? Everything ok?"

He heard a big sigh on the other end then, "Yeah I'm fine. You know who took off again to put out a fire somewhere."

Chase had heard this story before and couldn't understand why she kept putting up with it. He felt jealous hearing this and wondered why he had never acted on his attraction to Karen. They could have made a nice couple even though Karen had never exhibited much interest in his psychic world. At times they *did* act like partners, bantering back and forth and flirting from time to time. They even came real close one night after having too much wine. They had ended up in the pool skinny dipping and it was only through an act of God, literally, that they hadn't gone all the way. Right when they had come together in a drunken embrace, a bolt of lighting came crashing down and intercepted the rod up on top of the cabin. It was enough to wake them out of the moment and call it a night.

"Sorry Karen, I don't know what else to say."

"Don't worry about it Chase. I'll get over it like I always do. What's up?"

"Would you mind rounding up the troops and telling them hot coffee and chow will be on in 15 minutes?"

There was a slight pause on the other end, then, "Sure, what's the occasion? Trying to impress somebody?" she said slyly with a strange pitch in her voice.

"Who me?" Chase joked. "By the way Karen, don't wake up Ronnie or you'll bring down the wrath of Zeus on us all!" he said realizing that Karen was a little jealous herself.

"Got it! Are we having venison sausage and eggs to eat or what?"

"No, not yet" Chase said thinking about the buck again. "It'll be a few days before the aging and butchering get done. Have you ever had venison?"

"I don't eat Bambi burgers Chase, never have, and never will. Hate to disappoint you but it'll be a cold day down in the Saint Bart's before you get me to eat a deer."

"More for me then, see ya in a few." Clair disconnected the conversation and Chase trotted into his huge kitchen and looked around like he had never seen it before. He was a good cook but rarely, if ever, had guests over for any kind of meal.

"Good morning Clair," Chase said as he began getting fresh eggs, bacon, bread, and coffee out of the refrigerator.

Good morning Chase.

"Mail please"

Clair Began to read:

> *4 Messages*
> 1:30AM Louise Penta—Remote Access Report
> 1:49AM Jonathan Longworth—Benefactors Meeting
> 2:25AM Dug Waters—Richard Fox
> 3:00AM Wesley—please read ASAP

"Read Wesley" Chase said. And Clair began to recite the e-mail Wesley had sent him in the middle of the night. Chase kept breaking eggs while he listened to the short but revealing note. It caused him to think about the cryptic message he had received from Ghost regarding the three entities and all the deception. He decided he should talk to Wesley in person--soon.

"Reply"

"Wesley, your message sounds very familiar. I got a similar story from Ghost last night. I'll be on campus all day so call me when you have some time to talk this morning—Chase"

"Send"

"Read Longworth"

"Chase, just a note to remind you that the annual Benefactors meeting is only a week from this Friday at the Four Seasons. I still need a list of key personnel attending for the dinner arrangements. Can't wait to see you and catch up--Jonathan"

"Reply"

"Hi Jonathan, thanks for the reminder. I am looking forward to seeing you too. Things are going well and I'm all set to present this year's progress and achievements. I will send along a list of attendees as soon as I can—Chase"

"Send"

"Read Louise"

"Chase, I wanted to let you know that we had a remote log in from Karen's house last night. Not unusual by itself but the connection was still open and active when the security log placed her back here on

campus. It's the still open port part that gets me miffed. Thoughts?--
Louise"

"Reply"

"Hey Louise, what would we do without you? Thanks for the heads
up and great work on catching us in the act. I asked Karen to have her
boyfriend Tom set up that data mining application interface for me so I
could do some work last night. I didn't want to bother you with such a
mundane task. He was probably working on it after she left to come
back for the meeting late last night—Chase"

"Send"

 "Read Dug"

Chase listened to Dug reiterate their run in with Richard Fox last
night and about the air tight alibi he had going. He was glad to hear that
Dug and Connie were going to follow up on the loose ends first thing in
the morning and report back.

"Reply"

"Great job Dug. Way to keep your cool. My instincts tell me you
guys did the right thing by letting him go for now. I think it's very
interesting that both Fox and Ferguson had alibis for the events
yesterday. I'll have to think about this more and get some input from
Wesley later on. How is Connie working out? Is she behaving herself?
Has she talked to Henry White as far as you know?—Chase"

"Send"

"End Mail," Clair's voice announced.

"Thanks Clair" Chase said as he finished breaking up two dozen
eggs and started chopping fresh vegetables for the omelets—his mind
was moving a million miles per minute.

*****

Karen emerged into the guest courtyard through the tunnel. The
mist was dancing along the top of the stream as the bright morning sun
peeked over the lower hills to the east. Toting a bag of goodies for
Seville, including two changes of clothes, some makeup, fresh
undergarments, and a couple of pairs of shoes, Karen was in good
spirits and excited about being with her new friend. On the practical
side, one benefit of women checking out other women was the ability
to guess sizes, tastes, and colors. She and Seville were pretty darn close
in size; taste of clothes was another matter as she hadn't seen Seville in
more than one outfit. As she came around the bend along the stream

she practically bumped into Seville who was sitting on a rock reading a book.

"Good morning Seville!" Karen said in a bright and cheery voice.

"Hi Karen" Seville said, her face lighting up with a big smile. She liked Karen; she had spunk and could sense her loyalty to Chase and the others. "I didn't expect to see you this early. I thought you had part two of that hot date going on last night."

"That was the plan Seville. When I got home ready to burst at the seams, all I found was a note that Tom had to leave for Atlanta for an emergency network call. Not the first time, probably not the last."

"I'm sorry; you must've been pretty disappointed. But, the good news is you're here! I've been dying to talk you about anything other than work stuff."

"Really? I bet you just want to pick my brain about Chase."

"No, not really. I picked Ronnie's brain for almost an hour last night. I think I have all the dirt I need for now, unless of course, you have anything juicy you want to add!"

"Juicy about the Boy Scout? I don't think so, well, not really anyway." Karen said, not sure if she should fill in Seville about her and Chase.

"Then tell me how you got hooked up with this crowd Karen?"

"It's a long story. I grew up here, went to college out in Colorado, and spent almost 14 years out there chasing my tail, skiing, and men. Then my favorite Aunt became very ill and I flew back to visit and never went back. I was managing the operations for a small computer distributor over in Keene when one day in walked Chase and Louise for a presentation on a new networking something or other. My boss was late and I wound up entertaining them for almost an hour and learned all about what Serial Connections did. I was fascinated, and a few months later sent a resume to Chase in response to an ad in the paper. He remembered me and hired me on the spot."

"The man has great taste!"

Karen noticed that Seville was checking her out when she made the last comment and said, "If you say so Seville. I do think he's an excellent judge of character and has done a great job staffing. We haven't had any turnover since I've been here."

Seville grew silent for a moment then offered, "Karen, do you mind if I ask you a personal question?"

"Depends on what it is Seville."

"I get the feeling that there is or was something between you and Chase. Call it woman's intuition, but I would bet my life on it, and believe me the last thing I want to do is interfere."

It was Karen's turn to go quiet as she contemplated her and Chase's relationship, then answered the question sincerely, "You're sweet Seville. It's no wonder everybody likes you. The truth is, a couple of years ago we almost got together after a night of partying. We definitely have feelings for each other it's just that, well, it's been very awkward. He is a Boy Scout, and if there ever was a definition of gentleman, his name would be in it. I don't mind telling you that if it hadn't been for that thunder storm I would have gone all the way him in a second!"

"Thunder storm?"

"Yeah, we were out here one night on a hot August day and drank way too much. We ended up in the pool that night and got kinda playful. Just when things were heating up a thunder storm came racing over the mountain and a bolt of lighting struck the rod up there on top of his cabin." she said pointing up the hill.

You're kidding me?"

"Nope, he dragged me out of the pool so fast I didn't know what was going on. He disappeared up into the computer room with Louise and the two of them spent the night checking out all the electronics. The next day we didn't even discuss what had happened and ever since it's been pretty quiet. We still flirt and stuff but that's it. Not long after that I met Tom on an on-line dating service and the rest is history."

"Wow Karen. I'm not sure what to say."

"Don't worry about it Seville. Things happen for a reason and the relationship with Tom has been great. I'm not sure I'll ever get him to settle down though. So, tell me about you. Why aren't you hooked up with a great guy and married and all that stuff?"

"God Karen, that's an even longer story than yours. I went to an all girl college and to be honest, I wasn't even sure I liked men. Once I got out into the real world that changed. I'm still schizophrenic about the man/woman thing but I've just gotten used to it. I've seriously dated all of four men in the last twenty years and never found one that could or would settle down, Bob Fellows included."

"Not *the* Bob Fellows?" Karen asked shocked.

Seville lowered her head in shame and replied, "Unfortunately. I'm still so embarrassed that I know him let alone that he was the one who brought me here in the first place."

"That's ok Seville; we know the difference and haven't judged you one bit because of him. How were you to know that he was going to try an end run around us? So, hey, I brought you some stuff that you might need until you get home, if you ever do. Let's go to your room so you can change because the boss is upstairs right now breaking his neck cooking breakfast for the woman folk and this is one event I don't want to miss."

"Chase is cooking for everyone?"

"So he says. I haven't seen any catering trucks on the property so it must be true. I don't know about you but I sure could use a cup of coffee."

"Me too" said Seville as they started towards the hut. "Karen?"

"Yeah?"

"Thanks for coming down to get me. It means a lot. I really like you and hope you feel the same."

Karen felt a nice warm glow move through her body. She did like Seville and just realized there was more to it than just friendship. She hadn't really been with another woman before but the thought had always thrilled her secretly. She found herself fantasizing about being with her but quickly shook it off. "This is one of my favorite places here. The pool, the plants, the stream, the huts, I can never get enough," she ranted, trying to change the subject, then added, "Yes I do Seville, I like you a lot too. I'm glad you're here today," she said cheerily with an impish tone.

Seville reached out and took Karen by the hand as they walked past the green pool, mist still playing in the morning light. "The pool is *my* favorite. After Ronnie went to bed last night I came out here for a swim. That water fall is so awesome!"

"You did huh? Were you alone?"

"Of course!" Seville said sternly to Karen. "I did see Chase up on his balcony though as I was getting out. It looked like he was meditating or something."

"Oh drat." Karen said out of the blue. "I forgot to pack you a swim suit. I am so sorry; we'll have to take care of that today." Then Karen got a weird look on her face and said. "If you didn't have a suit to swim in just what were you wearing last night?"

Seville smiled that coy smile and said "Nothing Karen, nothing at all."

Karen's eyes swept up and down Seville's gorgeous body again without realizing it and said, "And you think Chase was up there meditating with you swimming around down here in the buff! Woman, what am I ever going to do with you?" and they began to laugh uncontrollably.

When they got to the hut, Karen settled down on a chair and explained all the clothes she had brought. Seville was riffling through the bag, ogling all the wonderful choices, and trying to match different colors. After laying things out on the bed she began removing the set of clothes she had borrowed from Ronnie. Karen found she couldn't take her eyes off her new friend and began twitching her legs together. Her body was nice and taught, undoubtedly the result of strenuous workouts at the gym. Karen marveled at the contours, her muscled arms and shoulders flowing perfectly to her rounded breasts. Karen giggled when she noticed a belly button ring sporting a large diamond right in the middle of her flat and toned abdomen.

"You like?" Seville smiled, standing up straight and pretending to model for Karen, slowly turning around.

"God you're beautiful Seville!" Karen said, exhaling deeply. Seville smiled back at Karen and picked up a small green pair of sexy lace underpants and worked them up her long, smooth legs. Karen handed her the pair of Calvin Klein jeans and watched as she slid the jeans up and wiggled her butt in.

"Hey these fit great. Let's see, which top do you think your boss will like today?" Seville said holding up two tops that Karen had obviously picked out with more than covering in mind.

"I like the light blue one; it brings out your eyes. They are stunning Seville!" Karen exclaimed.

Seville looked at the shirt, felt the material, and said "What do you think, bra or no bra?" she asked quite seriously.

"I think you should harness up woman. If I'm not mistaken Chase was really pissed at me last night for putting on my Bob Fellows distraction outfit. I have to admit I did have a great time doing it though. It's not every day one can be a semi-exhibitionist around here."

"I thought you looked fantastic Karen" she said while shooting over a little wink. You were the main attraction last night, especially Chase's. I felt like a nun with Ronnie's black robe on and was kinda jealous of you."

"You jealous of me? Come on Seville, you've got to be kidding. I bet you don't even wear makeup!"

Seville walked over to Karen and took her by the waist, her bare chest lightly pressing into Karen's, and whispered into her ear. "Girl, you and I need to have a serious self esteem talk one of these days." and she took one of Karen's hands and ran it gently over her full breast.

"You are wicked sexy and if I didn't like Chase so much I would be jumping your bones rights now." They both started to giggle and Karen realized that touching and being touched by Seville felt wonderful. Her cheeks were in full blush as she watched Seville finish getting dressed, bra, gun holster, and all, and then they headed back over to the building to round up everyone for breakfast.

*****

Louise Penta sat at her very elaborate command center in the heart of the Serial Connections computer center. She had simultaneous access to six flat panel screens sitting on multiple tiers in an array around a semi curved workstation. She had just finished reading Chase's e-mail regarding the remote access from Karen's house and was silently cursing Chase under her breath. *These damn people don't have a clue about security. If they only knew how hard I worked to make this one of the safest and impenetrable computer systems!* She couldn't believe that Chase actually let an outsider into the main computer to play with applications that, quite frankly, could become a portal into the entire system. She was looking at the activity log to check on what happened during that session just to make sure when she noticed that Tom (she had never met Tom but heard more about him than she cared to know) had indeed been working on the new data mining interface and had set it up for Chase's user requirements. She also noticed that he had done an excellent job. The session had lasted about two hours which was about right and he had tested the interface against Clair's extensive data files. She was going to have to write another memo to the staff about network security.

Louise was just wrapping up when a soft tone started to sound on the monitor system. She looked at "Terri," the monitor on the far right and saw that one of the operative's data communications gear or Data Gator as they called them was sounding the check in alarm. The check in alarm was one of the fail safe measures Louise had developed to keep track of the movements and whereabouts of the field teams. It was very simple actually. Every eight hours the owner of the unit had to engage the safe button on the unit declaring that A) The unit was in their possession and, B) That the operative was not in harms way. Once in a while they forgot and a quick phone call verified that fact. Louise said to Clair, "Dial Susan Kincaid" and she waited a few moments for the call to connect and listened to the ringing through the speaker system. The phone finally went to voice mail and Louise left a polite message for Susan to kindly activate the safe mode as soon as possible.

While she was leaving the message, Louise keyed up a screen that showed a map and details of Susan's travels over the last 12 hours. By the looks of things she had been out in front of the Samurai's house for most of the day and evening and had left to go home around 11:00 PM. According to the device signal it was at this moment in her house right outside of Seattle and had been there in that location for about five hours. Louise figured it would be 4:00AM there and that Susan had clearly had a long day and would get the message when she woke up. Satisfied for the moment about Susan and not one to procrastinate, Louise opened up her word processor and started typing a memo to the Serial Connections staff regarding network security.

*****

After changing, Karen and Seville had gone outside and over to the offices to see if anyone was in yet. They found Katherine and Samuel hard at work and invited them to come along upstairs. Samuel said to Karen "We're not having venison sausage are we?" he said with a yuk look on his face.

"Emphatically no" Karen replied, "As a matter of fact I have informed our beloved leader that the only way most of us will taste his venison is if he can find a way to make tofu out of it." That got a quiet chuckle out of everyone but Seville.

"Venison? I keep hearing venison jokes. Is there something I need to know about Chase that you guys are holding back?"

Katherine picked up on the delicate situation first. "Seville, all of us have our crosses to bear in life. Some of us smoke, some of us drink, some of us gamble. I'm afraid that Chase has one of the worst addictions of all—deer hunting. In fact, God bless him, until yesterday morning we all thought he had been kidding us about hunting because we've never seen a single deer come through this place other than in wild stories about how they got away. Apparently Chase got lucky yesterday and had a run in with this buck he's been after for years and got him. And even though none of us have seen this buck yet, he keeps telling us to warm up our Daniel Boone taste buds for the feast of our lives."

"I hate to be the bearer of bad news ladies" Samuel said "but I have seen this buck. It's not only true; the damn thing IS big enough to feed all of us for the entire winter."

"Since when did you get to see the buck?" Katherine exclaimed with a hint of jealousy in her voice.

"I had the distinct privilege of helping Chase take it to the check in station when we thought we were heading into town to meet with Mr. Fellows."

"So Chase is the great white hunter huh?" Seville offered, suppressing the feeling of approval for Chase's activities. Something inside her was quite comfortable and secure with that thought.

"Well" said Karen, "He certainly thinks he is. Katherine is right about the fact that we hear a lot more about it than we actually see. I've never tried venison but I hear it's supposed to be very good, especially prepared with certain sauces and marinades. I'm not sure I would like burgers or sausage though. We'll see."

"I've had it a few times" said Samuel as they entered the kitchen area of Chase's house.

"Chase! The place smells wonderful. What in the world are you cooking?" said Karen as they all filed into the large Kitchen and took stools around the curved center island.

With a big grin Chase announced "I just got the meat back from the butcher first thing this morning. Sausages and venison omelets coming right up!" he exclaimed.

Moans and groans rose from the group, hands raised in defiance, and signaling no thanks.

"Just kidding guys, we have regular ole Jimmy Dean sausage, western style omelets, English muffins, Danish, and some very special French roast coffee I've been saving for ever. If ya don't like omelets let the chef know and I am sure he can come up with rather mundane versions of the incredible, edible, egg."

Karen and Seville jumped right in taking orders and passing around coffee mugs, juice glasses, and setting places. Soon everyone was eating away and Chase was just starting to make a few extra plates for the stragglers i.e. Ronnie and Louise who he figured wouldn't come up for air for another hour or so. After eating and idle chit chat, Katherine and Karen got up and started to clear and the group settled in for another cup of coffee when Karen looked over at Seville and said, "Hey Seville, I'll bet everyone here is dying to hear about you. Why don't you tell us a bit about yourself while were cleaning up. That way you don't have to repeat the story five times later!"

"Thanks Karen" Seville said sarcastically. "Payback's going to be a bitch."

Karen sent Seville a teasing look and chirped, "I certainly hope so!"

Smiling at Karen's little advance she began, "Well, let's see" she said looking up at the ceiling pretending to be deep in thought, "Once upon a time there was....." and before she could continue had to duck as three napkins hurled through space at her from across the table, everyone laughing and chuckling.

"Ok—Serious. Well, God I hate doing this Karen." While tossing a dirty look over at the smiling cupid at the sink. "I was born in New Mexico, right near the border. My family emigrated from Columbia three generations ago and settled in the States back in the early 1900's. My great grandparents were pure Mayan and moved to the states to escape the civil unrest. They were one of the few families of the time that were able to make it on their own without having to work for other families as servants. My great grandfather was a traditional medicine man and built what you would consider to be one of the first modern medical practices based on ancient Mayan medicine techniques and practices. They had it rough for awhile because the locals thought he was some kind of witch doctor and didn't fully appreciate him until he started helping white folks with cases of small pox. After that, the locals left the family alone and in peace but never really did accept them into the community."

"Over the years more of us came across the border and the clan grew very large and began moving all over the states. My mother, who was one of the most beautiful woman I have ever laid eyes on ended up marrying a Dutch engineer who had settled down after making his fortune building drilling rigs across the southwest. They were married in 1956 and started their family right there. When I was 11 years old they were both killed in a terrible plane crash coming back from a house hunting trip in Los Angeles. After about a year of being passed around from relative to relative, we were sent up to Connecticut to live with my mother's younger brother whose wife could not have children and who still lives there today."

"I went to Smith College and studied criminal law and eventually became a police officer much to the disappointment of everyone in the family. We were the first round of totally college educated kids and they just couldn't figure me out. I joined the Providence PD about 12 years ago and worked my way up to Lieutenant just a couple of years ago on the special homicide team. I have never been married or had kids, but do have lots of nieces and nephews who just adore me. And the rest is history. Ok I'm done" Seville said picking up her mug of coffee and taking a gulp.

"I'm sorry about your parents Seville" said Karen, everyone else nodding in agreement. "That must have been terribly hard"

"It was for awhile Karen. My aunt and uncle are wonderful people and have kept the family together through a lot. If it wasn't for them I probably would have lost all sense of our Mayan past. My uncle still teaches us the old ways and spends a lot of time with the grandkids making sure they know and respect our Mayan culture."

"Mayan huh" said Chase with obvious interest. "Do any of your relatives still practice the Mayan medicine ways?"

"Sort of Chase. I have another uncle who lives in the mountains in New Mexico who is a spiritualist and practicing shaman. He has taken our ways and melded them into a more modern practice. He is a real doctor and works with the poor and the needy in the rural areas. We still keep in touch and he keeps trying to get me to pack my bags and come down to what he calls the "real world". He came up here to visit once and got physically sick because of all the bad energy."

"I can understand that" said Chase. "We grew up with all the big city energies around here and are used to it. The thing of it is that people around here need help too."

"I had that conversation with him once and his reasoning was very plain and simple in that if we are in touch with our higher powers and following the path chosen for us, we will be where we are supposed to be, doing what we are supposed to be doing. He actually commended me for taking on the law enforcement mantel against the wishes of the family. He has always thought me to be more in touch with our past and the need to follow the spirit than others in the family have."

"Then why would he ask you to go to New Mexico?" Katherine asked "If he thought you were following your path he wouldn't have suggested it."

"It was his way of telling me he loved me and that there is always a place for me to go if I needed to. I have no idea what my path is these days. I resigned from the Providence Police Department months ago because I lost my direction. I just woke up one day, walked in, and resigned. I'm still working because I want to get this Lumber Jack guy before I leave. I could make a call right now and never return if I wanted to."

"There you go!" Karen said looking hard at Chase with that hire her now or I am going to kill you look.

Everyone seemed to be on the same thought pattern for a moment and things got quiet. Chase stirred the pot by saying. "Sometimes we are compelled to do things not knowing why at the moment, because the path is not yet clear. It might be that your resignation was simply to put you in a position to make your next move if and when the path was made clear."

"Maybe Chase, but like I said, I feel more lost today than I've ever felt. That's not the kind of feeling that has me thinking I am walking in spirit."

"Who knows?" Chase offered as he shrugged his shoulders and looked around the room. All his people were still looking at him like they wanted him to make Seville an offer right there on the spot. He had already considered it of course, and it did feel right, but ultimately it was Seville's path, destiny, and decision. He almost tabled the thought but said "All I know is that today is going to be a long day and for now we are a team no matter who we work for, but just for the record Seville, if I asked you to join the team officially what would be your answer?"

It was Seville's turn to blush as she felt all eyes gazing at her. "Well, I...." she stammered, "I would have to say yes!" she blurted out with a huge smile that quickly turned to a frown.

Karen was all lit up and said "Why the sad face?"

"Because I haven't been asked yet!"

"I smell coffee and food!" the group heard from around the corner. "Chase, why don't you just ask her and let's get on with things?" said Ronni with a calm matter of fact voice as she walked into the kitchen from around the corner.

Hearing Ronni's vote of confidence pushed Chase over the edge. "I was just about too Ronni, you spoiled the surprise!" Chase said with a big smile looking over at Seville "Well?"

Looking around the table at all her new friends she said, "Wow, I feel like I'm home. Yes Chase. As of right now I'm on the team!" and everybody started clapping and cheering.

Ronni who had sat down and was looking around said "What's a lady got to do to get served around here!"

Chase walked around the corner and gave Seville a hand shake, and as everyone stood shocked at Chase for just shaking her hand, he pulled her to him and gave her a big bear hug and welcomed her to Serial Connections. His face suddenly turned serious and he said "We have a slight problem people, Seville can't operate until she gets her

Federal PI badge and stuff. We'll have to keep her tied up in the office until then I'm afraid."

Everyone stopped for a moment, and realized the truth in what Chase just said and that that could change Seville's mind at least temporarily. Seville smiled and said "Not to worry, the day after I resigned three months ago the first thing I did was to apply. I am already a licensed, gun packing PI!"

Chase looked over at Ronni who was sitting there very innocently with an ever so slight smile and he could tell that they had been up to no good behind his back. He just shook his head in amazement and started chipping in cleaning up the kitchen.

"I do need one thing" she said very seriously "and I don't want this to sound like I am stepping on anyone's toes" and she glanced directly at Samuel and Katherine, "but I made a personal commitment to work on the Lumber Jack until he's either caught or dead and I want to be able to follow up on that promise."

Chase looked around the table at everyone for a quick read and felt no problems so he said "Seville, the Lumber Jack, like all the others we are tracking right now are most likely going to take all the man power we can muster. From now on you and I work as a team and we split our resources across all three of these guys until we bring them in. What that means is yes, you will be able to work the Lumber Jack, but you'll have responsibilities on the other cases too. Deal?"

"Deal" she said still glowing, looking around the table at her new family and basking in the warmth.

*****

Emit had gotten up before sunrise that morning to head up to Maine to get some things squared away knowing the FBI was on to him. When he got in his truck, there was a note tucked into the driver's seat. At first he thought it was from the FBI letting him know they were watching but it turned out to be far more ominous:

Dear Emit,

I can only admire your handy work and wish that I was the master mind behind your very creative exploits. It is unfortunate that the FBI has become involved and that you are now going to be constrained in your movements. At this very minute you are being watched by the FBI but also by someone else. His name is Samuel Johnson and he is with an organization called Serial Connections out of Jaffrey, New

Hampshire. You can manage the FBI Emit, but the Serial Connections group is good. They are the ones who are going to bring you down: Unless you bring them down first!

The head of the group is Chase Benton, and he is the one pulling the strings and driving Samuel so hard to get you. If you can get Chase first, you can live and keep your dreams alive. I can help Emit, but you have to believe in me and believe that you can accomplish this. If not then you are doomed to die or be locked up like an animal in a cage.

First you must throw off the FBI and Serial Connections. At this moment they are both keeping track of your movements and whereabouts so the timing will perfect. Go back in the house and use your third vehicle to go pick up some friends of yours. The pastor and his wife must be expended so you can live. You will know what to do from there. I will be sending you more information on Samuel and Chase in a day or two so that you can focus your efforts where they will really count. In the meantime get this one job done; it is more important than you know. Do the job very quickly—today!

Your Admiring Friend

Emit had gone back into the house after reading the note, stunned, confused, and not knowing exactly what to do. It didn't take long for him to think about what his new friend had said and for him to see the logic and simple beauty of the plan. *How does this man know so much about me? How did he know about my other truck?* The answers eluded him for now but got him thinking about the Providence murders. *He's the one who did that job knowing that I was away and that I would have an air tight alibi. He's protecting me!*

That was all Emit needed to know to get him into motion. He got a few more things he would need and headed out the back of his house and across the long trail through the cranberry bogs to an old processing building that had a maintenance garage attached to it. He opened the padlock with his key and pulled open the large double doors to the garage and his brown King Cab pickup truck. He threw his duffel bag in the back, then got in and drove out of the garage heading back into town the long way around. He had to hurry because it was Sunday and soon the pastor and his wife would be up and getting ready for their holiest of days.

As he came back into town he drove by the top of his street first and sure enough there was a utility van about four houses down from his. He could imagine two or three people in that van drinking cold coffee and munching on a stale bag of doughnuts. Satisfied that the FBI really was laying in wait for him he headed over to the other side of town where he was sure they would not be watching the pastor. It was a good bet that the FBI would be around sometime today to visit with the pastor to issue another apology and to make sure he wasn't going to press charges.

It was around 6:30AM when Emit pulled into John's driveway and he was thinking they would both have to be awake by now considering the events of last night and knowing that John had not finished writing his sermon for today's service. He walked up to the door and rang the bell by the left side of the plate glass window. In a moment he heard footsteps coming from the kitchen and John's wife, Charli, came down the hall peering through the windows to see who could possibly be here this early in the morning.

"Good morning Charli" Emit said with a little bit of sheepishness in his voice because of what happened the night before.

"Emit, how are you? We were so worried about you last night. Is everything alright?"

"Oh yes Charli, I just couldn't sleep very well and I hate to disturb you and John but I really need to talk to John about what happened. I mean, I feel awful about him getting roughed up and cuffed right at my home!"

"Don't you fret about it one more second Emit Ferguson, John is a big boy and he just wants to make sure you're ok. Why don't you come into the kitchen and let me pour you a hot cup of coffee and we can chat for a minute. John is in the study finishing up his sermon and shouldn't be too much longer. As a matter of fact, you can ride over to church with us and come back for a nice home cooked meal after. The Seward's and Pratt's are coming over for a little pot luck and I am sure everyone would love to hear about the adventure last night." Charli said as she turned and headed back down the hall towards the kitchen.

Charli was in her mid 50's and had an average build for a woman her age. Her short brown hair was made up perfectly and that drove Emit crazy. He hated perfect happy people. Her figure wasn't bad either and she didn't look a day over 45. That drove him crazy too, and he could feel the anger starting to swell inside. All his victims were people that thought they were better than everyone else. Perfect happy people! Emit tried to settle down but his rage was already too far gone. He kinda felt bad because John and Charli had befriended him over the years when others wouldn't. *Too bad,* he thought. They were probably the happiest, most perfect people he knew. Why he hadn't clipped their happy wings a long time ago he would never know.

Damn them! How could they be so happy knowing he wasn't? He felt the rage growing stronger and knew he was getting close to letting his good feelings for these people go. His new friend had been very clear about trusting him and doing what he said in order to keep his dreams alive.

When they got into the kitchen Emit waited for Charli to pour a cup of coffee and bring it over to the table in the alcove. As she turned her back to get herself a cup, Emit pulled out an old lead police bludgeon from his coat pocket and brought it crashing down on the side of Charli's head, causing her to grunt in pain and her body to collapse onto the floor with a thud. He knelt down beside her and felt the pulse on the side of her neck. *Good, she's still alive!* And then careful not to touch anything in the house he turned and went through the family room and side porch to where John had a nice little *happy* study all to himself.

"John?" Emit called through the hallway, "Charli wants to know if you need a refill on your coffee?"

"Emit! Come in come in, I'm just wrapping this up. Be with you in a second."

Emit walked into the pastor's study he had been in so many times before. It looked much different today and Emit felt totally disconnected from the room where he had felt safe and loved over the years.

John saw Emit walk up to him in the reflection of the computer screen and couldn't quite make out what he was doing when he felt a searing pain on the side of his neck. The first blow stunned John but it did not knock him out as Emit had planned. John slowly turned his head towards Emit with a look of horror as he realized that not only was Emit here to kill him but he was indeed the man the FBI had been looking for last night. The realization that the man he had helped for so many years and had become close friends with was a mass murderer took his breath away and he began choking and fighting for breath.

John cried out to Charli to run. He saw a sad look come across Emit's face and knew that his beloved Charli was no longer there to hear as the blunt instrument in Emit's hand came crashing down across his forehead and turned his entire world dark. As Emit lifted John's body from the chair he looked at the screen on the computer in front of him and read the last few lines his pastor friend had written:

"Though I walk through the shadow of the valley of death, I shall fear no evil—AMEN" "Yeah, AMEN John, you and your fucking happy wife are soon going to see what it feels like to be really happy. You have no idea what evil is—but you will-- soon."

Emit picked up the pace knowing he had to get his prey up to Maine quickly. He wasn't worried about fibers and stuff because the place was full of his from being over here so much. He was worried about fresh prints though, and went back and wiped down everything he thought he might have touched. Loading the two into the back of the truck was easy work for Emit and he was soon on his way north.

Pulling into his place after the three hour ride, he could see the fresh tire tracks from the FBI raid the night before and was grateful for his new friend who was indeed protecting him. He quickly backed the truck into his large three stall barn on the side of the house and wasted no time getting John and Charli out of the vehicle. Charli had been awake for a while now and was terrified almost to death. Shock was more like it. Her eyes kept rolling up into the back of her head and she was shaking hysterically.

John was much worse off. His head was swollen in two places and blood still trickled down his forehead but he was still out cold. Emit figured he might never come out of it which pissed him off because he wanted Charli to see her happy husband suffer as Emit clipped his happy wings. He picked up Charli who couldn't weigh more than 120 pounds and dropped her in the back of a large utility ATV he kept at the rear of his barn, then got John and emptied him in next to Charli. Emit opened the rear door of the garage then went and got on the ATV and turned on the ignition. The engine roared to life and he took his captive's out a back road that went almost three miles into the dense Maine wilderness. Soon he saw cliffs up ahead signaling him to take a sharp right and he diverted the vehicle up into a less traveled trail that wound back and forth up the steep grade.

Blasting into the camp clearing he could see the small building his father had built almost 45 years ago for hunting. He still used the building for hunting once in a while and kept it stocked with canned goods, cut fire wood, and some other amenities. He looked up at the bright sky overhead and figured it was about 10:00AM and that if he could get back to the Cape by 2:00PM he would be doing well. The excitement was growing by the minute as he had never clipped the happy wings of anyone he knew and thought that it might just be a lot more meaningful.

He pulled out some smelling salts from his pocket and held them under both Charli's and John's noses. Both of them seemed to spring to life and he carefully took the pieces of cloth from their mouths. John was disoriented but his eyes were now open and he looked around frantically trying to figure out where they were. John saw Charli and his eyes went wide as he realized she was still alive. Charli had come around a little bit but was losing ground real fast.

"Emit, what in God's name are you doing to us?" shouted John to his old friend and new captor.

"Shut up John, it's time for you and your happy wife to get clipped."

"What do you mean Emit?" John said frantically, still looking around at the unfamiliar surroundings. "Where are we? This doesn't look like the Cape Emit."

"John, I said shut the fuck up! I don't want to hear your groveling. Just take it like a man so we can all move on please."

John went white as thoughts flashed into his mind about the night before and the FBI telling them they thought Emit was the Lumber Jack who had been stalking and killing people all over New England. He became completely terrified when he thought back to an article he had read about two weeks earlier describing the victims being found without any arms, legs, or heads.

"I'd been thinking that I would clip you first John because I didn't know if you were going to wake up, but since you did, I think I'll clip Charli first, she needs some rest desperately."

It was now very clear to John what was going on. His head was still throbbing but the pure adrenaline caused by this terror had him wide awake and not thinking of anything else but saving himself and his precious wife. He watched Emit as he walked over to what looked like a large industrial wood chipper and saw him begin to take apart an assembly inside the insert shoot. The blades on the unit didn't look like the normal, big, rough blades John remembered seeing on chippers, as they had somehow been replaced by much more refined blades; shaper, longer, and curved at slightly different angles. Emit had a foot long file in his hand and he was slowly running it along the sharp edges of the blades, back and forth with extreme care. John tried to struggle out of his bonds but it was no use. Emit had bound them well and the only chance he had now was to try to appeal to whatever shred of humanity remained in the man.

"Emit, why don't you stop that and let's talk for a while. I'm going to miss our sessions and perhaps we should have one more for old time sake?"

"John, I love ya dearly but your happy bullshit isn't going to work anymore. I wish I had more time with you all but I have to get going soon." Emit retorted to John, not missing a single stroke on the now very polished and sharp rotating blades.

"Just take me Emit, and leave poor Charli alone. She's been through enough. Can't you see that?"

"All I can see is two of the happiest people I've ever known and I can't believe I hadn't thought of bringing you two up here before. This is going to be really good John. You and Charli can finally be *really* happy wherever it is you think you go when you die."

"Emit please" John gasped as he watched the blades being returned to the housing and Emit walk over to the gas powered engine on the side of the chipper. John looked downhill from the back of the huge death machine and was horrified when he saw a pile of shredded bones and skulls at least three feet high and ten feet in diameter. It was a massive graveyard with at least thirty peoples remains heaped in a pile. The sun reflected off bright objects he realized must be watches, bracelets, necklaces, and other jewelry scattered around the ground.

"I said shut up John" Emit spoke one last time as he pulled the cord and the sixty horsepower engine roared to life, blue smoke coming from the exhaust pipe running out the side. Emit went over to Charli and pulled her to her feet and walked her to the platform leading into the mouth of the monster. He laid her down on the rubber conveyor belt, feet facing the turning blades, her eyes just a blank stare, still deep in shock. John watched in slow motion as Emit pushed a button that started the conveyor rolling towards the sharp teeth of the monster. He screamed at the top of his lungs as he watched the nightmare of Charli's body slowly moving into the turning rotors. The sound was unlike anything he had ever heard, bones being cut and splintered and spit out the back raining down upon Charli's predecessors. Amazingly she didn't make a sound as the lower half of her body quickly disappeared into the abyss, blood shooting and spurting all over the inside cover of the chipper. Emit hit the button and the belt stopped right before the blades ate Charli's upper thighs. He spun the platform around on its swivel and repeated the process until only her head remained. John had turned completely white with fear and couldn't utter a word as Emit went for the last extremity, finishing the first of his two clippings.

"Your turn John, Charli's waiting for you!" Emit said as he turned to look at the man in front of him who was paralyzed with fear. "Remember the last words you wrote John? *Though I walk through the shadow of the valley of death, I shall fear no evil.* You were going to preach that at us today John. Did you really mean it or were just going to blow more happy smoke up our butts?"

John looked terrible, and as he looked back at Emit, a feeling of calm came over him as he replayed his favorite scripture over and over in his mind. He resigned himself to peace knowing that he was moving on to a better place, a happier place.

*****

If it hadn't been for all the booze Richard drank on the way back in last night he was sure he wouldn't have slept at all instead of the few hours he did get in. After his encounter with the two cops at the dock last night he went straight home to make things appear the way they should and had stayed awake for three more hours wondering exactly what he his next plans would be. He was sure they didn't have any evidence on him other than a hunch, and the hunch being only because of the rental connection. Once the cops got down and dirty with their investigation it would clearly show that the Sawyers were an anomaly as far as he and his rental company were concerned. He had been very careful not to go after his own clients in the past so there would not be any direct link between the others and himself.

The Sawyers had been different though. He had first seen Susan the day they had gotten here for vacation. She had *the* look more than anyone else so far, and Kevin reminded him so much of his stepfather, beer in hand, terrorizing Susan and the kids—so sad. He had planned on saving a different family that was renting through another outfit who was coming up from Virginia until he had seen the Sawyer clan and decided he had to save them instead. Fortunately he had already made his arrangements with Luke and other than switching locations from Richmond to Gaithersburg, which was less of a drive anyway, all his plans remained intact.

Despite the threat of the FBI and the anonymous new friend, Richard was still basking in the glow of his latest mercenary work. He was so grateful that the Sawyer family could now rest in peace after having endured the sins of such an unholy, dysfunctional existence. He knew in his heart that Susan was now thanking him for his good work and for rescuing herself and her children from that monster forever.

That bastard Kevin had barely even come too during the ritual which had really pissed him off. He was supposed to have watched the ceremony so it would be etched in his mind for all eternity. His son Russell watched though. Russell was getting to be just like his father and Richard was very proud to have spared some poor woman and her children the same agony when Russell got old enough to have his own dysfunctional clan. And Katie, poor Katie, she had been horrified but Richard also knew she was now grateful having been spared any further torment from her father, brother or another man later on in life.

All in all, Richard was satisfied that he had done a very good work yesterday and no matter what happened to him now, no one could take away his good deeds.

*****

Dug and Connie had hit the sack right away when they got back to their hotel early that morning and had agreed to meet for breakfast around 8:00AM to start planning what promised to be a long day. Dug arrived at the restaurant and was reading his e-mails from HQ with a great deal of interest. A note from Karen to the staff announced that Seville Waters had just been hired from the Providence Police Department and that she was starting immediately. He couldn't remember the last time they hired a new employee at Serial Connections and was wondering what that was all about when he opened a private note from Karen explaining the Seville and Chase connection and couldn't help but wonder how that was going to work out over time.

"Good morning Dug!" Connie said as she strolled into the small but quaint 12 table breakfast nook at the hotel.

"Hey Connie!" Dug said looking up at his temporary field partner and becoming aware that he was really enjoying her company. She was dressed in jeans, hiking boots, wool button down shirt, and was looking very good compared to the formal FBI attire she had been wearing the night before.

"Sleep good?" She asked with a big smile on her face.

"Pretty well, but could've used a few more hours for sure."

"Me too, how does the menu look? I'm starving!"

"Depends on how you like your eggs or cereal" he said with a quiet chuckle insinuating that the menu was pretty basic.

"Three over hard for the protein" she declared without missing a beat.

"Looks like we have a pretty full day ahead Connie, are you ready for battle?"

"Sure. I was thinking while I was taking a shower that we have so much ground to cover it might make sense if we split up for the morning, cover some ground then meet up for lunch to go over what we've got."

"I was thinking alone those lines too. I don't know about you but Richard Fox scares the hell out of me. Last night was the first time I ever met him and whether he is the Devil or not he worries me."

"I felt the same thing too Dug, he had that very cold way about him, not cold being shy or withdrawn, but cold like evil."

"Well, thanks to the guys back at the ranch we have a pretty good idea it's him. We just need to hone in on the evidence or catch him red handed or both."

Connie took out a map of the eastern shore and laid it on the table and said "Let's mark all the locations we can, figure out which ones need some personal attention, divvy them up then get going."

Dug pulled out a pen and started circling areas on the map that they would have to go visit that day. "Figs Landing is going to be a haul, how do feel about taking the Bug down there to check out his story about gas and supplies?"

"Ok, I can get down and back in about two and a half hours. We also need to check out the location where they found the Sawyers other car this morning," as she circled a spot well north of Ocean City.

"When did they find the car?" Dug looked up amazed.

"I just got the call before coming down. A local was on his way out fishing early this morning and I guess he uses a shed to stash his fishing gear. When he opened it up there was a maroon convertible inside—without any plates. But it gets better Dug. The green sedan Richard left in the garage belonged to a couple from Virginia" she said looking down at a fax in her hands. "The car had been taken out of their garage in Richmond sometime last week and was reported stolen yesterday afternoon."

"Why not report it until yesterday if it was stolen last week?"

"That's the interesting part Dug. The Sutton's reported the car stolen when they arrived home from a week long vacation at—Ocean City Maryland!"

"Jesus" Dug whispered under his breath. "Are you thinking what I'm thinking?"

"Yeah, for some reason Richard or the Devil originally planned on the Suttons but for some reason changed his mind and took out the Sawyers instead."

"Yeah but why? Connie, you said that you've been to at least five of the murder scenes, what's your MO on the guy and the families?"

"Well, I have a theory that no one at the FBI buys. I think this guy is somehow recreating an event that happened in his own life. Somehow during his lifetime he was forced to watch a horrible event probably involving his mother and/or father."

"But why would he be recreating the event? Why wouldn't he just lash out randomly if he was so pissed off?"

"That's where it gets dicey. The evidence points to a man that is or was very religious because of the crosses etched into his victims. It could be that he is trying to find people or families like his own and maybe trying to save them from the same horror he went through."

"Ok, I could buy that, but why would he switch families at the last minute?"

"If my theory holds up then something about the victim families is reminding him of his own family. The way they look, the age of the children, status, or something is triggering him. Something about the Sawyers caused him to all of a sudden rethink his plans and he goes after them instead."

Dug thought about everything for awhile then picked up the Datagator and connected to Clair. They were scrolling through the information that had been gathered so far about all the cases and especially the Sawyers when he stopped the screen. "Look at this Connie; this is the list of credit card charges from the Sawyer's visit to Ocean City. What do you see?"

"I see a lot of visits to the package store," she said.

"Yeah, I wonder if the Devil and his family were abused by an alcoholic."

"Could be Dug."

"Hey, can you call in and see if someone can get over to the Suttons and get a little background on them including some pictures of Mr. and Mrs. and the kids?"

"What else would you need?

Are one or both in AA or Ala-non, the ages of the kids, religious backgrounds, stuff like that."

"Will do, I will call it in when I hit the road for Figs landing."

"Alright, let's get going. I'm going to head up to take a look at the Sawyers car. It should take about the same amount of time. When we get back we can compare notes then figure out how we are going to canvass this area. We still need to take some more pictures of the boat and buildings around Richards's office. It would be nice to find this garage the psychics saw in the session yesterday. It could provide a bunch of clues. Have whoever is in Virginia fax pictures and any information directly to Clair." He paused and wrote down a number that would send the fax to Jaffrey and passed it over to Connie.

"Ok Chief" she said, still smiling at Dug, not being able to shake the feeling growing insider her.

Chapter 22

Jaffrey/Ocean City/FBI/Cape Cod

After celebrating the news that Seville was joining the team and having finished breakfast, the group dissipated in all directions. Ronnie and Seville had gone back down to the courtyard and Karen, Samuel, and Katherine took their coffee cups and went downstairs to the office to get back to work. Chase went into his study to think about all the different directions his team was heading into. He didn't worry much about things but his instincts were telling him that the team was about to engage in a war of sorts, the enemy not who they thought, and the danger that surrounded them more transparent and deadly than ever before.

"Clair, please get Wesley on the screen." Chase said as he lit some sage and settled down in a plain flat back chair facing out the large picture window towards the mountain. He let his mind wander almost to a deep trance-like state in order to relax and prepare for the day ahead. In his mind the picture Ghost had drawn in the dirt came to the forefront and he began to overlay his sub-conscious mind on that picture to see if anything fit the puzzle his long time spirit mentor had gifted him. In a few seconds pictures and thoughts came rushing through the door to his mind and two kept cycling through like they wanted to stay. He had met Henry White years ago during the Hacker case and had briefly seen him on a number of occasions since. He already new Henry was involved somehow, but where he fit in the puzzle was the question. The image of the angler fish and Henry fit a little but didn't feel totally right. If that was the case then Henry was one of the lesser figures in Ghosts picture, dangerous but being deceived as much as the others. *But how could that be? Henry has to be the one pulling the strings!*

The other picture was of the man he had seen in the Providence Murder vision earlier. When this picture returned again the hairs stood up on the back of his neck which made him pay close attention. This man was definitely part of the picture but he couldn't get a good read on where he fit in the hierarchy of things. The interesting thing was that this guy didn't feel right as the Angler fish which left no one but Henry as the candidate. The only other piece that kept floating to the front of his mind was the Raven or Black bird. Somehow there was a person involved here who was like them--psychic. As he focused on that image only one picture kept coming into his mind—Ronnie! This really threw him for a loop. Ronnie couldn't possibly be involved in this mess! But she *was* involved somehow; he could feel the rightness of it.

"Good Morning Grasshopper!" Chase heard from the speakers coming from the wide screen flat panel display to his right. He shook his head and cleared his thoughts for a moment before he replied to his old friend.

"Fine mess we've gotten ourselves into!" Chase declared back to Wesley before turning his chair to face the screen.

"But if it were going to be easy then why would they need us?" Wesley retorted as if they had practiced this ritual greeting many times before.

"How's the Bride?" Chase said, not quite ready to cut into business.

"Ashley is doing well and sends her love."

"Back at her" Chase said asking Wesley to pass along the mutual thought.

"It looks like your plate is pretty full my friend. How're you holding up?"

Chase caught the mention of Seville in his last statement and said "Timing couldn't be worse Wesley, I think I have finally found the woman of my dreams and I just don't have the capacity to do anything about it right now."

"I don't understand Chase; it looks to me like you're doing just fine. You know that Seville was put here at this moment for a reason. Don't look for the reason, it will find you sometime in the future. Ashley and I were just reading Karen's note about Seville joining the team. I can't tell you how thrilled we both are, especially Ashley; she's been praying that whoever came into your life could become part of the family so to speak. Just keep an open mind, and as I always say….."

"I know, go *with* the flow, and don't *cause* it."

"Oh, by the way, did you do the past life regression Ronnie suggested last night regarding you and Seville?"

"No Wesley, I've been too focused on the business end of things. I went to sacred ground last night to find some answers about what is going on here. There is something very evil out there and it's not about the serials. It's about us. Someone is trying real hard to bring us down and I don't have a clue yet as to who, what, why, or where."

"When you mentioned finding Seville I think your choice of words was more appropriate than you think. Make sure you find the time to figure it out. Ronnie and I knew right away."

"Why don't you all just let me know so I can move on?"

"That would spoil the surprise Chase. I can't wait to hear your update!"

"Sure Wesley. Can we switch gears and go over this mess. I need to get settled into a better frame of mind so I can focus. All three of our top cases are coming to a head, there are one or more bad guys out there who have nothing to do with the serials and I really have to get into the zone. I need your help."

"And what would you do if I wasn't here Chase?"

"Come on Wesley, do we have to get into lessons right now? I really could use some help!"

"Need I repeat the question?"

Chase saw the seriousness on Wesley's face and decided to surrender to his teacher who had accurately directed him in most matters for decades. Chase knew that part of the process Wesley was initiating here was to get him relaxed and focused on a different sort of energy. That energy was discernment and it could not be conjured up well when pre-conceived notions were running rampant through his mind.

Wesley started the session by saying "The totem bear has already paid you a visit Chase, the answers to all your questions have been laid out in front you. How are you going to see them?"

"I'm not going to see them Wesley, they are going to present themselves to me at the exact moment I need them."

"Correct, but how is that going to help you now."

"By creating peace within I can flow with the present, instead of getting bogged down in what I think the future will be."

"And what about direction?"

"The path to travel, the fork to take, and the speed at which to move are also answers that will come with peace. Discernment comes from patience, wisdom, serenity and a true heart."

"And what do you already know Chase?"

"I know that our first mission is to stop the killing. The serials must be our first priority or we have already lost the battle."

"Who are you fighting Chase?"

"We are fighting ourselves."

"Expand."

"The dark forces will only succeed if we stray from our mission and allow their traps to misguide and direct us. In this we are fighting our urges to attack the wrong enemy. The dark force will depend on it's discernment of our potential actions in order to betray our mission and stop us from succeeding."

"So..?"

"Intuition and wisdom will guide the way and discernment will be about recognizing the true enemy and staying the course to victory no matter how strong other desires try to pull us away."

"It would appear to me that a very fine line exists between the serials and the negative forces. How will you tell the difference?"

"I won't, the difference will tell me."

"All right then." Said Wesley looking at his pupil through the video conferencing system and feeling satisfied that Chase was truly on the right track.

"Wesley, the warrior in me wants to lash out and attack these forces. I feel like I need to protect my people at all costs."

"You do have to protect your people Chase but knowing who and why will come in its own time. Keep the warrior at the ready, but not at the helm. The magician is the one who is going to win this battle and there may be casualties, but there will be victory."

Chase couldn't help thinking about all the people involved both on his team and the innocents out there getting slaughtered by mad men. At times like these he felt so helpless because he knew he had to let things run their course or even more damage would be done in the long term; a bitter pill to swallow no matter how you sliced it. "Alright Wesley, let's load the magician with the knowledge he needs. Tell me about your dowsing session last night, it looks similar to mine and I want to try to find some validation. If I am going to fight and win this war I'm going to at least need to know what the battle field looks like."

"Like I said in the e-mail, we have two very strong personalities out there trying desperately to stop Serial Connections. One of them clearly wants to destroy us literally, the other one wants to destroy us figuratively. I know you think Henry White is one of those two and I would have to agree, but I would be careful about those preconceived notions. I believe that the two are very much connected and driving towards similar goals but in my mind one of them is the ring leader, the other just doesn't know it. The truth is that both of them are very dangerous and capable of doing whatever it takes to reach their goals. And I mean *whatever* it takes."

"What about the psychic? Last night, right in the middle of my session, Ghost found an intruder and sent it back to this world."

"Whoever this psychic is displays a great deal of power Chase, but this person is not the one we must fear but rather the one who we must fool. The psychic is in the employ of one of the dangerous ones. I feel that the motive behind this person is first for money, then perhaps reputation, but not for revenge or destruction even though the work they provide could lead to it."

"Wesley, Ronnie came up in a meditation just awhile ago having some connection to the psychic. For a minute I suspected Ronnie and I feel terrible about it, but she is involved somehow."

Wesley smiled through the screen and said "That is the magician speaking to you Chase. Out of all of us who do you think would be best suited to put up our shields in order to fool this threat?"

"Shit" said Chase, "Ronnie of course, she's the one who'll be fighting that battle while we push on against the Serials!"

"Bingo! Give the man a prize."

"There was more to it Wesley. Ronnie is involved with this psychic somehow, I know it, and I just can't put my finger on it."

"I guess we'll find out soon enough" said Wesley not seeming to be too worried about it.

*****

Chase had just started his workout when Clair announced that Louise Penta was frantically looking for him and Wesley regarding Susan Kincaid. Chase immediately sensed the bad energy and went right down to the computer room. On his way he asked Clair to get Ronnie and Seville and have them meet them there.

"Good morning Louise" Chase said as he walked into the room. This room never ceased to amaze him with its dark covered windows, very little color other than what was on the monitors and he could not imagine spending so much time locked up like this. But it had been her design and it was just the way she liked it.

"Chase, we have a big problem. Wesley is just about to come back on line, we should wait for him."

"Ronnie and Seville are joining us too, can we wait until we're all assembled?" asked Chase still looking around the room, not feeling comfortable having a meeting in here. He decided to take a chance. "Louise, would you mind if I pulled the curtains so we can have some light in here?"

Louise gave him that look, then noticed that her boss was very serious about it and conceded knowing what she was about to tell them. "Ok Chase, this time it will be fine but don't get in the habit."

Chase walked over to the window section and pulled the heavy blackout curtains to the side. The sun streamed into the room and Louise automatically covered her eyes from the intense light. Chase stopped to look out the window and marvel at one of the best views the building offered and couldn't for the life of him understand why someone would want to cover it up. As if reading his mind (which she couldn't) she said "I do open those curtains on very cloudy days and at night when the moon is bright. I love the view as much as you do; it's just that when I'm working, I need low light to see the monitors.

"You don't have to explain to me Louise; you know I have a great deal of respect for individual workspace. I would never ask you to change a thing."

"Thanks Chase" she said as Wesley's thick moustache and smile came on screen.

"Good morning again" Wesley offered through the monitor.

"Hey Wesley" Louise said smiling at her friend and fellow computer geek. Before Wesley retired to the Saint Bart's he and his wife Ashley had run a small computer store and even though Louise reported to Chase structurally she really reported to Wesley in terms of all the computer stuff. They would sometimes geek all night long together trying to solve some of Microsoft's most baffling software mysteries.

Just then Ronnie and Seville walked into the room and everyone was gathered. Chase said "Seville meet Wesley Marks, our non-resident Vice President of Beach Erosion."

"Very nice to meet you Wesley, I've heard a lot about you."

Wesley looked at Ronnie for a moment and she just shrugged her shoulders back at him like she had just been doing her job filling in Seville on all the dirt. "It is my pleasure Seville" Wesley replied. "If Ashley gets back from the market in time I am sure she would like to say hello too."

Chase turned the meeting over to Louise who began with "Early this morning I got a check in alarm from Susan's equipment. At the time it was 4:00AM her time and I didn't really think anything about it. I did try calling but there was no answer and she has not returned the message yet.

So far everyone in the room didn't seem too concerned then Louise said, "Just about 20 minutes ago I decided to check her status and things got weird. Her Datagator is still at her house according to the tracking device and so is her car. The problem is that she's no longer at the house herself." She pulled up a tracking screen that had three items marked on it, the datagator, the car, and Susan herself. "Susan had recently traveled from her house to a street one street over from the Samurai's residence, and then the signal vanished."

"Clair, please ask Karen to join us in the computer room ASAP" Chase said into the air, then offered to Seville. "We have a number of tracking devices in order to make sure we keep our field operatives as safe as possible. I should have told you before you joined that all of us have a miniature tracking device embedded somewhere on our bodies. We only use that particular device as a last ditch effort to locate a lost operative, and quite frankly I can't remember the last time we had to activate it."

"I can" said Karen as she strolled into the room. "Remember the time you were up in Maine hunting and got lost and we had to use the tracker to help you get to a road?"

Chase blushed remembering one of the most embarrassing moments of his life. "Thanks for the history lesson Karen!" he said then returned the floor to Louise.

"According to the clocks she would have left her house around 6:00AM and gotten to the new location around 6:20AM. She's still not answering her cell or house phone."

"Wesley, Thoughts?" Chase said.

Wesley had his eyes closed and was in a semi-trance as was Ronnie. Both of them came back with nothing.

"Shit" Chase said. "Ronnie, you didn't get anything? How about you Wesley?"

"Not a thing" they both answered in unison and all of a sudden Chase realized that they were being blocked somehow. He had never seen an instance as long as he knew both of them where they were cold on the psychic front at the same time. He went into a trance and started to travel but ran into a black wall.

"We are being assaulted again folks" Chase said and Both Wesley and Ronnie nodded in agreement. "Wait a minute. Seville, they might not know about you yet. See if you can get anything and he looked at both Ronnie and Wesley silently asking them to channel some energy her way. Seville looked around the room at everyone feeling a little sheepish then decided to go for it. She closed her eyes lightly and thought of Susan Kincaid, the Samurai, and Seattle. In a few moments she started shaking and blurting out random thoughts. "Kitchen, broken stove, shattered glass, dead cats, fist in the face, man—no face, gun-floor, pain—lots of pain, blackness. Seville cut off and Karen came around from behind to hold her and help her into a chair. The group remained silent until Seville composed herself and shook off the shivers. "What happened? Did you guys do something to me?" Chase looked at Ronnie to provide an explanation.

"Seville, while you were thinking about Susan the three of us channeled some energy to you to enhance your receptivity. You did an awesome job. Do you remember what you saw?"

"Not a thing Ronnie, I just remember being in a very intense place for a minute and speaking but I don't remember what I saw or said."

"Clair, please analyze and play back session." Chase said.

"Chase, while Seville was working I was able to pick up some of what she was seeing" Wesley said. Ronnie confirmed the same thing.

"So did I" said Chase. "Wesley I think we just found the answer to one of the challenges we were discussing this morning."

"Exactly!" said Wesley calmly but with a hint of excitement.

"I want Seville to go through the playback before we offer any insights" Chase said to Ronnie and Wesley. They both nodded because they knew Chase wanted to give Seville the entire experience and they both already knew what Clair was going to come back with based on what they saw.

On another large screen Clair began to display columns of pictures. The first column had eight different pictures of kitchens, the second one was eight pictures of cats, and the last one had eight different front facing profile shots of woman. Seville looked up at the screen and knowing how the session worked began to rattle off numbers. "Picture number four, picture number 13, picture number 21 and then stopped. Clair made all the other pictures disappear and what remained caused silence in the room. On the screen the first picture was a shot of Susan Kincaid's custom built kitchen, the picture having been added to the archives about three years ago after a major remodeling. The second picture was of two cats seated on a window sill with their heads looking outside. This picture was a shot of Susan's two cats, Fuzz ball and Twinkles. The third picture was a front facing file picture of Susan Kincaid. They all knew that Seville had not seen a picture of Susan yet.

Wesley spoke first looking directly at Chase "The games a-foot Watson" he said with a mock British accent.

"Indeed" said Chase as he walked over to a chair near the window and looked out over the Mountain. The rest of group remained silent while Chase sat and stared out the window. In just a few moments he turned to the group and said "Gather round."

"Karen, I need you to get the jet ready for a trip to Seattle. I will be going by myself. Also, get another plane for Seville; she's heading for Ocean City. Wesley and Louise, please do whatever you can while I am in the air to check on Susan. I don't know what I am going to find but I am certain that this is a setup. Ronnie, I want you and your team to focus and concentrate on what or who is trying to block us psychically. Seville, when you get to Ocean City, hook up with Dug and Connie. I want whoever is out there watching us to think we are pressing hard on the Devil, and we are, but I want a major distraction down in Maryland. Wesley, help Dug and Seville come up with something good."

The entire group looked at Chase whose demeanor had suddenly turned to very calm, very firm, and extremely focused. Karen and Ronnie left the room right away, Wesley asked Louise if they could talk for a minute, and Chase invited Seville to join him upstairs while he packed a few things.

*****

Connie made it down to Figs Landing in record time and was looking forward to doing some investigative work that really had some meat to it. She had been chasing her tail for months on this case and kept coming up with nothing and could feel that they were getting real close to Richard Fox. Her instincts told her he was the Maryland Devil and now all she had to do was find the evidence they needed to bring him in. Her main problem was going to be navigating the tricky maze between the Bureau and Serial Connections. At the end of the day all she wanted was to stop the killings and bring the killer to justice-one way or another, and wasn't partial to either organization—yet. She couldn't stop thinking of Dug, Chase, and the rest of the Serial Connections team. Even though the FBI had been her life's dream she had become disillusioned by the agenda driving, politics, and molasses like response.

So far she liked what she saw from Serial Connections. The fact that they were a small, dedicated organization without all the bullshit was very appealing to her, but Henry White had made it very clear a few moments ago that she worked for him and the FBI and if her loyalties strayed even a little he would make sure her career was ruined forever. She had sucked it up instead of challenging him over the phone. Henry White was the epitome of what she found wrong with the

FBI, and knew that there were many others like her in the Bureau whose dreams had been shattered by its reality. But for now she would stick to her plan and use every resource available to catch Richard Fox before he could kill again.

Figs Landing was in a quaint little eastern shore town that was not all that big. Connie made it easily to the one and only marina and parked her car on a gravel lot nearby. Heading down the long wooden walkway she looked out over boats of all shapes and sizes. Some had been buttoned up for the approaching winter and others were still at the ready, owners anxiously awaiting more summer like days to head out to the Ocean and Bay. It was pretty busy this Sunday and Connie looked for the gas pumps she knew would be out along the day slips that docked incoming travelers for fuel and supplies. A tall man with a pot belly, old Marlboro hat, and greasy overalls was just finishing up with a customer when Connie walked up and introduced herself as Special Agent Thompson.

"Nice to meet you Miss." Gary Sikes said while he was hanging the pump back up into the slot marked Premium.

"Mr. Sikes, were you here yesterday manning the pumps?"

"Sure was Miss, this is my place and me and the wife run everything around here—including the help." He nodded over to a teenage boy running around cleaning things up.

"Have you ever seen this man?" Connie asked holding out a picture of Richard Fox she had snapped last night in Ocean City.

"Sure Miss, he comes around here once in a while. Don't remember his name but he was here yesterday, you can't forget that boat of his. It's a real beauty."

"She pulled out another picture of the boat and handed it to the man. "Is this the boat you saw here yesterday?"

"Yup, that's the one. He came in yesterday afternoon for some gas and bought a whole lot of stuff in the store. He must've had quite the party out there."

"Are you sure the man on the boat yesterday was the same man that always drives that boat?"

"As far as I know Miss; He was dressed just like the man in the picture your holding except he was wearing a baseball cap and had his sunglasses on."

"Was there anything unusual about his visit yesterday Mr. Sikes?"

"Nope! It was pretty busy and he was in and out of here in about 30 minutes. He said he had been out flounder fishing that morning and might do some crabbing that afternoon."

"Did he show you his catch?"

"Naw, not many do. I don't go on the boats unless I need to fix something or help some rookie boat owner figure out their rig."

"Mr. Fox was alone yesterday?"

"As far as I know I didn't see anybody Miss."

"Thanks Mr. Sikes, would you mind if I asked your wife and your dock hand a few questions before I go?"

"Help yourself. The Ms's name is Wendy and Tommy over there is the one who was working with me yesterday. Hey Tommy!" Mr. Sikes roared over the noise of the big boat engines. "Come on over here for a minute!" Immediately the red headed freckled face boy who looked to be around thirteen years old came running over.

"Hi Tommy, my name is Connie Thompson, and I wanted to ask you a couple of questions, ok?"

"Sure" he said with a bright greasy smile.

"Did you see this man here this weekend?" she said as she held out a picture of Richard Fox.

"Yeah, he came in yesterday. I remember because I couldn't stop looking at his boat. That's the same boat I'm going to get when I get older."

"Did you notice anything when he was here Tommy? Anything at all?"

"Well, when he was inside, I was pretty sure there was a lady peeking out one of the bulkhead windows. I saw the curtain pull aside for a minute and a face that looked like a lady's anyway."

Connie looked at Tommy with focus and said "Are you sure Tommy? This is very important. Was there someone else on that boat yesterday?"

Tommy looked over at Mr. Sikes who just stood there without any expression and said "I would bet my life on it Miss."

Connie thanked Mr. Sikes and Tommy once again and walked over to the building with the sign over it that read "General Store," and walked into another era. The store was right out of the 1920's with old wooden floors, antique coolers and ice chest, oak counter with a cash register that must have been well over 60 years old. Behind the counter was a gentle looking woman in her mid 50's, hair pulled up, white apron slung around her neck, and a warm smile on her face.

"You must be Mrs. Sikes" said Connie as she approached the counter.

"You can call me Wendy young lady. What can I get you today?"

"Well, actually I am from the FBI and we are conducting an investigation Wendy. Have you seen this man recently?" she said holding out the picture of Richard.

"Of course, he was in here yesterday. He spent a small fortune on supplies for that boat of his, mostly booze, but he did buy some fishing stuff."

"Do you remember exactly what he bought?" Connie asked still very curious about the possibility of another person being on the boat with Richard.

"Yeah, other than the liquor and beer, he bought some bait fish and chicken bones for crabbing."

"Bait fish? Connie countered.

"Minnows, the kind you use for flounder."

"Really, that's interesting. Did he buy anything else while he was here? Soda, Chap Stick, candy, anything?"

"Well actually, after he had paid for everything and was leaving he came back in looking kinda sheepish and bought some of those over there." Wendy said pointing to a rack down at the end of the counter.

Connie glanced over and saw a Trojan display with all kinds of assorted condoms in various size packages. She noticed Wendy blush and decided to let it go. "Thank you Wendy, you've been a big help. If you or your husband think of anything else would you mind giving me a call?" Connie said as she passed Wendy her card.

"Sure Miss Thompson. You be sure to have a nice day now."

"Thank you Wendy, you too"

Connie walked outside and started to head back over to her car when she noticed a couple walking out of another building that didn't have any markings on it at all. The woman was holding a brown shopping bag that looked pretty heavy that was dripping wet on the bottom. Curious, Connie walked over to the door of the building and the strong smell of fresh fish hit her like a brick. She looked inside the screen door and saw a fish counter so she opened the door and went inside for a look. A kid who looked like he was in his twenties was busy cleaning some mackerel in a large industrial sink but no one else was in the place. Looking into the case, Connie saw a wide variety of fish neatly stacked on ice chips. Some of the fish were whole and some were already cut into fillets. About two dozen Maryland soft shell crabs were moving around in a partitioned section trying desperately to escape.

"Can I help you?" The young man said nicely while slicing through the belly of another mackerel.

"How much are your whole flounders?"

"Two ninety nine a pound wrapped. Four ninety nine a pound wrapped and filleted."

"Were you working yesterday?" Connie asked.

"Nope just Sundays, Joey was on yesterday but he's out fishing today. He should be back pretty soon though."

Connie walked up and laid her card on top of the counter. "Would you mind having Joey call me at this number as soon as he gets back?"

"Sure, did he do something wrong?" The kid asked when he glanced over and saw the FBI logo on the card.

"Nothing at all, I just want to ask him a couple of questions." She said before turning and walking out the door.

*****

The timing couldn't have been better for Emit. He had made his way back to the Cape, found a nice little spot in a secluded section of Truro to drop off his handy work and made it back to his shed by 2:00 PM that afternoon. Another note had been left for him, this time at the shed, and it told him that neither the police nor the FBI had been to his house yet today. The time on the note had read 1:30PM.

He had changed his clothes and burned the working set back up in Maine after he was finished clipping the Peters. He had put them into old army surplus body bags for the trip back to cape. He was smiling on his way through the backyard. The note had praised him about his ability to think and act so quickly; his ego and pride swelling immensely. His new friend also told him that he would be making another move very soon and to stay put until he could be in touch again. No sooner had Emit come around the corner of his house then a blue sedan rolled into his driveway occupied by two men wearing dark suits. He walked up to them with an apparent interest and waited for them to get out of the car. Looking casually down the street he noticed the same utility truck sitting where it had been that morning.

The driver got out of the vehicle and said "Emit Ferguson?"

"Yea, that's me" he said with a sudden burst of confidence aroused by an outside protector.

"My name is Special Agent Fellows from the Boston Bureau and I am here to speak with you about our little incident last night."

"Oh yeah?" said Emit with a hint of skepticism in his voice "Haven't you guys bugged me enough yet?"

"Were not here to bug you Mr. Ferguson, we are here to offer an apology and hopefully just ask you a few more questions so we can wrap this up."

"I haven't talked to my lawyer yet so I am not sure I should be speaking to you."

"That is your right Mr. Ferguson, but I think you'll find that we don't have all that much left to discuss and I would be happy to speak with your lawyer if you like."

Emit saw the man looked pretty harmless and said. "Alright, I got a few minutes before I need to clean up."

Bob Fellows looked down at Emits legs and his waders and noticed a muddy mess running up and down the boots and said "Out working in the yard today?"

"Nope, I was out in the bog picking some fresh cranberries"

"Nice" Bob said. "Mr. Ferguson, first of all I am here to officially extend an apology from the Bureau and to tell you that if there is anything we can do to help because of last night to let us know. Also, I wanted to ask you why someone would call us about you regarding the Lumber Jack. That piece still has us baffled and quite frankly a bit concerned."

"Apology accepted Mr....What was your name again?"

"Agent Fellows"

"Agent Fellows, I'm going to be alright but who I'm really worried about is the Peters. The Pastor almost wet his pants last night and I am sure his wife was pretty damn upset too."

"Emit, can I call you Emit?" Emit nodded yes. "One of the reasons we are concerned is that sometimes mass murderers like the Lumber Jack will call in false reports to throw us off track. But sometimes they will make the call regarding someone they were planning on killing. We think that Mr. Peters was here just by coincidence but since the call came in especially for you we are going to keep an eye on things around here just for your safety. Speaking of the Peters, we haven't been able to find them this afternoon. Apparently they left a note at the church that they were called away for a family emergency early this morning and missed the service. No one has heard from them or seen them since last night."

"They didn't tell me about anything going on Agent Fellows. As a matter of fact I was going to call them to apologize for last night and for missing Church today myself. I couldn't sleep after what happened and ended up sleeping in a bit this morning."

"And you've been home all day?"

"Yeah, here in the house and out in the bog."

Bob was not going to question him further on that because the team out in the van had confirmed that Emit had not gone out all day. "Are there any people that you know who might be playing a trick on you Emit?"

"Not that I know of Agent"

"Is there anyone that doesn't like you enough to try to get you into trouble? If it hadn't been for the Pastor and the fact that you both were at that retreat we would have picked you up and this situation would be a whole lot more trouble for you."

"Some prank. If I ever catch who called me in you doesn't want to know what I'll do to them." He said before thinking through his reply.

"Well, I understand your anger Emit, but why don't you let us take care of that when we find out who it was. I wouldn't want you getting into all kinds of trouble over this."

"Yeah, your right, but you can give me 5 minuets alone with them can't ya?"

"We'll see Emit. Tell me about this place you have up in Maine? Why two homes?"

"The ex-wife moved back down here from Maine after the separation. I bought this place to be closer to the kids. Works out pretty good, I got customers both here and in Maine and during the winter when we don't do much up north I can still get plenty of contracting work down here."

"I see. Sounds like a good setup. When was the last time you were in Maine?"

"Just a couple of weeks ago I was up there getting the place semi-closed down for the season. I'll go up some this winter for a little hunting and ice fishing. I still have a lot of buddies up there you know."

"That would have been the week of the 5th?"

"I guess so why?"

"I am just checking out some dates Emit. Even though we don't think you're a likely candidate for the Lumber Jack, we still need to find the guy and right now you are the closest link we have."

"Boy I feel real special Agent Fellows" Emit said sarcastically. "I really hope I don't have to talk to my lawyer."

"Me too Emit, here is my card, if you think of anything else please give me a call anytime. Enjoy the rest of the day."

"Thanks Bob, I can call you Bob can't I?" Emit said with a final grin as Bob Fellows walked back to his car and drove away.

*****

"I want you to keep 24 hour per day surveillance on Emit Ferguson Bob. I can't believe he was out all day off in the bogs and we didn't know about it. What in the hell are you guys doing?" Henry White screamed into the phone at special agent Fellows. "I want to know every time that little weasel wipes his ass, you got that?"

"Yes Sir" Bob said into the phone he was holding a few inches from his ear. "I just got down to the Cape this afternoon and hadn't had time to brief any of the people. They were all under the impression that Emit was just a victim and not the prime suspect based on what happened last night."

"Did you find that preacher and his wife yet?"

"Not yet, they didn't talk to anyone before leaving that we know of, they just left a note at the Church with a copy of his sermon for the day for one of the lay people to read at the service."

"Find them Bob, pull out all the stops. Emit is our man, I know it and I am counting on you to get the evidence I need to nail the bastard."

"I am Henry, I've got 3 full time agents working the area now and we should have something real soon."

"What is Chase doing Bob? Has he shown up at the Cape yet?"

"No, and no one has seen Samuel Johnson down here either. I think we scared them off big time with that little stunt last night." Bob told Henry with a barb in voice.

"Chase Benton doesn't scare off Bob. Find out what they're doing and let me know immediately because I will be dammed if they are going to get this guy. Call Seville and see what she knows since you're not welcome up there anymore."

"I already talked to Seville Henry. She quit the force today and joined up with Chase. It seems our back stabbing got to her too. She wouldn't tell me a thing when I called her and basically told me to have a nice life. She did say she was on her way to Maryland but wouldn't tell me what she was doing down there."

"Why in the hell would she be going to Maryland when they haven't pulled in the Lumber Jack yet? Isn't she vested in bringing this guy in?"

"Yeah, that's the only reason she was still on the force this long, she promised to stay until the Lumber Jack was caught."

"Shit" Henry said out loud to himself. "They must be getting close to nailing Fox on the Maryland Devil case. That's the only thing I can think of that would take her away from Emit."

"Maybe" said Bob "Didn't you say that one of our people has hooked up with a Serial Connections guy down there?"

"Yes, Connie is glued to his hip. I talked to her this morning and she assures me that they trust her and that she is going to get as much out of them as possible, including first shot at this Richard Fox guy, if he's the guy."

"Be careful Henry, you don't want a replay of last night with Chase and his team. If we shut them out again, they'll go completely underground and work ten times harder than before."

"Don't tell me what to do Bob, especially since your methods have turned up zilch. I told you I am going to do whatever it takes to bring these Serials in first and I could really give a rat's ass about how I do it."

"Whatever Henry, I have to go catch a bad guy, are we all done?"

"Call me the minute you have something Bob. Anything at all! I don't want any decisions being made without my input. Clear?"

"Clear Henry, see ya."

Henry folded his phone down and leaned back against the seat in his limo. He usually slept pretty well on planes but this trip he didn't sleep much at all and he needed to get some rest. He just couldn't get all this madness out of his head. He sat back up and pulled out his private cell phone which had started to vibrate.

"Yes?"

"I'm in Seattle now and just called to check in. Any new developments" Tim said on the other end.

"Nothing yet, what's your plan out there? Have you been able to find Susan Kincaid yet? Is she still tailing Masanori?"

"Susan doesn't seem to be around" Tim said with an uncertain tone. "I have been outside watching the house for the last 3 hours and other than your boys down the street, there are no signs of any other surveillance."

"What is your guy there doing?"

"I sent him to watch Susan's house as soon as I got here. He saw her pack up and head out from here last night about 11:00 and hasn't seen her since. Her car is still at her house but that doesn't mean she's home."

"Look, forget about Susan for the time being. I want you to formulate a plan to catch Masanori red handed and take custody of him.

It has to be discrete and when you get him you will not under any circumstances be visible. Once you have him in custody let me know and we will make an anonymous phone call to the Seattle FBI to have him picked up."

"Ok Boss, but it might mean getting very creative if you get my drift."

"Get as creative as you need to Tim; just don't ever let me know about how you did it. Got it?"

"Got it Henry. It looks like things are starting to heat up down in Maryland too. Do you want me to get the creative juices flowing down there?"

"No, I have someone else working close to the situation. Just have your man down there stay in touch and keep close in case I need a little extra push."

"Will do, I will get back to you."

"Good Bye" Henry said collapsing back into the seat again. His head was spinning but he felt like things were starting to turn in his favor. It was starting to look like the Lumber Jack was going to have to be put on the backburner for a few days unless Bob came up with something useful. Henry closed his eyes and started running scenario after scenario through his mind.

*****

Dug was just finishing up entering his information into Clair when Connie came striding through the lobby door with a bright smile on her face looking around for her new colleague. Seeing him at a table off the foyer she changed direction and took up a chair opposite Dug.

"You'll never believe what I turned up down at Figs Landing!" She said with a great deal of excitement.

"Richard was with a woman?" Dug said casually back to her as if reading her mind.

A big pout came over her face as she uttered "Don't tell me your one of the psychics too!"

"No" Dug said, pleased that her response verified that she had discovered the same thing. "Let me go first Connie. I went up to where they found the Sawyers car and ran into the old timer that found it. After talking to him for a few minutes he finally warmed up to me and started spilling his guts. It seems our friend Richard left his boat tied up to an old dock early yesterday morning and some guy and woman ended up taking the boat out until 7:00PM last night. The old timer lives right on the water about a hundred yards away and saw Richard Fox leave the boat, saw the couple show up a couple of hours later, take the boat, then dock it up again after having been gone for about 10 hours. That's all he saw though. He never did see who took the boat later that night only that it was gone this morning. The old man came down and was snooping around after the boat disappeared again and that's when he found the Sawyers convertible stashed in an old shed down the road a ways from the dock. He never thought to tie the two things together and didn't mention the boat to the police."

Connie felt deflated for a moment then realized that both of them had very important pieces of the puzzle. She filled Dug in on what she found and that she was pretty sure whoever was on that boat had bought the fish and crabs Richard was showing off as his catch of the day last night. Neither one of them had any idea who the other man and woman was, only that they were sure Richard had set up a very clever alibi. Dug was doing some calculations when he discovered the discrepancy on the boats radar/tracking system. He had wondered why the trip Richard showed him started about a ¼ mile out from the dock. Now he knew why. Richard had wiped the system clean of his first trip north and had programmed it to start again when the boat reached a certain point outside the Ocean City Marina. Whoever was manning the boat for him must have had instructions on where to take the boat and what to do.

Chapter 23

Jaffrey/Seattle/Boston/Ocean City

Karen drove Chase and Seville to the airport in Keene soon after they had discovered the situation with Susan. When they got to the private hanger they both said their good byes to Karen who seemed to be very worried and uptight. Seville had grabbed Karen and held her tight for a moment trying to assure her that they would all be ok and would be back soon. Chase followed suit and said to Karen "Listen kiddo, I need you to keep things hopping around here, Ronnie is going to need a lot of help today, be there for her, and keep in touch with me while I'm up in the air."

"That's easy for you to say Chase!" Karen said with half tears running from her eyes. "You two mean more to me than you know and you better get your sorry asses back here in a hurry."

"Karen, you are the last person on earth I would want to be coming after me. I'll be back" said Chase as he gently pushed her back in her car and waived goodbye. He turned to Seville, took her hand and walked her over to the twin prop waiting on the outside of the hanger. When they got to the stairs he turned her around and pulled her into him. Seville melted against his chest; head nuzzled into his shoulder, arms firmly around his waist. *Why does this man feel so familiar to me? My desire for him is far stronger than I could ever have imagined, and he makes me feel so safe and warm. I know him from somewhere, it's like we have been together before.*

Seville lifted her head and took Chase's head in her hands and tasted his lips for the first time. Their embrace left them both reeling and lightheaded, conjuring up an anticipation that would have to wait for another time.

"Goodbye Seville, you have everything I gave you?"

"Yes Chase" she said, her blue eyes penetrating into his spirit.

"*Everything*? He said once more with emphasis.

She looked at him with a sly grin and said "Yes Chase, *everything*. I hope you'll be ready to fetch your equipment when we get back!"

Chase looked into her eyes once more full of emotion and said "Be careful and come back in one piece."

"You too." She said and walked up the stairs and disappeared into the cabin.

He waited on the tarmac until her plane lifted off and turned south towards Maryland then climbed aboard Jonathan's specially configured Lear Jet for the long 6 hour flight to Seattle.

He had spent the first hour or so of the flight checking e-mails and sending off some notes to Ronnie, Karen, Louise, and Wesley with a few last minute dictums and suggestions regarding things to do today while he was away. He was not certain at all where things were going but he did feel like he was traveling in the right direction. He hoped the team down in Maryland was going to come up with some good stuff to keep Henry White and his goons occupied long enough for him to get things wrapped up in Seattle—God willing. After sending off the last e-mail he sank back into the large leather recliner and closed his eyes to rest. His thoughts went straight to Seville and in his minds eye he pulled up a picture of her standing at the bottom of the stairs of the plane at the airport. Her long silky black hair was hanging down almost to her waist and her smile was so sweet and genuine. The feelings that stirred inside were new yet not unfamiliar. He thought back over time and remembered the woman he had been with over the years. He loved woman, their softness, their gentle spirits, their warmth but he had never fallen in love with any of them. It had always been like his heart had been closed off somewhere along the line and he couldn't make that deep spiritual connection needed to take a relationship to the final level. In fact, it was Karen of all people who had come very close. Even though they had never been together, he had always felt a kinship to her and at times had been tempted to do something about it but something in the back of his mind kept telling him to wait.

At that moment he knew he had to go to that place both Ronni and Wesley had encouraged him to visit.

About 20 years ago, during a past life regression class he was taking with Ronnie as a teacher, and Wesley and his wife Ashley as fellow classmates, he had journeyed to a place filled with sunshine and warmth, but for some reason he had not been able to look any further. Ronnie and Wesley had been trying all these years to get him to go back to that place until one day the student became the teacher and advised them that when the time was right for him to understand that life he would know and then would fully open that door. He had visited many of his past lives over the years and was not afraid of the experience, but rather embraced them as a very important part of his growth in this life. This one life however, had something very different in it that was not meant to be discovered—until now.

"Hey John, are you guys still awake up there?" Chase said into a speaker on the side of his chair then heard some mock snoring coming back at him through the cabin speakers. "Thank God for auto pilot! I could use some real quiet time back here for about an hour, any of you have to go to the bathroom or need coffee?"

"Naw, we're all set Chase. You have a nice nap and let us know when you get up."

"Thanks guys" as he switched the speaker to the off position.

"Clair, please pull up the past life meditation sequence"

Almost immediately the screen in front of him went blank and soft flute music began filling the cabin accompanied by sounds of birds and flowing water. Chase settled back in his chair, put the recliner up, stretched his legs, and began relaxing his entire body to the point of near numbness as the recording of Ronnie's voice came on and started guiding him on a journey he would never forget.

The sky is a deep warm blue with small wisps of white clouds floating gently on the mid summer breeze. As you look out into the distance all you can see for miles is a bed of beautiful wild flowers glowing with bright summer colors of blue, orange, white, purple, yellow, and red. The flowers are moving in rhythm with the wind creating a sensation of something that is alive, joined, and thriving all around you. The warmth of the sun beating down upon your face feels like hope and joy and radiates down into every fiber of your body.

As you begin walking through the field, you suddenly become aware of all the wonders Mother Earth has created and placed in your path on this marvelous journey. Dozens of butterflies dance across the tops of the flowers being tossed further along towards their destination by the breeze. Bees of all shapes and sizes enjoy the cycle of life, tasting the sweet nectars of the flowers as they pass from one wonderful blossom to the next.

A hawk stands still in the air as her spread wings dig into Mother Earth's breath blowing from across the great valley towards the mountain ranges she calls home. The faint sounds of a tiny field mouse ring in your ears as he scurries for shelter having sensed the Hawks silent flight above. A doe and her twin fawns raise their heads in alarm at your approaching footsteps and after catching your scent and feeling the joy and happiness emanating from deep within you drop their heads back into the succulent new grass shoots coming up through the soft warm summer soil.

As you continue on, the path you follow turns into the forest and you begin walking up a slight incline along a well worn and traveled trail. Forest creatures begin to emerge as the trail goes deeper and deeper into the darkened woods. You come upon a stream that is gently flowing down from the steep hill ahead of you. As you approach the hill, the most magnificent set of granite steps, covered with vines and moss reach up to the top of the hill and wind out of view. You can see and hear the birds all around you; squirrels and chip monks dance through the trees and scurry along the forest floor delighted by your presence in their space.

You begin the sharp climb up the stairs and notice monoliths with ancient markings on them peering at you through the dense brush and you wonder who might have left these giant stone carvings behind and what they mean. At the top of the stairs you pass through an archway into a small courtyard and you step out into another field, this time green with newly sprouted wheat swaying in the breeze. As you continue on over a ridge you gaze upon a large lake that runs for miles in either direction and see a small pier reaching into the water, a one man boat tethered to the wooden structure, waiting for its next passenger. As you seat yourself in the firmly made boat, the sails magically fill with the warm summer wind and you begin gliding across the shimmering mountain water. After a few moments you can clearly see the other side and view another pier, this time leading into a large cave mouth carved out of the side of the mountain. As you dock the boat you can see huge oak doors set into the entrance of the cave, each one hand carved with beautiful scenes from the heavens. The doors beckon you to open them to continue your journey into the past. As you walk through the doors the bright sunlight begins to dim and the flickering light of torches illuminates the inside of the cave. At the far end a single door silently opens and you continue walking into the next chamber which turns out to be a very long hallway with many doors on either side, each door representing a past life.

Ronni's voice begins to fade as Chase becomes aware of his destination. The door he needs to open is familiar to him as he has passed it many times. He walks up to the door and slowly pulls up the wooden latch holding it in place and steps in with his eyes closed. After a moment he looks down and sees the small darkly tanned feet of a young boy standing in the sand, water rushing around his ankles. Looking up he is overcome by the bright sunlight beating down on his partially clad body and looks out over the bright blue Mediterranean Ocean. The waves are light blue and green and gently wash the white sand beach stretching for hundreds of yards along the massive cliff walls. Not far away a bright colored tent rests upon a flat and he can see his parents sitting in chairs enjoying the afternoon sun and entertaining some merchants selling fine linens. His Mother keeps a keen eye on her small son as he dances in the waves. He feels free inside, no cares or worries and the whole world around him is new and full of adventure and excitement.

In a flash he is older, perhaps ten, and playing swords with some friends in and around the rocky hillside. The play is serious and he can feel the sting of the wooden swords as they graze him here and there in mock battle. The stings cause him to become the aggressor and soon he has his mates pinned to the ground begging for mercy, blood trickling down the forehead of his best friend and the other nursing a swollen shoulder. He can feel the exhilaration of battle and victory, his proud ego swelling like the moon torn tides. Off to the side a small group of girls watches the boys, pretending to be uninterested in their childish games but never the less watching him in awe as he bests two of the most popular boys in their small sea side town. He looks over at the girls and notices Phoenicia peeking at him from behind an outcropping, her long black hair and olive skin gleaming in the light. He knows that she will be his wife someday and seeing her there charges him back up as he encourages his wounded mates to joust just one more time.

Yet another time flashes into his mind, this time he is at the war academy, 15 years old and already standing close to 6 feet tall, his muscles beginning to form into the solid mass that will catapult him to the top of his class in the coming year. He has gained the favor of his teachers and drill masters and they keep him in the forefront, driving him harder and longer than most of his classmates. His extraordinary talents transcend the physical as he is a natural leader and instinctively adept at stealth and strategy on the battlefield, consistently besting the academies most experienced soldiers and commanders in mock battlefield simulations.

All of a sudden he is walking on the beach with Phoenicia. She has blossomed into the most beautiful woman on the island and they are madly in love. He is going away soon and they spend the hot summer day near the water, dreaming of their future, frolicking in the waves, teasing their fleshly desires, and making plans for their marriage when he returns from his first campaign.

Phoenicia is now with child, arms and hands wrapped around the underside of her full term belly. She is waiting for him to return once again, praying that he will bear witness to the birth of their first son. In the distance a lone cloud of dust comes over the ridge with a rider bearing down on the town with obvious haste. He is dressed in full armament and riding a tall grey stallion that adds to his large stature. He can see her in the distance and whips up the speed of his battle exhausted mount. His returning embrace is full of passion and warmth, and although a hardened soldier now, tears of love and joy run down his bruised and scarred face as he holds Phoenicia like he will never let her go.

Years have passed and he is returning yet again from another campaign. His flesh is still hard and solid yet he looks tired and haggard, deep running scars covering much of his visible skin. From afar he can see his villa amongst the trees, workers scurrying about in the vegetable gardens and tending the farm. He can see Phoenicia standing on the great terrace looking up at his approach, a smile creasing her aging beauty, her never dying love still shining through her eyes. A group of teenage boys are jousting with carved wooden swords on the side of the nearby hill and the young girls are making busy, setting the tables for a late afternoon meal.

Another flash: The field before him is immense, two powerful armies lined up for a final battle, winner takes all. He is atop his stallion, all eyes upon him as he sends hand signals to his legion of archers who begin their deadly rain upon the advancing column. The long day begins as carnage and death rule the battle. Nightfall is now near and through the dust and death he can smell victory closing in. One last signal sent far to the north brings a thousand fresh Calvary charging over the hillside into the tired and torn field of honor. He had kept them well in the rear so that spies would not count them before the battle and he can see the horror and fear on the opposing faces as they feel the ground rumble from the massive advance. His infantry surge back to life as they see the face of doom on their enemies and the intensity of battle rises to a peak. Victory had been won at that very moment and he could have taken the army in surrender but his orders had been very clear that this battle was to end the war once and for all, leaving no troops for future resurgence. He felt a great sadness wash over him for although these men were his sworn enemy they had earned his respect over the years and they would be missed.

A family gathering is in full swing, he is no longer dressed in uniform but rather the robes of a politician. A foreboding is in the back of his mind as he surveys the fruits of his life before him. Phoenicia, ever regal and beautiful, masterfully directs the servants to attend their guests; their grown children and grand children cover the grounds with laughter and play. They steal a glance at each other, the warmth and passion of their youth still fresh despite the tolls his military life had imposed on them. A feeling of deep gratitude washes over him in that moment and once again soldiers tears well up in the back of his eyes. In the distance his keen ears hear the approaching horses over the sounds of the gathering. He takes one more look at his wife and disappears into the villa and out the front to meet his uninvited but expected guests. There is a small troop of soldiers and a commander of the newly formed army approaching. He had been lobbying the people to stay at peace, and to let at least one generation pass through life without knowing the ravages of war. He was born a warrior, not a politician, and his labors in the chambers had not been of equal success. The Commander dismounts from his horse and without hesitation or remorse approaches him and plunges his blade deep into his heart. He can feel the cold of steel and imagines the deaths of hundreds of men at *his* hands over the years. He shows no fear nor does he attempt to fight knowing that his benefactors had given their oath that his family would be spared and allowed to thrive. His last thoughts were of Phoenicia, his life and his love, and as he fell to his knees, death by the sword, he swore by the Gods they would be together again.

Chase awoke from his deep trance, sweat running down his face, right hand intensely clutched over his heart. The picture of Seville or Phoenicia was still fresh and vivid in his mind as was the pain from the sword. He deepened his breathing and relaxed his tensed muscles to the point where his body and mind settled. He felt through his shirt and rubbed a birthmark that was three inches long knowing now that he had carried that scar through dozens of lives. He looked at the clock on the wall and discovered that he had been under for almost three hours. He closed his eyes again and fell gently asleep.

*****

With a weary smile on his face the man scrolled through screen after screen of information. *I wonder just how all of this is going to turn out* he thought as his smile turned into a wicked grin. Chase was now on his way to Seattle but for different reasons than he had planned. According to the computer system Susan Kincaid had gone missing and that had caused a premature trip by Chase to the West Coast; *Very*

Interesting. Now he would have to rethink his plans. Originally he had hoped everything would be focused on the Lumber Jack and that Seattle would not get caught up the maelstrom. *Got to learn to go with the flow!*

Pressing the speed dial on the phone he waited patiently while the phone rang and rang.

"Yes" the female voice said on the other end.

"It's me. I wanted to update you on a change of plans."

"But I was ready to begin the ritual for the Lumber Jack" she said in protest.

"And so you should have been, but, there has been a new development and I am going to need you to table that for now."

With hesitation and frustration in her voice she said "Very well, you're the boss"

"Yes, that's true. Now, Chase is in route to Seattle very unexpectedly. I was hoping that we were going to have the final confrontation with him soon but it looks like we have to wait until he gets back. Also, Seville is on her way to Maryland and I wanted to make sure that she was part of the final plan as well.

"Ok, so what would you like me to be doing?

"Well, it looks like Veronica is still meeting with her group today in Jaffrey. I want you to tap into that meeting somehow and let me know what they are working on."

"But that's what I was getting ready to do anyway!"

"Yes, but for a different reason. Instead of just gathering information, I want you to figure out a way to fuck with them. I think Veronica is scared of you even though she doesn't know who you are yet."

"But she does, she just doesn't know it!"

"Right, but I want you to make a major impact on that meeting. Even if you can't mess with her make sure you mess with anyone in that meeting that can be messed with. As a matter of fact, plant as many false images with them as you can."

"Like what?" all of sudden getting interested.

"I am sure that they will be doing some work for both Chase and Seville today instead of working on the Lumber Jack. Chase won't be in Seattle for a while yet but Seville is just arriving and they might just start to get a read on our friend Richard Fox. Mess with them to the point that they think Richard is some kind of Samaritan and that he couldn't possibly be the one doing the Devil killings."

"That will be easy, what about the stuff in Seattle?"

"I'm not sure yet. Let me think about that for a while, just concentrate on Maryland for now and the psychic group. Is there any more on Wesley? I want you to make sure that you have a better handle on him. I am not so sure that he is the weak link you make him out to be."

"I have been working on him. He comes and goes but like I said to you before, I don't get the feeling that he's terribly engaged in this thing psychically."

"Try harder; my instincts are in high gear on him. Put someone else on him if you have to."

"Ok, like I said you're the boss."

Hanging up the phone the man went back to his computer. Toggling through some screens he brought up all the data on the Maryland Devil and immersed himself into Dug, Connie, Richard, and now Seville.

*****

Connie sat in the Beetle on the edge of the private airport in Rehoboth Delaware as the light drizzle ran off her windshield. Dug had asked her earlier if she wouldn't mind driving the 45 minuets to pick up Seville as he wanted to do some more snooping around that might require actions not befitting an FBI agent. She had given him the look when he mentioned this then smiled knowing that Dug wouldn't do anything that might ever compromise the case should it end up in court and let him have his way.

She had been waiting about 15 minuets when the Serial Connections plane landed and headed over to the hanger where she was parked. She had been apprehensive about meeting her since she learned that Seville had jumped ship on the Providence PD and joined up with Chase and his team. She had also been briefed by Dug about what Bob Fellows and Henry White had pulled and was not looking forward to another situation where trust was going to be an issue. Glancing over the wet tarmac she saw the most stunning woman she had ever seen coming down the short stairway from the plane. *Wow!* She thought as she watched Seville glide down the stairs and begin walking over toward the Beetle.

Connie got out of the car and met Seville with her hand stretched out and introduced herself. Seville took her hand and reciprocated the gesture and the two got back into the car for the drive to Ocean City.

"Gosh, I haven't been down here since I was a kid" Seville said, trying to break the ice with Connie for the long drive. "We came down here one summer from Connecticut to stay at the beach. I miss the French fries and vinegar most of all."

Connie chuckled at the thought. For some reason when people thought about Ocean City Maryland and the Delaware sea shore they mostly thought of the local French fries which, quite frankly were not that remarkable, but putting vinegar on them, and the special local salt made them unforgettable.

"Well, if we get the chance we'll have to hit the Boardwalk and see if any of the places are still open" Connie offered. "Dug sent his apologies for not meeting you but he thought he could get some ground covered snooping around while we were driving."

"That's ok Connie. Actually, you and I are kinda the new kids on the block and I was hoping we could get some time together anyway."

"Me too Seville; I wanted to let you know that I think it was a bold move to join up with the Serial Connections team the way you did. I don't think I could ever quit the Bureau even though there are days when walking away wouldn't be a bad idea."

"Well, I don't know if they told you that I had actually put in my notice over three months ago and have been working on an at will basis until the Lumber Jack was caught. I really didn't know why I had resigned in the first place until this morning and I guess I am still reeling from the decision."

"That's awesome Seville. I don't know anyone up there except Dug but I get a good feeling about Chase and the team. I guess I am a little envious because it would be great to work on these cases with a lot more latitude than I have with the FBI."

"I know the feeling Connie. I've spent the last day with them and I already feel like they are family. I also have a great deal of respect for their methods and codes. Even though they aren't an official agency, Chase has built a great deal of ethic into Serial Connections and I admire the entire staff and how they run the business."

"So you haven't met Dug yet?"

"Not in person anyway; we were introduced over the video conferencing system last night. He seems like a nice guy who knows what the hell he's doing."

"He is a good guy. Yesterday when we met he did a great job pulling an end run around me." And she quickly told Seville about how he ditched her at the High School field and his Clarice Starling routine in the house.

Seville was laughing hysterically at the story and said "I can't wait to meet him Connie. Tell me about you and Henry White." Seville said all of a sudden taking Connie completely off guard.

"Tell you what Seville? I report to Henry on a dotted line basis, don't care for the man at all, and have very little respect for his agenda's and the way he runs roughshod over everyone in his path."

"I can understand the way you feel about him Connie but I was referring to your current relationship with Henry regarding the Maryland Devil and the fact that he knows you're hooked up with us."

Connie let out a big sigh and said very defensively "Look Seville, I still work for the FBI and as long as I do I have to play the game. Henry has called me three times since I got hooked up with Dug and is trying to shove his agenda down my throat and I don't like it one little bit."

Seville took a few minutes and carefully told Connie about the incidents with Bob Fellows and Henry the day before. "You have to understand Connie that we are just being cautious. We want to bring in these bad guys. That's all we do and we don't have any other agenda's. We were working with the FBI supposedly as a team, shared a great deal of information, and got really burned. The truth is a very dangerous serial is still out there because of what happened. It's not right."

"I understand Seville. I hope you guys trust me, I really do, because bringing in this Richard Fox guy is the only agenda I have. I have been giving lip service to Henry as much as possible and will have to take my lumps with him once it's over. I haven't told him anything that you guys are doing that is going to compromise the efforts of Serial Connections or anyone on the team. I hope you can believe that."

"Chase and I discussed it again this morning and agreed that giving you the benefit of the doubt was the right thing to do. In this business we either have to trust our partners explicitly or not at all. You have our trust and you know that that means we are putting our lives in your hands. Don't let us down like the other guys did."

"Thanks Seville. I won't, and I want you to know that I would jump in front of a bullet for you guys."

"Hopefully that won't be necessary but you should know that we would do the same for you."

Seville looked up and noticed that they were on the main drag in Ocean City now and started to get her head back into game.

"Where are we meeting Dug?"

"Over near Richard Fox's office. He was going to snoop around a little at his office, condo, and near the dock. I am supposed to call him when we get to 90th street and he will meet us out on the main drag. Actually we are close enough now to call" and she pulled out her cell phone and punched in Dugs number.

Seville was staring out the window while Connie worked the phone trying to see if she remembered any of the buildings or miniature golf places dotting both sides of the street.

"That's funny" Connie said. His phone keeps going right to voice mail. I wonder what's up."

"He could be on a tail. Maybe he ran into Richard and is following him. The first thing I would do is shut down the phone."

"True, but I just keep mine on vibrate and you know what? I think Dug did too. He got two calls this morning while we were eating breakfast and I didn't hear the phone either time."

"Then let's just head up to the end of Main Street and walk around for a while. I am sure he'll surface soon enough. Hey, maybe we can sneak out to the boardwalk and get some fries?"

"Yeah that sounds good to me" said Connie taking a left to find a parking spot off near the boardwalk. When they got out of the car Seville took a long draw of the crisp ocean air into her lungs and let out a big sigh. "I love the smell of the ocean Connie it makes me feel so alive."

"I know what you mean. Come on I can smell grease coming up from the south. If it's the place I'm thinking of they have the best fries of all."

As the women headed down the long side street towards the beach the smell of the salt air became more pronounced and the sound of waves crashing not too far in the distance began to overpower the sounds of the car traffic behind them. Sea gulls floated in the air near the old wooden boardwalk waiting for the tourists to drop a piece of fried dough or some other piece of food so they could swoop in fearlessly to fight over the spoils. The smell of the boardwalk was mixed with the faint smell of wood and tar used to keep the piles and planks from rotting in the ever present harshness of sun, rain, and salt. Connie went up to the counter to get some fries and Seville walked over to the edge of the boardwalk and leaned her body against the top of the rail and soaked in the beauty of the day, the long slow rollers and white caps visible as far as the eye could see. As she looked out over the beach she got the feeling that she had seen this exact view before and tried calling forth memories of her visit here when she was a child.

The she heard Connie say behind her "Richards's office is the one right over your left shoulder."

Seville turned around and looked up at the second floor over the shops and her eyes were drawn to a set of windows. Then she recalled the session with Clair which showed the view of the boardwalk, the beach, and the ocean and realized that it was that picture she was seeing, not one from long ago. As she looked up at the windows she got that sense of foreboding that signaled to her something was wrong.

"Connie, I need to call the office for a minute, save me some of those fries." And she pulled out the phone Karen had giver her and hit the speed dial.

"Serial Connections, how may I help you?" she heard Karen on the other end.

"Karen, it's Seville, I am down in Ocean City with Connie and I have this bad feeling about Dug. Can you put Louise on the phone please?"

"Hey, nice to hear from you too" Karen said back with a slight edge. "How was the trip down?"

"The trip was great Karen. Listen sweetie, something's not right down here, can you please patch me into Louise. I will call later to catch you up on stuff."

"Sorry Seville, Louise is coming right up" Karen said and then scolded herself, forgetting that they were all in pretty dangerous places right now and she needed to be a little more serious.

"Hey Seville, what's up?" she heard Louise say on the other end.

"Hi Louise, I just got to the beach and we were supposed to hook up with Dug but he is not here and is not answering his phone. Is there anything you can do to help us out?"

"Sure, hold on." Louise said as she turned to one of her monitors and started stroking the keyboard. "Shit, Dugs electronics are not turned on. He's not showing up on the screen. Wait a minute" and she hit another button and Seville could hear the sound of Dug's voice mail through the open line. "Your right, he's not answering his phone either. Let me try one more thing." She said while Seville waited patiently still staring up at the windows on the second floor.

"I just ran the log on Dugs equipment. It seems the unit is turned off and the last GPS signal it sent out is within 4 blocks of where you are transmitting from right now. Also the log says that the battery on the unit had a full charge and was not malfunctioning. He must have turned it off for some reason—which is not like Dug by the way."

"Shit" Seville said. "Louise, I know Chase doesn't like to use the transmitters unless absolutely necessary but can you do a quick ping on Dug's. I have a really bad feeling about this."

"Sorry Seville, Dug was the last holdout on the personal transmitters. He doesn't believe in having anything electronic planted on or in his body, which is one reason his Data Gator is usually turned on."

"Can you try to pinpoint the last location? Four square blocks is a lot of ground to cover?"

"Sorry again, unless the units are hand calibrated for a specific search they are set on the default area which is what we got."

"Shit, Shit, Shit" Seville said in rapid succession. "Louise, is Ronnie there with her team?"

"Sure is, I will keep playing with the system Seville, if I get anything I will call immediately. Hold on."

"Seville this is Ronnie, what's going on?"

"Hey Ronnie, are you working with your team right now?"

"Yes, but so far we haven't gotten a thing. It looks to me like a whole bunch of psychic garbage. I think some one is really playing games with us here!"

Seville quickly filled Ronnie in on what was going on and then said "Would you mind keeping the group focused on this for a while? Connie and I are going to check around to see what we can find. My phone is on; call me as soon as you get anything at all."

"Will do, and Seville?"

"What Ronnie?"

"Be careful—real careful!"

Seville hung up her phone and turned to Connie who had been listening to the conversation "Connie, we need to split up and start looking around. Do you know all the locations of Richards haunts?"

Connie pulled out her notebook and a pen and started to make a diagram of the vicinity. "This is where we are." she said and circled the point with her pen. "Here is Richards's condo, number 16 Bay Street, second floor. Here is the dock and the boat, the boats name is the 'Redemption'. Why don't you go down and check around the condo, also on the corner of that street is a small bar called the 'Dune' which Richard has been known to hang out in. I am going to go up and check out his office, look around for his car, then head over to the marina. Why don't we meet at the boat in about 30 minutes?"

"Good plan Connie, give me your cell phone number and here is mine."

"Great, see you in a while" as Seville headed back out to the street and Connie made her way up the boardwalk to the entrance of the rental offices.

*****

The psychic team had been working for about an hour and had gotten lots of hits regarding the Maryland Devil. Ronnie had a feeling that something was amiss and had kept quiet just watching and listening. Generally speaking the information coming over the psychic channel was pretty tame. It almost painted Richard Fox as a Church going Saint in the Community. They even got hits from his child hood, him and his Mother walking to Church or sitting on the pews during a service.

After the call from Seville, Ronnie told the class to take a break and went over to a woman sitting by herself in the corner of the room, gently tapping on some hand made drums. Cori, a Native American from Vermont had come down at Ronnie's request. She was well known in the Serial Connections circle but was not a member of the team at her own request. Ronnie invited her down because they were close friends and because of Cori's very unique intuitive powers and had a feeling that she was going to be able to help break through this psychic wall someone was putting up.

The rhythm of the drums was slow and searching, her beats purposeful as she reached out into the other world for answers through her Spirit Guides. Her eyes were half open and the eyelids were fluttering slowly almost in beat with the drums. As Ronnie approached her and sat quietly next to where she sat on the floor Cori began to speak softly.

"I am walking through a place that is dark and wet. The walls are covered with a moss that is old, ancient, and waiting. I can feel the energy of a circle nearby. The energy is familiar, like I have sat in it's presence before. I can barely see the circle in the shrouded mist that is flowing from the source of the moisture in this place. Three figures are gathered around a talisman, focusing and concentrating on things that make my stomach churn. As I reach out with my energy I can feel that one of them, a woman, is leading the ritual and has become the beacon for the gathering energies. I can see her focusing her desires to some place far in the distance with great intention. I can feel the excitement of her own desire, for the task they are completing is filling her with enormous satisfaction and gratitude. There is a forth presence in this place. It is lurking off to the side; its breath is heavy with anticipation. I cannot feel its energies though as a great shield has been molded to it both for protection and for stealth. The circle is done with their work for now. I can see the figures, like reptiles, slithering back through the mist to the dark places from which they came."

Cori became silent as the beating of the drums slowed and the tempo became one with the beating of her heart. At last her eyes fluttered open again and she became aware of Ronni and her surroundings.

"Ronnie, I have seen the people that would stop you from your good works. They are not bad people but rather misguided. The one who was leading the circle is someone you know! She is familiar to you and vice versa. It is her motives that I find the most interesting. Her agenda is not the same as the other one. He is evil, she is not. She is doing his work so that she can get to you Ronnie. You are her goal."

"Can you tell who it is?"

"No, she too was shrouded in a cloak of stealth. I was feeling her energies after she projected them out into the world."

"Could she feel you Cori?"

"No, I was in the outer realm, just at the edge where I could see but not be seen. By tapping into the energy she was releasing she would not have been able to feel my intrusion."

"Are they Wicca?"

"No Ronnie, they're like us but they are feeding off the desire for gain instead of the desire for Love."

"Turning to the Dark Side?" Ronnie said with a slight chuckle.

"Yes! You're almost right. Except they feel that what they are doing is building strength that will someday be used for good. They have been misled by the other one."

"Time is dwindling Cori, any thoughts on what we can do?"

"I do have some thoughts but I need a quiet place to go over things. In the meantime I would keep on with your group like nothing is wrong."

"Yes, I agree. I will meet you down in the courtyard after we're finished here."

*****

Connie had given Richard Fox's office building as good a sweep as she could without a warrant and decided that he was not anywhere on the premises so she headed back outside and started the 4 block walk across the peninsula to the marina to check out the Temptation. The rain was moderate and the fresh ocean air swept much needed energy into her lungs. She hadn't been that worried about Dug until now. He would not have been over an hour late and definitely would not have turned off his electronics. She was walking down the street looking at the old buildings from the original part of Ocean City and noticing the eastern seaboard architecture of wood and clapboards when she happened by an old two story garage that looked like it was used for utility trucks. She glanced at the building with a certain interest when a voice behind her called out.

"Hello Officer! Nice day for a walk."

Recognizing the voice Connie spun around quickly and carefully to face a man in a bright yellow rain coat standing not 10 feet away.

"Mr. Fox, fancy meeting you here. I didn't notice you coming down the street." She said thinking that he must have just popped out of the alleyway between the garage and the office building next to it.

"Nothing fancy about it, I live in this neighborhood, but you…"

"Come on Richard, you know why we're here." She looked to her right at the garage then back at Richard Fox.

"Well, here I am what can I do for you today? I assume you checked everything out from last night?"

Connie's mental wheels started spinning as she felt goose bumps all over her. "Sure did Richard, as a matter of fact I have some questions for you regarding your alibi and some of the information you gave us."

"Like I said last night, anything I can do to help Officer!"

Just as Richard finished speaking, a large truck came barreling down the narrow street causing Connie to divert her attention for just a split second. When she looked back at Richard he was gone. She quickly looked around but the only place he could have gone was back into the alley. Reaching behind her back she slowly ducked underneath the glass windows of the garage and pulled out her service pistol. Carefully she worked her way to the corner of the building and peeked around the wall into the alleyway. About halfway down there was a staircase leading up to the office building on the left and a side door into the garage on the right. Making her way down the wet, roughly paved surface, she nosed up to the door and found that it was open just a crack.

"Richard?" She said through the opening. "I just want to talk to you; there is nothing to be worried about!"

But there was no reply and no sounds coming from inside the building so she jumped across the doorway and crouched on the other side and listened for another minute. Still hearing no sounds from within Connie stretched her right leg around the outer door frame and nudged the door open with her foot. Now she could at least see into the front part of the garage. It appeared to be empty from the front to the middle. Keeping in her crouch, she moved quickly inside the building and immediately turned her body from right to left, gun out, and swept the room. Sill nothing; as her eyes adjusted to the near dark she could see the wet footsteps on the floor coming from outside and heading towards the rear of the large industrial size garage. As she followed the tracks she saw that they led to a staircase that went up along the back wall.

Suddenly out of instinct she looked up but too late. She had just enough time to discern that the floor of the upstairs did not cover the entire area and a large sandbag came crashing down on her face and head. The impact forced her to drop her weapon and all she could see were bright blue/white lights dancing in her vision as she fell to the floor in severe pain. She lay there for a few moments trying to reach around on the floor with her arms to retrieve her gun when she heard footsteps coming down the stairs and approaching her across the concrete floor. Survival instincts coming alive she started rolling her body away from the direction of the footsteps hoping that she would roll on top of her gun. The very second her vision started to return something covered her nose that had an awful smell and the blue/white lights turned to black.

Looking down at Connie, Richard Fox felt the grin on his face. *This was way too easy* he thought thanks to his new friend sending him messages regarding his adversaries. He looked around and saw Connie's 9mm on the floor, went over to pick it up, then went back to get his prey. He grabbed her legs and began pulling her along the floor to the stairs in the back and then with great effort was able to get her to the top before he needed to rest for a minute. He looked over at Dug who was strapped into a chair, gagged, and just starting to wake up. On the right side of his forehead a bloody "R" dripped down the side of his face. *This one might be my last but it's definitely going to be my best* he thought as he picked up Connie again and pulled her over to a waiting cot sitting right next to Dug.

*****

"Nope, haven't seen him in a couple of days" the bartender of the Dune said to Seville as he handed back a picture of Richard Fox. "Hey Gordon, have you seen Richie around today?"

Another "Nope" floated back across the room from a man engrossed in the afternoon news.

"Thanks" said Seville as she headed back out into the drizzle. Getting her bearings she headed off to the west towards the Marina to hook up with Connie. *I hope Dug is ok.* She shook from a combination of the damp cold and the thought that Dug had somehow met up with Richard Fox and had not fared well. As she walked along the street her thoughts began to push inward and something started to come into her mind. At first she just thought she was having a waking dream but the visions that came into her head were much more vivid than she had ever experienced. Losing her physical senses she stopped on the sidewalk and grabbed onto a staircase railing for support.

Letting her body go she felt a tightening of her muscle groups and could feel a strength in her that was many times greater than her natural strength. In her vision she was looking out over a vast canopy of green with snow capped mountains in the distance. She was perched high up on a stone structure that she now realized was a small pyramid that had a large bowl on a pedestal in which flames shot out on one side and two large monoliths about 8 feet high on the other side. In between the two a steep staircase ran down to a lush floor of wild grass below. A man, or more like a peasant, was standing in between the pillars, both arms tied to either side, a look of shear terror filling his face as he looked at her across the platform.

As quickly as it had begun it faded and Seville continued holding onto the railing with a death grip as she tried desperately to regain her composure. *What in the fuck was that!* Seville screamed into her mind. She sat down on the damp steps and tried to figure out what was going on but couldn't for the life of her gain a connection with what had just happened. After a few moments she got up and continued her walk to the marina. On the way she kept processing what had just assaulted her. At first she was thinking about what Ronnie and Chase had said about someone planting stuff in their minds but after a while she began to feel like it was a part of her somehow. As terrifying as the vision and feelings were they had felt comfortable at least at the level of familiarity. Soon she found herself walking down the old, wet, gangplank at the marina looking for the Redemption and Connie. Following Connie's directions she soon came across Richards's boat. It was very impressive and she estimated that it must be worth a few hundred thousand dollars.

She clamored onto the boat and began looking for anyone or anything that might help. As she went up to the bridge she put her hand on the back of the captain's chair and suddenly had another vision of the man tied between the two stone monoliths on top of what she was feeling was a sacrificial alter. At first she tried to withdraw from the vision then for some reason began to embrace it, getting in touch with the feeling, the emotions, and the reason for the event. As she stared at the man she had the same sensations as before with her muscles beginning to tighten up and could feel a great deal of strength flowing through her body. She was feeling angry at the man like he had done something terribly wrong and that she was the one who was going to meter out his judgment. She felt herself begin walking towards him and as she did his face began to contort even more to the point where he looked like his head would pop from the strain. Again the visions stopped. This time though, Seville had gained a level of acceptance with the vision. She actually felt as if she was a man in that scene and that she was about to do something terrible to the peasant.

Enough of that she thought as she kept making her way around the boat finding nothing at all. Worried, she picked up her cell phone and dialed Connie's cell. It went right to voice mail which meant she had turned it off. Why would she have done that? Picking out another number she called Karen again.

"Karen, it's me. I need to talk to Ronnie real quick!"

This time Karen cut the pleasantries and said "Hold on Seville, I will patch you right through."

"Ronnie here" she heard through the phone in a moment.

"Ronnie its Seville, I'm at the marina and Dug is still missing and now it looks like Connie has gone missing too. I have covered all the areas we had talked about and no one is around. Were there any other places that came up in the sessions for this area that I have forgotten about?"

"Hold on" she heard Ronnie say "I am pulling up the case file on Clair right now. Seville, I want you to be very careful down there. Do you think we should call someone in to help you?"

"I've already thought of that Ronnie. I don't think it will help just yet but believe me if I think anyone is in danger I will call for reinforcements faster than you can say speed dial."

"Good to hear. Ok, here it is." Ronnie spoke to Seville over the phone and described Richards's office building, his condo, the marina, his boat, and then said "What about this garage hit that came up. Has anyone figured out what that is yet?"

"That's right!" Seville said into the phone. "Connie didn't mention any garage a while ago when we were splitting up the places we were going to cover. Help me out a little Ronnie, there must be a dozen garages around here. Any idea where it might be?"

"Can you stay put for a little while? I need to do a little work and I'll call you right back."

"I'll be here" she said as the phone disconnected and she put it back in her pocket, walked over to the railing of the boat gazing out over the cloudy, rainy day. *Should I tell Ronnie about what just happened?* She was thinking, trying to remember as much as she could about the man on the platform, her, and the mountain temple she had been on. *They felt more like memories to me than anything else. Funny, I felt as though I was a man not a woman for just a brief second. If that is what it feels like to be a man! I also felt like I was full of rage at the man strung up between the posts and that I was going to take that rage out on him.* She felt a brief vibration coming from her pocket and pulled out her phone.

"Yes"

"Ok Seville, here is what we have. There is a garage. The color is white and it has two oversize doors on it that would allow large trucks to get in and out. We are not sure exactly where it is but think it is within 1 or 2 blocks of Richards's office. Going to his office it would be on the right hand side. That's all we got."

"That should be all I need Ronnie. You guys are great. Ronnie, I need to talk to you about something after I find these guys. I just had two very vivid psychic episodes that came out of nowhere. They scared the shit out of me and at first I thought it was whoever is messing with your team. But the more I think about it and after the second one it feels more like a past experience. It felt like I was remembering."

"That's odd Seville. A past life experience usually comes out during a carefully planned session with a counselor or psychic. What were you thinking about when this happened?"

"I really wasn't thinking Ronnie. All I can remember is that I was getting angry about Connie and Dug disappearing and projecting that anger on Richard Fox. That and the feelings about all the people he may have killed."

"Anything else?"

"Yea, I felt like I was a man Ronnie, I mean I could feel the muscles in my body actually getting stronger and I could feel things about me that were definitely not feminine in nature."

"Humm, you're right Seville. When you get back up here I want to work with you on that. I think what's happening is that all of a sudden you have been thrown into a pool of psychic activity, which you're not used too, and this may simply be your inner psychic coming awake after a long time of being dormant."

"I'm not sure I like it Ronnie!"

"I can appreciate that Seville. Without the proper training the psychic self can be a terrifying place to be. But like I said, you're in the right place now, and over time we will train you to manage and control that psychic self to the point where you won't be able to imagine ever having lived without it."

"If you say so. Hey, have you heard from Chase?"

"Not yet as a matter of fact. He should be landing in Seattle within the next hour or so. When he checks in I will tell him you said hello. You had better get going and don't forget to call the locals if you run into trouble."

"I will. Thanks Ronnie. I'll check back as soon as I can." And Ronnie disconnected on the other end. Seville looked back out over the water, calm, yet dotted with the disruptions of a million rain drops and the picture of the man attached to the pillars came back in her mind, taunting her, and suddenly reminding her of Richard Fox, his face actually taking the place of the one in her memories. Without warning the feeling of rage began to swell inside her again, and an anxiousness and desperation was born into her thoughts that caused her to thoughtlessly turn and begin the walk towards Richard's office on the other side of the peninsula.

The rain had picked up and Seville walked at an even, determined pace covering a couple of blocks, carefully studying each building with her eyes and her senses when suddenly up ahead the garage came into view. There was no doubt in her mind that this was the place. She also had the feeling that Dug, Connie, *and* Richard were inside. She just knew it, and she also knew that Connie and Dug were in a great deal of trouble. Instinctively she pulled out her Glock, slowed her pace, and began reaching out with every ounce of energy trying to feel the people and the place. Approaching the front of the building she carefully took a look through one of the windows but it was too dark inside too see anything clearly. Stepping back from the building she could not see any lights on and there were no windows upstairs so she decided to go down the ally to check things out. Walking around the side and then in back of the garage she could feel the rage quickening inside her. As she walked around the third corner to the other side the door came into view and she found herself putting her pistol back in the holster and just walking right into the first floor level. Looking around into the near blackness a soft white glow came from over her head and she was overwhelmed with a sensation similar to the last two episodes but much more powerful. Her entire body started to spasm, her sight became blurry and then turned to darkness.

Chapter 24

Seattle/Ocean City

"Chase!" the pilot yelled at him through the open doorway to the jet parked at the private landing strip about 15 miles south east of Seattle. "We have Wesley on the video system; He say's its urgent."

Almost at his car Chase stopped, turned around, and headed back to the jet with a quick pace. He couldn't remember the last time Wesley was urgent about anything and the thought immediately had him worried. He doubled up the stairs and rushed back into the cabin facing the large screen on the inside bulkhead. There he saw a split screen with Wesley, Ronnie, and Dug each occupying a section, all of them sporting looks of both excitement and something he couldn't quite peg. Looking at Dug he could see blood stains on his sweater and some kind of wound on his forehead. He looked a little white but he seemed to have his wits about him. Before anyone could say a word to him he blurted out to Dug.

"Dug, what happened, is everything alright? Where's Seville?" But before Dug could answer Wesley cut them both off.

"Chase, take a seat and listen up. Dug, let me start this off and then I want you to go over the same story you just told Ronnie and me." Dug nodded his head on screen and let Wesley continue.

"Chase, first of all, Dug, Connie, and Seville are all going to be alright. Secondly, Richard Fox is dead. He was the Maryland Devil, the team has proof, but he was killed about an hour ago after abducting and torturing both Connie and Dug." Wesley let the words sink in for a moment and watched Chase's reaction through his video monitor in Saint Bart's.

"And Seville?" Chase asked through the screen, eyes darting to both Wesley and Dug for an answer.

"Seville is going to be ok Chase. She suffered a gunshot wound to the left arm which according to Dug is more like a graze. She is still unconscious though and that's where the rest of the story comes in. Clair, rerun the Maryland video." Chase watched as the monitor changed to single screen and the video began to play, Dug's voice providing the usual commentary.

The picture on the screen was Dug standing about 5 feet in front of the camera recapping the series of events. "Connie and I had both been taken by Richard earlier in the day. I will get into all those details later as I am still reeling from having been taken out by this guy. I was restrained in a chair with leather straps, naked, and had been cut by Richard on my forehead and legs. Connie had been captured a little while later looking for me and was just getting prepped by Richard when Seville came onto the scene and things got really weird and out of control. God I wish the Data Gator hadn't been turned off because you're never going to believe what happened.

I was in the chair and just starting to clear up after having been drugged by the guy. Connie was out cold and Richard had been getting her ready on the cot similar to how you saw Mrs. Sawyer in the Gaithersburg tapes. Richard had his back to the stairs and was bent over working on Connie when all of a sudden I see a figure walking slowly and silently up the stairs. At first I thought it was a guy because of the walk and the posture but when the figure got to the top I saw it was Seville. I took a double take because she did not look like the person I had met on the video conferencing system the day before. I mean she looked like Seville but she looked like a man. She was barefoot and didn't have a coat on and her blouse was bulging like it was two sizes too small and the buttons on the front had mostly popped off. Her face and eyes barely looked like her at all. It was like she had morphed into something else. And her eyes, my God I will never forget them as long as I live. They were glowing a fiery red around the rims and the pupils were fully dilated and as black as black can be.

She kept walking right into the room straight at Richard who sensed or heard her coming and stood up startled. He yelled at her to stop and pulled out Connie's pistol but she kept walking straight at him like she could care less he had a gun pointed at her. The funny thing is she didn't have her gun out. I saw she had her holster on but she was not holding the gun. I yelled at her to draw but she didn't seem to notice that Connie and I were there. Richard finally shot a round up into the ceiling to startle her but she kept walking very slowly right at him never taking her eyes off of his. I could see him getting scared and he finally aimed at her and fired but the shot went wide but she kept coming. He squeezed off two more quick shots and I could see one hit her in the left arm but she didn't even flinch. Now she was right on top of the guy. His back was to me so I couldn't see real good but I did see her right arm shoot towards his chest and his body freeze up like it had been sent into instant shock. Just one second later there was blood shooting all over Seville and I thought she had taken another bullet but there hadn't been another shot. Then Richard went down right on his back and there was Seville standing there with a blank stare on her face, her right hand curled into a claw and dripping blood. When I looked down at Richard there was a gusher of blood squirting out of his left chest from five separate holes. It was the most amazing thing I've ever seen. Seville just stood there and I swear to God her blouse started to right size, her eyes lost the red, and the look of shear anger on her face turned to calm, then she just collapsed to the floor."

At this point Chase could see Dug walk towards the camera, take it and start to pan the room. Connie was sitting on the cot tending to a wound on her leg and as he moved the camera they could see Richard Fox lying in a pool of blood, small rivulets of blood still flowing from his chest. His face was frozen with a look of terror none of them had ever seen before. As the camera moved even farther they saw Seville crumpled on the floor, blood coming from the arm, blouse covered with blood, and her face looking like that of a sleeping angel.

The footage ended and all three screens came back on the monitor. For a moment everyone kept silent until Chase broke the ice.

"She transfigured a past life into a present moment." He said not really looking at any of them and slowly moving his hand up to his chest, rubbing his scar through his shirt.

"I think your right Chase." Said Ronnie who then told the rest of the group about the conversation she had with Seville on the boat just before this happened.

Dug was the only one astonished by this news. The others had all experienced some kind of transfiguration in their pasts but he had never seen a result quite like this.

"The question is was she consciously aware of what she was doing?" Wesley threw out to the group.

"I don't think so." said Ronnie. According to her some kind of emotional reaction to the situation caused those flashbacks. I believe that when she walked into the situation knowing that Richard was going to be there something inside took over. I honestly don't think she had any awareness of what she was doing."

"I would tend to agree with Ronnie." Chase offered. "Where is Seville now Dug?"

All of sudden the picture of Dug swung around and they saw Seville lying on a stretcher, her arm being attended to by an EMT. State

Police Officers were walking around in the distance and a medical examiner was bent over the body of Richard Fox, a finger poking into one of the holes in his chest. Connie was in a corner surrounded by three FBI suits, one of which was holding a tape recorder, capturing her every word. Sensing the remote groups question Dug spoke up quietly.

"Connie and I already explained to the police that Seville is a third degree black belt and that her gun jammed causing her to reflexively use her hands in defense."

"Smart." Wesley offered. "Dug, I want you to get back to work. Don't let Seville out of your site and as soon as she comes too and gets the green light from the Dr. I want both of you to get on that plane and up to Jaffrey. I will call Karen and have her begin preparing Serial Connections official statement of the capture and write the description of the method myself."

"Thanks Wesley." said Chase. "Ronnie, you look as concerned as I am! What are your thoughts?"

"Chase, I think we all knew that somehow Seville was special and that over time her gifts would unravel. Remember her story this morning regarding her Mayan background? I am beginning to think that she has traveled in that life plain for some time. If that's the case her memories and instincts are going to be much stronger than that of a person who just passed through the Mayan culture once or twice in a past life. She must have been caught up in a recurring lesson situation, going back over and over again until she got things right or the universe got tired of her stubbornness. Regardless of why she had so many lives in that culture, the fact remains that because she was there so often her instincts and knowledge of that period, peoples, customs, and behaviors have become encoded in her spirit DNA."

Chase could hear Wesley let out a big sigh of concurrence at the comment and say "And although there is not much empirical evidence of Spirit DNA it makes sense that a spirit can manipulate their current body which could explain Seville's extreme transfiguration."

Chase found himself rubbing his scar again while he thought through what he just heard. "So Seville was in a particular culture for so many lives that her very spirit has become encoded with her Mayan instincts?"

"Exactly" said Ronnie. "Consider that scar you keep rubbing Chase. I suspect you had the time to finally go to that place and are now aware."

"About time too" Wesley threw in with a chuckle.

Chase just looked at the two of them wishing that some day they would just tell him things instead of making him figure them out the hard way.

"I think you were in the Greek culture for a long time as well, and I would bet that with some work you would find quite a bit of that Spirit DNA within yourself." said Ronnie.

"Chase, have you wondered why your transition from Mouse Warrior to Magician is taking so long and why it is such a struggle?" Wesley offered.

"Because I was there for so many lives and my spirit is encoded with the warrior thinking!"

"Exactly Chase. And how about your spirit guide Ghost? Tell me what you think about him?"

Chase sat back and they could both see his mind churning and then say "Ghost kept coming back as a Shaman time and time again throughout his physical lives. It became so much of a part of his spirit self that that's all he could ever be."

"Right" said Wesley. "In his case, because that was all he could ever be, the only way for him to continue to grow and be productive was to eventually shed his physical self and move on consciously to a whole new astral plain."

"Ok, so what about Seville?"

Ronnie and Wesley both smiled at the same time and Ronnie said "What did we do with you Chase? She needs to get into training as quickly as possible. Consider her to be the Hope Diamond in the rough."

"In the rough—that's for sure. The problem is she should have been killed by Richard and would have if he hadn't been a pretty lame marksman. Not to mention her method of killing Richard, I think that's scares me the most."

"Chase, you forget the time you were in college and ran down that serial rapist with a horse. I know for a fact that you never rode a horse in your life, not to mention bare back, and from all accounts you rode that horse like it was part of you!" Sounds a little like Greek Calvary to me."

"God Wesley, I haven't thought about that in years. But you're right. I always thought it was out of pure adrenaline but thinking about it I can actually feel the experience and naturalness of what I did."

"Sure you can, it was clearly Spirit DNA following you around. That's why I would like to see you spend more time in your past life studies. I would bet that you have some wonderful DNA to pull from on the conscious level if you knew it existed."

"Yea but Wesley, imagine the exhilaration of jumping on the back of the horse for the first time and not only riding it like the wind but taking down a pretty nasty bad guy too! Wouldn't you want that to be a surprise?"

"Oh Grasshopper!

"Just kidding, ok you got me sold on this DNA thing and I promise to put it on my list of things to do once we get through this mess. Now back to work. Ronnie, you're going to make sure Seville is comfortable when Dug gets her back?"

"Yes, and I think Wesley should head up here today too." she said.

"A day late and a dollar short Ronnie." said Wesley holding up a pair of e-tickets in his hand. "Ashley and I are on our way up first thing in the morning."

Chase's eyes lit up as he hadn't seen his old friend in person for over 6 months. "You guys are welcome to stay up in my place if you want. Speaking of my place, Ronnie, you might want to see if Seville would be more comfortable up there too."

"What about me?" she said with a fake pout.

"If I thought for a minute that you would leave your sacred courtyard I would extend the invitation immediately."

"You know me so well." She said winking through the camera.

"Ok guys I have to go find Susan. Wesley, can you check with Louise and make sure I get an update on her locator while I am driving over to her place?"

"Will do and remember the conversation we just had. You're running straight into something bad Chase. Be the magician and make sure you've got the warrior for back up!"

"Gotcha, I'll check back in about 25 minutes."

*****

The long, slim Lincoln Town car pulled up to the police tape stretched across the road on the tip of Ocean City. The driver lowered his window and flashed his FBI identification at the State Police Trooper standing guard and he lifted the tape so the vehicle could pass through and park in front of the two story garage now known to be the staging area for the Maryland Devil.

Dug and Connie were standing outside next to the stretcher carrying Seville when Henry White stepped out of the car not 30 feet away. Connie noticed him first. Henry was about 5'10" and sported a stocky build that was easily 30 pounds more than he needed. His hair was as white as his name and his bright red complexion was a combination of Irish decent, high blood pressure, and a few too many pints. Connie saw instantly that Henry was not a happy man, and she immediately began conjuring up the story she was going to have to tell him after he reamed her out. The EMTs were just about to load Seville into the back of the ambulance when Henry bellowed out to everyone within ear shot.

"Hold it right there! Don't put her in that ambulance yet."

The bewildered EMTs looked around to see this red faced madman approaching them waving a leather ID case and decided that they should stand down for the moment.

"Henry White, Director of the FBI Serial Group. Hold that stretcher right there for a minute." he said as he slightly changed direction and quickly advanced up to where Connie and Dug stood.

"Agent Thompson I need to have a word with you." Henry said while giving Dug the once over and wincing like he wasn't very impressed.

"Hello Director White, I would like to you to meet Dug Masters from the Serial Connections group in New Hampshire. Dug and his team mate Seville Waters are responsible for bringing down Richard Fox."

"What do you mean they are responsible? You were here weren't you? You were leading the investigation Agent Thompson and as far as I am concerned this is an FBI collar."

Dug couldn't keep himself leashed any longer and said boldly "Henry, I think you have the facts all backwards. It was Serial Connections who invited Agent Thompson to participate along with our preliminary investigation of Richard Fox in regards to the Maryland Devil case. Our Director, Chase Benton gave me special permission to bring Agent Thompson along to assist in obtaining proof that Richard Fox was indeed who we suspected…"

"I don't want to hear your drabble" Bellowed Henry, "This is our collar and Agent Thompson will stand in front of the press and tell them exactly what I want her to tell them."

"Forgive me Connie" he said with a sheepish look on his face while thumbing through some pictures on the screen of his video recorder. "You see Henry, it was Seville who actually brought Fox down and she was shot in the line of duty." And he flashed a picture of Seville lying on the floor next to Fox with blood everywhere. "Connie was unconscious, restrained, and about to be brutally raped by Richard when Seville came in and basically saved both our asses." next he flashed a picture of Connie laying flat out on a cot, stripped naked, and obviously still out cold. "After the shots, a passerby on the street called the police and they showed up a few minutes later. They undid my restraints first because I was awake from the effects of the chemical agent he used on us. These pictures and others are already back at Serial Connections and a press release has been written and is about to go out over the wire."

Despite his ruddy red complexion Dug could see all the color quickly draining out of Henry's face and could feel the anger swelling from inside him.

"Of course Chase would never release these pictures and to my knowledge has mentioned Agent Thompson as a valuable asset of the Serial Connections team regarding the final outcome of this case."

Henry stood there completely dumfounded, looked over at Seville on the stretcher and said to the EMT "Ok, you can get her to the hospital now" and looked back at Connie and Dug saying "You two; into the crime scene with me now!"

Dug looked at Connie with an apologetic face and started walking over to the ambulance and jumped up into the back with Seville.

Henry looked like he was having a bowl movement and screamed at Dug "Mr. Masters, I don't you think you heard me. I need you inside with Agent Thompson right now to go over the crime scene and I am going to need a copy of that tape you made."

Dug looked out the back of the ambulance and held the door open for a moment while he said "Sorry Henry, I have my orders to stay with Seville. She has been badly hurt, is still in shock, and I am not going to leave her alone. You are a real piece of work!" and pulled the door closed as the vehicle sirens came on and the SUV speed away from the curb.

"Come with me Thompson, you have a hell of a lot of explaining to do" and he trudged along the police tape into the alleyway with Connie in tow.

"This is where I entered the garage Henry. I entered the building using standard entry posture and had swept the room when I noticed one second too late that there was on opening above. That sandbag right there was dropped on my head and while I was semi-conscious Fox drugged me with the same chemical mix he used on his victims. From what Dug told me he then dragged me up the stairs and got me ready for his little redemption ritual." Come with me upstairs and you can see the rest.

As Henry got to the top of the stairs the first thing he saw across the room was Richard Fox's body still in the same position on his back and a massive amount of drying brownish red blood in pools on both sides of the body. Henry walked up and bent down to take a closer look at his wounds.

"You said that Seville did this to him with her bare hands?"

"Yes Sir, I didn't see any of it because I was still knocked out but that's what Dug shared with me."

"He's full of shit. No woman could plunge her fingers into a very strong man's chest and puncture his heart."

The coroner who had been standing nearby finishing a form looked up and said "She didn't just puncture the heart. Her fingers went into the chest perfectly around his heart. What killed him was the heart being crushed by her fingers."

Henry looked up astonished. "You mean to tell me that she dug her fingers into this man's chest so that they surrounded the heart muscle then she squeezed it with her fingers?"

"Yes, except she didn't just squeeze it. She wrapped her fingers around the heart and popped it like a small balloon filled with water."

Henry rose from his crouch and continued looking around the room. He saw the cot where Agent Thompson had been tied up and a chair right next to it where he supposed Dug Master had been lashed. Connie pointed over to the far wall to a wooden ladder than was built into the side of the wall and disappeared up into what looked to be an attic.

"We found his staging area up there along with his trophy case. A foot locker had press memorabilia for over 30 unsolved murders over a span of 20 years. We found hair brushes, jewelry, undergarments, and photographs all nicely dated and labeled. We should be able to close the books on most of them with matching crime scene evidence."

"What kind of person can rip into a chest and crush his heart muscle like that" Henry threw out into the room.

The coroner spoke up once again. "To be honest I had a hard time believing it was a woman that did this, especially the one we just sent out on the stretcher." He said looking at Henry. "According to the Serial Connections guy, the victim, or killer in this case, was standing up straight and was not leaning against a wall. You see, if the victim's back was against something it would seem much more likely that someone could leverage their own strength to penetrate their fingers right through hard muscle and flesh. But without something behind the victim imagine the skill and strength required to do that!"

"All we know is that Seville is some kind of triple black belt" said Connie to the room of listeners. "Who knows what kind of skill she has".

"And what about her weapon?" asked Henry.

"It must have jammed somehow." said the coroner. "We found it on the floor about 5 feet behind her. It looks like she dropped it before she was shot by Fox."

"Where is the gun?"

The coroner turned around and went into a large plastic container he was using for evidence and pulled out a large one gallon zip lock bag containing a nine millimeter Glock and handed it over to Henry. He took it out of the bag and without any concern for contaminating evidence he examined the weapon thoroughly checking out the cartridge, ammunition, chamber, and breech.

"There is nothing wrong with this gun." he challenged. "I want to know what in the hell really happened here. Thompson, you had better get the entire footage of video that Serial Connections guy took or you will be mopping floors in headquarters for the rest of your stellar FBI career."

"Director White, I will do my best but you know I cannot control that group. They are licensed and quite frankly know that anything they have will have to be turned over for the concluding investigation."

"I can't wait for that. I need that video now—today Agent Thompson—can you spell job security?"

Connie twitched back into her posture at those words and felt a rage begin to swell up in her belly. "Did you just threaten me Sir!" she asked with a calm but ragged voice.

Henry White backed off for one second as he heard Connie's remark and moved just a little bit closer to her, lowered his voice so no one else in the room could hear him and whispered "You breached FBI protocol today by coming into this place without agency knowledge or backup. I could run you in right now Thompson, but I like you. In certain ways you're just like me—you won't rest until you get what you want. You need the Agency as much as it needs you so I would consider my comment not a threat but rather a major career event in the making—do I make myself perfectly clear?"

Connie felt herself going into a tailspin emotionally and drew upon every ounce of strength to maintain a semblance of control. She desperately wanted to reach out and attack this awful excuse for a human being but gained enough sense to realize that he was baiting her and that this was not the place and time to do battle with this monster. At that very moment a brilliant idea popped into her head and she offered to Henry. "Seville is still in shock Henry; Dug has orders to get her back to Jaffrey as soon as possible. If you want me to get that video I need cart blanch to get it. Even then I am only promising to do my best. You know damn well that they trust us about as much as they trusted Richard Fox—Deal?"

She could see the wheels turning in Henry's mind and without so much as a change in heart rate or facial expression he said "Deal—Just get me that tape AND anything else we need on the other cases. You feed me and I'll keep feeding you—well." He turned, took one more look around the garage, and then disappeared down the steps.

*****

Chase's mind was swirling now with so many thoughts and directions. He was just leaving the private airport and heading to Susan Kincaid's house on the outskirts of Seattle. Seville was on his mind a great deal and more now that they had become aware of the power that had seemingly lain dormant within her. As he thought about her transfiguration it brought back the memories of his college days and one of his first experiences using his gifts to go after darkness.

It was his sophomore year and in the middle of winter when something ominous had begun on the campus. A serial rapist had come to the attention of the community and over the course of a month several girls at the school had been abducted, held for a couple of days and been repeatedly sexually abused. The entire campus was up in arms and most of the causal and not so casual conversations in the classrooms, dorms, and other venues focused on the brutality of this person and bringing him to justice.

Chase had opted out of the Fraternity aspects of college life as his demeanor and self isolation did not mix well with the testosterone of that environment. Instead of pledging a fraternity he had chosen to live in the dormitories and made good use of his spare time studying things that most of his peers could not or would not understand. His freshman year he found himself playing musical rooms because his roommates found him to be scary and aloof with his constant meditation and the strange things that occurred when he was around. This year he had made arrangements to have a single room and that suited him just fine.

He was able to piece together his own little sanctuary where his quest for peace and serenity prevailed.

For the most part he kept to himself but did have some interaction with an on campus coven of witches. His motivation to be with this group was all about learning their beliefs and ways not so that he might practice witchcraft but rather have a keen understanding of its workings, strengths, and weaknesses. He had consulted Wesley on this desire before introducing himself to the group and Wesley had simply told him to follow his instincts and to search for clarity in all things. Over the course of a couple of months, one of the Witches, Tara, had made it very clear that she desired a deeper relationship with him. He had never been attracted to a girl in this way before and for a period of time he found the emotions of a blossoming relationship and the sexual energy to be extremely exhilarating.

Wesley had taught him that throughout his life time he would encounter new feelings, emotions, and desires and that he should always embrace them because they were building blocks in the foundations of his character and spiritual growth. At first he found himself fantasizing about being with Tara. She had dark blond hair and a Celtic look about her. She was very attractive in the physical sense and even though he had never been with a girl, he seemed to sense what it would be like and what he should do. After a month of courting, flirting, and heavy petting sessions Tara finally ended up in Chase's room one night. It was magical.

As if on cue, Tara had stood up from the bed where they had been entwined and engulfed in passion, smiled down at Chase and began unbuttoning her blouse. His body ached as she opened the silk garment and exposed her milky white breasts to him for the first time. It was happening in slow motion and although he felt embarrassed to be staring at her he couldn't help but study her rounded contours and aroused nipples that seemed to be calling him. She gently ran her hands down along her breasts, down her sides, and then continued the ceremony with her jeans and panties. He thought she was a Goddess as she stood there completely exposed with a look of utter desire and lust in her eyes. They made love all night long, barely stopping between orgasms, not wanting the ecstasy to ever end. At first Chase found himself stumbling through the awkwardness of touching and being touched but Tara, who had more experience, was wonderfully patient coaching him through the art of sensing a woman's sweet spots and how to perceive when to move between gentle and firm strokes. Over the next couple of months Chase blossomed in ways he could never have imagined and his relationship with Tara remained exciting and passionate.

Having gone home for a long weekend he found himself at Wesley's house on a Saturday afternoon sharing the newness of his new spiritual experiences when he got a phone call from his Mother next door. A friend of Tara's had called looking to see if she had gone home with Chase for the weekend and his Mother had said no. She explained to Mrs. Benton that Tara had gone missing Friday afternoon after classes and could not be found. They were all concerned because the campus serial rapist had not been caught yet and over the last few months more women had been abducted. When Chase hung up the phone Wesley knew there was a big problem and Chase went on to explain about the madman who was loose and what he had been doing. As he was getting up to head back to school to look for Tara, Wesley had practically pulled him back into his chair and asked him to be still for a moment. Wesley closed his eyes and began to focus on the situation and Tara in particular when his mind began to flash with thoughts and pictures. He asked Chase to join him and before long they were sharing those mental flashes back and forth. Chase was visibly shaken. As with Timmy years ago he had just seen Tara in a place that was not good and could feel her terror, pain, and hopelessness. In the visions he could see her in a stall of some sort, hay strewn all over the ground and a closed, locked door holding her prisoner. He could feel that she had already been abused and that there was more to come. He also saw a picture of three men walking down a street on campus and realized that one or more of them were involved—he knew these guys!. A look of rage came over Chase and Wesley realized the time had come.

He broke up the session and spoke very carefully to Chase. "You are about to enter a new phase of your cycle of life. One we have spoken about many times. The warrior has now been let loose and this will be your first encounter with the truths that will guide your life until you are ready for your next phase. Walk softly and carefully Chase. Do not let your emotions or feelings for Tara get in the way of what you need to do because if that happens you may very well be jeopardizing her safety and her life. Focus on the enemy and not the passion; concentrate on your powers and your spirit and not on what you think you ought to do; let your guides and your instincts take you through this without thought or pre-conceived notion and justice will prevail."

Two hours later Chase was back on campus and he visited with Tara's roommate and had also spoken to the police. On his way back *he had consulted one of his spirit guides. The message was very simple and succinct; Walk into the night and the enemy will find you. So that's what he did after making sure that Tara was still missing and that there weren't any new developments. As he took off into the streets and began walking the campus he noticed that a lot of students were out on this cold February night and that he seemed to be the only one walking alone. He bumped into a couple of kids he kinda knew and they asked him if they had found Tara yet. They handed him a flyer that had been printed up by a student security organization which had Tara's picture and description on it along with contact information. Chase was informed that the flyers were being passed around and that quite a bit of the campus population was out looking. He thanked the guys and kept on walking but as he unfolded the paper in his hands and saw the picture of Tara staring back at him he found himself being filled with a deep red rage that was both new and terrifying to him. Another face on the flyer jumped out at him. A face he knew very well and had seen earlier in the day with Wesley.*

Harry Jenkins was one of the most popular kids at the school. He was a senior and not only belonged to the most prestigious fraternity on campus but he was class president AND the head of the student security group called the "Campus Busters". Chase stopped in his tracks and let the visions flow. He saw the stable again but this time he saw Harry too, he was coming out of a stall door, pulling a ski mask off his head and was covered with hay and dirt like he had been rolling around, but when he saw through the door the girl that laid in the soil was not Tara and his hopes began to rise until he realized that the girl had been one of the first victims months ago.

The blood was coursing through his veins now and all he could think of was finding Harry and making him take him to Tara. He began to plan his assault on Harry and had already determined how he was going to bring him down and make him talk. His pace quickened through the streets and as he came around a corner he saw a large group of students huddled around in a circle way down at the other end of the street. All at once the group broke up and three figures emerged and began walking in his direction. As they got closer Chase saw that it was Harry and two of his frat buddies and the rage quickly blossomed. As soon at it rose he felt a hand on his shoulder and spun around but no one was there. Turning back to Harry and friends he heard a familiar voice begin to coach him. "Focus on the enemy but not the passion; Now is the time for stealth and patience, you must wait and follow this man."

Shaking off the anger as best he could he kept his direction and walked right at the three students. When they approached him he could tell that Harry knew who he was and also his ties to Tara. "Hey Benton, sorry to hear about Tara, we are working like dogs to find her and get this asshole."

"Thanks Harry, it looks like you guys are doing a great job. Do you have one of those flyers?"

Harry pulled one out of the pile in his hands and handed it to Chase. "Here Benton, how come you're out here alone? We are recommending that any students on the search be teamed up with at least two other people."

"I just got back to Campus and haven't been able to find my friends yet. Hey, how about I go around with you guys?" he said looking carefully at the responses of the three.

Eyes darted back and forth between them and Chase new right away that it was more than just Harry involved in this insane crime.

"I think we should have as many groups out there as possible." Harry said rather awkwardly. "Why don't you find your friends and create another search team?"

Chase looked Harry right in the eyes as if he were trying to burn them with laser beams, took a quick glance at the other two who could not hold eye contact, and went along his way. He kept walking like he was heading somewhere but quickly backtracked off into the side yards and began following his prey. The night lasted much longer than he thought and he found himself dodging search teams and police for well over three hours... All of sudden the group split up, Harry going in one direction and the other two taking off down a back street. Chase stopped in his tracks and settled his spirit. He got a picture in his mind of the two others going towards a stable and knew that they were on there way to visit Tara—he had to stop them! As soon as he decided to follow the two another vision came into his head. It was Harry walking out of a court room with a huge smile on his face—He had not been found guilty! Confused, Chase settled into another path and focused on following Harry and what he saw turned his stomach inside out. The two others were having their way with Tara while Chase was following Harry but his last vision was that of Harry being cuffed and taken away, and there were no more rapes after that. Chase's heart sank into the ground as his decision to either stop Tara from being abused more or catching the ring leader crushed him. Reaching into his bowels for all the strength he could muster, he changed direction and went after the single figure walking down the street.

Harry stopped at the school pub for while and Chase set up watch across the street at the Student Union building. About an hour later, Harry came out and began walking back to fraternity row. When he got back to the expansive 3 story Victorian house Chase expected him to head in the front door but instead Harry darted around to the side and disappeared into the darkness. Chase treaded softly now that he was on enemy ground. He had never been behind this building and had no idea what to expect. Fortunately the night was clear and there was enough ambient light for him to see his way around. In the distance he heard a door squeak open then shut and he followed the sound down a trail that lead into the woods until he came to a very large barn. As he drew closer to the structure he heard the door open again and soft voices began to float over the night air. He ducked into the woods behind some hemlock trees and waited for the voices to draw nearer. As two figures passed by he could tell they were the two that had been with Harry earlier, and he could hear them telling of their adventures with Tara. He came a hairs width close to jumping the two right then and there but remembered that Harry was the enemy and as he withdrew his intent and fell back into the shadows he got a satisfying feeling that those two would soon be undone.

After a few moments Chase stepped quietly up to the building and listened for sounds coming from within. He quickly walked around the barn and found that the far end stable doors were wide open and he could peer inside from a distance. There was a small utility light on in the far corner that provided just enough light for Chase to get an idea of the layout of the ground floor. He could hear horses in the stalls stirring restlessly, obviously sensitized to the muffled sounds coming from the stall right in the middle. He could hear Harry talking but could not discern what he was saying as he approached the door. Suddenly the door burst open and Harry came storming out of the room. When he saw Chase standing there a look of rage and terror jumped onto his face. Instinctively Harry charged at Chase and with full force pounded into him, sending him crashing to the floor and knocking the wind from his lungs.

It was that moment things began to happen in slow motion. Picking himself up from the floor Chase began to feel an energy surge into his body and mind that he was unfamiliar with but was very powerful. In seconds Chase seemed to be on auto pilot, a surreal feeling that he could see what he was doing but was not controlling his thoughts or actions. Before Chase new it he was in a stall grabbing the mane of a beautiful white grey stallion and throwing his body horizontally up and onto the horses back. The horse rebelled at this intrusion until it could feel the power and intent of its new rider and began to respond to the pulls on its mane and heels digging into its sides. Lunging from the stall with amazing urgency the stallion turned at full gallop and headed out the stable door into the night, its nose picking up the scent of their quarry and charging blindly down the darkened trail.

Running as fast a he could, Harry had almost made it out to the riding fields when he heard the powerful hoofs coming at him from behind. Startled by this he slowed and turned in time to see a white blur emerge from the trail heading straight at him, a rider on its bare back, eyes black with furry. The horse quickly overtook Harry and kept pouncing from side to side preventing him from possible escape. All Harry could feel was an intense energy coming from the horse and rider. Feeling backed into a corner he lunged at the rider to try to pull him off his stead. The stallion was faster though and reared up and to the right, its massive leg and shoulder crashing into Harry like he was a rag doll. He went down and rolled in the dirt but was frozen with fear and laid there looking at the rider's wild eyes and watching him pull the mane of the horse in Harry's direction. He could see a white leg rise in the air over his head, stop, and then come crashing down at his head. Screaming in the night Harry could feel the column of flesh brush by his face, smell the familiar scent of the horse and the pounding vibration of the ground as it shook under the impact of the hoof next to his ear. That was all he remembered as the shock to his psychic took him to another place.

Chase shivered as his recall of the event brought back memories that he had somehow repressed over the years. Tara had left school after that horrible violation and moved back to Florida with her parents. They had kept in touch for while but the damage that had been done was too great and they were never able to reconnect. Harry and five others were found guilty of multiple kidnapping and rape charges and disappeared into the state penitentiary system.

His mind wandered briefly back to the event with the horse and the realization that that had been his first encounter with his Spirit DNA. He had never ridden a horse in his life, let alone bareback, and as he replayed the scene in his mind he could feel the intuitive familiarity of the horse, the ridding style, and especially the intensity of running down of his quarry. This had not been his first time! He couldn't wait for all of this to be over so that he could sit quietly for a few days and really immerse himself into this concept and perhaps conjure up a couple more of his past lives.

A sign on the side of the road caught his eye and he quickly hit the turn signal just in time not to miss the exit off the highway to Susan's house. It had already been a long day and promised to get even longer yet but he was catching a second wind now, getting closer to his quarry and to Susan. He began reaching out into the current situation, feeling for those thoughts and visions that have always been there as a guiding force. He couldn't shake the feeling that Susan was no longer on this earthly plain and that bothered him more than he ever thought it would. In 17 years they had all been in many dangerous situations but other than some scratches and scrapes no one in Serial Connections had ever been seriously hurt. All of a sudden Seville, her first day on the job had been shot, Susan had been kidnapped (he was pretty damn sure) and only God himself knew what else lay in wait for the team over the next few days. Of course, even though the team had always been engaged on multiple projects they had never had more than one come crashing down on them at the same time, and never had so much extraneous interference blocking their every move. Chase was all of sudden very proud of his team and Serial Connections. They had and were making a difference in world. Countless lives had been saved over the years. Some pretty amazing technologies and capabilities had been developed and all in all it continued to be a very rewarding path and journey.

Before he knew it Chase turned down the long driveway into Susan's little hideaway in the woods. He had been here more than a few times in the past and found her home to be very pleasant and filled with good positive energy. As he pulled up the driveway though that thought came crashing down on his head as he was struck with a series of very unpleasant waves of energy coming from her home. As he pulled in he saw the front door wide open, her car pulled off to the side where it might always be, and as he got out of the car the eerie quite consumed his senses.

Before he went into the house he pulled out his phone and speed dialed Louise Penta to see if she had had any luck with Susan's tracking system.

"Hey it's me" he said into the phone as moved slowly towards the front porch of the house.

"Hi Chase, I trust you had a nice flight?"

"An interesting flight Louise; very interesting!"

"You'll have to share with me when you get back." She said.

Although she was the supreme computer geek, Louise always wanted to spend time with Chase, listening to him talk about "his" world. He had a gentle way of explaining things to her that frankly were way beyond her comprehension and the clarity he provided on the esoteric things helped her immensely when it came time to codify his world into Clair.

"Will be my pleasure as always Louise, I am at Susan's house standing outside and things are not good here. Before I go in I wanted to check the status of her transmitter to see if you have anything."

"Nothing Boss" she said back into the phone. "I have tried everything I can think of including hypertensing the frequency in order to pick up minute traces but all that has managed to do is pick up other beacons all over the place."

"Ok, keep me posted if anything comes up will you?"

"Will do Chase—be careful."

Chase hung up the phone and slowly walked up onto the porch which was just starting to get covered with pine needles as the trees began their yearly pilgrimage towards winter. He carefully stepped into the house which smelled like the fresh pines from outside but also something else. He knew the smell of death, always had, and at once he knew for sure that what he had been dreading was indeed true. He could see the carnage in his mind as he came to a juncture of the living room and kitchen but headed into the kitchen first anyway. As they had seen back in Jaffrey the kitchen was the remnants of a battle ground. Broken glass covered the floor in front of the stove, and pockets of blood spotted the floor over by the window and to the side of the oven.

That is when he saw what he knew he would find; a trail of smeared blood leading out through the side door of the kitchen onto the three season porch on the side of the house. He turned on his electronics and began cataloging the scene in the kitchen before he swept the camera towards the porch and slowly advanced into the next room. His spirit was settled and prepared for what he had already seen. He looked into the LED on the unit just when Susan came into clear view.

Chase turned off his feelings just for a moment more while he panned the room, capturing the essence of death that surrounded him. Susan's two cats were on the floor over by the back door, their heads bent unnaturally at angles that suggested a quick and painless end. Susan was sitting in a chair, her hair dangling down the front of her chest, bare legs and arms white and limp. Her arms had been lashed to the chair and he could see random cut marks up and down her legs and arms which were curious to say the least. He barely noticed that on her left forearm there was a crater in her skin that was all of 2 inches long. Over her head, on the wall of the porch was a single Japanese Kanji drawn with her blood. Chase did not speak Japanese but knew the ornate character was that of death. He finished his examination with the camera, set it aside, and took a closer look at the arm. He flinched in pain when he realized what it was and quickly pulled out his phone.

"Louise, punch up Susan's security profile." He said tersely through the phone sending an immediate alarm to Louise.

"Got it" he heard her say.

"Tell me the location of Susan's tracking implant please!"

"Chase, Susan's transmitter is on her left forearm approximately 4 inches down from the elbow and 5 inches up from the nape of the wrist."

Louise could hear nothing from the phone for a few moments then heard Chase say "Louise, give me 20 minutes, no less-no more, then call the local police and tell them there has been a murder."

It was Chases turn to listen to silence on the other end, but the silence never broke as he heard the phone being gently hung up all the way across the country. He slowly cradled his phone and went back over to examine Susan. He could feel for an instant that she died a slow death, not wanting to reveal to the perpetrator where her transmitting device had been implanted. She had either conceded at the end or the device had been found through the random digging done by a very sharp knife. He chose to believe that she had conceded, hoping that she had realized that her life meant much more to him than any company secrets ever could.

Stepping back a few paces he knelt down on the floor in front of her. He pulled out a small bag from his carryall and laid it on the floor in front of him. He lifted out a small, perfectly polished abalone shell, placed a sage stick in the shell and lit the end. As the smoke wafted up into the air around them he thanked Great Spirit for this woman, friend, and associate. He asked that she be honored and brought quickly to that place of peace where she could find rest until a new life was born. *A Falcon glided through the thick forest surrounding her home and landed quietly on a large stump not far from the porch. Chase and the bird silently acknowledged one another with nods of their heads. The beautiful female raptor then called to Susan in a language that Chase could not understand but knew was asking her to follow its flight to a better place. He watched as the Falcons head followed something unseen coming from the porch then push its powerful legs off the stump and thrust its wings into a slow, steady rise through the trees. As the Falcon disappeared into the canopy Chase found peace within and a single tear fell from his cheek and gently landed in the abalone shell.*

*****

As Ronni walked into the courtyard from the cave entrance to meet with Cori, she heard in the distance the most beautiful rhythm coming from across the yard. She had heard Cori drum this beat before and knew that things had changed here forever. They had just lost one of their own, a soldier, and a friend, the first casualty after almost two decades of fighting the good fight and keeping the faith. Somewhere in the back of her mind she had seen this day come, but had kept it in the far recesses, not wanting the foretold reality to hinder her work all these years. Removing her glasses she continued walking through the sanctuary allowing her eyes to cleanse with sorrow. She took her favorite seat by the brook and gently plucked the closed fall blossoms off the vines of her precious morning glories. As she held them in her hand, gently pulling apart the individual petals, Karen and Louise stepped in behind her, placing their hands on her shoulders, all listening to the beat of the sacred drums. Ronnie handed the girls some petals and together they placed the brilliantly blue velvet into the brook and watched as they floated away forever.

Turning towards Mount Monadnock, Ronnie gazed upon the vista. To the west a light thin line chased after the setting sun, and to the east the bright full moon began its dance into the night. A shadow came across her spirit causing her to turn and face the south. The sky was dark and ominous—a storm was coming. She shivered at the thought.

*****

The blue lights and sirens of the cruisers whooshed by Chase as he headed back onto the highway away from Susan's house and on towards his new destination. He was holding a map he printed back on the airplane and figured he only had about 15 minutes until he got to Masanori's neighborhood. He could feel the edge starting to build up inside him, that familiar tingle that almost always brought about the warrior. He tried with all his might to suppress the awakening and felt it push back, not all the way, but just far enough for his spirit to start the process of bringing forth the magician. Soon he was heading back down off the highway and could feel the presence of his adversary but could also feel his guide, Merlin, floating in the air around him. He was about to push the accelerator harder to head up the rather steep hill in front of him when what looked to be a very large cat strolled out into the street causing him to swerve to his left. Fortunately there was a left hand turn there and he simply kept going down that street knowing from the map that he could circle back up the other way.

About halfway down the street he had to slow for a blue station wagon that was backing out of a driveway on the right. Slowing his car to almost a stop he waited for the car to switch gears and head off, but before that could happen his mind went into a flurry of visions. He could see a dungeon holding a woman, and an oriental man walking through a passageway, and then the shocker hit him. He saw the oriental man driving a blue station wagon just like the one in front of him now! It was Masanori! But it didn't make any sense. His house was up on the hill on the other side of the block. He slowly followed the car in front of him and eventually slowed and pulled over towards the end of the street and let the wagon continue on its way.

In his minds eye he sent himself up into the air over the neighborhood houses and began to hover. There he could see Masanori's house, the same as it was in all the pictures Susan had taken. A straight line from Masanori's house ended up at the bottom of the hill at the house where the blue wagon had just come from. He could see energy coming up through the overgrowth between the houses and the revelation hit him like a brick. Somehow Masanori used both houses for his work and the reason they could never see him leave his real house was because he rarely did. He had a passageway between the houses and left the bottom one when he didn't want to be noticed. Off to the right of the line of energy he could see the same reddish glow about 20 feet away from the major path of light. It was a circle about 3 feet in diameter and just the edges had that same eerie glow. He knew what it was.

Rejoining himself back in the car he picked up the phone and called into headquarters to talk to Louise once again.

"Hey, I have some news. I am pretty sure that Masanori is using two different houses connected to each other underground. I am also pretty sure that the passageway is what Ronni's group keeps seeing. It is where he holds his victims and if I am right there is a way into the passageway that doesn't require me going into either house. Masanori just left the other house so I might have some time inside before he gets back"

"I've got your tracker on Chase, so I can keep an eye on where you are and create a map of the place. Be careful and Chase? I am so sorry about Susan and I hate to say this but, nail that bastard. Nail him to the fucking wall!"

Understanding her anger Chase didn't feel the need to provide her with a lesson on the dangers of vengeful thinking and simply said "Sure"

He grabbed his bag and got out of the car. It was still pretty light here and as he walked back down the road to the other house he began to tune into the neighborhood, listening for dogs, watching for people, to make sure he could slip off the street without being noticed. As he approached the house his instincts kicked in again and he went one house further before sprinting between the homes and disappearing up into the brush at the rear of the yards. He knew just where to go and slowly navigated up and through the heavy thickets until he came to the place he had spotted earlier. It wasn't hard to find as he stepped right onto a circle of dirt and leaves where nothing grew in the middle of heavy growth. Pulling out his pocket knife Chase began to jab the blade into the soil and soon heard the unmistakable sound of metal upon metal. He put down his equipment and began to remove the 6 inches of top soil covering the 100 year old manhole cover. Finding the finger holds he worked the heavy metal plate until it finally broke the bonds of sitting undisturbed for decades.

His flashlight revealed a 10 foot drop down into a dark recess, a wrought iron ladder system melded into the cobblestone walls. Taking his gear he descended into the tunnel. Clearing his nose and throat from the damp musky air he wiped his hands of the moss and grime that had been covering the ladder rungs. The soil below him was damp and lay undisturbed for many years. Old footsteps still remained etched in the dirt coming from within and leading out to the ladder. His light did not have to travel far, just 20 feet or so until the beam hit a dead end, or so it seemed. As he examined the side walls he found what he was looking for. A very small latch system was recessed into the cobblestone bricks and as he firmly pulled it with his fingers he heard a bolt system disengage within the wall and air hiss through the cracks in the wall in front of him. He hadn't noticed before but there was a metal rung protruding from the wall that must be the door and when he went to pull it the large stone structure barely moved. Once again he put down his equipment and with his legs as leverage heaved against the ring and felt the stone slowly pull through the almost invisible seams of the door frame. Very fresh and clean air rushed passed his face when the seal finally broke and a faint light shone through telling him he had hit pay dirt.

Not five miles away as Masanori traversed the isles of his favorite supermarket a faint buzzing sound could be heard coming from his front pocket. Picking out his PDA, he saw it at once—the pressure system in the dungeon had been breached or was malfunctioning. Quickly punching icons on the screen with a very sharp fingernail he found the control panel and discovered that all the main doors were still sealed and neither of the houses had been intruded upon. He tried to reset the system remotely but each time he did it still read FAILED. He decided to abort his shopping trip and casually abandoned the cart he had filled with goodies for him and Greta, and quickly but carefully left the store.

Chase marveled at the interior of the passageway as he carefully slipped into the dungeon. His senses came alive as the energy of the past, present, and future began to invade his psychic. He already knew what this place was—a bad place—and other than the innocence of some of the victims, all he could feel was deep sadness, hopelessness, fear, and terror. There was another energy presence here though that was ominous and oppressive. Depravity, loath, hate, anger, lust, and a savagery the likes he had never felt came wafting over him. He acknowledged the spirit of his adversary then went to work. He headed down the stairs first for two reasons. Proximity told him that if and when Masanori returned he would be coming in the same way he went out—through the previously unknown house at the bottom of the hill and wanted to get a lay of the land and set his bearings. He passed a room that looked just like an operating room and quickly shielded himself against the onslaught of visions that came streaming towards him. *The death room he thought.* He went down one more flight and turned to his right into what looked like a sparsely furnished office. On the wall in front of him and behind the floor desk his eyes fixated on the two swords on the wall. The sword of the Samurai: known to be the sharpest of all swords, the ancient art of folding the steel into razor sharp perfection could cut almost any object when wielded by a master. Chase went to the desk and his eyes gravitated to the flat panel computer screen on the top right. Masanori's e-mail program was up and Chase's eyes were drawn to the subject line of the one on the very top "Susan Kincaid" was all it said. All he could do was stare at the words, and try to keep restrained... He was about to open the message to read what it said and to figure out who it came from when the program chimed and another e-mail filled the top space. This one was more ominous than the last "Benton is coming—He is at your place now!" was all Chase could see. Without hesitation Chased grabbed the mouse and the keyboard and forwarded the last message to Louis Penta. She would know what to do. Feeling an increased sense of urgency, Chase left the room quickly and headed left and back up into the long cobblestone hallway. He came upon a door that had a sliding plate just below his eye level and quietly opened the portal. Looking inside he saw a young woman lying on a bed, wearing a long flowing night gown. Stepping back from the door he looked around the edges to find out how to open it. Right in front of his eyes he found two buttons recessed into the wall. Reaching towards it and figuring that the one on top was the "open" button he was about to push it when instinct pulled him back sounding the warning clangs in his mind. Stepping back again he followed the door frame up and around until he saw what he was looking for. Another thin latch like the one on the outer chamber he had come through before. Reaching up he slowly brought the latch down and the door unsealed itself and he easily pushed it open. Greta came alive with fear and curled up into a ball on the bed at the sound of the approaching monster.

"I am here to help, my name is Chase and I have come to take you out of this place." as he cautiously approached the girl on the bed.

"Get away you fucking mutant!" she screamed into the soft bed cover as she started kicking her legs and feet viciously in Chase's direction.

"What's your name?" Chase said with a soothing voice.

Something inside Greta heard these last words and she could tell that this was not the man who had been brutalizing her but someone else. Turning her head slightly in his direction, and seeing that this was indeed someone else caused her to slow her actions just slightly, natural curiosity bringing her defense mechanism back a notch.

"My name is Chase Benton; I am a private investigator and have come to take you out of here. What is your name?"

Sputtering through a haze of confusion she said "Greta"

"Greta, I am a good guy and we don't have much time. You are going to have to trust me and move quickly." he reached out his hand for hers.

Looking up at the man with the kind voice once again, Greta could feel something very different about him. He was not smiling but somehow she felt that he was and it was a smile of warmth and caring. She sat upright on the bed and reached out her hand. As she felt his touch, energy came through her arm that startled her into this new reality and began to talk to her mind. *"Move quickly!"* she could hear but not from spoken words and she allowed Chase to guide her from this horrible place.

Masanori had parked the car in the garage and had dashed into the bottom of the passageway. As he moved up the stairs a sight he had never seen struck terror into his soul. An open door sticking into the hallway where there had never been a door before froze him in his tracks. Eyes darting around, all his senses coming to full alert, Masanori knew his kingdom had been invaded and that his new enemy Chase Benton was near—very near. Quickly ducking into his office he reached up the wall and pulled off one of his swords and almost ritually pulled the Katana from its sacred covering. As he did he noticed his monitor and saw that a new e-mail had arrived since he left only 25 minutes ago. But it had been read! Clicking on his mouse he opened the message.

Masanori My Friend and Fellow Madman,
Chase Benton has arrived at your lair and your time has come. Chase must die or none of us will ever to be able to tread safely in the world doing what we do best. Fate has chosen you to be our deliverer, the one who will lead us against those that do not allow us to practice our religions, our faiths.
Fight well and live!

Chase led Greta by the hand out of the room and stood in the hallway for a moment getting his bearing and planning their exit strategy. He was sure that if he went up into the top house he would trip an alarm and who knows what else. The door into Greta's room had been wired with a false entry mechanism and he felt that if those buttons had been pushed something dreadful would have happened to whoever was in that room and perhaps even the one who pushed the buttons. The only safe way out would be the passageway that he found leading in from the outside. Clearly, Masanori had not found that entry way and would be quite surprised to find it and his prey missing.

He reached out again to try to find any dangers but saw nothing more than he had already felt in this horrible place. He took Greta and they began walking down the slightly lit corridor until they came upon the door he had opened from the outside. Masanori's office was down to the right and out of the corner of his eye he noticed something different from when he had left that room moments earlier. Looking around and keeping his senses at full alert he diverted Greta over to the office door to take a look inside. As he scanned the room everything looked the same until he came to the wall behind the desk. One of the ornamental swords had been taken off the wall!

As quickly as he could process that sight his minds eye opened up and fell into a state of mental slow motion and felt a blade begin its backward arc through the light air. All in one jerk Chase pulled Greta's arm with brute force and hurled her into the office just as he could feel the energy and path of the blade bearing down on him. Judging the impact of the blade by the energy it was emitting placed its contact at his neck and with precision he threw his head backwards and to the left just as the blade hit the side of the doorway where his head had been. The wood and metal frame exploded into tiny shards that showered his face and eyes with amazing force.

He could feel the sting on his eyelids and see the shiny razor of a blade inches in front of his face. The blade was buried in the wood frame and taking advantage of a few seconds of reprieve he darted into the office to protect Greta at all costs. She had fallen on the floor from the shear force of his unexpected shove and was still rolling towards the desk. Chase leapt over her and the desk with one bound and found himself ripping the last sword off the wall. Behind him he could hear the grunting sound of Masanori trying to reclaim his weapon from the door frame and turned to face the man they called the Samurai for the first time.

As Chase stared down his opponent, never breaking eye contact, he advanced back into the middle of the room and placed himself between the Samurai and Greta. She had started to scream again but her cries were not heard by either man. The sword in Chase's hand began to talk to him, and the feel, the balance, the weight, and the destruction it could wield all felt right. The men began to posture. Masanori held his weapon with both hands sticking out in front of his body and began to slowly move to his right. Chase carried his in his right hand holding it out to the side and raised his left arm up to the front of his body as if to shield himself. He realized the shield he could feel attached to his forearm was a thought and not a reality—an instinct from the past.

Masanori lunged at Chase and swept his Katana behind his head and brought it crashing down towards Chase's body. Reaching his sword hand up and over, Chase grabbed the end of his blade with his left hand just as the two steel razors met, sparks flying and metal screeching. Pushing back the blow with both hands Chase brought his knee crashing up into Masanori's solar plexus sending him reeling back across the room, shoulder splintering against the hard cobblestone wall. Masanori looked in horror as he could see Chase's hollow dark eyes penetrating and detached, planning their next move. Chase could smell the fear coming from his prey and slowly sidestepped to the left seeking the shoulder he now knew was wounded from the impact. Bringing his sword back up and to the right, he saw Masanori swing his right arm instinctively to the left to place his weapon in front of the impending strike. As soon as Masanori committed, Chase found his body continuing to spin to the right instead of stopping. His left hand came up and joined his right as his body leveraged its weight, catapulting his blade around to the unprotected left side of the killer. The impact was brutally powerful and as the sword came all the way through Chase thought for a moment that he had somehow missed his target. Seconds went by and as Chase straightened up and stood in a defensive crouch, he saw a thin red line begin to from around the waist of Masanori.

Masanori glared at Chase for besting him then dropped his eyes to the now gushing stream of blood flowing down his hips and legs. He tried to move to his left not realizing the extent of his wounds and watched as his body came apart into two pieces tumbling down to the ground. Greta's screams began to slowly enter Chase's consciousness as his body and mind crept back to the present and he became fully aware of his surroundings and the ordeal he had just faced. The warrior still at the fringe of his mind took over one more time as Chase approached Masanori's desk, opened the last e-mail, hit reply, typed out a few words then hit enter.

Chapter 25

New England

Louise sat straight up in the day bed she kept in her large computer room, startled, scared, head throbbing. She reached her hands up into her hair and found that she was soaked from sweating and realized that she had fallen asleep for over an hour from shear exhaustion. Her mind was foggy but as she focused, the dream she was having, the very bad dream, started to come back to her. She had been inside Clair, an electron, traveling around Clair's hardware circuits at the speed of light looking for anything that might be causing a problem with her precious system when far up ahead a shadow briefly appeared that she knew shouldn't be there. The shadow saw her coming and bolted through another circuit before she could catch up. She had been speeding around the inside of Clair checking every little nook and cranny, desperately trying to find whatever that thing was and neutralize it before it could do damage—thank God it was just a dream.....

For Louise, an intruder in her computer system was the worst kind of nightmare and all day she had been trying to process a nagging feeling that something WAS inside Clair, or someone, looking, probing, stealing information--postured to wreck havoc with the system if it wanted to. Her ego kept pushing the thought away because she knew she had built the system using all of the most sophisticated technology available, and then some, and kept telling herself that it was virtually impossible for someone to break into the computer. Even if an unauthorized user was on the system using one of the employee's user ID's, a program she had developed herself called "Watcher" would have picked it up. She had originally developed watcher as a tool to monitor the usage and training of the users, especially the psychics who by and large were computer illiterate. Watcher maintained a log and profile of each user's interactions with every piece of the system including the mouse, keyboard, and applications. Louise could run automated reports showing how well they had progressed in their learning of the system and how proficient they had become using it. It wasn't until later that she figured out that Watcher would also make a great security system. First, it was a training application and any hacker would not consider looking at it if they were trying to disable the real security apps of the system. Second the very nature of the program was such that by just looking at the real time statistics she could tell you if it was Karen because of the way and speed she typed, or Samuel because he checked his e-mail program religiously every 4 minutes or so, or Ronnie because it took her 7 seconds exactly to type in her password and she always went directly to the horoscope section of her on-line news program. This kind of real time monitoring and logging would bring a normal system to its knees but Louise had the luxury of having a very large computer system with more off peak processing capacity than God and a very small base of employee's to monitor.

Louise shook off the horrible dream feeling and grabbed her cup of 3 hour old coffee, looked into it and took a long gulp. Chase had been working with her on her intuitive skills and she just realized that there was indeed an intruder in the system. She pulled back her hair, wiped the sleep from her face, plunked into her large swivel chair and lit up all 6 monitors. She let her fingers and mind flow as she worked the keyboard like magic and soon there were four application names staring her in the face:

> Data Mining
> Tracker Program
> Clair 1.0
> Remote Wireless Connections

"Ok you little sucker, I know you're in there, all I need is for you to show your face just one time and I got ya! Louise thought to herself and began a full night of vigilance.

*****

The long trip back to the east coast came alive for Chase when the plane had come in for a landing and he could see Mount Monadnock waking in the distance with the rising sun from the east. Magic Mountain was alive and powerful, the morning shadows and bright light creating majesty and awesomeness that stirred him every time he saw it. Although he didn't sleep deeply after yesterday's ordeal he did sleep and his dreams were mellow and soft allowing his internal batteries a much needed charging. Before he left the Samurai's house he had left a long note to the local police, then escorted Greta out of that dreadful place and brought her to a neighbor's house for temporary refuge. Once he got in his car he placed a call to the local State Police, identified himself and gave them all his credentials. He told them where to go, what to do, and let them know that the FBI was stationed out in front of the other house and to please let the agents know about what happened at the State Police's convenience. They had tried to convince him to remain but told them he had pressing business and was already in flight but that his foundation was always available and would be lending a hand with post cleanup details and statements soon.

He was very grateful that he had been the one to find Susan and that he was able to honor her death and follow her passing. She would be back someday in another life he knew deep inside. All of a sudden a smile creased his face as he remembered that Wesley and Ashley were flying in early this morning from the Islands. Also, he was looking forward to seeing Seville after her very extreme first encounter as a member of Serial Connections. Before he had gone to sleep on the plane he had talked to Ronnie for a while as she was the only one still awake at that hour. Seville and Dug had made it back mid evening and apparently Seville was doing just fine. Ronnie said the wound to her arm was superficial and that she seemed to be acting like nothing had happened at all. She also noted that Seville had developed quite the edge during the day. She said that Karen had decided to stay overnight and that the girls had gone up to Chase's to retire.

Ronnie briefed him on the work that Cori had done and according to her she would have a good idea who the psychic perpetrator was and where to be found by morning. Cori always amazed Chase. A pure blood Native American, Cori had her roots deep inside Mother Earth and an inside track to the Great Spirit. He fondly remembered his first encounter with Cori at her home in Vermont many years ago. A few spring fly's had gotten onto her porch and had been dive bombing them relentlessly when Cori looked up at the old metal fly swatter hanging on a nail by the door. Within seconds the Fly's seemed to disappear and quiet was restored to the porch. Noticing the funny look on Chase's face she had simply offered that a pact had been made. She had explained to the fly's that she had no desire to swat them into another existence, but certainly would if they continued to harass the gathering—amazing.

He couldn't wait to find out who had been wrecking havoc with Serial Connections, and more importantly—why? His mind kept wandering to the drawing Ghost had provided him the other night regarding the principles and powers that seemed to be converging on them from all directions. In the back of his mind everything seemed vaguely familiar, a presence that was not unknown to him, yet hidden behind a curtain of energy that concealed its true nature and identity. He was at peace with this now, especially after his run in with Masanori. The stars had already cast the future in stone and his job was not trying to change the things he did not know but rather embrace them with all the resources he could muster. He smiled as he got off the plane and saw that Karen had left his truck for him, looking forward to the short drive around the mountain and home.

*****

Tim sat at the computer console, his fingers whizzing through the keyboard checking his locator map of the Serial Connections personnel to verify where Karen was at that moment. He had been slightly amused that both Karen and Seville had shared the same location during the night and couldn't help but wonder what that was all about. He was also curious about Susan Kincaid, her locator device went missing then she turned up dead at her house. What confused him was that he knew it had not been Masanori who killed her—then who? Masanori had now been taken out by Chase, who was already back in New Hampshire heading from Keene to the compound in Jaffrey at that very moment. This was getting good…..

"Where in the hell is she?" a rough voice announced from behind Tim. "We've been here all night waiting and I need to get up to my place."

"Shut up Emit, she'll be here when she gets here. Don't forget she's the bait that lets us take Chase out once and for all."

"Yeah, well, you'd better be right Tim. Things were going just fine for me until you stepped in and messed everything all up."

"Don't forget my friend, they already had your number and if I hadn't stepped in you'd be dead or behind bars right now."

"Maybe, but I got things to do and people to clip, so let's try to move things along a little faster ok?"

"Like I said Emit; Shut up! Hey, looks like she's starting to move." Tim said as he watched the screen and saw Karen's beacon coming out of the building and over to her car. Tim watched as the beacon stopped then began moving a little faster but instead of heading out the driveway it took a sharp left up towards Chase's place.

"Bonus Ball!" he said to himself.

"What's going on? Emit grunted.

"It looks like we get two for the price of one. Seville just hopped into Karen's car and they are headed in this direction. Emit, Karen is going to be a piece of cake but I'm not so sure about Seville. This is what I want you to do when they get here....."

*****

When Chase pulled into the compound he looked at the clock on the dash of the truck and saw that is was only 6:48AM. Thinking that Ronnie had probably just gone to bed and not knowing Cori's sleep habits he decided that it would best if he just went straight to his place, take a shower, check on the girls, and get some hot coffee going. He pulled the truck off to the right and headed up his long, winding driveway to the top of the hill. As he ascended the steep grade he slowed the truck down to a crawl so he could take in the scenery off to the right. A small heard of deer had wondered into the alfalfa field he planted every year and were quietly grazing with their heads down. They didn't seem to mind until the truck slowed then they all came to attention, heads perking up with quick checks to the left and right to get their bearings. A small sprite who barely sported 1 ½ antlers took a few steps forwards as if to protect the herd but retreated just as fast as they all turned and thundered off into the thick forest, white tails waving goodbye. He smiled to himself as the truck pulled up to the front of his place and he nosed the vehicle into his favorite spot that looked out over the back of the hill into the mountain ranges on the other side of the valley.

He quietly walked into his home and reached out with his senses to check things out. The fresh smell of coffee hit him first and a smile creased his face thinking that the girls were up, looking forward to catching up on the last days events with real live bodies. Turning into the kitchen he found a half full pot of coffee on the counter and two mugs sitting on the wonderfully carved semi-circle table perfectly fitted into the back end of the cooking island in the middle of the room. Looking more closely he saw a hand written note on the table next to a third mug, empty and dry, meant for him:

Welcome Home Chase!
Seville and I have gone to my place to
change clothes and freshen up.
We should be back around 7:30.

See ya soon!   Karen
PS: We will clean up when we return!

He read the note and looked at the clock again and saw that he had about thirty minutes to freshen up himself and some quiet time to boot. He looked around the kitchen and aside from the mugs there was no mess at all leaving him curious about the end of the note. Pouring a mug of java, he walked around through the house towards the back bedrooms. He was expecting the see the guest bedrooms all messed up from their sleeping there last night but none of them looked disturbed. Walking into his room provided a great deal of clarity. His rather large futon platform sat right in the middle back of the room and the sheets, blankets, and pillows were strewn around like there had been 10 kids engaged in a huge pillow fight. It was then it all hit him as his eyebrows raised and face contorted into a very surprised look of revelation. None of the guest rooms had been slept in and this bed was much more of a mess than one person could have possibly made and even then two people just sleeping wouldn't have even come close to the damage. A sly look came across his face as he walked up to the bed and held out his right arm, palm facing downwards as if he was going to touch the crime scene. He pulled his hand back thinking that he didn't really want to invade their privacy but then grinned again thinking *"Hell, this is my room"* and his palm dove onto the futon. At once pictures began flashing into his mind of the activity that had taken place there during the night and his look of amazement turned to one of blissful disappointment as he thought *"Jeeze, you guys could have waited for me!...."*

*****

"A what!" roared Henry White into the radio.

"A Moon Light Hikers Club" said Agent Tom Sands. "Every full moon this club takes hikes all over the Cape. Early this morning they found these two body bags, called in the locals here in Truro who knew we were still here and had us over for a look. It's the remains of the Pastor and his wife. They are missing their extremities and it looks just like the Lumber Jacks M.O."

"How can you be sure it's them if the extremities are missing?" barked Henry who was sitting down on the door step of Emits Cape Code house not a mile away.

"I don't for sure Henry, but they have been missing since yesterday morning and the two bodies, what's left of them anyway, fit the descriptions to a tee. At this point I have to make the assumption that it's them."

"Agent Ward just shared with me that Emit has gone missing again John. She said that when you got the call and checked his house he was long gone. Furthermore, when they fanned out around the house they found and old garage or shed way out in the bog behind his house with fresh tire tires tracks going into and out of the garage a couple of times. What in the hell have you guys been doing here?"

"Henry, I don't know what to tell you. We had no idea the bog had an access road into it from the other side. Our local maps made no indication at all, so we never even thought of the possibility."

"We'll talk about that later Tom." He looked out over Emits front yard and eyed the FBI S.W.A.T. van sitting in the street. "Tom, get your ass over here to Emits right now. I am going to have Agent Ward suit me up. You and I are going to Maine."

*****

When Chase got out of the shower and was starting to get dressed he heard voices floating down the hallway from the kitchen. Wesley's loud boom was unmistakable and a cheer came across his face. As he hurried down the hallway and turned the corner, Wesley and Ashley were sitting on one side of the table and Ronni and Cori were at the other side. He went up to Cori first and hauled her out of the chair for a huge hug. "Cori, it's great to see you. How are things up in Vermont?"

"Same old same old" she said returning the hug, always glad to see Chase no matter what the circumstance. "You're looking a little older than the last time I saw you boy!" she exclaimed, running her hand through his long blondish grey hair.

"Thanks a bunch Cori, just what I needed to hear." And he bent over and gave Ronnie a squeeze on the shoulder and kiss on the check. "Good morning Ronni. Or should I say middle of the night. What in the heck got you out of bed so early?"

"Are you kidding? The morning prayer drums have been going off for the last hour and short of throwing them in the lagoon there was no chance I was going to stay asleep." she said with a friendly glare at Cori.

Cori just rolled her eyes, smiled and said "You gotta do what you gotta do!"

Chase practically ran around the table and picked Ashley's entire 4'11" frame right off the ground and held her tight. Putting her down he held out his forearm against hers and said "Jesus Ashley, if it wasn't for that full head of blond hair I'd swear you were one of the locals down in St Bart's!" then he stepped around her and approached Wesley. The two men reached out their hands and grabbed each other in the Indian wrestle style and pulled into each other, Wesley's massive 6'5" body towering over Chase. "Good to see you Chase" Wesley said in a soft voice, letting go of his long time student, teacher, and friend.

"Great to see all of you too, I just wish it was a couple of weeks from now at the benefactors meeting and not here under these circumstances."

"True" Wesley said in his stoic tone while other heads nodded in agreement. "Hey, where are the ladies? We are dying to meet Seville and see Karen. I heard they were hold up here last night"

"They were, I just got in about 30 minutes ago and found a note that they went over to Karen's to get some fresh clothes and would be back by 7:30 or so."

"Ronni, did you get to talk to Seville yesterday when she got back?" Wesley asked.

"Not really, she was tired and a little wound up so I figured it would be best not to start picking her brain about what happened."

"Probably a good idea; It's been a while since I've heard of something like that happen to an untrained person."

"It happened to me last night!" Chase offered to the group causing all heads to turn in his direction.

"How so?" said Wesley with a look of alarm.

Chase described the entire Seattle encounter to his friends starting with finding Susan's body at her home then ending with the sword fight he had with Masanori in the dungeon.

"Did you do that guided meditation on the way out to Seattle yesterday?" Ronni asked astonished at what she just heard.

"Yes. I was under for over two hours guys. It was the most amazing past life recall I've had yet. They were very vivid movies running through my mind from the time I was a little child until the time of my death." He lifted his sweatshirt and exposed the scar on his lower chest over his heart. "I finally know where this birthmark came from. This is how I was killed well over two thousand years ago."

Ronni and Wesley just looked at each other with smiles on their faces and Cori and Ashley were still in a kind of shock.

"When Masanori came at me yesterday with that sword it was like somebody else took over inside me and all of sudden I was fighting like a champion gladiator. I still had my conscious thought but my instincts were definitely not my own. I remember when I came crashing down on him with that fatal blow I knew exactly what I was doing and what the outcome would be. I had set him up so that I could decisively take him out. It was very scary and at the same time one of the most awesome and exhilarating experiences I have ever had."

Just then Dug walked in and greeted everybody and Chase went around and started fixing another pot of coffee before he said "Dug, how would you like to fill us in on what happened down in Maryland yesterday? How's your head doing?"

"I figured as much" he said sizing up the table then choosing a stool right in the middle so he could see and talk to everyone. "My head will be ok. The Dr. said we can get the R out with a little plastic surgery. I'll live. As for Seville, it was the weirdest thing I have ever seen, even though I have seen some pretty weird stuff coming out of this group. Connie and I had been taken by Fox, and Connie was still out cold, getting prepped by Richard for only God knows what when I saw a shadow coming up the stairs very slowly and quietly. Richard had his back to the stairs and Seville came up and into the room without being heard. I was keeping my peripheral vision on her so that Fox didn't see me gawking at what was just about to take him out. He must have sensed something because all of a sudden he got up and spun around holding Connie's pistol and told Seville to freeze. She had her gun with her but it was tucked into her waist holster behind her back and she didn't even make a move for it. You should have seen her eyes Chase. They were the most vengeful red glowing eyes I have ever seen. I could tell it wasn't her. When he realized she wasn't going to stop he got scared and fired a shot up into the rafters but she didn't even blink. That's when he leveled the gun and started pinching off shots right at her. The first ones missed completely but I could see the third shot graze her shoulder and she kept right on coming. Before he could get off another shot I could see her right arm shooting out at him with incredible speed, his body looked like it was hit by a jack hammer but before it could repel backwards from the impact his torso stopped and began moving towards Seville. That's when blood started spurting out all over the place and before I even had a chance to conceptualize what was going on she pulled back her arm and he literally fell over on his back in slow motion. Blood was spouting out the holes in his chest like a bunch of geysers. One second after he fell, Seville changed. Her facial features softened up, her upper body muscles became loose, and her eyes fell back to what I guess is normal then she collapsed on the floor. Luckily some one heard the shots from out on the street and came barging up. I had the guy untie me then go get the police. I had just enough time to figure out what had happened even though I was scared shitless and took her gun out and put it on the floor behind her. Then I quickly took the videos you have probably already seen before the cops got there."

Wesley whistled through his teeth and Ronni gave a glance over to Chase. The rest of the group just remained silent. Chase broke the ice and said "Dug, you did an awesome job. I'm not sure I would have been able to keep my cool the way you did."

"Chase thanks for the kudos but you know damn well I really screwed up bad. I could've gotten all three of us killed by letting Fox take me out in the first place."

"Dug, it is what it is" offered Wesley from his perch. "Things are meant to happen for a reason and in this case, other than a few scrapes things worked out just fine."

"Right" said Chase. "Dug, is it true that Henry White showed up?"

"Yeah, what a you know what he is" said Dug.

"Dug we all speak French here" said Ronni with a smile. "It pains me to hear you restrain your natural language."

Dug looked at Ronni and a thin smile broke across his face. "Gottcha—thanks Ronni. Mr. Prick was there all right. He was wicked pissed off at me, at Connie, and especially us." He said looking around at the group insinuating Serial Connections. He had the balls to order me back into the crime scene instead of going in the ambulance with Seville. I basically told him to F-, fuck off. So tell me guys; what happened to Seville?"

"Spirit DNA" was all Chase got out of his mouth before the large screen monitor on the wall came to life and Louise Penta barged in on the party.

Wesley noticed it first. Louise looked like a piece of shit left out in the sun to dry. Her hair messy and greasy, she had large bags under her eyes that dropped down her cheeks, and perspiration was dripping down the side of her head.

"Chase, we got big problems." said Louise as she started rambling at 60 miles an hour.

"Wooaaah Louise, slow down and start from the beginning."

"Last night I got this awful feeling that Clair had been hacked and that somebody was, still is, controlling certain parts of the system. But wait, it's that and, I think Karen and Seville are missing. I have been in the tracker program for the last three hours trying to figure out what happened to Susan's transmitter and trying to find a footprint of the hacker and about 15 minutes ago both their signals just turned off. At first I thought it was a glitch because of the work I was doing but when I couldn't get the signals back I called over to Karen's house and didn't get an answer. I tried her cell phone and its shut off and same with Seville's. I got a really bad feeling then all of sudden I got this e-mail and I knew for sure."

Benton, Emit and I have your women. If I were you I wouldn't expect them to last until sunset today. First goes Karen, then your precious new addition Seville. Emit has a real good surprise in store for both of them and I have a really big surprise for you!
See ya in Maine

The room had already turned quiet and as the psychics in the room intuitively reached out to the energy of the sender to try to pick something up they all started to experience a dull throbbing in the sides of their heads. Cori saw what was going on and immediately turned her energetic self invisible so that she would not be picked up by the very strong energy sent to block the group. She once again reached out to the energy beam and silently followed it to its origin, very careful not to get close enough to be detected. This time she saw the same group as before but instead of being in a dark dank cave they were circled in the living room of an old house. Concentrating as hard as she could she kept hold of the energy beam and backed up and out of the house until she had a good view of the dwelling they were in. Taking a mental picture of the house she noticed that it was in a very congested area and backed up even farther to try to get an idea of where this place was. Nothing looked familiar but as she inched back one more step the top of a building came into view that evoked a long ago memory. Just a little farther and all of sudden she was looking at the roof of a house that was hundreds of years old. Quickly counting in her mind she added up seven gables on the roof of the house that was only a block away from where the psychic terror was. Now she had it.

Chase was looking at the e-mail and despite the throbbing in his head felt like there was something right within his grasp. He strained even harder, reaching out the arm of his third eye towards the object right there in front of him. Just as he was about to grab the object he felt it begin to fade. "Nooo" he screamed and just as he began to think he was going to fail he felt a very familiar nudge come up from within him. Wesley was helping! With an amazing last reach his psychic hand extended right at the object and just before it disappeared his finger touched it and for a very brief instant a very blurry picture of a man came into his mind. He tried with all his strength to smooth the picture out but couldn't and the picture faded before he could identify the man.

"What is it Chase" Wesley said very concerned.

"I missed it Wesley. I was so damn close. Thanks for trying to help." And he sat back on his stool for a minute to regain his composure. "Louise, what is the status of the computer system?"

"Clair just shut down. So did the tracking system and the remote connection program."

"Louise, do you remember a couple of days ago when Karen's boyfriend Tom was connected in to do the data mining interface?"

"Yeah sure, I wasn't happy about that but you're the boss."

"Well I think—no I know that our intruder is Karen's boyfriend Tom."

Wesley chimed in and said "I don't get it. What's in this for him?"

"You guys will just have to trust me on this. Wesley, I need you and Louise to rout out this problem and get Clair back on-line. Cori, what's the plan of attack for nailing whoever is sending this damned psychic block at us?"

Cori looked over at Ronni with a sly look and said "We're going to Salem!"

"Salem New Hampshire?" Ronnie said.

"No Salem Massachusetts."

"Why?" Ashley asked with a quizzical look.

"Why girls, haven't you noticed the date today?"

Everyone looked around the kitchen and spied a long cloth calendar on the wall and as they honed in on the date they heard Cori say "Ronni, call out the troops, its Halloween, and were going on a witch hunt!"

Chase looked at Cori and Ronni and shook his head. "I hope you know what you're doing. Since Clair is down I want everyone in the field to have headsets on. Wesley and Louise are going to be our command center until they get Clair up and running." Then he looked over at Dug and the bandage on his head. "Are you up for some field work?"

Dug lit right up. "You bet boss"

"Good, go get Connie and make sure you're both dressed for the woods, the three of us are leaving in 15 minutes. It seems everybody else is ghost hunting today and we're no exception."

*****

The two men and their cargo moved quickly though the uneven terrain on the large utility ATV headed up and into the heavily forested ridge. Once they reached the top they could see Emits cabin coming up quickly and Emit moved the machine expertly around to the side door of the dwelling. Tim got out first and stretched as he looked around. He had been here before although Emit did not know it, and had no reason to find out. He had used this place over the years from time to time for some of his own fun and games.

"Tim, why the hell do you have it out for Chase Benton so bad?"

"He screwed me over a long time ago Emit. He killed my brother and now its time for him to pay."

"How in the heck did he kill your brother?"

"My brother and I had a little side business going Emit. Just like the one you've got here and my brother got caught in the crossfire, Chase took him out but didn't catch me."

"That really sucks Tim, sorry to hear about that."

"My brother and I were very close and to see him killed was one of the most painful things in my life. That's why I have it out for Chase Benton and that's why he's not going to last the day. Ok Emit, I figure we have about 30-40 minutes before the storm troops get here. I want you to take Karen and get her all set up on that little contraption you have out back. Get the engine going and set the timer on it for exactly one hour. Then get your rifle and set up over on the top of that ridge and keep a sharp eye out. The FBI is going to be coming here too and I want Henry White almost as bad as Chase. He didn't kill my brother but he sure was involved. And Emit, make no mistake about it, it's either them or us."

"What are you going to do?"

"Seville and I are going to be a little further up the ridge where I have a good view of what's going on." Tim said as he pulled his duffel bag and hunting bow out of the back of the vehicle.

"You sure you don't want a riffle? I got a few in the cabin."

"No thanks, Chase is going down the same way my brother did."

Karen and Seville were in the back of the ATV tied up with ropes, duct tape wound around their heads and mouths. Seville glanced over at

Karen after listening to their captor and she saw that Karen was sinking deeper and deeper into shock. Her eyes were practically swollen shut from non-stop sobbing since they both came too in the van a couple of hours ago. She could only imagine what Karen was thinking and feeling about this man she had put every ounce of her trust in. And now listening to the fact that he had been using her for over a year to launch his vendetta against Chase was pushing her over the edge. Seville had been kicking herself in the ass for walking right into their trap and at that moment did not feel very secure in the fact that they were going to get out of this.

As Tim/Tom yanked Seville out of the van she glared at him and as she did she actually felt her muscles twitching the same way they did down in Maryland. Then she realized that whatever happened to her yesterday just might be her friend again today. As Tim pulled her along the leaf covered trail she began to go within, searching, feeling, for this thing that she hoped would come out again—soon.

Karen could barely walk and Emit ended up picking her right up and carrying her around to the back of the cabin. When she saw the large apparatus and figured out just what it was, she let go and fainted. Emit was just fine with that, she wasn't the type he would have picked to clip the happy wings anyway.

*****

"Ok folks lets get the system check under way" everyone heard Wesley bellow through their integrated headphones. "We are going to have to do this the old fashioned way except we have real high tech equipment to do it with. In case you were wondering the headsets you are wearing can receive and send our signal three miles below the ocean surface so you won't have to worry about being out of range. Let's check in one at a time starting with the Maine contingent."

"Chase here, Dug here, Connie here."

"Ok, now the Ghostbusters; Ronni and your class."

"Ronnie here, Cori here, Ashley here, Jan here, Amy here, Linda here, Gerry here."

"Great, we are all talking and set up. Logistics: Louise is going to be primary with the Maine group and we are going to switch them over to a different channel when we're done with the check. I am going to be primary for the Salem group and will also be keeping my ear on things on the other channel through a speaker. Ronni, where are you guys now?"

"We are all in the van a couple of doors down from the house."

"Chase?"

"We are just pulling into the back road that leads up to the old logging trail on the other side of the mountain from Emits place. We should be at the trail head in another 15-20 minutes."

"Ok guys anything else?" Wesley announced.

Chase came on and spoke to the entire group. "Alright team, this is it. Remember we already lost Susan and whoever is behind all this obviously doesn't care who he takes out or how. Ronni and Cori, any sign of violence on your end and haul your guys out of there faster than you can say boo."

"Got it Chase" he heard them all say in unison.

"We know that Emit is here and that there is at least one other wild card with him and one down in Salem. Until we get the psychic block down I am not going to be able to see a thing. Wesley and Louise are able to track all of us now with the headphones so whatever you do don't take them off or we won't be able to find you. You guys back at the ranch keep working to get the system up and let me know as soon as it is. Good luck everybody, and don't forget we all have a date at my place tomorrow night for a venison feast!"

*****

"Well, Well" Ronni said as she looked from the window of the van down and across the street. The van was loaded with 5 of Ronni's most promising students. A woman had just come to the front door, stepped out, looked around, and headed back in the house.

"Who's that?" asked Cori.

"That is Rosemary Cullet, an old pupil of mine from about 15 years ago."

Jan piped in "I remember her Ronni; she was a Pagan and belonged to that Church over in Athol Massachusetts."

"That's right Jan. I had nothing but trouble with her for three years. She was one of the most insecure people I had ever met. She couldn't get over the fact that some of us had developed to be stronger than her and ended up not coming to class any more. I haven't heard a word from her since."

"She obviously remembers you Ronni." Cori said.

"And she has developed to be pretty strong too." Ronni added.

"What was she just doing at the door?" Nancy asked from the back seat.

"I just knocked on the door." Cori said, tickled to see her ploy work.

"What?" asked Linda.

"I just sent a little psychic knock to the door to see who might come out."

Heads from the back of the van came to attention when they heard this.

"Here's the plan ladies and gentleman: we need to break up the circle they have going on inside which means we have to do two things. One is to keep Rosemary distracted and her influence over the dark circle to a minimum. The second thing is we need to build a huge shield around this house to keep the circles blocking energies contained. Distracting Rosemary is going to easy and we need to the get the shield up while she's busy. As soon as she knows the shield is up and gets back to the circle it won't be so easy. They are going to try to attack each link in the shield, i.e. us, with all kinds of crap. All you need to remember is that no matter what you see or feel, it is only an illusion and do your very best to keep your concentration and focus on our job."

Jan spoke up. "So how do we distract Rosemary?"

"Funny you should ask Jan."

"Oh boy! me and my big mouth."

*****

Chase's truck was parked off the side of the road at the head of an old trail that headed east into a valley. He had a map out on the back of the truck and was going over the layout with Connie and Dug. "Here is Emits house" he pointed to a spot about three miles from where they were and ran his fingers along a valley towards their current position and stopped about half way.

"It makes sense that he has something set up right around here in this valley. Searches of his house showed nothing going on there so I am suspecting that he has a cabin or some kind of work area up here in these ridges. By the looks of the map it is very well protected simply by the sheer drop and if they have the place canvassed we may very well be climbing up these walls to get up to where they are."

Pointing to a spot on the map Chase said "Connie and Dug, I want you two to focus on Emit here and try to keep him busy or take him out: We're beyond proof at this point. I'll bet that the girls are somewhere in this area and there should be a steep but climbable trail that he can get up with his ATV. If you can take him out head up that trail as fast as you can and look for Karen and or Seville. Once we get to about this point keep a sharp lookout and stay alert. He is a hunter and will no doubt be keeping sentry with a high powered rife and scope. He'll see us coming well before we see him unless those guys down in Salem break down that wall sooner rather than later."

Chase pulled out two large crates from the back of the truck and cracked them open. The first was filled with ropes and climbing gear and he passed completes sets of equipment to Connie and Dug, then pulled out one for himself. Next he opened the other crate that was filled with 4 assault riffles, ammunition, marine issue combat knives, flashlights, and colt 45 pistols with shoulder holsters.

"You might want to bring the 45's instead of your weapons because they are much more rugged out in these conditions and will give you a little longer distance for close in combat" Chase said as he hauled out one more container and moved it over to the side away from Connie and Dug. As they began putting on their gear, Chase began getting his stuff ready.

"You're not taking a riffle?" Connie asked.

"No Connie, me and firearms don't mix very well. I will take one of those pistols though just in case."

Dug watched Chase pull his things together and begin to load his bow with some very sharp looking broad head arrows. The bow quiver held 4 arrows and when he was done filling it he pulled out another old fashioned over the back quiver and loaded another 6 arrows into it. When he slung it over his shoulder Dug noticed an arrow lashed to the outside of the quiver, pointing upward. The arrow looked very old and was very rusty and he could have sworn it had dried blood caked on it.

"Chase, what's with the arrow on the side of your quiver?" he asked.

Chase looked to the side as if he could see the arrow and said "It's my good luck charm guys. That's the arrow that brought down the Hacker 17 years ago and I never go out hunting without it."

Just then a series of rifle shots went off in the air due east of where they were and they could here smaller caliber shots fired in return.

"Sounds like Henry White just ran into Emit!" Connie said remembering her conversation with Henry on the cell phone just 40 minutes earlier. He had told her that he and Agent Sands were just about to Emits place, and tried to convince Connie to stall Chase until they were able to pull in Emit themselves.

"FBI or not we had better get going, lets double time and get over there before all hell breaks loose." Said Chase as the trio started running up the trail and right towards hell.

*****

"I got it!" cried Wesley as his fingers moved over the keyboard with a fierce determination. "Louise, he was getting in through your test and development system "Clair 1.0". I can see his paws all over the place.

"Wesley that's impossible. I spent two hours going through Clair 1.0 last night and I didn't find a damn thing."

"That's because you were looking in the wrong place Louise. He initially got in through the remote connection program as we suspected but was using one of your integration connectors to actually get into the program and manipulate applications and data" he said as his fingers came to rest and Clair came roaring back to life.

"Wesley I feel like a total schmuck."

"Don't you dare think like that, you're one of the most brilliant tech's I have ever met and without you and that brilliance Serial Connections would be ten years behind the times in terms of its technology capability. Has Chase told you that I have been pushing him to patent this system and start marketing it to law enforcement agencies around the world?"

"Thanks Wesley, but I still feel like a schmuck. No, he hasn't told me about that."

"Well, he doesn't want to and the only reason he doesn't is because he wants to keep us all pure in terms of mission and focus. He's right, but Jonathan has started turning up the volume on that one too because he is a business man and would love the foundation to be able to turn some dollar profit too."

"Ok Wesley, later, lets get our baby back up and running. The guys in the field are going to need our help!"

"Right" and as if on cue they both turned their swivel chairs back into the command center and started playing Clair like she was a fine musical instrument.

*****

The front door opened and a woman, not the same one who came out before, poked her head out and looked at Jan. "Yes, how can I help you?"

"I'm here to see Rosemary please."

"Rosemary? There isn't a Rosemary here I'm afraid."

"Yes the woman who just came out the door about 15 minutes ago?" Jan spoke.

The tall red head thought for a second and said "You mean Selena. Yes she's here but I'm afraid she is very busy right at the moment."

"Please tell Rosemary that some old friends are here to see her. I am sure she will want to visit."

"Whatever, wait here." The woman closed the door and Jan stayed put on the front step until a moment later when the woman who called herself Selena opened the door and looked out doing a double take. "Jan, is that you?" she said with a look of astonishment and recognition.

"Yes Rosemary, it's really good to see you again. Selena? When did you come up with that name?"

"Well, you know, it's a business name. What brings you all the way out to Salem? How did you find me?"

"I didn't find you Rosemary, Cori and Ronni did." And she stepped aside to let Selena peer out into the large front yard. Jan heard her gasp as her eyes found Ronni off to the right and a woman who she didn't know but had heard of standing off to the left. While Selena was trying to comprehend what was going on, Jan backed slowly down the walk and entered the circle they had formed around the house and the battle began.

*****

Dug was leading the way as the three of them made quick time of the trail between them and the sound of gunfire; the terrain was starting to change dramatically and the sides of the valley turned from wooded slopes into walls of rock up to a hundred feet tall. Rounding the next bend Dug suddenly came to an abrupt halt and signaled the team behind him to stop and crouch. A hundred yards ahead they could see a body lying on the ground, gunfire hitting all around it. Right in between them and the body was a very steep trail that cut straight up into the ridge, fresh ATV tracks cut into the smoothed over soil and rocks. Everybody got out their binoculars and starting taking a look around both below and up in the rocks. Suddenly a shot rang out from the trail from somewhere near the body and Connie pointed her glasses at the source.

"It's Henry White. It looks like he's pinned down in those rocks off to the left. The guy down must be Agent Sands. He's not moving but that doesn't mean much. He could be wounded and playing dead."

"Louise, how are we doing getting Clair and the tracking program up and running? We're here and I need to know where the hell the girls are."

"Chase, Wesley got Clair back up and we are working on the tracking system right now. We are almost there."

"What's the report from Salem?"

Wesley chimed in this time. "The team is on location and things just got started Chase. You should be clear any time now."

Chase could still feel the dull ache in the sides of his head so for now he was on human power and started pointing his glasses way up the ridge. Another shot rang out from above and Dug whispered into his headset. "I got the shooter; he is wedged into the rocks about 9:30, midway up the hill. He's got good protection and clear shooting lanes all in front of the trail going up."

Connie was still looking over at Henry White and said "Chase and Dug, can you guys cover me so I can go over and get Henry out of that mess?"

"Connie, do you think you and Henry can get up the wall on the far side? If you guys can get up there then Dug and I can start our ascent from this side and get him in between us."

"I can go up first if I have cover, then secure a rope and let Henry climb up after me. I see your plan. We can hold Emit down once we are up and then you guys will have an easy climb."

"That's the thought" said Chase. "We still don't know where the other guy is but I am sure he is up there somewhere just waiting for us to show. Can you see the smoke coming from the North East? I can hear an engine running too. The smoke smells like a gas engine. I wonder what that is.?"

"It's probably a generator Chase, and I'll bet that's the cabin and where the girls are."

"Ok Connie, get ready to go. He hasn't seen us yet so once you start sprinting I'll start spraying his location." said Dug, checking his weapon and clip and on the count of three Connie dashed out into the open trail and sprinted the 60 yards totally exposed. Dug waited until he could see the shooter stand up to take a bead on his new quarry then let loose four rapid fire shots right at the man. The rocks around him exploded and he quickly retreated back into his crevice never getting off a shot. Dug could see her jump behind the group of rocks to join Henry. Just then Chase turned his head up into the hill and told Dug to duck right at the very second a hunting arrow came whistling by Dug's head burying itself into the soft sand in the trail.

"Hello there whoever you are!" said Chase in a whisper. The battle had begun here too.

*****

Ronni had coached the team on the way in on visualization and what they needed to accomplish in order to put up a super strong shield around the house in Salem. Now, she and the team completely circled the two story dwelling, each member having two other members in their line of sight in order to maintain a closed and connected energy field. While Rosemary was standing on the front doorstep still in shock, Ronni and Cori wasted no time. Eyes open they all started to imagine a bright gold light extending from outstretched hand to outstretched hand until the circle had been completed. Now the light began to lift into a beautiful arced dome until it met at the pinnacle over the top of the house and closed itself, sealing off any way for energy to escape.

Almost at the same time Rosemary disappeared back into the house and in moments long black whispery tentacles began floating from the house, reaching out, striking the newly created wall and testing the strength of the shield. Each time they hit the golden light, sparks shot into the air and the tentacles bounced back into the empty air within, trapped, unable to continue their mission.

*****

Connie was almost at the top of the rock wall and as she looked up was grateful that a huge boulder just to her left would provide natural cover for her while she secured her climbing rope and helped Henry get up the rock face. She slid her agile body up and over the edge of the cliff and quickly found a tree suitable to hold the weight of the man following her. She threw the coil of rope over the side then looked over as it unwound itself and landed on the floor of the trail next to Henry. Henry set up the rope and began his climb.

Chase was peering into the rocks and ridges off to the left of where he and Dug were. Dug was pinging off a shot up into the rocks once every minute or so to keep Emit occupied while Connie and Henry made it up to his level. He could see Henry awkwardly begin his climb and Connie up about 120 feet silently coaching his ascent.

The arrow had come from way up in the hill and as Chase looked around the natural horseshoe indentation of the cliff he checked out all three sides of the walls but could see nothing but rocks and thick, short pine trees providing great shelter. Chase looked at the arrow in the ground and began mentally back tracking it based on the angle and direction of its impact into the trail. He followed a path up high and to the right. When he zeroed in on the area he still couldn't see a thing.

Just then all hell broke loose.

"Chase this is Louise, we have the tracker up."

"Shit" he heard Wesley spew into the speaker. "We have doubles. Chase, I am looking at a topo map of your area with the tracker beacons lit up. I have doubles for you and Dug. I need to take out the headset beacons for you and Dug because the doubles are screwing everything up. There. Ok, I got Karen now; she is stationary and about 20 meters from where Connie is. There's Seville. She is almost directly over your head Chase about 150 feet high."

As Chase was listening to the computer team the dull ache in the side of his head disappeared and almost instantly a wave came over him like he had been hit by a truck. He knelt down on the ground holding his head causing Dug to get immediately worried. He had been fighting the block so hard that when the block went away all his psychic energy exploded and he was picking up shit from all over the place and couldn't process any of it.

Wesley sensed what was happening and said "Chase, pullback and reground yourself. Settle your spirit and focus on what you need to accomplish."

As Chase did what he was told he grabbed hold of his own mind and gained control over the visions and pictures flooding through his third eye. He reached out with one thought: Where do we need to be? And as quickly as the thought left his mind he saw a picture of Karen way up in the hills, her body roped and tied, laying on what looked to be a conveyor belt. At the end of the conveyor belt were very sharp blades spinning in perfect synchronization, waiting for her to come.

*****

The psychic team in Salem could feel the power and the energy of the shield that was in their command. Between Ronni and Cori they could see all the team members and kept a sharp eye out for any threats coming from within the house. Looking down her line Ronni could see Amy standing with her eyes closed, a look of peace and love on her face, radiating the glow of the shield. Then out from the house another long black tentacle shot straight at her and rammed the shield right in front of her face. Amy's look turned to horror as her eyes opened and she saw the head of a large serpent, foot long fangs dripping with venom, repeatedly striking the golden canopy. Her concentration disrupted, Ronni watched in disbelief as that side of the shield came tumbling down and more black tentacles shot through the air escaping their cage.

"Focus Amy!" cried Ronni. "Remember it's all in your head, the snake is not real!"

With all her strength Amy closed her eyes and put her thoughts on her children, causing her spirit to regain control and swell over with love. The golden light began to rise again and more black tentacles racing for freedom became trapped in the enclosure. Cori could not see Amy but did see the large snake come out and attack her. She looked at Gerry to her left and Ashley further down to check on them when a figure came dancing out of the side of the house. It was a Witch Doctor, dressed in ceremonial headdress and he was staring Cori down with the most evil eyes she had ever seen. He was carrying a gourd with seeds and shaking it at her violently throwing his magic at her, trying to get her to back down and run away. At that moment Cori realized what the dark circle was doing. They were reaching through the shield to discover the deepest, darkest fears they had and then were conjuring up apparitions of those fears for the attack.

"Is that all you got!" Cori screamed at the Witch Doctor and just as suddenly her lack of fear disintegrated the black magic into dust.

*****

Chase was just telling Connie and Dug where they could find Karen and that he felt she was in severe danger when he got whacked in the head and he lost all of his senses again. "Wesley, what's going on in Salem, I just lost it again."

"It's just temporary Chase. They are still securing the site."

Chase looked through his binoculars to see how Henry was doing when he noticed Henry snagged on a jagged out-cropping. All of sudden his body jerked free and the pocket that was caught ripped open spilling credit cards and loose change down the side of the cliff to the ground below.

"Connie, is everything all right up there?"

"Yeah Chase, Henry just caught his pants but he's on his way up again."

"You guys have to hurry Connie; Karen doesn't have much time at all."

"Got it Chase!"

Louise and Wesley were just about finished re-calibrating the tracker system when both their eyes caught sight of something very eerie. Just below Connie a new light began to blink on and off and drop precipitously down about 75 feet. When the beacon settled on the ground the initials of the person wearing the device blinked on screen. It read SEC. Susan Elizabeth Kincaid.

"Chase and Connie, listen up for a minute. We have another problem. Connie what just happened underneath you?" Wesley said, all three of the field agents hearing the great concern in his voice.

"Nothing Wesley." Connie replied. "Henry just got caught up on a rock but he's loose now and on his way up."

"Wesley what's going on?" said Chase.

"Chase, we just found Susan Kincaid's transmitter. It's on the ground right beneath Connie."

Silence fell over the entire group as each of them thought about the ramifications of what Wesley just said. Chase replayed the picture of all the contents of Henry's pockets falling down to the ground just a moment before and his concern turned a bright red shade of rage as he stared at the man through his field glasses scaling the steep wall.

Connie was still sitting on the edge of the ledge with the rope holding Henry between her legs when the shock wave hit her. Chase had told her and Dug every excruciating detail of finding Susan dead on her porch, disfigured, and beaten. He had told them that he figured it had been Masanori who killed Susan as a ploy to get Chase out in the open with his guard down. They had no reason to believe otherwise: until now.

Connie's mind started flashing: Her grandfather, the academy, the turmoil and the strife at the hands of people like Henry White at the Agency. Her eyes turned dark as she looked at the man slowly approaching up the rope. "Henry how was your trip to Seattle?" she asked, calmly and deliberately.

"What trip to Seattle?" Henry gasped as he struggled up the rope.

"Henry now's not the time for lies. Tell me about Susan Henry?"

Everyone was listening to Connie through their headsets and Chase got an awful feeling that she was about to do something very stupid and started trying to talk her down. She couldn't hear a thing.

"Why did you kill Susan Henry?"

Hearing Susan's name caused Henry to come to attention. He looked up from his precarious position at the dark penetrating eyes just 10 feet above him then looked down more than 90 feet to the jagged rocks below.

"Connie, pull me up so we can talk."

Connie stopped pulling the rope and let Henry hang on the side of the sheer cliff. "We can talk just fine right here Henry. Go ahead, tell me. Why did you kill Susan?"

Henry felt trapped; his forehead was dripping sweat from the climb and more so from his own revelation that what he had done was horrible. For just an instant he came out of the ego driven stupor that had been driving him for years and crystallized a picture of himself—a monster.

"Connie, you don't understand; the pressure at the Agency was brutal. There was talk about disbanding the Serial Team altogether because of our lack of results. I had no choice."

Chase was still talking to Connie when the psychic block lifted again and his eye went right to her. He saw in an instant what she was about to do and cried into the headset. "Connie, wait, just let Henry hang there. He's not going anywhere. Susan will have her justice." But as he reached out to her again she was not backing down in the slightest. He couldn't let this woman ruin her career over a man like Henry White and he desperately searched for a way to stop her when he felt the bow in his hands. He knew what he had to do as he plucked an arrow from his quiver and loaded it into position. Standing up right in the face of potential fire, Chase drew the string back with his mechanical trigger and sighted in the man hanging on for his life. Judging for wind and distance he closed his eyes and let the arrow loose.

Connie was looking down at Henry with pure hatred and disgust and without hesitation pulled out her marine knife and cut the rope. Looking down at the man whose face now showed horror at what she'd just done Connie yelled "You fucking Bastard, rot in hell."

In slow motion Connie watched Henry fall away from his perch just as an object came soaring through the air space where Henry's head had been a nano-second before. The arrow struck the side of the wall and careened off into woods as she watched Henry plummet to the ground and his bones shatter into a thousand pieces.

*****

Ronni could feel a momentary break in the energy from inside the house and for a moment thought they had given up and had broken down when the front door opened and Rosemary stepped out into the front yard followed by her minions. All at the once the dark circle broke rank and each of Selena's minions picked one of Ronni's group and walked right up to the shield. Ronni looked astonished as she saw a circle around the house. Her people facing in and Selena's group paired off facing out. Selena stood back from the circle and her eyes kept a dual focus on both Ronni and Cori.

"No Cori, that's not even close to all I've got." And she dropped her hand signaling her people to begin the next invasion.

Ronni looked around again and all of a sudden a very pronounced feeling of pride welled up in her. She was looking at her students who for years had dedicated themselves to self development and spiritual growth. She sent out a vibration from each of her hands and kept it circling until she felt the energy join on the other side of the house. They all felt it, drank its warmth and courage, then turned back to face the enemy. Ronni found herself thinking that in all her years this was truly a defining moment. Success or failure meant life or death for those she loved the most in this world. Failure was not an option.

Calling out to Cori to close ranks, Ronni broke the line and walked through the shield of her own design into the lions den. Cori already knew what Ronni was up to and sent some added energy her way. When Selena saw Ronni break through and walk into the yard she began to tense up, sending that energy right at Ronni."

"What's a matter Rosemary? Not feeling quite so powerful all of a sudden?"

"Stop right there Ronni, you don't know what your dealing with!"

"Really?"

"That's right Ronni, things have changed. I'm not the weak little insecure person you used to ride roughshod over years ago with your holier than now attitude."

"Then what are you Rosemary? All I see is a woman who doesn't care about innocent death and destruction. Are you telling me that you have become the angel of death?"

"I'm not responsible for anyone's death Ronni, you know that. My powers are for hire just like yours. I don't kill people."

"But the man you work for does Rosemary. Do you really believe that you are innocent because you didn't pull the trigger?"

"I don't know what you're talking about Ronni. My benefactor hasn't killed anyone."

"People have already died because we have been unable to work." Ronnie carefully planted a vision of Susan Kincaid into Rosemary's mind, then a picture of the Pastor and his Wife, and kept flooding her psychic with the knowledge of the death she was enabling.

"You see Rosemary; your quest for power has blinded you. You're no better than the man you work for."

"Fuck you Ronni, get your people and get the hell out of here while I can remain tolerant."

Just then they heard a sound rising up through the wind. It was the faint beat of the drums. Ronni looked over at Cori and saw that she was now sitting on the lawn slowly playing her drums, increasing the beat with intensity and rhythm. As the two armies fought each other through the golden shield, pushing and shoving psychically, animals began to appear at the fringes of the yard. These were not the domestic variety of cats and dogs but rather wild animals, bathed in a soft white glow. A large mountain lion leaped through the shield and planted itself right in between Ashley and the man fighting for her ground. A moose, large and lumbering came crashing through, landing in front of another of Selena's people. One by one the adversaries were blocked by the Spirit Animals Cori called to help win the battle. Rosemary stood in disbelief as she looked at Ronni and Cori, and felt the energy and power drain out of her. Rosemary's eyes suddenly darted to the ground behind Ronni and watched as the last of Cori's creatures approached, this one meant for her, and a little white deer mouse paused right in between them and stood its ground.

*****

After Chase and Dug watched Henry White fall to his death Dug looked up at the crevice where Emit was just in time to see him slip away further up into the rocks.

"Shit" Dug yelled "Emit is taking off. Connie watch your back, Emit is on the move up near you."

Chase had taken cover again behind some deadfall trees and regrouped his mind. "Dug, you and Connie have got to get to Karen, there's not much time."

Dug looked at Chase with the bow in his hands then across the long opening to the trail up into the ridge and decided that the bow wasn't going to do. He took off the sling for his riffle and handed it to Chase. "Here you go boss, your going to need this to give me cover." And he watched Dug pull the .45 out of his holster and load the chamber.

"Right" Chase said taking the assault weapon from his colleague and getting a feel for the heavy gun in his hands. "Once you get to that trail head go straight up and hook up with Connie. She's just off to the right. Follow the sound of the engine: that will lead you to Karen; hurry Dug."

Dug didn't look back but exploded from his position and raced across the loose dirt and rocks. Chase raised the riffle to his chest and began plucking off shots up into the rocks high above. No fire was returned. He saw Dug reach the path and turn sharp left before disappearing up into the woods.

Satisfied for now, Chase dropped the riffle and talked into his mouthpiece. "Ok, Wesley, lets work on Seville, where the heck is she?"

"Chase, tracker says Seville is just due North of you about 150 feet higher than you are. The topographical map places her in a tree line somewhere along the ridge."

Chase looked out over the cliffs again. His eyes went straight up to the edge of the cliff and began slowly working from right to left, carefully scanning everything he saw. Nothing! He pulled out his binoculars and started the search over. About halfway across the ridge, he saw it: A thin line running vertically from a branch on a tall pine tree down into what looked like the top of another, smaller pine. He slowed down and began moving his search in small increments to the left and right of that pine until he came across another man made object. A hat! The rim of the hat was just barely visible poking out behind a tree about ten feet from the first. It was moving too.

Just as Chase started to focus his mind on the hat he saw another line being pulled up from the ground behind the tree with the hat. The line became taught and he could see that it ran to the first smaller pine to the left. The line pulled hard and all of a sudden the small pine was yanked off its base and came crashing down the sheer wall of the cliff. Chase didn't bother to watch the tree fall because what he saw behind it had caused him to freeze right in his tracks.

*****

"Wesley, we're in trouble, the Salem police just showed up with three cruisers. One of the neighbors must have called in after seeing all of us out here on the lawn."

"Don't sweat the small stuff Ronni, it's good that they are, it will tie up the situation long enough for Chase and his team to finish things up in Maine."

"But I've never been arrested before" whined Ronni.

"There's a first time for everything my old friend. You guys did an awesome job. Tell the group to keep their energy focused on Chase, Dug, and Connie. Emit and the other guy are still loose and they haven't actually found Karen and Seville yet. With Chase's mind free though, I feel much better about the odds."

"Ok Wesley, I'll make sure the cops stay here for as long as I can."

"Offer to read their cards or something before they haul your butt in."

"Funny Wesley, wish Chase good luck from all us. Don't forget to come down and bail us out later—Ok?"

"I'll be down first thing in the morning Ronni" Wesley said with a smile on his face.

*****

Dug was carefully winding his way up the steep trail keeping his eyes up ahead for Emit when he saw something blur by to his left. Looking over he saw a small pine tree just in time to see it crash. He slowed down and ducked behind a tree then followed a line of sight from where the tree came to rest back up the cliff wall. When his eyes got to the top of the wall his breath stopped.

"Chase this is Dug, are you seeing what I'm seeing? But Chase didn't answer.

Connie came on and said "Dug, what's going on?"

"You're not going to believe this." He said as he took out his field glasses to get a closer look. "Seville is up on top of the cliff all tied up with a noose around her neck. It looks like she is standing on a cut log that is barely four feet from the edge."

Hearing Dug describe what he was seeing himself broke Chase out of the trance.

"Dug, you and Connie go get Karen. Forget Seville. Move it now!"

Dug heard the seriousness in Chase's voice and said "Right Chase. Connie, I figure you're about fifty yards to my right. I can just see the top of a cabin up ahead and the noise from the engine is coming from that direction. I am going to keep going left, you go right and we'll meet around in the back. Emit is still loose so keep your eyes peeled."

"On my way Dug!" Connie whispered back as she began darting back up through the tall pines. Just as she passed by a large Elm tree a shot rang out and exploded just behind her head into the bark. "Emits out" she called into the headset and heard return fire coming from Dug's pistol. Connie figured that Dug was pining Emit down and continued the race to Karen.

Dug advanced on the position where he thought Emit was and when he charged around a large rock expecting to catch him in a crouch, Emit was not there. Dug looked up and the cabin was now very close but there was no sign of the man with the riffle. Suddenly he heard the faint sound of another motor starting up behind the cabin and decided he didn't have any time to waist. He advanced quickly to a spot where he could see around the edge of the building and shook at the sight. He could see the back of a head laying on a flat conveyor system that had just started to slowly move. At the other end he saw the whirling blades of the wood chipper anxiously awaiting its meal. He lunged out of his crouch not caring about being exposed and dashed towards the monster machine but his sense of distance and time told him he was too late. Running at full steam he caught a movement off to his left. A man with a riffle had stepped out from behind a tree and was taking aim at something in Karen's direction. Without hesitation Dug swiveled his gun hand to the left and began to empty his clip into the man. The riffle shot rang out as Emits body shook from being riddled with five .45 caliber slugs. Dug kept running and looked at Karen just in time to see the sole of her foot whip violently to the left as the blades of the machine connected with her body. His heart dropped into his soul at the realization that he had failed his friend. Just then another blur came from around the building and right before his eyes he saw Connie's body flying over the conveyor system, roll to the left, and jam her riffle into the stainless steel teeth of the monster. Sparks shot out of the sheet metal collar as blades ripped and broke, gears jammed and the motor on the monster ceased to turn.

Dug raced up to the contraption and was able to hit the off button for the conveyor belt just as Karen's legs started to jam into the twisted, broken metal. He saw Connie get up off the ground and head over to check on Emit so he pulled out his blade and quickly cut Karen's bonds and gently ripped the duct tape from her mouth then scooped her up off the platform. She wrapped her arms tightly around his neck as he sat down on a rock and held her fast. Connie came walking back over from checking to make sure Emit was finished and saw Karen's face swollen from the tears and fright, knelt down beside her and ran her hands through Karen's long brown hair. Karen looked up at Connie with a look of gratitude just as Connie's eyes rolled into the back of her head as she collapsed to the ground.

Dug looked down thinking that she was just exhausted until he saw the blood red stain spreading through her shirt at her lower abdomen. Karen withdrew from Dug and they both rolled Connie over, and when Dug lifted her shirt up he saw a gaping bullet hole that had tore right through her stomach. Karen reached down for Connie and held her head as Dug pulled out a first aid kit from his pack and began to try to stop the bleeding.

"Wesley, this is Dug. Connie's down. She's taken a riffle shot in the stomach. We are going to need medics up here and quick. Karen is safe and is with me."

"Got it Dug; I'll see if I can get a chopper to the area. Get her flat on her back and work on the shock and bleeding." Karen gently laid Connie's head on the soft bed of pine needles then stretched her legs that had been terribly cramped. Looking down at her foot she saw the end of her sneaker had been torn and fully realized that she had come way to close to loosing her foot. Anger began to swell inside her.

"Thanks Wesley." Dug said as he looked down at his new friend and tears came into his eyes. He had been looking forward to getting to know her better and started to pray that help would get here in time. He opened the buttons on her blouse so he could wipe the blood and dab the wound with an antiseptic swab he retrieved from the kit. She was not responding but her breathing, although shallow, was steady and firm. He put his own shirt under her head, his jacket across her torso and just tried to make her comfortable. Then with a rush he remembered Chase and Seville. He rose to tell Karen that he would be back as soon as he could but when he turned Karen was gone and so was his .45.

*****

At the top of the hill the man called Tim to some and Tom to others sat behind a large pine tree getting ready for his next shot. Looking over to his left he could see Seville precariously teetering on the small cut log almost on her tip toes and smiled regarding his ingenuity. The noose around her neck was fit in such a way so that if she were to fall over her neck would snap immediately and that would be that. Tim's biggest concern now was getting Chase before any more of his troops arrived. Having heard the last round of gun fire and the motors on Emits wood chipper stopping he had to assume that Emit was gone and that Chase might have reinforcements up here at any moment. As he looked down he heard the screech of a raptor flying somewhere nearby but could not see it. He took that to be a good omen and pulled the hunting hood over his head, locked an arrow into place in his bow, stood up and appeared from behind the tree. He could just see Chase heading up an uncut trail over to the right. Pulling back the arrow, Tim set his sights well ahead of Chase and let the long aluminum tube fly into space.

Chase had figured that his only shot at getting to Seville would be to try and navigate up the rock wall somehow. He had sent his Falcon out to find a path that would ensure safety and concealment as he made his way up. Sure enough, Falcon had come through and in his minds eye Chase could see a clear, navigable trail up to the top of the wall. A few more meters and the wall itself would provide shelter from an attack up above. Another screech from above warned Chase and he ducked just as an arrow embedded itself in the path ten feet in front of him. Looking up he saw his adversary for the first time standing near the ledge, face covered, and boldly loading another arrow. Already with an arrow in his bow, Chase stood up quickly, took aim, and let his own salvo loose. The arrow speed through the air and thumped into the large pine behind Tim just as Tim let another of his own go. The duel had begun.

"Chase Benton, you don't know how good it is to see you here." Tim yelled out over the expanse.

"Your right, I don't know how good it is. You seem to know me but I don't think I recall knowing you." He volleyed back.

"We've met before Chase, some time ago, along time ago."

"Really, it's hard to say when I can't see the face of the man addressing me."

"You're the great psychic Chase why don't you tell me where we've met before."

"If you really know me than you also know that I don't play parlor games. Speaking of parlor games, I understand your little team of psychic wana-bees down in Salem gave up."

"They served their purpose didn't they? So did Henry White. By the way, thanks for taking him out. Working for him under the table was getting to be terribly boring and you saved me another shot later on."

Things were starting to add up in Chase's mind now but he still didn't have a clue as to who this man was so he let the bantering continue as he loaded another arrow.

"You appear to be pretty good at using people, especially Karen. I have to admire the way you kept yourself a secret for over a year while dating her." His next arrow flew up the ridge and planted itself almost directly between Tim's legs. Tim didn't even flinch.

"Karen was the easy part Chase. Henry on the other hand took years of wooing to convince that he needed a special team on the outside of the agency. He actually paid me big bucks to learn everything I could about Serial Connections and you. He wanted you almost as bad as I did. It was easy feeding and very self serving."

Chase watched the orange blur of feathers come at him from above and let the arrow race by his right side missing by only a foot. At this distance neither man was going to get hit because of the slow speed of the arrows, they were simply toying with each other. He saw the explosion on the tree behind Tim before he heard the shot from the assault riffle. Looking to his right he saw Dug tucked into the same crevice Emit had sat in earlier, riffle aimed up towards the top of the ridge. Tim quickly ducked back behind the safety of the pines and Chase took advantage of the moment to advance to the bottom of the wall...

"Dug it's good to have you back!" Chase said into the headset.

"No problem boss. I can keep the guy pinned down from here."

"Good, where are Connie and Karen?"

"Connie is still down Chase. I don't know where Karen is. She took off while I was tending to Connie, she took my .45, I grabbed Connie's rifle"

Chase heard what he said and a slight panic set in. The last thing he needed was Karen running around with a weapon she didn't know how to use. "Dug, be careful, Seville is not in a good position up there. We need to keep Tim away from her at all costs."

"I can see that Chase—Shit!" Dug roared as he felt an arrow clip his forearm. Tim had moved to the right and was completely concealed.

Chase started climbing up and around the 20 foot tier of rocks. He was exposed big time but was counting on Dug to keep up the cover fire. Just as his hand reached for the next finger hold in the rocks he felt another arrow coming right at him. He had no choice but to let his body fall backwards knowing that he would slide down the 10 feet he already gained. As he let go the arrow that would have pounded into his chest bounced of the rock and ricocheted into the woods. As he fell, the extra arrows in his backup quiver came sliding out and he could hear them jangling down into the valley floor below.

"Crap" he said as he quickly regained himself and sized up the situation. He only had one more arrow in his bow quiver and the others were now gone. "Dug, I have got to get up this rock. Keep him down."

Dug loaded a new clip in Connie's riffle and started slowly walking his shots into the woods where he thought Tim was. Chase climbed like there was no tomorrow and finally made it to the top and cover. Suddenly Dug's riffle jammed and he looked down at the weapon. It had been chewed up pretty badly when Connie shoved it into the wood chipper and he cursed under his breath too late to realize that he was in the open. His right shoulder whipped back as the steel broad head penetrated his flesh and shattered bone. The hot searing pain shot through his body as he dropped the riffle and retreated back into the rocks.

"I'm hit Chase! Dug cried out through his pain. "My riffle is jammed and I couldn't shoot it now anyway."

"Stay down and keep safe Dug. I'm almost at the top of the ridge. Keep your eyes open for Karen and wish me luck."

"Got it" Dug said as the color drained out of his face, warm blood running down his upper torso.

"Ok Chase, it's just you and me again." Tim yelled out over the cliff.

Chase kept quiet this time and sat back in the rocks to calm his breathing and get focused. Things were happening too fast and getting out of control. Reaching out he found Seville first. He could feel her fear but could feel her anger even more. She was going to be ok for now. Then he found Tim in his minds eye. Tim had been completely elusive because of the psychic blocks from the group in Salem but was now wide open. Chase went inside Tim's mind for the first time and almost screamed.

Thoughts and visions and contradictions went racing through his brain as the true identity of the man named Tim showed itself. A picture of a man came into his mind, the man being pinned to a cabin door with the most evil look on his face. Impossible Chase thought to himself. Edward Feeny was dead and had been for over 17 years!

Edward could feel Chase in his head and feeling safe stepped back out onto the ridge and pulled the hood from over his face. He could just barely see Chase in the rocks and could have taken a shot but wanted revenge the old fashioned way—an eye for an eye—and that was Seville. "That's right Chase. It's nice to see you again after all these years."

Still in shock, Chase didn't have much to say. He was busy drawing lines and measuring distances from himself to Edward and Seville trying to figure out what his next move was going to be. Thinking things through he decided to keep Edward talking.

"I didn't know you had a twin brother Edward. It wasn't in the records anywhere."

"My brother Tim and I were separated at birth as orphans. I assumed his identity after you killed him."

"How did you find each other?"

"Quite by accident Chase, but we did become very close and worked together for many years as young adults."

"I guess so. He was your partner in crime?"

"My partner in revenge was more like it."

"God Edward, that's so cliché."

"Fuck off Chase; it's your turn now." He yelled down at his nemesis while he turned his back to the cliff and jumped back into empty air.

Chase watched as Edward launched himself off the cliff and for a brief moment thought he was taking his own life until he saw the rope attached to a harness. In ten seconds Edward was down on the ground and running for cover behind a group of boulders in the clearing. Chase had not been expecting that move at all but then realized what he was planning to do. He had been set up from the start. Chase looked up and judged his distance up the rest of the cliff and over to where Seville stood on the top of the log. Not wasting any time he made a dash for it while keeping an eye on Edward far down below. Edward was loading his bow again and taking aim at Seville. Chase watched as the arrow came up from below and just missed the log Seville was teetering on. There was no way he was going to make it in time. Looking down below at Edward re-loading and the last 80 yards to Seville, Chase put his last arrow in. Both men fired toward Seville at the same time. Edwards's arrow hit its mark and sent the balanced log tipping over just as Chase's arrow creased the rope tied to Seville's neck.

Chase held his breath as he watched Seville's body fall downward. The rope becoming taught as her body jerked to a stop, her feet inches from the ground. She wiggled desperately, every muscle pushing out against the ropes to prevent the noose from crushing her throat. Chase was 40 yards away still rushing to Seville when the rope finally broke, his arrow having cut through enough of the tendons to weaken its strength. Seville came crashing down on the hard rock ledge, legs hanging out over the side, barely able to keep her balance.

Edward looked up in total anger as he saw his perfectly laid plan fall apart. He loaded his bow one more time thinking he could still get Seville before Chase got to her. He raised the bow, looked through the sights and was about to pull the mechanical trigger when a voice sounded behind him.

"I wouldn't do that if I were you Tom."

Edward's focus was obliterated by the sound of Karen's voice and he slowly lowered the bow and turned. Twenty yards behind him Karen stood, arms raised, .45 automatic pointed right at his head.

"What I wouldn't give to pull this trigger right now." She said, pure venom coating every word.

Edward briefly considered talking his way through Karen but thought better of it. "Your not Seville Karen, but you'll do." Was all he said as he began slowly raising the bow. Karen needed no more coaxing and squeezed of a round from the large handgun. The gun jerked her hand high and too the right and missed him by more than a foot. She had never fired a pistol this big and was completely taken by surprise. Her look turned from pissed off to scared as she watched Tom's face turn into a wide grin.

Chase had gotten to Seville and pulled her back from the ledge. He couldn't believe Karen was down there all by herself facing Edward. He reached down for an arrow but his quiver was empty and he cursed himself. His eyes darted over to where Dug had been hoping to high heaven that he would be able to do something but couldn't see him anywhere. Just when he thought Karen was doomed he heard Seville grunt through the duct tape over her mouth. Turning he saw her eyes desperately trying to tell him something. He followed their path until he saw his empty quiver resting on the ground, one lone rusted arrow lashed against the outside of the ornate leather pouch.

The shear irony struck him like a brick as he quickly untied it and fixed it into his weapon. As he sighted in Edward Feeny he could see Karen pull the trigger on the gun one more time. A click echoed through the valley as the hammer of the gun struck nothing, all the bullets having been emptied into Emit by Dug. Karen's face became ridged and calm as she watched Tom getting ready to fire. The thought of running away did not occur to her. Her dignity was at stake and she stood her ground with her head high, staring down the man that had brutally used her to get to Serial Connections.

As Edward began to pull the string back a smile spread across his face, victory was his. Just as he was about to fire Karen looked up and saw a bright green light streak towards Tom. It looked like an Angel.

Epilog

Chase looked out over the balcony and saw the whispery white/grey clouds in the distance, the full moon once again rising and sliding across the sky towards Mount Monadnock. Soft music rose up from the courtyard below; bright string lights crisscrossed the entire expanse, illuminating the grounds like he had never seen them before. Dozens of overhead air warmers placed throughout the paths and open spaces created a spring like temperature in the middle of a cold November night. Buffet tables and beverage booths were being stocked by the small army of attendants dressed in 13th century attire and the green/blue flood lights in the waterfall, great pool, and brook highlighted the swirls and light mist coming off the warm water into the cool night air. It was more perfect than he could have wished for.

After the mayhem of Halloween and its preceding days, Chase had contacted Jonathan Longworth and asked him to postpone the annual benefactors meeting until this date so that his team could regroup and lick their wounds. Jonathan had been more than willing given the circumstance but had not been very open to moving the venue from Boston to out here. He had asked Jonathan to trust him on this one.

The reality was that with three major serials caught and killed, two FBI Agents killed in the line of duty, one being a high ranking official, and the loss of Susan, they had been non-stop for the last four weeks filling out mountains of paperwork, writing and filing reports, and spending hours and hours with lawyers from all fronts giving depositions and expert testimony. He had been out to Seattle four times, down to the Maryland Shore once, FBI Headquarters 3 times, and back and forth to Maine. He was exhausted but all the loose ends were coming together and soon they would be back on track to opening up the Foundation full time for business. And that was just the administrivia!

The real work had been with his team who had suffered a great deal of emotional, physical, and spiritual pain during those three days from hell. With absolutely no resistance from them, he had asked Wesley and Ronni to help him work with all the Foundation employees to help build them back up, restore their confidence, and to constantly remind them why they were all here, and that their pain and suffering came to be in order to spare dozens of others even more horrible experiences. Easier said than done!

His work had started even before he left Maine on Halloween day. The FBI had sent in 20 agents to scour the place and were not happy to find Henry White laying at the bottom of a cliff smashed to pieces. He had a brief moment to talk to Connie about it after she came to and she had told Chase that she was adamant about taking responsibility for what she had done. Wesley had been listening to the conversation through the headset and whispered to Chase that the laws of Great Spirit had been satisfied and that no further pain and suffering for what Henry did needed to occur. Chase ended up convincing Connie that the Henry White issue was closed and that all she needed to know was that his rope had snapped while she had been returning fire from Emit—end of story.

Karen had ended up collapsing after she watched the horror on Tom's face when the old rusty arrow that had belonged to his twin brother ripped through his chest and planted itself right in front of her. She had never seen anyone die, peacefully or violently, let alone someone that had meant so much to her. After a couple of weeks of healing walks and talks she had asked Chase if he would sponsor her in some law enforcement courses and martial arts training. He had given her a huge hug and told her that she could have whatever she wanted; she was the boss after all.

He could see Seville and Karen down below in their formal gowns looking absolutely ravishing as they walked slowly down the brook path towards the pool. The thought just occurred to him that no one had ever brought up their little slumber party in his room that night—he still wondered about that and it made him tingle. As if they could read his mind they both looked up and saw him standing there on the balcony. They leaned into each other and Seville grabbed Karen by the arm and whispered something into her ear causing her to giggle.

"Hey Wesley" he said before his friend had announced himself from behind.

"Not bad grasshopper" he said stepping up alongside Chase and leaning out into the night.

"Dressed for success I see" Chase commented seeing that Wesley was still in his shorts and T-shirt, barefoot, and unshaven.

"Yeah, well, I've been up here in the woods way to long. I can't wait to head home right after this shindig tonight."

"I can't thank you and Ashley enough for everything you've done. Look at Karen Wesley; she looks like a million bucks. I really wasn't sure if she was going to make it back."

"You can thank Ronni, Ashley, and Seville for that. I really didn't have anything to do with it."

"Ok Mister Modest. Hey, you never did tell me about your sessions with Seville regarding her Spirit DNA episodes."

"Nor will I Chase. That's something you'll have to take up with her personally. I didn't share your stuff with her either. You don't seem very excited about the trip to San Francisco tomorrow?"

"God Wesley, it's almost an anticlimax at this point. Of course I am excited, especially since I've barely seen her over the last four weeks. It's almost like she's been avoiding me."

"Who's been avoiding who Chase?"

"Wesley, it just hasn't felt right at all with all this other crap going on. Susan's death, Connie and Dug mending, Karen, you know."

"You're such a woman sometimes."

"Would you like to hear some French?"

"Oui"

"I'm sure I will be fine once we get out of here. Karen has strict instructions not to bother us for any reason for at least the first week."

"Ok-Good; so here's the ten million dollar question. You've done a great job making sure everyone has been taken care of. What about you? How's Chase?"

"I'm fine Wesley"

"I didn't ask you how the tough guy was, I asked how Chase was."

"You know Wesley sometimes I could just...."

"Ok, so let's keep this simple. You know the drill. I just posed a question, what just ran through your mind?"

"Wow, do you really want to know?"

"Shoot"

"The truth is I hadn't thought about it at all until you just mentioned it."

"Tell me something I don't know?"

"What just flashed through my mind was a whole bunch of feelings. I felt like a Father, Mother, Brother, Sister, Employer, colleague, fighter, friend. It was pretty amazing."

"Amazing that you *are* all those things or that you *felt* those feelings?"

"The feelings; I guess I could get pretty overwhelmed if I really let them lose."

"That's the point Chase; you've got to take the time to do just that. A lot happened, not only to the team but to you. There are a ton of nuggets in the last four weeks. I'd hate to see you miss that stuff. The more time you let pass bye the less the feelings will be there. I'll tell you what; have Karen make arrangements to have you dropped off at my place on your way back from San Fran. I'm sure Seville will be fine for a few days. I've got some great techniques to try on you....."

*****

The weather was cold and dry and the bright blue sky streaked into nowhere as the car pulled into the private hanger at the Keene airfield. Chase, Seville, and Karen all got out of the car and at once looked up into the morning sky. Chase walked up to Karen and gave her his signature bear hug and kisses and thanked her for driving them in. Seville stepped right in and grabbed Karen too and the three of them just basked in the light for a moment.

"Ok kiddo" Chase said to Karen. "Off you go, you know where we'll be and short of a nuclear disaster please keep everyone away from us."

Happy tears rolling down her face Karen said "Bye guys, I wish I could come with you. Are you sure you don't need help with the luggage?"

"I'll tell you what." Seville said "If I start getting board after a couple of days I'll talk the boss into flying you out for the rest of week!"

"You won't be getting board" Chase countered, giving Seville that sly look. "But you just might want to make those plans anyway." He said in Karen's direction giving her the permission she desired.

"Yeeesss!" Karen hissed with a big grin on her face and grabbed them both once again before getting in the car and driving off.

Standing on the tarmac, her arm around Chase's neck, Seville pulled him into her side and said "You're quite the guy Chase. Hey, what's with the two planes?"

"I have a little surprise." He said as he took a box out of his pocket and walked over to the private jet and stepped up to meet the Captain. He handed him the box then turned and walked back to Seville. In a second the plane roared into life and zoomed out on the runway and took off.

"Not to be nosey Chase, but wasn't that our ride to the West Coast?"

"Sure was." he said coyly, taking Seville by the arm and walking over to the second plane and escorting her up into the cabin.

"Ok, I wasn't born a turnip. What is that little ole warped mind of yours up too?"

"Let me tell you a story." He said with a look of thought and happiness. "Years ago when I was a kid, and Wesley was beginning his mentoring role in my life, he used to challenge me in lots of different ways. My favorite was his challenge to sneak up on him whether it was in his house, out in the woods, or anywhere. No matter how hard I tried he always knew I was coming and right before I got to him he would turn around and surprise me. Even Ashley tried to help me by letting me in the house when he was out and I would hide someplace, but he always knew I was there. To this day I haven't been able to best him. Today's the day!" he said with a wicked grin.

"I just put two duplicates of our tracking devices in the jet that is now heading off to California. This morning right before we left I went into Clair and turned off our implanted ones so no one can find out where we really are. My dear, we are now headed to the Saint Bart's by way of plane, then sailboat. I figure that with all that's been going on, Wesley is exhausted and not thinking clearly. He should just be getting home now and we should be arriving in a small diving boat off his beach late this afternoon. Today's the day babe!"

"You are crazy Benton. You mean to tell me we are taking another detour before you and I can be together? I should kick your butt off this plane right now."

"Come with me...." and he led Seville by the hand to a door halfway back in the cabin. Walking through the door her heart stopped. Behind the door was the most beautifully decorated room, adorned in the ancient Greek, smelling of incense and Mir. On the floor were at least 40 brightly covered pillows, bright white sheep skins peeking through. Bowls of fruit and goats cheese dotted the perimeter and earns of water and juice stood next to golden goblets on the floor.

Seville turned and shut the door behind them then turned back to face Chase. Their hands touched and they stared into each others eyes and let the energy of centuries gone by fill back into their beings. A yellow and gold rainbow engulfed their aura's as they melted back into a time and place so long ago. The awareness and the memories were just like yesterday.

"Anstiss!" she said softly to her lost lover.

"Yes Phoenicia." as his hands took her shoulders and pulled her into his chest, tears welling in her eyes, sliding down her check.

She pulled back gently, and with one last look of doubt, took his shirt in her hands and slowly exposed his bare chest. Looking him in the eyes her hand slid up his belly to his left breast, feeling and searching until the tips of her fingers found the proof her spirit so desperately needed. She glanced down and ran her hands across the straight smooth scar resting on top of his heart and whispered into his ears "Apollo kept his word my love."

"Yes Phoenicia. He needed his wars to continue and could not with me there."

"I died that day too Anstiss, my heart bled a thousand deaths."

"My heart has bled a hundred lifetimes waiting to have you back."

"Do you remember our last night together? After the children had settled and the moon had risen up over the fields?"

"A memory forever etched in my soul."

"We made love for hours under the stars like we had never loved before." and she stepped back from her lost lover and let her clothing fall to the floor, watching him drink in her beauty and seeing the love and the lust spark in his eyes. "Come to me Chase, come to me Anstiss, and be mine again, forever......."

*****

The four man zodiac came buzzing around the point leaving the fifty five foot sailboat they had sailed in from Antigua off in the distance. Seville was glowing with warmth and a radiance she had not felt for way too long. The short 5 hour flight down was not nearly enough time but she knew that they would have many more adventures in San Francisco and basked in the after thoughts and the anticipation of the days ahead. Chase slowed the motor and brought the craft to a stop about a hundred yards off shore. Over the rise of the bluff on the beach he could see the top of the house Wesley had built years before and imagined him sound asleep under the quiet whirl of one of the many ceiling fans. He put up the diver's buoy and helped Seville finish getting her gear on.

"Ok, we are going to jump in here and swim over to the left side of the beach over there." as she followed his finger up the beach. "Once we get to the beach, we dump our gear and get up to the house— Wesley will never know what hit him!"

Chase helped Seville over the side and waited until she was clear of the boat then turned to the open ocean and fell backwards into the warm blue Caribbean water. The bubbles from the splash caused a brilliant disruption in his vision as millions of them danced in the sunlight as they floated up to find freedom above. As his vision began to clear he could vaguely see Seville in front of him and began to follow. As soon as the bubbles were gone he noticed that she had turned around and was facing him holding up a divers sign. He saw a huge grin of white teeth surrounded by a long moustache staring at him through the clear water. Reading the sign he screamed through his air piece:

Hey Chase! Welcome to Saint Bart's, have a nice day!

In the early pioneer days in Southern New Hampshire, an explorer named John Butler was working his way along the Souhegan River where Greenville New Hampshire is today.

As he rounded the river he came across a ritual murder being conducted by a black shaman from a local tribe of Indians. As the shaman was sacrificing his human offering, John took aim with his musket and mortally wounded the Indian named "Black Antler". With his last breath Black Antler swore: ***"For every cycle of the Medicine Wheel, for one thousand years, one of your blood will die. Not until then will your family rest from your deed. They will die at the hands of Mother Earth's messengers: The bear, the wolf, the bird of prey....You're clan will not know peace......"***

Five generations of Butler first born Son's carried the grim secret of Black Antler's curse and chronicled the annual sacrifices in the Butler Diaries until finally Robert Butler enlisted the help of a medicine man to capture and contain the spirit of Black Antler for all eternity.

In 2007, a group of small boys were exploring along the river by the old mill In Greenville. The water level was very low and they found the secret passageway into the cavern that contained the tomb of the spirit. Not knowing the danger, they opened the sealed door allowing Black Antler to escape.

After 180 years of imprisonment, the spirit of Black Antler begins to make up for lost time and seeks out descendants of John Butler starting a killing spree that no one can comprehend.

Chase Benton and the Serial Connections team discover something dark about the apparently accidental but gruesome deaths and begin their own investigation. All over New England Chase and team stalk an unseen force that will not stop until the curse of Black Antler is fulfilled!!

Serial Entity©

By Mark De Binder

Please register your book so we can send
you updates and information on new works!

The Author would love to read your
comments about Serial Connections!

Personalized autographed copies
of Serial Connections available!

All at:

www.whitefalcongroup.com

Printed in the United States
96638LV00001B/100-558/A

9 780979 589706